M000206456

DEATH AT THE FALLS

Books by Rosemary Simpson

WHAT THE DEAD LEAVE BEHIND

LIES THAT COMFORT AND BETRAY

LET THE DEAD KEEP THEIR SECRETS

DEATH BRINGS A SHADOW

DEATH, DIAMONDS, AND DECEPTION

THE DEAD CRY JUSTICE

DEATH AT THE FALLS

Published by Kensington Publishing Corp.

DEATH AT THE FALLS

ROSEMARY SIMPSON

KENSINGTON
PUBLISHING CORP.

www.kensingtonbooks.com

KENSINGTON BOOKS are published by

Kensington Publishing Corp.
119 West 40th Street
New York, NY 10018

Copyright © 2022 by Rosemary Simpson

All Kensington titles, imprints and distributed lines are available at special quantity discounts for bulk purchases for sales promotion, premiums, fund-raising, educational or institutional use. Special book excerpts or customized printings can also be created to fit specific needs. For details, write or phone the office of the Kensington Special Sales Manager: Kensington Publishing Corp., 119 West 40th Street, New York, NY, 10018. Attn. Special Sales Department. Phone: 1-800-221-2647.

Library of Congress Card Catalogue Number: 2022940965

ISBN: 978-1-4967-3336-8
First Kensington Hardcover Edition: December 2022

ISBN: 978-1-4967-3337-5 (ebook)

10 9 8 7 6 5 4 3 2 1

Printed in the United States of America

"The Waters which fall from this horrible Precipice, do foam and boyl after the most hideous manner imaginable, making an outrageous Noise, more terrible than that of Thunder. . . ."

—Father Louis Hennepin,
A New Discovery of a Vast Country in America, 1698

CHAPTER 1

Prudence MacKenzie stared out the window of the train she and her partner had boarded in New York City's Grand Central Depot early that morning.

"It's magnificent, Geoffrey. I had no idea how glorious they would actually be."

Hundreds of thousands of gallons of whitewater cascaded down Horseshoe Falls, American Falls, and Bridal Veil Falls while far below the steel suspension bridge spanning the Niagara River, a child's toy of a boat pitched its way through swirling waters and a brilliant rainbow. Passengers on the *Maid of the Mist* wore slick oilskins to protect them from the heavy sprays churned up by the action of the falls and dozens of spiraling whirlpools; they counted a voyage aboard the *Maid* a highlight of their Niagara experience.

For exceptionally adventurous souls not content to marvel from the dry safety of the river's banks and bluffs, the guidebook Prudence cradled in her lap recommended a foray into the Cave of the Winds beneath Bridal Veil Falls. She'd marked everything the author described as either too exciting or too dangerous for ladies to attempt.

"Look behind us," Geoffrey urged as the train passed the midpoint of the river and entered Canadian territory. "Look back at the banks on the American side."

Streams of filthy wastewater gushed down high cliffs as far as the eye could see. Brick chimneys jutting up along the banks of the river like a forest of unnatural trees belched out clouds of dark smoke. Piles of rotten lumber, stacks of rusty metal, and small mountains of indistinguishable debris teetered on the edge of the precipice. As they watched, fragments of rubble tumbled down into the water below, swept away by the swift current.

Prudence rubbed at the car's window with a lace-edged handkerchief. "Those must be the factories we read about."

The *New York Times* had run a series of articles on the efforts of Frederick Law Olmsted and the Free Niagara movement to eradicate the area's worst industrial development in favor of preserving its natural beauty in a free public park. Bitter controversy and rancorous opposition had delayed the project for years until the Niagara Reservation Act was pushed through the New York State Legislature and signed into law by the governor in the spring of 1885. Five and a half years ago.

"I hadn't thought it would take so long," Prudence mused, facing forward again, folding the now-grimy handkerchief into a tiny square.

"What you see is the power of money," Geoffrey commented. "Those mills and manufacturing plants are ugly and probably stink to high heaven if you get too close, but operations like that make their owners wealthy. They're not giving them up without a fight."

"Is that why we're here? To wade into a dispute between the Free Niagara people and the factory owners? I wish Aunt Gillian had been more precise in her letter. '*My dear friend Ernestine Hamilton needs your help. She knows you've passed the bar. I've told her you're on the way. Don't dawdle. Be discreet.*' And then she blithely hies off to Scotland for the grouse shooting and doesn't mention whose estate she's visiting so we can't contact her. Typical, typical!"

"Lady Rotherton is predictably unpredictable," Geoffrey said. The corners of his mouth turned up in a wry smile. He'd realized very soon after meeting her that there was no defense against Prudence's very British and formerly American aunt. Much simpler to go along with whatever schemes she dreamed up and hope her attention would be diverted before too much damage had been done. "At least there's still an ocean between you again."

"I think she convinced herself I'd sail back to England with her last spring."

"Even when she was pushing hard for it, I couldn't envision you stepping into the arms of a chinless English aristocrat with empty pockets, a moldering London town house, and a country estate with nothing to recommend it but the scenery." He shook his head and then chuckled. "On second thought, Prudence, you might want to reconsider. You'd wear a tiara and a title very nicely."

"I'm going to pretend you didn't say that."

Prudence had paid little heed to the bantering that had always marked their relationship and occasionally took on a sharp, quarrelsome edge until Geoffrey was seriously wounded on a train very like the one they were riding in today. The tension that had once reverberated between them like a taut violin string no longer tightened her jaw and etched frown lines across her forehead. She drew away from the brink of a quarrel now, mindful of words that could not be taken back, invisible injuries that were harder to heal than bullet wounds and broken bones.

Geoffrey had almost died. Prudence nearly lost him. And that had made all the difference. Edging her way cautiously toward a commitment she had been loath to make, Prudence was almost ready to let down her defenses. The verbal swordplay had lost much of its bite.

But not always and not entirely.

" *'Be discreet.'* I wonder what Aunt Gillian means by that," Prudence mused. "We're going to have to ask questions to find this mysterious friend of hers. At least we know she lives on the Canadian side of the falls."

"If Ernestine Hamilton is embroiled in a land dispute in American Niagara, she may not want it known that two New York City lawyers have entered the fray."

"I think of us less as lawyers than private inquiry agents. Don't you?"

"Hunter and MacKenzie, Investigative Law. We've created something new," Geoffrey said.

While the courtroom had always remained a possibility, most of the cases they'd accepted in the past two and a half years had been more investigatory than legal. He had thought that might change after Prudence became only the second woman to be admitted to the practice of law in New York State, but the clients she had been hoping for had not materialized.

Despite their best efforts, they hadn't been able to quash rumors of the case that had taken them into the squalid streets of Five Points and the sordid world of sexual slavery. The notoriety of what they had discovered repelled a conservative clientele averse to newsworthy impropriety. For better or worse, private inquiry agents were often tarred with the same brush as the beleaguered individuals who hired them.

"You'll never be able to walk away from your Pinkerton years," Prudence said. She'd grown adept at interpreting the expression on Geoffrey's face and reading his thoughts.

"I no longer want to. Now that I've come to terms with them." He had accepted the fact that there would always be cases he could never discuss with anyone, incidents that tortured his conscience, nightmares against which there seemed to be no defense. He was counting on the passage of time to dull the memories and hoping to spare Prudence the worst of what it meant to battle crime and exploitation.

"We'll check into the Clifton House, order tea, and see what a waiter or the desk clerk can tell us about our client," Prudence decided. "Discreetly, of course." When she smiled, her light gray eyes sparkled, and her face radiated a compelling beauty.

"Josiah claims it's the finest hotel in Canadian Niagara."

"He would know," Prudence agreed.

Someday, their secretary would leave them to pursue his own interests, but not for the foreseeable future, she hoped. Josiah Gregory was as intrinsically important to the smooth function of their fledgling enterprise as either of the two principals. On more than one occasion, he'd proven to be a valuable operative as well as a skilled practitioner of shorthand and a master at keeping complete and orderly files. For this case, he'd bought the train tickets, made the hotel reservations, and secured the travel guide Prudence had been reading during the long ride from New York City. The one thing Prudence hadn't thought to ask him to do was uncover who Ernestine Hamilton was and why Aunt Gillian had decided she needed the services of a newly minted lawyer.

"We're pulling into the station," Geoffrey announced, checking for items that needed to be returned to his pockets and the briefcase he never allowed a porter to carry.

Prudence secured the pins of her elaborately befeathered hat, tugged down the jacket of her pinch-waisted traveling suit, and inspected the tiny buttons of her gloves. The drab secretarial garb she wore when she wanted to be unnoticed and unobserved lay packed in her valise. Any friend of Lady Rotherton would expect Gillian's niece to present herself suitably and fashionably attired. So would the staff of the Clifton House Hotel. Sometimes being discreet meant playing the role that was expected. A practice at which Prudence had long excelled.

Their trunks and valises loaded into one of the open buggies dispatched by the Clifton House to meet every incoming train,

Geoffrey and Prudence breathed in the clear, crisp October air and listened to their top-hatted driver's welcoming spiel. Within minutes of beginning the ride up toward the bluff that gave the three-story hotel the finest views of any of the tourist establishments in the area, they learned that it had been built in the 1830s and then become so popular that it more than doubled in size to 150 rooms. Every person of note who visited the falls sought accommodation at Clifton House, he informed them, including Jenny Lind, the Swedish Nightingale, and a Prince of Wales. It had even been the site of abortive peace negotiations between North and South during the war.

Prudence cocked an eyebrow at Geoffrey, who shook his head and leaned slightly forward as if eager not to miss a word of the patently oft-recited monologue. A talkative buggy driver was not someone you could count on to be discreet. New York City hansom cabbies knew everyone and everything that went on in the city, including what they heard and saw in their vehicles that never made it into a newspaper or a society parlor. They were notorious gossips among themselves and willing tittle-tattlers if the price was right. Why would a Niagara Falls coachman be any different? She tamped down her impatience and concentrated on the scenery.

The buggy climbed a steep hill, their driver touching one forefinger to the brim of his hat as they met descending carriages and groups of Clifton House guests strolling the extensive grounds. The closer they came to the hotel itself, the more they became aware of the rumble of the falls. At first just a suggestion of sound, the soft roar gradually increased in volume and power until it was like listening to a sustained roll of far-off thunder.

"Wind's blowing in our direction," the driver remarked. "That's why you're hearing them so good. Some days it's as quiet as a church up here. Then again, it'll get so loud you can't hear the person standing next to you."

"Do you drive visitors around to see the sights?" Prudence asked.

"Used to, but not no more. Nowadays I work for the hotel, bringing new arrivals up from the station and taking them back down when they leave. There's hacks on both sides of the river that do nothing but drive tours. You tell 'em you want to go one place, they'll take you to ten. They've all cut deals with the concessionaires."

"I thought the Niagara Reservation was supposed to be a free park. That's what we read in the *Times*," Geoffrey commented.

"The park's free, but that's about the only thing you don't have to pay for. That's what the fighting was all about when Olmsted came up with the idea. Folks were making a good living charging to see the falls. They threw up wooden fences to block the view, then drilled holes in them you had to fork over a quarter to put your eye to. Nobody was too happy about the idea of a free attraction except the Parker family. New York State paid them half a million dollars for Goat Island." The driver snorted and shook his head. "Eminent domain was what the government called it. Folks had to accept what they were offered or spend money they didn't have going to court for a case they were gonna lose anyway."

"That was on the American side," Prudence remarked. "What about the Canadian?"

"Not much different. We passed by Queen Victoria Park down at the bottom of the hill we're climbing right now. Clifton Hill. They opened it two years ago on Victoria Day, Her Majesty's birthday." He figured that Americans, judging by their accents, wouldn't know what Victoria Day was unless he explained it to them.

"Which do you recommend?" Prudence asked.

"I'd see 'em both. You can hire a buggy and guide on this

side of the river and he'll drive you across the suspension bridge to wherever you want to go."

"We came across the suspension bridge today. By train," Prudence protested.

"Yes, ma'am, you did. But underneath the train tracks there's a passageway for carriages and pedestrians. It'll cost you twenty-five cents to walk it, thirty-seven for a one-horse carriage. Like I said, nothing much in Niagara is free."

"Except the view," Geoffrey said. He shaded his eyes with one hand the better to see the falls in the distance and the Clifton House's white painted verandas gleaming in the sunlight. The hotel looked to be as fine and no doubt as exclusive as anything to be found in New York City.

"Only from the parks," the driver reminded them. "Anywhere else you go somebody will have a hand out." True to his word, their coachman lingered over unloading their trunks and valises long enough for Geoffrey to dole out a sizable gratuity.

Josiah had arranged for a suite of two bedrooms separated by a comfortably large parlor on the side of the hotel that directly faced the falls.

Sharing a suite without adequate chaperonage was still unthinkable in most social quarters, but Nellie Bly had circumnavigated the globe without a female companion in tow and Clara Barton had become president of the American Red Cross. A vote on Woman Suffrage had been defeated in the U.S. Senate, but the movement for equality was regrouping and growing stronger by the day. Times and the way people lived them were changing.

The bellman who carried up their luggage opened the French doors leading onto the veranda, checked that the flowers, the fruit basket, and the champagne cooling in ice were satisfactory, accepted Geoffrey's generous tip, and finally, blessedly, left them alone.

"It looks like the telephone has come to Niagara," Prudence said, picking up a thin directory. Its cover boasted a photographic print of one of the famous winter ice bridges that froze portions of the falls and tempted foolhardy young men out onto the river's dangerous surfaces. She thumbed through its meager pages. "I don't see an Ernestine Hamilton listed. And I don't know her husband's given name or if some other family name or title would be used. Aunt Gillian didn't see fit to provide us with that information." She flung down the useless booklet. "No Hamiltons at all."

"I doubt many private homes have a telephone," Geoffrey said. "Except for a few business owners who want the connection with their offices. The bigger hotels, of course." He pulled out his gold pocket watch to check the time. "Electricity will be next. As soon as some genius of an engineer figures out how to harness the power of the falls. I have a feeling that if what we're here for is a land dispute, it's because either Thomas Edison or George Westinghouse is angling to ensure that only one of them holds the power monopoly. Electricity is the future, Prudence, and it could prove to be even more lucrative than Carnegie's steel mills, Rockefeller's oil fields, or Vanderbilt's railroads. My money, for what it's worth, is on Nikola Tesla's alternating current."

"I've been looking forward to a decent cup of tea for hours now," Prudence interrupted, moving toward the suite's entry hall. Once Geoffrey started rambling on about the scientific mysteries of electricity, power grids, and the conflicting claims of alternating versus direct current, there was no stopping him. She'd heard the arguments many times before. "And some tiny, crustless sandwiches. Petits fours or scones perhaps. We are in Canada, after all."

With a final, speculative glance out the French doors toward the unharnessed power of the falls, Geoffrey picked up his briefcase. "Don't leave anything here or in your room that would mark us as private inquiry agents. And lawyers," he warned. "We don't know yet what we're walking into."

"The dining room first," Prudence said, nodding agreement. "Or maybe a table on the veranda."

"Are you sure you don't want Lady Rotherton to make an Englishwoman out of you?" Geoffrey teased. "Then you'd have all the tea and scones you could wish for."

"Not worth the price," Prudence said. "And even Aunt Gillian complains about the London weather."

CHAPTER 2

They decided on a table that overlooked the falls from the hushed elegance of the Clifton House dining room. Floor-to-ceiling windows framed the view, while starched white linen, monogramed silver, and crystal bud vases ensured that afternoon tea would be as elaborate a ritual in Niagara as it was in London.

"I want a taste of everything," Prudence decided, ordering the cream tea that included three varieties of finger sandwiches as well as scones, clotted cream, and strawberry jam. "Darjeeling, please," she told the beardless waiter who looked hardly old enough to be a kitchen boy.

Geoffrey's preferences ran to thick, chicory-laced New Orleans-style coffee, but he'd learned to substitute a strong black India tea. "Assam," he ordered. "And I'll also have the cream tea." He smiled across the table at his partner, wondering not for the first time how tightly corseted women managed to eat and drink anything at all. Prudence would consume all of her sandwiches and scones and probably some of his as well. It was always that way during the first days of a new case, as if she were squirreling away energy for whatever lay ahead. It was one of the charmingly odd quirks about her that he cherished.

"We'll have to ask the maître d' about Ernestine Hamilton," Geoffrey said as they waited for their tea to arrive. "I assume townspeople as well as guests frequent the hotel restaurant."

"From what we saw on our way here, there isn't anything on either side of the river to rival the Clifton House. So if Niagara does have a sophisticated population, I imagine this is where they congregate," Prudence agreed.

In New York City, deals tended to be brokered over elaborate meals at places like Delmonico's, the Astor House, or the private dining rooms of the Fifth Avenue Hotel where Geoffrey leased an apartment. She didn't imagine that Niagara's important men conducted themselves any differently. "'Be discreet,'" Prudence said, quoting Lady Rotherton's letter. "I think that one word intrigues me more than anything else she wrote. Nothing my aunt has ever done could be called discreet."

They fell silent as the waiter rolled a serving cart to the table. Triangular crustless sandwiches lay stacked on a three-tiered silver serving stand, fronds of bright green parsley nestled among them. Another tiered stand held plain and currant scones, and a third boasted bite-sized cakes and delicate pastries. Everything testified to the presence of a skilled master chef in the Clifton House kitchens.

As the waiter poured their first cups of fragrant Darjeeling and Assam tea, Prudence quirked one eyebrow at Geoffrey, who gave an infinitesimal nod. *Might as well,* he seemed to say.

Laying her copy of *The Humbugs of Niagara Falls Exposed* on the table where its title could be easily read, Prudence smiled encouragingly as the waiter managed the tea pouring without spilling a drop on the immaculate tablecloth. "Are you familiar with this guide?" she asked. "It's a fascinating read, but I'm not sure what to believe."

"Mr. Young might exaggerate a bit sometimes, but we do recommend his book to all our guests."

Prudence plunged on. "It's not a complete guide to Niagara Falls, though, even though it claims to be." She ran a manicured finger across the book's secondary title. *With A Complete Tourists' Guide.* "For one thing, it doesn't include the information I wanted. Nor are its maps at all comprehensive." She made a clicking sound of dissatisfaction. "Geoffrey, do you have that address we were looking for? This young man might be able to help us."

"I don't believe I brought it down with me." Geoffrey patted his coat pockets, doing his Pinkerton-trained best to look befuddled and forgetful.

"That's rather bothersome," Prudence said. "Never mind. We're hoping to spend some time with a family friend whom I've never actually met." She fluttered her eyelashes and looked appreciatively at the laden table. "Mrs. Ernestine Hamilton. She might take tea here from time to time."

"Lady Hamilton?" The young man glanced toward the entrance to the dining room, where the maître d' kept his reservation book and a watchful eye on the staff. "I don't think I can be of any help," he mumbled, running a crumb scraper over the pristine linen cloth, fidgeting with the tiered serving trays. "Enjoy your tea, sir and madam."

"That was peculiar," Geoffrey commented as he watched the discomfited waiter make a beeline toward the swinging doors that led to the kitchens. He sipped the Assam tea appreciatively and took a bite from one of the cucumber-and-chive sandwiches.

"*Lady* Hamilton." Prudence stirred a few drops of milk and a scant spoonful of sugar into her Darjeeling, then helped herself to a currant scone and liberal portions of clotted cream and strawberry jam. "Delicious," she murmured. "I shouldn't be surprised that Aunt Gillian's friend is titled. I doubt she's acquainted with anyone in London who isn't."

"We still don't know where Lady Hamilton lives or how to go about contacting her," Geoffrey took another of the tiny sandwiches.

"But she *is* here somewhere." Two pieces of frosted seed cake disappeared rapidly from Prudence's plate. She cast a quick look toward the falls. "We have at least an hour of daylight left, according to the *Complete Tourists' Guide*. Shall we have another cup and then stretch our legs after that long train ride?"

"We'll try the maître d' on the way out, and then the desk clerk or one of the doormen if all else fails," he agreed.

Prudence poured Darjeeling for herself and Assam for her partner. The sandwich and cake trays were nearly empty.

"Neither of them wanted to give up any information," Prudence commented as she and Geoffrey made their way down Clifton Hill on one of the hotel's well-maintained paths.

The maître d' had kept a blank face when Geoffrey asked about Lady Hamilton, but the rapid blink of his eyes told a different story. He'd refused to say any more than that the lady was an occasional honored guest in the Clifton House dining room. They'd done better with the desk clerk, who begrudgingly revealed that Lady Hamilton lived in Niagara's most exclusive residential neighborhood, located not far from Clifton Hill. An easy and enjoyable walk, the clerk admitted, accepting another circumspectly folded bill in exchange for directions.

"Your aunt's friend appears to be well-known in the city," Geoffrey said. "But nobody wants to talk about her."

"It could be Lord Hamilton who puts people off. Maybe he has a vicious temper. Or he's a rake and a gambler. Aunt Gillian was very closemouthed in her letter. It's not like her." Gossip, scandal, and rumormongering were staples of society on both sides of the Atlantic.

Prudence shuffled through the few brilliantly colored leaves that had escaped the Clifton House gardeners' rakes, delighting in their crunch beneath her shoes. Walking always helped focus her mind, never more so than when a mystery beckoned. She warbled a tiny hum of satisfaction.

They found Lady Hamilton's stone mansion exactly where the desk clerk had directed them, at the end of a street of impressively large homes atop another of the high bluffs overlooking the falls. White cedars, black walnut, and spectacular tulip trees protected the area from the worst of the fall and winter winds described in the *Tourists' Guide* yet did not entirely obscure the view.

"Imagine what this will look like once winter settles in," Prudence said. "Christmas here must be like living in a child's wonderland."

"You'd probably be risking your life trying to get up and down these hills in a carriage," Geoffrey said. "A horse could easily break a leg."

"You sound like Josiah," Prudence chided. "Always practical. I prefer letting my imagination wander."

"Then by all means, don't let me interfere." Geoffrey shifted the cane he didn't really need and patted the hand Prudence had slipped into the crook of his arm as the ascent grew steeper. His partner's mix of hardheadedness and fanciful flights of creativity never failed to delight. He suspected that the only time she gave unrestrained voice to the softer side of her nature was in the nightly journal entries every well-bred young lady had been trained to compose. And perhaps not even there, if the self-protective side of her nature warned that someone else might read what she had written.

The desk clerk had not provided an address, but he'd given a detailed description of Lady Hamilton's house. "You can't miss it," he'd said.

"It looks like a wedding cake," Prudence murmured, taking in the soaring turrets, round-topped dormer windows, and gabled roofline. New York City's older mansions, like Prudence's own, tended to be austere cubes of dark red brick, brownstone, or gray granite. The string of imitation châteaux being built along Fifth Avenue by various Vanderbilts and Mrs. Astor's Four Hundred bore no comparison to this whimsical architectural creation.

A dozen stone steps led to porticoed double doors flanked by three stories of bay windows, all set in blindingly white stone embellished with intricately carved trim. Prudence stepped back from the elaborately curlicued iron gate to allow Geoffrey to open it.

"Shall we?" he asked when they'd mounted the steps and caught their breath.

At Prudence's nod, he rang the bell.

Lady Ernestine Hamilton was taller than the average woman, slender, and so graceful in her walk, that she seemed to glide effortlessly across the parlor into which Geoffrey and Prudence had been ushered by a dignified elderly butler. Arms outstretched to welcome Lady Rotherton's cherished niece, Lady Hamilton broke all rules of social restraint by clasping Prudence's fingers in her own and bending forward to lightly kiss each cheek. "My dear child, I am so grateful that Gillian was able to persuade you to come," she said, only releasing Prudence to allow Geoffrey to bow over one delicate hand. "You look so much like dear Sarah. Same lovely hair, same wonderful eyes."

"You knew my mother?" Prudence asked.

"We were debutantes together, Gillian and I. Sweet Sarah was the baby sister I never had." Lady Hamilton shepherded her guests to a pair of green silk French Empire-style armchairs, then sat down opposite them. "She took it very hard when Gillian married her English lord. And then I followed less than a year later. The letters we wrote! Every week without fail, back and forth across the Atlantic. Gillian and I were never so happy as when Sarah told us about meeting your father. We knew right away he was the one. She married for love, and that was rather rare in those days in social circles like ours." She smiled at Geoffrey. "I hope this family history doesn't bore you, Mr. Hunter."

"Not at all, Lady Hamilton. I had the pleasure of meeting Lady Rotherton two years ago in London and then again last winter when she came to New York."

"We're both widows now." Lady Hamilton smoothed the black silk skirt of her mourning gown.

"My condolences," Prudence said.

"Thank you, my dear. Lord Hamilton had been in ill health for a good many years, so when the time came, it was both a release and a blessing."

Stock phrases spoken without any real emotion, Prudence decided, glancing at Lady Hamilton's long, exquisitely tapered fingers. She wore beautiful black star sapphires and carved onyx in gold and silver settings, but no wedding ring.

"I wonder, Lady Hamilton, if you could tell me why Aunt Gillian was so insistent that I travel to Niagara. All she wrote was that you knew I had been admitted to the bar and that you urgently needed my help."

"Canadian women haven't won that right yet, although not for want of trying."

"I can't practice law in Canada, Lady Hamilton. I can't represent you here. In fact, I'm not sure it would be ethical for me to give you any legal advice at all."

"I don't need a Canadian solicitor or barrister. The suit I intend to fight will be brought in an American court," Lady Hamilton explained. "What do you know about having a child declared illegitimate?"

"Are the parents living or dead?" Prudence asked.

"Mother dead, father absent. Not yet declared dead but I suppose that's next."

"How old is the child we're talking about?" Geoffrey asked.

"Are you a lawyer, too, Mr. Hunter?"

He handed her a HUNTER AND MACKENZIE, INVESTIGATIVE LAW card.

"They're planning to ask the court to invalidate the parents' union on the grounds that it never happened, automatically making the child a bastard. There's no marriage certificate to prove the couple ever took out a license or appeared before a justice of the peace," Lady Hamilton began. "It gets worse. They're also intending to persuade the court to rule that the child is not her presumed father's issue, that the mother's history of loose living and immorality makes it highly likely she conceived while having an affair. Multiple affairs, so that even the mother, were she still alive, couldn't swear as to the identity of the man responsible."

"Who are *they?*" Prudence asked, her quick mind organizing facts and suppositions into separate categories. Cases she'd read about and studied flashed across her memory as she searched for precedent.

"The grandparents," Lady Hamilton said. "The grandmother, in particular."

"I assume we're talking about a substantial inheritance?" In Geoffrey's experience, lawsuits were always about money, no matter how lofty the avowed sentiments of the plaintiffs.

"There's a great deal of land involved. Land means money in Niagara, especially property that fronts on the river. You've seen what the towns look like now. Imagine them ten or fifteen years in the future, when the factories have been regulated and the shantytowns cleared away. Hotels and restaurants will have to be built for the tourists who have already started flooding into the free parks. Niagara will become every bride's wedding destination. But that's just the tip of the iceberg. The falls are being fought over by rival electric companies. Anyone who holds on to his land long enough will be able to sell it for more than he ever imagined it could bring. Hydroelectricity, Mr. Hunter. If you believe in the power of electricity, you know that once people are convinced it's safe, they'll never willingly cling to kerosene and gaslight."

"How old is the child?" Geoffrey repeated his unanswered question.

"Not quite eighteen. That's why I sounded desperate when I wrote to Gillian after she told me you'd passed the bar. There's a trust to be challenged, you see."

Out of the awkward silence that fell, Prudence asked the question whose answer she believed she already knew.

"No other lawyer will take the case if and when there's a court battle. You've made inquiries and been turned down by every attorney in American Niagara. I'm right, aren't I?"

Lady Hamilton's silence was the only confirmation they needed.

CHAPTER 3

With a commitment to meet again the next morning, Prudence and Geoffrey rode back to Clifton House in the comfort of one of Lady Hamilton's elegant carriages.

"I promise all of your questions will be answered tomorrow before the day is out," she had told them, "but for the moment I must beg your indulgence. The story I have to tell is not a simple one, nor is it entirely mine to reveal."

Adamantly refusing to discuss the particulars of the case for which they had been summoned to Niagara, Lady Hamilton had nevertheless amused her visitors for over an hour with vignettes of two wealthy young American women entering a world that craved their fortunes but despised their lack of aristocratic lineage.

"Every social event was excruciating," she'd told them, "especially if royalty was present. Our curtsies were never deep enough, and wagers were laid on whether our tiaras would fall off. Dear Gillian was set free after a year of wedded bliss. I had rather a longer sentence to serve."

The smile with which she eventually dismissed them was charming and guileless, but Prudence read implacable determination in Ernestine Hamilton's eyes and an iron will in the set of her spine.

"If I didn't know better, I'd swear we've just had a visit with your aunt Gillian," Geoffrey said, catching a brief, farewell glimpse of the lady outlined by soft gaslight illuminating the hallway of Hamilton House.

"They were dollar princesses," Prudence reminded him. "Trained from their first corset to be as unbending as Carnegie steel. It took that kind of upbringing to convince them that money and title were the only things in life that mattered. Once Aunt Gillian sets out on a course of action, nothing can sidetrack her. I suspect Lady Hamilton is the same."

And that was that. Not enough facts to construct a case, not even the name of the young woman whose legitimacy and rights of inheritance somehow tied her to the woman who'd espoused her cause.

Taking Prudence's gloved hand in his own, arranging a fur lap robe over their legs, Geoffrey gestured out the carriage window into the twilight. "We had best enjoy the moment while we can," he said, bending so close that his breath stirred the tendrils of light brown hair peeping out from beneath his partner's fashionable hat.

Pinpoints of gaslight and yellow lantern flames glowed and flickered in the hills and valleys of the two towns on either side of the Niagara River as dusk deepened into night. The falls thundered and shone silvery white under the rising three-quarter moon.

The Clifton House doorman sent a bellboy up to their suite as Geoffrey and Prudence were finishing their first cups of coffee before going down to the dining room for breakfast.

Lady Hamilton's carriage awaited them at the portico entrance. As promised. But earlier than anticipated.

"Once the tourists leave their hotels, Niagara becomes like a swarming anthill," she told them as they climbed into the four-wheeled barouche. The leather roof had been raised to afford the ladies some privacy and shelter from uncertain fall weather. "I trust you slept well?"

While Prudence framed a polite answer, Lady Hamilton ordered the coachman to make good speed down Clifton Hill before the hotel's buggies began to transport departing guests to the railroad station. She maintained a steady stream of commentary on every landmark they passed, never pausing long enough for either of her passengers to slip in a question.

"This is what I wanted you to see before we cross over to the American side," she informed them as the carriage turned onto the manicured grounds of what appeared to be a very large private mansion. "Our Lady of the Falls Academy. Launched fifty some years ago by an order of French nuns from Montreal, although many of the sisters are Irish now. And English is the primary language of instruction."

Tall pines lined the pebbled drive, creating a vista leading to a four-story redbrick building topped with cupolas at each corner, sprawling wings to either side, and a bow-shaped white porch so deep that the building's doors were hidden in shadow. Rose beds bordered in ferns hid the mansion's foundation; well-manicured lawns, the grass now brown and edging into dormancy, stretched as far as the eye could see. At the rear of the building rose a tall steeple, marking the site of the school's chapel. Not a sound broke the early-morning stillness.

The carriage pulled to a halt in the circular driveway. "We won't get out," Lady Hamilton informed them. "But I wanted you to have this image in your minds when you meet Rowan Adderly."

They had a name now. *Rowan Adderly.*

"The Academy was established to educate the daughters of our best families," Lady Hamilton said as the carriage began to roll again. "Students come from throughout the province and across the border. The nuns believe that young women of socially prominent families should be educated to influence their important and powerful future husbands in the ways of Christian charity and loyalty to the Church. Among other virtues."

"One of which is to donate generously to Our Lady of the Falls Academy." Prudence kept her voice low, but there was no mistaking the implied censure.

"The order staffs mission schools, also. And an orphanage."

"On the Academy grounds?" Geoffrey asked.

"The abandoned and parentless girls they take in are trained to become housemaids, cooks, laundresses, and seamstresses," Lady Hamilton answered, shying away from his question. "That's all you need to know for the moment."

As the carriage rolled toward the Academy's gates, Prudence heard the resonant tolling of the chapel bell calling the nuns to prayer. She pictured in her mind's eye a row of silent, black veiled figures moving through gothic doors, pale white fingers reaching out to dip holy water as they passed within.

While the nuns prayed, rows of privileged girls from good families slept on in the white curtained alcoves of silent dormitories.

Prudence imagined that somewhere else on the property, the orphans Lady Hamilton had alluded to tumbled out of iron cots, shrugged into rough cotton work dresses, and bound their hair in gray scarves. Work-roughened fingers tied the day's clean aprons around bodies thickened by years of porridge, potatoes, and unrelenting manual labor.

Everything Prudence had learned in the past few years about class distinctions, hopeless lives, and the crushing weight of poverty painted the other side of the picture Lady Hamilton had brought them here to envision.

She felt the arrow of Ernestine's gaze and turned her head to meet it. Lady Hamilton wasn't smiling. Her mouth was set in a thin, straight line. She had had them driven to Our Lady of the Falls for a purpose, though Prudence did not yet know what that might be.

Whatever Geoffrey was thinking he kept to himself.

* * *

As they approached the railway suspension bridge over the Niagara River, a thin stream of working men and women funneled onto the yawning pedestrian deck beneath the railroad tracks. Two tough-looking toll keepers exacted payment from everyone crossing to the American side. The floorboards of the tunnel deck vibrated like the prongs of a tuning fork under the wheels of heavily laden carts and carriages.

"You get used to it after a while," Lady Hamilton reassured them. "As far as I know, none of our bridges has ever collapsed, though they do have to be rebuilt from time to time. The rotten wooden beams and struts on this one were replaced with steel a few years ago."

Morning mist obscured the falls and the river below, but no matter which side of the river you were on, there was no escaping the steady roar of the cascading torrents that were Niagara's livelihood. Beautiful, awe inspiring, and dangerous to the unwary and the foolhardy.

The *Tourists' Guide* recounted so many horrific tales of death and nearly fatal exploits that Prudence had tired of summarizing them for Geoffrey's benefit, concluding that there was no lack of daredevil idiots in the world. Now, as the carriage rolled on to American territory, she glanced back, half expecting to see a taut wire stretched over the narrowest part of the river, a stuntman making his precarious way across, fighting the wind and maintaining his balance with a long, horizontal pole.

"There's a barrel plunge planned for later today," Lady Hamilton said, noting Prudence's quick search of the empty airspace behind them. "We can stop to see it from below if the timing is right."

"What kind of barrel plunge?" Geoffrey asked. "Surely not a person going over the falls?"

"Not yet. But that's the goal. It may be a sheep this time. Or a chicken. There's no end to the livestock Crazy Louie has already consigned to the whirlpools and the rapids."

"Crazy Louie?"

"His proper name is Louie Whiting," Lady Hamilton said. "Stark raving bonkers. I doubt he'll be the first human being to survive a descent of the falls, but it won't be for lack of trying. His barrels are sturdier now than the initial contraptions he built, but they continue to crack and splinter into small pieces."

So perhaps the stories in the *Tourists' Guide* weren't so exaggerated after all, Prudence thought. Some of them, she remembered, sounded less far-fetched than Crazy Louie and his animal-filled barrels.

"The town is waking up," Lady Hamilton commented as they passed groups of tourists moving sluggishly along the sidewalks, guidebooks in hand. Souvenir shops were opening, proprietors setting out racks of postcards and tables piled high with everything from ladies' handkerchiefs to wooden toys for children. All with NIAGARA FALLS painted, printed, or carved across their surfaces. Cafés propped blackboard menus against their front windows; the smell of fatty sausages, burnt sugar, and boiled coffee filled the air. A hum of conversation, arguments, and the shrill demands of hungry children mingled with the clop of horse-drawn vehicles and the cries of street vendors.

"I'm always glad to leave the noise and hustle behind," Lady Hamilton remarked as the carriage turned onto a narrow dirt road well out of sight and sound of the village that had sprung up at the foot of the suspension bridge. "The hawkers are everywhere now. And they've gotten so brash that it takes real determination to push past them. They count on most tourists being too intimidated not to give in."

"Some of the streets in New York City are like that," Prudence said, thinking of the crowded neighborhoods around Five Points where she often volunteered at the Friends Refuge for the Sick Poor. "Worse, actually."

"It's the same wherever quick, easy money is to be made from people who should know better than to let themselves be cheated or manipulated. Isn't that right, Mr. Hunter?"

"I quite agree with you, Lady Hamilton."

Prudence caught the shadow of a smile on Geoffrey's lips and knew he was thinking something else entirely. Probably drawing up a mental list of the ways in which two seasoned dollar princesses of a certain age resembled one another.

The temperature dropped a few degrees as they drove deeper into what looked to be virgin forest.

"It's been a long time since I've seen trees like these growing in the wild," Geoffrey said, listing the names aloud. "White cedar, sugar maple, hemlock, shagbark hickory."

"I'm impressed," Lady Hamilton said. "You didn't tell me you were a student of nature."

"I grew up spending hot summer days in a forest like this one," Geoffrey explained. "We were punished if we couldn't name the trees we climbed. My brothers and I." He gestured toward the thick layer of pine needles, fall leaves, and creeper vines that carpeted the forest floor. "Even when all of that is covered with snow, the deer know to burrow down to the moss and grass below."

"Do you hunt?"

"When I was younger. Southerners are born with rifles in their hands. Wild turkey, deer, even squirrels." A trace of his past softened Geoffrey's vowels.

Her partner seldom reminisced about his early life on the cotton and tobacco plantations in eastern North Carolina where his father and grandfather had amassed enormous wealth on the backs of hundreds of slaves. Prudence said nothing, waiting for another question whose answer might give her one more glimpse of the life Geoffrey was usually reluctant to talk about.

But Lady Hamilton chose not to pursue the topic. She studied his face for a long moment, watching him take in the glory of sunlight filtered through the tree canopy. She, too, turned her head toward the breathtakingly beautiful spectacle of a pristine wood in late October. The barouche rolled deeper into silence as the hurly-burly of Niagara faded away behind them.

"We'll have to walk the rest of the way," Lady Hamilton announced when her coachman signaled that the dirt road had become a track too narrow for the wide carriage to navigate. "It's not far."

"Are we expected?" Prudence asked.

"I told Daniel Johnson about you when Gillian wrote that you'd passed the bar. But I also informed him that I couldn't be certain you'd come."

"Lady Rotherton isn't to be underestimated," Geoffrey said, swinging his cane at the undergrowth crowding the path. Forced to use a walking stick by a bullet that to this day remained lodged in his right leg, he'd gradually adapted to what he'd initially rejected. The handcrafted sword cane he carried now was precisely calibrated to his height and the length of his arm. It was one of the deadliest weapons he'd ever used, wholly unexpected by any adversary foolish enough to challenge him.

"She isn't infallible," Lady Hamilton retorted. "Not entirely and not always."

Prudence came to a sudden halt when she glimpsed the outline of a cabin through the trees. It stood in a small clearing, surrounded by a thick layer of fallen leaves and pine needles. Impossible to approach without stirring up a warning rustle of disturbed forest debris.

Lady Hamilton took the lead, striding forward with the energy of someone eager to begin getting on with things.

Prudence and Geoffrey followed close behind, alert, watchful, intrigued by the little they knew and the great deal they did not.

A tall man with the sinewy arms of a bowman appeared on the cabin's porch, beside him a dog whose head nearly reached the height of his master's waist. Enormous and shaggy coated, its cold yellow eyes stared at the strangers with unblinking menace. Low-throated growls rumbled from a muzzle bared to display teeth sharp enough to rip prey or enemy to shreds.

Lady Hamilton stepped closer to the cabin, gesturing Prudence and Geoffrey to remain where they were. She waited until the dog caught and identified her scent. The animal ceased growling, gave a single, welcoming tail wag, rolled down its lips over the unnerving rows of teeth.

"Good morning, Daniel," she said quietly. "I've brought the young woman I talked to you about. Prudence MacKenzie. Her partner is with her. Geoffrey Hunter."

The man nodded, laid a hand on the dog's head. Said something to the beast in a language neither Geoffrey nor Prudence recognized.

"You and they are welcome."

Only when Prudence took the first step onto the cabin's porch and looked up to examine the face of the man standing there did she see that the pupils of his eyes were milky white, filmed over with the cobwebs of old age.

Daniel Johnson was blind.

CHAPTER 4

"Shall we walk together?" Daniel Johnson suggested.

He smiled an invitation and stretched out the fingers of his right hand, descending the porch steps without hesitation when he felt the support of Geoffrey's arm.

The dog never left Johnson's side, muzzle nudging the blind man's left thigh, huge head nestled under its master's free hand. Snow-white fur around muzzle, chest, and underbelly set off a mottled brown and black coat.

"His name is Hero," Daniel said. "I found him as a pup near the river. Overlooked when the others in his litter were tied in a burlap sack and drowned. He's been with me ever since."

Ignoring Lady Hamilton's warning shake of the head, Prudence held out an ungloved fist. Yellow eyes flicked upward. Hero's tongue licked warmth across Prudence's knuckles.

"He'll guard you now, the way he does me. And Rowan." Daniel didn't seem to require sight to know what was happening around him. The hand that had held Geoffrey's arm reached out toward Prudence. "May I?" Sensing her unspoken permission, Daniel's forefinger brushed lightly over Prudence's cheeks, the bridge of her nose, her forehead, closed eyes, chin. Lastly, her lips. "I am surrounded by beautiful women," he said.

Taking Geoffrey's arm again, Daniel paced slowly across the clearing toward a stand of trees beyond which a rush of running water could be heard. The dog nudged his master's leg whenever a small obstacle blocked the path.

"Surely he doesn't live alone with just the dog for company?" Prudence asked softly, suspecting that Daniel's hearing had become more acute as his eyes failed.

"He told me the blindness crept across his vision for years before sealing him into permanent darkness. It gave him time to prepare," Lady Hamilton answered. "I brought Rowan to him in April. They needed one another and I knew she would be safer here than anywhere else."

"Safer than at the Academy?"

Lady Hamilton ignored the question.

Daniel stopped, turned. Waited for the two women to draw near. "Listen."

At first Prudence thought she was being urged to pay attention to the trill of birdsong, but a few moments later she realized it was a human voice echoing through the woods. An untrained but gifted contralto, she thought, years of attendance at the opera making it second nature to identify a singer's range.

"Rowan," Lady Hamilton said, smiling with unmistakable affection. "Her mother sang for a living before she married Lucas Adderly. Grace had the voice of an angel, but the Adderlys have never forgiven the taint of public performance. Only women of dubious virtue appear on the stage."

"How much have you told them?" Daniel asked, moving away from Geoffrey and into a shaft of sunlight, braided gray hair and weathered brown skin drinking in the warmth. He wore a long, belted shirt of loosely woven fabric, woolen trousers, and shoes fashioned of soft, undyed leather.

"Only that Rowan's grandmother wants her declared both illegitimate and not their son's daughter." Lady Hamilton pitched her voice low so it wouldn't travel through the trees to the songstress. "I've left the rest of it to you. And to Rowan."

"Perhaps now is the time," Geoffrey urged.

Daniel motioned Hero to sit, then positioned himself in a storyteller's stance, feet planted slightly apart, blind hooded eyes turned toward his listeners.

"Lucas Adderly was a serious and predictable young man until he stepped into the Niagara Music Hall one rainy night and heard Grace Malone sing," he began. "They left Niagara together when she became pregnant. After Grace died, Lucas brought Rowan home. She was as beautiful an infant as anyone had ever seen, but his parents wanted nothing to do with her. Even when she was a tiny little thing, she had her mother's bright red hair and hazel eyes.

"Lucas was willfully ignorant about some things in those days, refusing to admit that Grace's child would not win over her grandparents' hearts. He tended his father after the accident that left Cyrus Adderly alive but chair-bound and mute, and for a while it looked as though he would be able to put Grace behind him. Like most other widowers. Having to take over as head of the family left little time to grieve or brood. But he was using whiskey to keep the memories at bay night after night. Drink always takes its toll. When Grace was five years old, he disappeared without warning, leaving behind instructions for his bank and his lawyer. We heard he'd gone to San Francisco. The town saw Lucas once a year after that, when he came back to Niagara to spend a week or two with his daughter in late spring or summer. And then he would bolt again. Rumor had it he'd made another fortune out west, this time in shipping."

"Whenever Lucas wasn't in residence, Myra Adderly consigned Rowan to an upper-floor nursery, with a nanny and a maid in attendance to make sure she didn't have to lay eyes on the child," Lady Hamilton said, taking up the story. "Cyrus was oblivious to what was happening. Still is, as far as I know, though I haven't laid eyes on him for years.

"Rowan grew up healthy, intelligent, and so much like her mother that it must have pierced Lucas's heart at every visit. When the girl turned seven, he agreed to enroll her in Our Lady of the Falls Academy. Myra's idea, but Lucas went along with it. That was also the year he made the legal and financial arrangements that tied up the family wealth in a trust so skillfully constructed that it hasn't been broken to this day. Except in matters of the heart, Lucas Adderly was never anyone's fool."

"Rowan was to be a day pupil at the Academy, but Myra persuaded the Mother Superior to take her on as a full-time boarder. The nanny who had loved and cared for her was dismissed. As she grew older, Rowan began staying at the school through many and then all of the holidays. Christmas, Easter, the summer months when the other pupils went home," Daniel said.

"The only time his daughter set foot inside Adderly House was when Lucas sent word that he was on his way. For a few short weeks she played with imported dolls and wore dresses fit for a princess. Then back she went into school uniform and a bleak dormitory cubicle at the Academy."

"And Lucas never knew?" Prudence asked.

"The trust he established paid Rowan's tuition, but it also authorized Myra to approve other expenses his daughter might need. It wasn't difficult for her to add room and board. I've always believed he chose to ignore what was happening. Rowan never complained, their time together was limited, and he didn't ask the questions that would have required him to intervene."

"That can't be the whole story," Geoffrey said when Daniel fell silent.

"You're wondering how Daniel and I became involved." Lady Hamilton took a handkerchief from the sleeve where she had tucked it. "The late Lord Hamilton was on the Academy's board of trustees. Charities and patronages come with a title, so even when we were new to the province, he was deluged with requests to sponsor this organization or sit on that board of directors. He deflected to me anything that didn't involve horses, dogs, or hunting. I heard Rowan sing at one of the first award assemblies I attended. She couldn't have been more than ten or eleven, but her pitch was perfect and her range astounding. I learned her story for the first time that summer.

"Everything in Niagara changed when New York State paid the Parker family half a million dollars for Goat Island and a few other waterfront properties. Suddenly everyone realized what the future promised for those who could move fast and hard enough." Lady Hamilton sounded abruptly and briskly businesslike.

"That was also the first year Lucas stayed away," Daniel said.

"Rowan sat alone in her bedroom at Adderly House waiting for him. Myra had her driven to the Academy as soon as she was sure her son wouldn't put in a late appearance, but you could see the wheels turning. Lucas had fixed things so his daughter would be a very rich young woman someday, but nobody knew the exact terms of the trust.

"The next summer, when there was still no word from Lucas, Myra didn't bother taking her granddaughter home from the Academy. Rowan became a slip of a ghost haunting empty corridors, pale and lonely, only coming alive when she sang. And that wasn't very often. Nuns observe silence when they're by themselves."

"How terrible for Rowan," Prudence murmured.

"It got worse. Word went around that the Adderlys had begun to doubt whether their son was really Rowan's father. And no one had ever seen a marriage certificate."

"The next we knew Rowan had been transferred from the Academy into the orphanage." Lady Hamilton's voice took on the angry crack of a whip. "'Where she belonged' was what Myra was supposed to have said.

"She was put to work scrubbing floors where her former

classmates stepped around her or tracked through what she'd just cleaned. She scoured pots in the school kitchens, and when winter came, she hung out wet sheets in the freezing wind."

"Lucas's parents were trying to get rid of her," Prudence whispered.

"And they almost succeeded," Lady Hamilton said. "Rowan was frequently ill, but sickness in an orphanage doesn't excuse you from the work you're assigned. No work, no food."

"These are nuns we're talking about. How could they be so cruel?"

"One of them wasn't. A very young, very timid sister wept over what had happened to Rowan and slipped me a note one day when I was at the Academy for a board meeting. Could I help her?" Lady Hamilton folded her handkerchief into a tiny square.

"How did you manage it?" Prudence asked.

"I played their own cards back at them. Wealthy patrons have the pick of the orphans when the time comes to place them in service. I simply moved up the schedule. Blackmailed the Reverend Mother into releasing Rowan into my employ."

"Blackmailed a nun?" Prudence exclaimed.

"The Academy has always received generous monetary gifts from patrons eager to buy their way into heaven. Mismanagement of funds is one of the great secrets of religious life." Lady Hamilton brushed aside the question she saw forming on Prudence's lips. "It's always best to have more than one winning card to play. Remember that.

"When Myra insisted that Rowan belonged in the orphanage, it signified that the Adderlys believed they had no family connection to the girl. And therefore no interest in her future. I knew I couldn't keep her as a guest in my house. She had to disappear into the community, become invisible until Lucas returned. Daniel's cabin in the woods was the perfect solution. I let it be known that she'd proved unsatisfactory and that I'd arranged other employment for her."

"A white person reduced to working for an old, blind Indian is as demeaning as it gets," Daniel reminded them. "She has become the granddaughter I never had."

In the silence that followed, Rowan Adderly's voice floated through the trees above the echo of the river.

Every fiber of Prudence's being wanted to ensure that the girl whose story she had just learned would not become another casualty of familial greed and callousness. But the law was a stern taskmaster, justice as capricious as the weather. And she herself was untried in the arena of litigation. If she was likely to lose because of lack of evidence, should this be her first case?

Lady Hamilton had taken Daniel's arm, Hero moving out in front of them.

Geoffrey remained quiet, but as Prudence raised the collar of her jacket against the October chill, he took the cashmere scarf from beneath his coat and draped it around her neck.

"We have a lot of work to do," he said matter-of-factly. "This is not going to be an easy case to win."

"But we will win it?"

"If I've understood Lady Hamilton correctly, the Adderlys haven't moved against Rowan yet. Not in a legal sense. But from what she's told us, it's inevitable. There's an experienced attorney in the family law firm already calculating his fee."

"So we investigate before we defend."

"Lucas Adderly is the key. Someone clearly hopes he's dead."

"That being so, our first job is to find him. Then convince him to come back to Niagara one last time. Marriage and birth certificates in hand."

"If he's alive," Geoffrey said. "There's a reason a person can be declared dead after seven years of no provable contact. Corpses are silent witnesses even when they're identifiable."

*   *   *

Daniel, Lady Hamilton, and Hero waited at the tree line for Prudence and Geoffrey to catch up.

"Sorry," Prudence murmured. "We started talking."

"I'm going to assume that means you'll take the case," Lady Hamilton said.

"The Adderlys haven't filed a brief yet," Geoffrey reminded her.

"We can't afford to wait. Gillian told me you have ex-Pinkertons on retainer to do your investigatory work."

"We do."

Daniel raised his hand from atop Hero's head. "Later," he said. "She's seen us."

None of the three sighted individuals had noticed the young woman walking toward them from the bluff overlooking the Niagara River. She carried a large woven willow basket, a knitted shawl draped over one arm.

Long red hair the color of a blazing sunset danced in the wind. Large hazel eyes examined them from a perfectly oval face. Rowan Adderly's skin was the pale, translucent white of someone who never tans, a scattering of freckles across nose and cheeks the only sign of outdoor color.

She moved straight as an arrow to the man on whose chest she placed an open palm. "Grandfather," she said. A second, unfamiliar word.

Daniel's large hand covered hers and then released it.

It was, Prudence thought, as ritualistic a greeting as a spoken hello and a handshake. But far more tender, measured, and courtly.

Rowan stepped into Lady Hamilton's arms as though she had been born to their embrace.

"My dear girl." Ernestine's fingers entwined a long tendril of the bright red hair. "You've let the wind make tangles it will take forever to comb out." The proud look she turned on Prudence and Geoffrey was evidence of the deep affection she held for this child not of her blood. "Prudence, Mr. Hunter, I want you to meet your prospective client, Rowan Adderly."

The ungloved hand Rowan extended was slender and long, her fingers those of a musician. But there were faint calluses on her palm that bore witness to a far different type of work than plucking strings or striking piano keys.

She spoke with a contralto's low, slightly husky voice. "Have they persuaded you?"

"We've listened to Lady Hamilton and to Mr. Johnson," Geoffrey answered. "Now we'd like to hear from you."

CHAPTER 5

Rowan settled the man she addressed as *Grandfather* into a spindle-back rocker on the cabin's narrow porch. She folded a quilt around his legs, set her basket on the top step, then perched herself next to it.

Prudence and Lady Hamilton refused the offer of chairs from inside, positioning themselves on the steps just below Rowan. Geoffrey leaned against the porch railing.

"The nuns weren't always cruel," Rowan began. "They told us they had to be strict for the good of our souls and to think of punishments as penance for our sins." She picked a small, embroidered purse from the basket and threaded a long needle with clear crystal beads. "Tourists buy these," she explained. "The clan mothers are teaching me the patterns, but I'm not very good at it yet." She bent over the beadwork, long red hair falling around her face like a fiery curtain.

"What did your father tell you when he spoke about your mother?" Lady Hamilton urged. "Weren't there favorite stories he repeated?"

"My father was always very gentle with me. But quiet. He hardly talked during the times we were together. He held my hand as we walked but never picked me up or cradled me in his arms. Sometimes I sang to him. He said he didn't need a photograph of my mother, that all he had to do was look at me and he would see her.

"I learned not to ask questions because my father rarely answered them. He didn't grow angry the few times I persisted, but he seemed sad and disappointed. When I listened to the girls at the Academy talk about their families, I always wished I had something to contribute. But I didn't.

"I know so little." Rowan's shoulders hunched forward. Then she lifted her head and looked directly at Prudence and Geoffrey. The concealing curtain of red hair fell back, revealing a pained but determined face. "My Adderly grandmother is claiming that my parents never married and that my mother was . . . promiscuous. She says that because I look so much like her and don't resemble my father at all, I must be some other man's child."

"Do you have a christening bracelet?" Geoffrey asked. "A written account of your birth? Anything that might indicate your father believed you to be his child?"

Rowan frowned. "I have nothing," she said slowly, setting aside the beadwork, mentally reaching back into her empty childhood.

"What about the nanny or the nursemaid who took care of you until you were sent to the Academy?"

"There was only one person who looked after me."

"Where would we find her?" Geoffrey prodded. "Do you remember her name?"

Rowan glanced at Daniel.

"Elizabeth," Daniel said into the stillness. "My daughter. She was this young one's milk mother."

"I remember the warmth of her arms around me," Rowan said, "Elizabeth turned the nursery into a refuge shared by just the two of us. I had no blood mother, but I hardly needed one as long as I had Elizabeth."

And there it was, Prudence realized, the connection between Rowan Adderly and a log cabin at the end of a narrow, seldom-trod track into the forest. The blind man's child had been the infant Rowan's wet nurse.

In time they'd have to find out what had happened to the baby Elizabeth must have borne. So many tiny creatures died in the first few days or weeks after leaving the safety of a mother's womb. And Elizabeth herself? The husband or lover who fathered her child? Years of unspoken pain had seeped into the damp October air.

"When Rowan was sent to the Academy, they dismissed Elizabeth with little more than the clothes on her back and the carpetbag she'd taken with her to Adderly House," Daniel said. "A scant handful of coins was all she had to show for seven years of devoted service. It broke her heart to be turned out, but she was already ill, though neither of us suspected it until many months later."

Prudence wanted to ask how much of Rowan's early story Lady Hamilton had already known before these moments on Daniel's porch. But Lady Hamilton had a habit of drifting into a stubborn silence when asked a direct question she didn't want to answer.

Did she have secrets of her own? Did she step into the narrative then out again when a fact or memory came uncomfortably close to a hidden personal life that had to be protected? She was as much an enigma to Prudence as the aunt who was neither entirely American nor completely British.

And there was Rowan to consider. How many times should she be forced to remember hurtful moments from years that should have been filled with more than the love of a nurse-maid? To sense that your own grandmother despised you had to have been devastating and incomprehensible to a young child.

"We have a decision to make," Geoffrey said, breaking into her thoughts.

"Before you do, you should be aware of something else," Daniel said. "There is more to Rowan's story than a vengeful woman's hatred of her son's marriage."

His speech was measured and deliberate, like the physical movements with which he moved through his sightless world.

"Some time back, a young Tuscaroran man came to me. He was troubled by things he had witnessed but not understood at the time they were happening. Martin works for anyone who will hire him. He is willing and able but has little formal education."

"He doesn't read," Rowan said, "but he can add and subtract long strings of numbers in his head and on his fingers."

"When the planning was being done for the State Reservation, Martin was hired by the surveyors. He carried equipment, led them through uncharted forest, provided the names of people whose land they were traveling on. Did whatever needed to be done, whatever task he was given. Never asked questions. Martin's great gift, in addition to his physical strength and skill with numbers, is his deep silence. Choosing to speak to me about what was troubling his conscience was not something he did lightly or without struggle.

"When the surveyors called out their coordinates, Martin framed in his head the maps they were creating. Over time he realized that new calculations didn't always match previous ones. The mental maps he drew changed, though no one noted the contradictions.

"He believes that some of the survey maps have been altered, that parcels originally included in the stretches taken by the state government through eminent domain were redrawn and redeeded to individuals who paid generously for the service."

"Tourist development and hydroelectricity?" Geoffrey asked, glancing at Lady Hamilton.

"Fortunes to be made," she murmured. "As I told you."

"In the years before he disappeared, Lucas bought multiple tracts of land. Martin suspects that at least one of the government surveyors has been bribed to make changes that would affect those parcels. He came to me because he is convinced that harm has been done to Rowan and that more is being planned."

"How can that be?" Prudence asked.

Daniel shrugged. "Numbers are confusing to most people. To Martin they're as clear as raindrops."

"Niagara is ripe with corruption, just like any other rapidly growing city. Recently, more so than most," Lady Hamilton said. "You said it yourself, Mr. Hunter. Tourists and hydroelectricity. Cheaper and more certain of rich reward than mining for gold."

"We'll need to talk to this Martin."

"Martin Fallow," Daniel said. "He builds barrels for Louie Whiting when there's no other work available."

"How long ago did he bring you his concerns?" Prudence asked, careful to frame her question without assigning blame to anyone.

"It was after Lady Hamilton rescued me," Rowan said, deft fingers sweeping the thick fall of her hair into a neat bun secured with a carved comb she took from her basket. "I was just learning how to bead. Martin came through the trees so quietly that only Hero heard him. I remember looking up from the mess I was making and thinking he looked like a tribal ghost from the past. He seemed unsettled by my presence. That's not quite the right word, and perhaps it was only because he didn't expect anyone but Grandfather to be here. I stepped inside the cabin to give them privacy. I overheard the conversation from there."

"Crazy Louie is sending another barrel over the falls this afternoon," Lady Hamilton reminded them. "If Martin Fallow isn't employed elsewhere, he'll be on the riverbank to gather up the fragments."

Before they left the clearing, Prudence turned for a last look at the cabin.

A young girl stood quietly in the shadows of a porch overgrown with vines and strewn with autumn leaves. Behind and beside her sat an old man who lived in blackness and a half wolf dog that had narrowly escaped being tied in a sack and drowned.

Geoffrey had said they had a decision to make.

Prudence no longer felt they had a choice.

A crowd had gathered along the shoreline opposite Horseshoe Falls when Lady Hamilton ordered her coachman to pull the carriage off the road.

"Crazy Louie sends whoever is working with him to the spot where he predicts the day's barrel is most likely to wash up," Lady Hamilton commented as she worked her way toward a massive outcropping of rock. "It's always slippery because of the mist, so grab on to those overhanging branches as you work your way up. We should be able to see Martin Fallow standing at the edge of the crowd, close to the river."

"What does he look like?" Geoffrey asked. He'd clambered over the boulders just behind Prudence, ready to catch her should she fall.

"Tuscaroran," Lady Hamilton said. "Tall, thick through the shoulders, braided hair, wearing the same type of long shirt Daniel favors. Rubber boots to wade through the cold water, fisherman's gloves to protect his hands from splinters. He'll probably be holding a long shepherd's crook to snag the barrel as it drifts toward land. Or rake in the pieces if it's another failure."

"You've watched these retrievals in the past," Prudence said, catching her breath as they reached the top of the outcropping.

"Someday a live human being will be inside a barrel or whatever contraption the fool thinks will protect him. Crazy Louie is as mad for adventure as the wire walkers who perform stunts over the river. It's like going to the circus to watch the trapeze artists or the lion tamers. There's always a tinge of disappointment when no one plummets to the ground or is mangled by an angry cat."

"He publicizes when he's sending a barrel over?" Geoffrey asked.

"Word gets around. And he sends boys out into the crowds to pass the hat. Both before and after."

"Do spectators gather at the launch place?"

"It's mainly people who want to be certain he's actually nailed or bolted a living creature inside the barrel before he releases it into the current that sweeps it over the falls."

"What about local newspaper coverage?" Prudence had spent many an hour dirtying her hands on newsprint in search of a clue.

"Sometimes. But unless Louie's touting something new or different, the paper doesn't bother sending out a reporter anymore, let alone a photographer." Lady Hamilton took a pair of opera glasses from her reticule. She scanned from left to right, then back again.

"That's odd. I don't see Martin anywhere. I suppose Louie could have hired someone else for today, but I hadn't heard that more surveyors were in town. That's usually the only time Martin misses one of these shows. He's as intrigued as the rest of us who know how hazardous the falls are. Tourists are awed by them, but they have no understanding of the danger."

"May I?" Prudence held out a hand for the opera glasses. She could just make out a group of dark figures above and to one side of Horseshoe Falls.

"Sometimes he sends up a flare when the barrel goes over," Lady Hamilton said.

"I overheard that the unlucky passenger today is a sheep." Geoffrey gestured toward the chattering crowd along the riverbank.

"That means Crazy Louie is edging toward a human being before too much longer," Lady Hamilton said. "Somewhere between one hundred fifty and two hundred pounds, I expect, if the sheep's any clue."

"How do you know how much a sheep weighs?" Prudence asked.

"The home farm," she answered ambiguously. "Lancashire. The late Lord Hamilton was as incompetent a landowner as he was everything else he tried his hand at. A full-grown ram of one of the smaller breeds usually runs less than three or four hundred pounds, so it's a good substitute for a man."

"The poor thing must be terrified when they shove him inside a barrel and nail it shut," Prudence said, holding on to the opera glasses.

"Crazy Louie mixes up some sort of sleeping concoction and feeds it to the beasts. It keeps them from kicking out the sides of the barrel or beating themselves to death inside it when they're tossed into the water."

"There," Geoffrey said, pointing. "A flare."

Prudence focused the opera glasses on the foaming spray of the falls, searching for and quickly finding a dark object hurtling through the water, bouncing in and out of the swift moving cascades into the river's whirlpools below.

"How long does it take?" Prudence asked, tracking the barrel as spectators cheered the descent.

"Only a few minutes for the actual fall." Lady Hamilton stepped precariously close to the edge of the granite outcropping on which they stood. "It's retrieving the barrel once it lands in the river that takes the time. If it's not in pieces, that is." She held out an imperious hand for the opera glasses. "Where on earth could he be?"

"I see someone carrying a hooked pole," Geoffrey said, "but he doesn't match your description of Martin Fallow." He gestured toward a group of four or five men, one of them several yards into the river. He wore a rope wound around his waist and an oilcloth jacket and trousers to keep out the worst of the wet cold.

"They've charted the whirlpools and the currents," Lady Hamilton said. "He may be crazy, but Louie Whiting has been known to estimate to within a few feet where one of his barrels will come ashore. Some of the other harebrained idiots aren't as well informed. A barrel or a small boat can bob around for more than an hour or disappear entirely and never be found."

Crazy Louie's sheep in a barrel was floating steadily closer to the man with the curved staff.

"Can we go down?" Prudence asked. "I'd like to be able to see inside when they open it up."

"We can, of course. But I warn you, Prudence, it's likely to be a very bloody sight."

Lady Hamilton took a different path than the one they'd used to climb to the top of the outcropping. Sliding pebbles and crushed vegetation made the descent faster but more slippery. "Hold on to the branches or one another," she warned.

Geoffrey went down directly in front of Prudence. "In case you lose your balance," he explained when she protested. "Better to land on me than these rocks."

Two of the men waiting on the shoreline grabbed the six-foot-long barrel as soon as it glided within reach, rolling it onto level ground. The crowd surged in that direction, but except for a few intrepid onlookers, didn't venture too close. Most of them had read or heard stories of the often-gory remains that frightened children, caused ladies to faint, and turned the stomachs of strong men.

"I still don't see him," Lady Hamilton complained, threading her way through the audience of onlookers. Prudence and Geoffrey followed in her wake. "I suppose he could have remained up above this time, but Martin is usually the one to retrieve the barrel. I don't recognize this other fellow."

"How will they open it?" Prudence asked, relieved to see that the iron-banded contraption seemed to be intact.

"The bolts keeping the latches closed on the lid have to be knocked out with a hammer," Lady Hamilton explained. "When they hold, that is. Sometimes they screw or nail the lid shut, but this time it looks to me like latches."

"I don't see any serious damage to the body of the barrel," Geoffrey speculated. "So perhaps the sheep will still be alive."

"Crazy Louie maintains that a man can go over the falls as soon as a barrel is designed to consistently make the descent without breaking apart. This one looks more well-constructed than some of his other models. More iron bands and thicker wooden staves, I'd say." Lady Hamilton nodded approvingly. "We may have to stop calling him Crazy Louie if he manages to pull off this stunt successfully."

The clang of chisel and hammer rang out over the muttered speculations that grew quieter as first one then another bolt was loosened, removed, and dropped to the ground. The barrel was eased on to its side, then a crowbar forced the waterlogged wooden lid that barrel makers called a head. The crowd held its collective breath, listening for the first indignant bleat that would signal the sheep was about to dart to freedom.

"Holy Mary, Mother of God!"

"Get him out of there!"

"Who is it?"

"Is he alive?"

The body pulled from the barrel was almost unrecognizably battered. It looked to the spectators as though the man's head had lolled about on a broken neck, smashing repeatedly against the inside walls of the cask as it crashed over the falls and into the raging river below.

One by one the bystanders turned away, walking slowly, silently, back toward their carriages or the footpath that led to the village. Soon enough they would burst out in morbid speculation, but for the moment the sight of a badly damaged human corpse had shocked them into speechlessness.

"It's Martin Fallow."

"Are you sure?"

"I recognize the belt buckle."

"He's big, like Martin."

"It was supposed to be a sheep. That's what Louie said was going over today."

"That's not a sheep."

"It's Martin, all right."

The man who'd worn the oilskin jacket when he waded into the water, took it off and laid it over the body.

"We've always known Louie was crazy, but Martin had a good head on his shoulders."

"Looked to me like his neck was snapped."

"Please God it happened as soon as he went over. Before the battering began."

"There's not even a blanket or a pillow inside to soften the blows."

"It was supposed to be a sheep," someone repeated. "A sheep."

"Are they right?" Geoffrey asked as he led Lady Hamilton and Prudence away from the scene. "Is that the man Daniel said came to him with suspicions about what the surveyors were doing?"

"It's Martin," Lady Hamilton said. "He did odd jobs all over town. We all know him. Knew him."

"Why didn't someone stop him from climbing into the barrel?" Prudence asked. "Surely they realized what would happen if he went over the falls without any kind of padding inside?"

"No one saw him get in," Geoffrey said. "Not under his own steam, at any rate."

Lady Hamilton stood stock-still. "What are you implying, Mr. Hunter?"

"He means this wasn't an accident," Prudence said, nodding agreement at her partner. She'd come to the same conclusion herself.

"Martin Fallow was murdered," Geoffrey said. "We're taking the case."

CHAPTER 6

Lady Hamilton, pale and unsettled, ordered her coachman to drop Prudence and Geoffrey at the spot where Crazy Louie had watched the fall of his doomed sheep.

Moments after they'd climbed out of the carriage to mingle with the crowd, the spectators learned that it hadn't been an animal who'd made the drop over the falls after all.

"That's impossible," Louie Whiting shouted at the breathless man who'd barely managed to describe what he'd seen before cries of disbelief erupted all around him.

"It was Martin Fallow inside," the bearer of bad news continued. His name was Allen and he'd never had to deliver a report as bad as this in the three years he'd been associated with Louie's barrel-over-the-falls project.

"Dead?" Crazy Louie asked. The brisk Niagara wind whipped the words from his mouth.

"Neck snapped like a chicken's. His head had banged around in the barrel so much, it was hard to recognize him."

"But you're sure it was Martin?"

Allen nodded. "It was Martin, no doubt about it. All of us

who pulled him out had worked with him at one time or another. Always wore that long shirt and the fancy belt buckle."

Prudence and Geoffrey had edged their way through the tourists and barrel launch regulars until they were close enough to overhear the conversation. After his first bellow of incredulity, Crazy Louie lowered his voice and took a few steps away from the appalled onlookers.

"Has anybody sent for the police?"

"I rushed up here as fast as I could, so I don't know," Allen said. "Someone's bound to have called for them by now."

"What did the barrel look like?"

Crazy Louie took out a pocket notebook to sketch what Allen described to him. He'd designed today's container to be bigger and sturdier than the last failure. The sheep had been calmed with a few drops of chloral hydrate, nowhere near enough to render it unconscious.

"Looked fine, looked good. All in one piece, hardly a dent or scratch except what you'd expect from being in the water and hitting a few rocks. Swear on a tick, Louie, we thought the sheep would come bounding out as soon as we got the head off."

"No sign of it?"

"We pulled Martin out and then looked inside. No sheep."

"That's impossible," Crazy Louie said again. "I bolted that barrel shut myself in front of witnesses. Everybody saw the sheep trot inside; even after the head was put on you could hear it bleating. We all stood there waiting until it quieted down. There was no way anyone could have made a switch."

"All I know is what I saw with my own eyes," Allen said. "That weren't no sheep went over the falls. Swear to God."

Crazy Louie raised an angry fist, then let it drop, almost striking Geoffrey as he whirled away from the assistant who had brought him news that might end the wild dream he'd spent half his adult life pursuing. "No interviews," he snarled. "You keep your damn questions to yourself."

"I'm not a reporter," Geoffrey answered, standing his ground.

"Private investigator." He held out a Hunter and MacKenzie business card.

"Crooked cop for hire. You're as bad as the press. Always poking your noses in where you're not wanted."

"Ex-Pink."

That stopped Louie in his tracks. Pinkertons had a dubious reputation for honesty and a penchant for violence, but they got results.

"I don't need anyone looking into my affairs. Couldn't afford you even if I did."

"My partner and I already have a client," Geoffrey said, nodding in Prudence's direction by way of introduction.

Crazy Louie snorted. He had no patience with interfering women and would have barred them from attending his demonstrations if he could. They were too softhearted to understand that animals had to die in his barrels so a man wouldn't.

"What's that got to do with me?"

"Maybe nothing." Geoffrey kept his voice low and even, persistent without being pushy. "A few questions, though?"

The man who had brought Crazy Louie the news of Martin Fallow's death stepped between Geoffrey and the cask maker. "I've seen these two before. Down below the falls where the barrel came ashore. They were in the crowd when we took the head off and saw the body."

"What were you doing there?" Louie asked, suddenly suspicious. He had a lot riding on being the first man to go over the falls and live to tell about it. "Nobody steals my designs."

"Our client isn't interested in how you build your barrels," Geoffrey said.

"But we are," Prudence said. "We'd like to know how a man replaced the sheep you say you personally sent into the water."

"Over the falls," Louie muttered. "Over the falls."

"P.T. Barnum would look for a false bottom," Prudence continued, aware that some in the crowd had stepped close enough to hear what was being said. "Have you seen any of his shows?

Magicians make solid objects disappear into thin air every day of the week and twice on Saturday. Once you get the hang of deception, it's not that difficult to pull off a stunt. An accomplice distracts the crowd for a moment, you make the switch, and the gullible are fooled again. Barnum would claim it's because they want to be."

Heads nodded. Everyone knew who P.T. Barnum was.

"I'm betting the barrel was supposed to be smashed to pieces when it hit the river," Geoffrey said. "Whoever paid you to get rid of Martin Fallow's body counted on the corpse disappearing into one of the whirlpools or not being found until it was too damaged to identify."

"But something went wrong, Mr. Whiting, didn't it? Your barrel was too well built. It didn't break apart the way it was supposed to," Prudence declared. Witnesses and informants sometimes cracked under the shock of interrogation by an assertive female.

"How much were you paid?" Geoffrey demanded.

"It won't be enough if the police decide to charge you with murder," Prudence added before Louie could deny the accusation. She watched the hand stroking his beard begin to shake.

"Were there two identical barrels?" Geoffrey asked. "Is that how you did it?"

Heads swiveled toward Louie, waiting for his answer. The popular daredevil inventor had transformed into a murder suspect. Greedy for money and recognition. Spectators who'd been skeptical about his announced intent to be the first man to survive the falls murmured that they'd known all along there was something not quite right and downright criminal about him.

Allen tugged urgently at Louie's arm, nodding toward an approaching horseman. "The constable is coming. You'd better get back to the American side."

"Nobody paid me a dime to get rid of a body or pull any kind of trick," Crazy Louie snarled, pushing through the small audience that stared at him in fascination. "I don't know where you get your harebrained ideas, Mr. Ex-Pink, but I put one hundred eighty-five pounds of Cotswold sheep in my barrel. That's what went over the falls. I don't know how Martin got where he ended up, but I had nothing to do with it."

Moments later Louie had blended into the remaining crowd. Prudence tried to follow his progress, but he'd disappeared.

When the Canadian constable arrived, there would be nothing for him to see, no one except stray tourists to interrogate. And on the American side of the river, Crazy Louie was as tolerated as an entertaining pet dog with a few odd habits. Someday he might make them all famous.

"Do you think he was telling the truth?" Prudence asked as she and Geoffrey walked toward Clifton Hill and their hotel.

"We won't get to the bottom of this until Amos Lang and Josiah get here," Geoffrey said. "I'm not trying to avoid your question, but we don't have enough facts to answer it yet."

"Do you have an opinion?" Prudence persisted, frustrated by her partner's refusal to venture a hypothesis based on pure speculation. There were times, and cases, when Prudence's hunches had proven at least as useful as the most cooperative of witnesses. "Why do we need Amos and Josiah?"

"Amos can worm his way into any situation without being noticed, something I don't think we'll be able to do now that we've appeared in public with Lady Hamilton. It's obvious that she's well-known in both Niagaras, which means we're objects of curiosity by association."

"And Josiah?"

"Nobody is as good with documents as he is. He can read between lines you or I might not even suspect are there. And he's tireless. Whatever is being manipulated inside the records offices won't stay hidden for long once Josiah gets a look at their files. He can stay at another hotel so there's no connection to us."

"What about Amos?"

"Amos makes his own arrangements. Nobody has ever been able to track him. That's how he earned his nickname. The Ferret." Geoffrey plainly enjoyed and envied Amos Lang's ability to disappear at will.

"Will you send a telegram?" Prudence asked.

"Lady Hamilton can dispatch one of her people to another town. I'll write out the message so all he has to do is hand it to the operator."

"Do you really believe the death we witnessed this morning is connected to Rowan? Wouldn't it be enough for the family to get the court to declare her not Lucas Adderly's child? Without any inheritance rights, she would no longer be a threat. That's the case Aunt Gillian sent us here to resolve."

"But it's not the case we've stumbled into. Think about it, Prudence. A surveyor's helper is killed, and his body disposed of in a way that should have resulted in it never being recovered in a condition that would allow for an autopsy. Unless I'm mistaken, everything revolves around that death. Rowan may be nothing more than a peripheral figure in a much larger scheme. We'll keep our heads down until Amos and Josiah get here."

"You gave our card to Crazy Louie," Prudence reminded him as they approached the main entrance of Clifton House. "You told him we were asking questions on behalf of a client." She didn't often have reason to criticize something her partner did, but this time she thought she was justified. "Now that he knows who we are, there isn't any point backing off. Accusing him of conspiring to murder Martin Fallow was not keeping our heads down."

"Touché," Geoffrey said.

The slightly smug tone of his voice told Prudence he hadn't blundered when he'd handed Crazy Louie their card.

"You did that deliberately," she said. "You want it known that a pair of private investigators is poking around and that by association we've been hired by Lady Hamilton."

"Metal filings to a magnet," Geoffrey said.

Prudence immediately pictured a host of small iron fragments flying through the air to land in ever-increasing clumps on a lodestone in the shape of a horseshoe. She knew there would be too much information, some of it deliberately misleading. Too many informants, some of them lying with calculated intent to deceive.

"The more players in the game, the more likely it is someone will make a mistake," she said, laying a hand on Geoffrey's arm as they stepped into the Clifton House foyer. "That's it, isn't it?"

"When is a sheep not a sheep?" he answered. "Tea?"

Later that afternoon they rented two horses from the livery stable behind the hotel and set out along the bridle path that ran beside the river above Horseshoe Falls. Prudence's tweed riding habit flowed gracefully over the sidesaddle around whose top pommel she'd hooked her right leg. Although they affected the air of a couple riding for idle amusement, Geoffrey had sketched out a specific itinerary. Some of it was going to be through uncleared forest.

"We know the barrel went into the river about a quarter of a mile above the falls." He was thinking aloud as their horses ambled side by side away from the livery stable and the hotel lawns where strolling guests enjoyed the view.

"Crazy Louie supervised the tranquilizing and loading of the sheep, left an assistant to do the actual launch, then went downriver to the place we met him, just opposite where the barrel would shoot over the falls," he continued. "It was crucial to be able to observe what happened during those few minutes of freefall and then when it landed in the water. That's why he posted spotters and a retrieval crew below, on the American side."

"You're convinced there were two barrels, aren't you?" Prudence asked.

No matter how often they'd gone over the discovery of Martin Fallow's body, there didn't seem to be any other logical explanation. If Crazy Louie was telling the truth.

"The switch had to have taken place after Louie had left the launch location."

"Which doesn't make sense if there was a crowd there as well as at the falls and at the recovery point. Someone would have noticed that there was a pair of barrels when there should have been only one."

"We'll know better once we can poke around without having to pretend we're casual tourists," Geoffrey said. Like Prudence, he was dressed as though for a jog in Central Park: tweed jacket, jodhpurs, bowler hat, and a pair of well-polished English riding boots.

"Is anyone following us?" Prudence reined her horse to the edge of the bridle path and threaded her way through the trees until she was sure someone riding by would not see them. Geoffrey dismounted by her side, placing a hand on each animal's muzzle. Five minutes passed in unbroken silence.

"All clear. I don't think we've attracted any unwanted attention." He tried not to wince as he swung back into the saddle, but the bullet he carried in one leg had a way of reminding him of its presence. Annoying, but no longer the crippling handicap he'd had to endure for nearly a year before the pronounced limp eased into a normal stride again. Prudence had learned to pretend not to notice it, though Geoffrey didn't think she'd ever stop worrying that the bullet would migrate out of the bone in which it was lodged. He'd been warned what to expect if it did. He refused to worry about what he couldn't control.

They found the site of the barrel launch easily enough, a trampled-down grassy verge almost level with a relatively calm portion of the Niagara River. A swath of current had carved out a shallow spot perfect for setting a boat into the water. Wagon ruts stretched off into the trees, proof that more than one adventurer had found the natural ramp site.

Prudence unfolded the map they'd picked up in the hotel

lobby. "There's a dirt road at the end of those tracks," she said, marking their location with the pencil stub Geoffrey handed her. "It meanders back toward town."

Hitching their horses to adjacent saplings, they began walking the area, pacing a mental grid that ensured nothing would be overlooked. A weak sun streamed through the woods, and after a few quiet minutes, they heard birdsong again and the scrabble of squirrels gathering their autumn harvest of acorns.

They didn't bother discussing what they were searching for. The best answer was that they'd know it when they found it. Signs of a second barrel stashed out of sight of the witnesses to the launch? A tool left behind by a careless conspirator? Wagon tracks where there shouldn't be any? Chewed tobacco plugs spit out by a man forced to wait until he could leave without being spotted and questioned? If there really had been two barrels, this was the most logical place to look for proof.

Late-afternoon shadows were falling across shoreline and bridle path when Prudence and Geoffrey finally admitted there was nothing to find. It had been a thorough exploration, but without the hoped-for results. They'd crisscrossed the launch area twice and ventured deep into the trees, discovering an abundance of animal tracks and scat, but only faint traces of human presence. None of them suggested anything but brief forays to the riverbank, almost certainly to witness one of Crazy Louie's barrel launches.

"There had to have been two containers," Prudence maintained, almost too tired to remount her horse. "Nothing else makes sense."

"We're missing something," Geoffrey said, leading the way back toward Clifton House. "And it's got to be because we don't know enough about the Niagara currents or what's happened in the past when boats or people were swept over the falls. Did any survive? Where did human remains or wreckage come ashore?" He sounded impatient with his own ignorance.

"We'll have to mend the breach with Crazy Louie," Prudence said. "Or find someone else with his knowledge and experience of the river. Daniel should be able to help with that." She hesitated for a moment. "I'll leave that part of the puzzle to you to solve. At least for the time being."

Geoffrey nodded. He'd been contemplating another visit to Daniel's cabin. He also wanted to see the workshop where Crazy Louie built his barrels. But he needed to know what Prudence had in mind to do next.

"Were you planning another conversation with Rowan?" Geoffrey asked.

"No, not Rowan. I don't believe she has that much more to tell us."

Prudence had done her best to put behind her the events that had nearly ended her life after the Great Blizzard of March 1888, but now she deliberately pulled them from the locked compartment of her brain where she'd consigned them. Greedy, unscrupulous stepmother and her equally unprincipled brother. The death of a fiancé, the suspected murder of her father, a brush with laudanum addiction that would forever haunt her.

"I know something about families whose members try to destroy one another," she reminded Geoffrey.

"The Adderlys?"

"Myra Adderly, to be precise. What we're lacking is context. You've always told me that for an investigation to be successful, we have to be able to place a suspect into the background that made him who and what he came to be."

"How will you manage it?"

"Lady Hamilton. She's so much like Aunt Gillian, they could be sisters instead of old friends. And no one is better at manipulating people."

"Amen to that," Geoffrey said. "Amen to that."

CHAPTER 7

"I don't know how true it is," Lady Hamilton said as the carriage entered the lower deck of the suspension bridge over the Niagara River, "but some of the older residents maintain that there was a time when people paid little attention to whether they lived on the American or Canadian side. Then the first bridge was built and began to play an important role in conducting slaves to freedom on the Underground Railroad. Before that, a few brave abolitionists ferried runaways across in small boats, usually at night."

Looking down at the water far below them, Prudence shuddered. "That must have been unspeakably frightening. And dangerous."

"I can only imagine the desperation," Lady Hamilton agreed.

"Rowan's situation is nowhere near that dire," Prudence said. "Challenging, yes, but certainly not life threatening."

She'd had a good night's sleep in a comfortable bed and a delicious Clifton House breakfast to start the day. Between the two of them, she and Geoffrey had crafted an initial investigative strategy and written the cryptic telegram to summon Amos Lang and Josiah Gregory. By the time they'd finished their coffee, steak, eggs, newly baked bread, fresh churned butter, and last summer's strawberry jam, Prudence had also decided the approach she would take with Myra Adderly. If Lady Hamilton managed to arrange a social call. Which, it turned out, she had.

"We're pushing things a bit," Lady Hamilton admitted, "but what's the use of a title if you can't use it to leverage your way in to where someone doesn't want you to go?"

"How does the social structure of the two Niagaras work?"

"We're different, separate," Lady Hamilton declared, "and determined to remain so, at least on the surface. One Niagara as British as it's possible to be on this side of the Atlantic, and the other very American. We work together whenever it's politically or economically useful, as when the province was nudged into creating Victoria Park after the New York Reservation was established."

"I remember you saying that both Canadian and American daughters of good families attend Our Lady of the Falls Academy," Prudence said.

"It's been that way from the beginning. The nuns would deny it, but the Academy's board of trustees is as much a political tool as any other organization in the area. The meetings are sometimes a dress rehearsal for upcoming discussions of a much less religious or educative nature." Lady Hamilton's smile was as lipless as a snake's.

"Rowan had very little to say about her time there."

"You'll find she's reluctant to reveal anything that might be taken as a complaint or grievance. I think she's been more severely punished for past honesty than she would have us know."

Educated by a French governess who was scrupulously supervised by her judge father, Prudence had never experienced living away from home in an institution governed by strict adherence to unbending routine and rigidly enforced rules of conduct.

"What kind of punishments?"

"Being locked inside a dark closet to learn obedience. Whipped across the backs of the legs and the palms of the hands. Writing the same absurd sentence over and over for a minor infraction. Wearing a dunce's cap in front of one's classmates. Called out by name and verbally chastised in the daily assembly. If you can imagine something so embarrassing it would bring you to tears, a boarding school directress has already thought of it."

"How much worse it must have been in the orphanage."

"That's one of the reasons I decided to take her to Daniel's cabin," Lady Hamilton said. "The Tuscarora clan mothers could be counted on to heal and care for her."

"But you told the Reverend Mother you were bringing her to your house to work as a servant," Prudence said.

"Lying is a necessary skill for a woman. If you haven't learned it yet, I suggest you start practicing immediately. You might consider Myra Adderly as a model. She's very good at making an untruth sound like gospel."

The carriage came to a stop high on a hill overlooking the falls from the American side.

The Adderly mansion bore no resemblance to the wedding cake house in which Lady Hamilton lived. Built of red brick with bands of patterned white inlay, surrounded by tall wrought-iron fencing between evenly spaced brick columns, the house sprawled across an expanse of lawn wide and deep enough to hold several large city homes. A curved carriage driveway beneath white birch trees led from the public road to the imposing front entrance and covered portico.

"I'll introduce you to Myra as the niece of a London friend visiting Niagara for the first time. That should put her off her guard. We'll save your professional credentials for later in the conversation."

"How will you bring up the topic of Rowan?" Prudence asked.

"Directly," Lady Hamilton said. "But not right away. She won't expect it, so watch for her reaction."

"I understand you're staying at Clifton House, Miss MacKenzie." Myra Adderly poured coffee into delicate Chinese porcelain cups. It was too early in the day for tea in American Niagara, so the coffee was a subtle rebuke to Lady Hamilton's insistence on this late-morning visit. Society ladies didn't usually welcome callers until the afternoon hours.

"I was told it was the most comfortable hotel in the area," Prudence replied.

"And do you find it adequate?"

"More than I expected. The view is magnificent, and the dining room as elegant as one might find anywhere."

"High praise indeed, but Niagara must seem a backwater to someone from the city."

"Nothing comparable to the falls is to be found in Central Park, Mrs. Adderly." Prudence wasn't sure where the conversation was going, but she had agreed to maintain a flow of inconsequential chitchat until Lady Hamilton picked her moment.

"One gets used to them, living here as we do."

"And the sightseers? We saw a great many of them as we drove across the bridge and through the village. Do you get used to them as well?" Prudence kept her tone light, and her gaze slightly distracted, as though she didn't really expect a serious answer to her question.

"We ignore them whenever possible. They're a seasonal nuisance, like flocks of migratory birds."

"I wonder that you haven't asked me about Rowan." Lady Hamilton set down her cup and fixed a gimlet-eyed stare on her hostess.

The temperature in the room dropped by several degrees as Myra met and held her guest's icy blue eyes.

"You'll be glad to know she's safe, in good health, and growing stronger every day."

"The girl's welfare is of no personal concern to me or any member of the Adderly family, Ernestine. I'm surprised you would believe any differently."

"Miss MacKenzie isn't here to marvel at the wonders of nature," Lady Hamilton said.

Prudence raised her eyes from contemplation of coffee cups and slices of raisin cake.

"Oh?"

"She's a lady lawyer, recently admitted to the state bar. I've engaged her services on behalf of your granddaughter."

"I don't have a granddaughter." Myra Adderly rose to her feet, a few short steps away from the bellpull that would summon a servant to show out her unwelcome guests.

"Rowan Adderly is your son's daughter by Grace Malone," Lady Hamilton said. "We'll prove it in court, if necessary. If that's the route you choose to take."

Myra froze in place.

"Sit down," Lady Hamilton directed. "Unless you want your butler to hear what I have to say." She gestured toward the servant standing in the open parlor doorway.

"That will be all, Simons," their hostess said without raising her voice. "I'll ring if we need something."

The butler disappeared, closing the door behind him. Myra seated herself in a pale blue silk armchair as though it were a throne and she a queen granting regal audience to a pair of beggars. It was a pose that had long intimidated family members and social inferiors, as much a part of her personality as the frame of mind that created it.

Lady Hamilton wasn't the least impressed.

"That's better. Rowan was badly treated in the orphanage you had her sent to. You knew that would happen. I wouldn't put it past you to have told the Reverend Mother that she deserved special attention for the airs and graces she had no right to assume."

"The girl was dealt with exactly the same as every other foundling. No more, no less. Those were my explicit instructions."

"You knew the town would be abuzz with the change."

"The family decided it would not be appropriate to continue paying the girl's tuition and board once we became convinced she wasn't one of us."

"*The family?* Don't you mean *you,* Myra? No one has seen or heard from Lucas in years, your husband is paralyzed and cannot speak, and your daughter, Daphne, rarely emerges from the purdah of widowhood into which you pushed her."

"My daughter supervises the care and education of her two sons."

"They have a tutor to do that."

"Daphne's health has always been fragile."

They were dueling, Prudence realized, exchanging precisely placed barbs where they would hurt the most. These two well-bred women nursed a grudge of such longstanding bitterness that it had to stretch back for years, long before Lady Hamilton's rescue of Rowan Adderly. The *girl,* as her grandmother called her, was only the most recent skirmish conducted under cover of a deadly polite exchange.

"To get back to your granddaughter," Lady Hamilton began.

"Despite the use of our family name, that girl is *not* my son's child."

"Of course she is. More to the point, she's his heir."

"The court will disagree. If it comes to that."

"The whole town knows Lucas set up a trust for her."

"Trusts are private documents. They don't have to be filed with a court and they certainly don't have to be shared with outside interests who ask for their particulars."

She was right. Prudence was on the point of agreeing when

she realized that Lady Hamilton had known all along that she had no right to any of the information contained in the provisions of Lucas Adderly's trust. She'd been goading her hostess in the hope that Myra could be pressured into losing her temper and divulging the details of what was coming Rowan's way when she turned eighteen in a few weeks' time.

"What you're telling me is that during all the years Lucas came back to Niagara every spring or summer, you accepted that Rowan was his daughter. But as soon as you could reasonably doubt that Lucas was alive, you denied her. That's what it looks like to me. Don't you agree, Prudence?"

"I think the pertinent documents will tell the story," Prudence answered. It was a favorite quote of Judge MacKenzie's, usually when he had no idea on which side of a dispute the truth lay.

Lady Hamilton flashed her a look that could have frozen the falls.

"I can assure you there is neither marriage nor birth certificate to prove that Grace Malone ever entered into any legal liaison with my son."

Myra's assertion had the confident ring of truth. Which meant, Prudence decided, that someone had taken care to destroy whatever documents had existed that might prove a valid marriage and legitimate birth.

"I wish I'd met her," Lady Hamilton said. "Is it true Grace was the most beautiful woman ever to have favored Niagara Falls with her presence?"

"She was a slut, a shanty Irish trollop who only avoided selling herself on the streets because she could sing well enough to entertain the drunks in a saloon." Myra's teeth ground against each other and her breath came in short bursts.

"I've been told her voice was operatic in quality, and that Lucas first heard her when she was booked into the Niagara Music Hall. That's hardly a saloon."

"No lady of decent reputation struts about on a stage."

"Sarah Bernhardt, Lillie Langtry, Lillian Russell, Eleonora Duse . . ."

"The women you've named are not ladies. They are creatures of a certain class who entertain the masses and therefore do not merit social recognition."

"Rowan has inherited her mother's voice. It's a gift I'm sure enchanted but also perhaps saddened her father."

"My son was *not* her father."

"Then why have you taken such an interest in her? Why is it rumored that the Adderly family will do whatever is necessary to disprove her claim that she is, in fact, Lucas Adderly's legitimate daughter, born within the bonds of matrimony? Is there a great deal of money at stake, Myra? Will the reins of power pass from your hands into those of a young woman you openly despise?"

"Mother? I heard raised voices. Is something wrong?"

Daphne Adderly Yates resembled Myra not at all. Where her mother commanded, Daphne cowered.

Trembling hands knotted together, she stared at Lady Hamilton and Prudence as though she'd never before seen guests in the Adderly House parlor.

"I'm s-sorry. I didn't mean to interrupt. It—It was just the raised voices. I thought there might be a problem," she stammered.

"I haven't seen you in such a long time," Lady Hamilton gushed, crossing quickly to the parlor door no one had heard open. She took Daphne's hands in hers and led the young woman toward where her mother frowned and Prudence waited to be introduced.

"We were talking about your niece, Rowan," Lady Hamilton continued smoothly, settling Daphne beside her. "How fortunate that the cousins are so close in age. I imagine they're one another's best friends."

Daphne stared at Lady Hamilton in horrified dismay, then burst into tears.

CHAPTER 8

They were waiting for him when Geoffrey emerged from the tree line, as if he'd sent word on ahead that he was coming. But he hadn't.

A woman sat beside Daniel, one moccasined foot resting on Hero's back. The dog thumped his tail in greeting but did not rise or leave his master's side.

"You knew I'd return," Geoffrey said as he approached the steps.

"You haven't been told the story you came to hear." Daniel said something in the language Geoffrey could not decipher. The woman nodded.

"My name is Susanna Landers." Cradling a small basket on her lap, one hand threaded beads onto a needle while the other held a lady's purse onto which Susanna was sewing a complex pattern of green leaves and purple flowers. She smiled at Geoffrey. "Rowan has many natural talents. Beading isn't one of them."

"She said tourists buy the purses."

"Purses, belts, book covers, hair ornaments . . . If we can attach beads to it, we can sell it." Susanna chuckled as if laughing to herself at the inexplicable ways of Niagara sightseers. "Rowan sings to the women when we gather to bead. It makes the hours fly to listen to her."

"Susanna knew Grace Malone from before her daughter was born," Daniel said by way of explaining Susanna's presence. "She's here to answer the questions you haven't asked yet."

"I'm a midwife," Susanna explained. She set the beadwork aside, empty needle secured in a spot of undecorated fabric. "Grace sought me out when she suspected she was pregnant. She only requested confirmation, not the herbs I could have given her."

"Did Lucas Adderly know?"

"He came with her. Anyone seeing them together would have realized they were in love. The first thing he said after I had examined her was that they would get married. Right away. The smile on his face was as bright as sunrise."

"What happened?"

"Myra Adderly intervened. His mother. When he told her they were getting married, she forbade it. Made such strong objections that they ran away together." Susanna shook her head over the foolishness of the young and the intransigence of the old. "I told them they were making a mistake not to stand up to her. They were both of legal age. Myra couldn't have stopped them taking out a license. But it was what she would have done to Grace that made up Lucas's mind. Myra has an adder's tongue and she hated what Grace was. She would have made her life miserable. No one could have borne it for long."

"Tell him," Daniel said. "Tell him everything."

"Grace Malone was an Irish immigrant, born in the middle of the Atlantic on a coffin ship in conditions so bad that sharks followed along behind for the bodies that were thrown overboard every day," Susanna began. "Her mother died giving birth. No one, including Grace's father, expected the baby to survive, but she did.

"Malone found work on the towpaths along the Erie Canal among the Irish who had settled there after the waterway was built. He remarried and there were other children, but Grace was the jewel of the family. She told me the reason her lungs were so strong was because she cried day and night for the sugar water she was fed when there wasn't a nursing mother available. Her father poured whiskey in the bottle to put her to sleep."

"I've been told she was a beautiful woman," Geoffrey said.

"Lucas Adderly had never seen anything like her," Susanna said. "Neither had anyone else in Niagara. Rowan is captivating, but Grace was nothing short of glorious. The piano-playing half brother who traveled with her had the same general coloring, but he was a carrot top. Washed-out red hair, skin as pale as skim milk, freckles that looked like dirt blotches he'd forgotten to wash off. His name was Thomas Malone. They called him Tommy Ginger. He was a drinker. But he loved his sister."

"Grace and Tommy were touring with a show that got booked into the Niagara Music Hall for a two-week run. Everyone in town went. There wasn't much else to do here then," Daniel said. "I remember some of the acts on the bill. There was a family of acrobats, a pair of comics, trained dancing dogs, and a minstrel group." He smiled as if he could see them capering behind his sightless lids.

"Grace was the lead act, the showstopper. You could hear a pin drop when she sang. When she was done, the audience jumped to its feet and cheered and applauded until she agreed to sing an encore. They tossed flowers everywhere; she was surrounded by them. Lucas came to the Music Hall on opening night. He was smitten as soon as she walked onto the stage. By the time she'd sung her last song he knew he had to have her or die trying.

"The run was extended for another two weeks, then a second month. Sold out every night. Tommy Ginger never knew what

Grace and Lucas were up to. He started drinking when the bartender put a glass of whiskey on the piano before the curtain went up and didn't stop until he passed out."

"She must have gotten pregnant right away," Susanna said. "So much in love, there wasn't a grain of common sense between the two of them."

"Go on," Daniel urged.

"Myra would have seen to it that Grace never felt a part of the Adderly family," Susanna said, "but that wasn't the real reason Lucas took her away." She ran one hand through the crystal beads in her basket, letting them drop through her fingers like teardrops. "Myra has a still room in that big mansion of hers. She makes fruit cordials and syrups for the croup. Sachets of lavender and rose petals to put in the linen drawers.

"She almost bled to death when Daphne was born, and even though she'd had two children in three years' time after she was first married, she never quickened again. Or if she did, she knew the herbs that would resolve the problem."

"Lucas was afraid she'd give Grace a concoction that would abort the child she was carrying," Geoffrey guessed.

"He knew she would. He'd let himself believe his mother would welcome a grandchild, but he didn't make that mistake twice. He read the obstinate look in her eyes and realized that in order to save the baby's life, he had to take Grace away from the woman who would find a way to kill her and the unborn infant."

"Did he explain to Grace why they had to leave?"

"I don't know," Susanna said. "The bond between Myra and her only son was a strange one. Unbreakably strong, but loveless."

"The story around town was that Grace and Tommy Ginger had welshed on their contract and left the show," Daniel explained. "Tommy sobered up long enough to smuggle Grace out of the hotel without being seen. They stayed with Susanna until Lucas settled things with the bank and the family lawyer. That's where I met her."

"The trust?" Geoffrey asked.

"That came later," Daniel said. "Lucas wanted to be sure that wherever he and Grace ended up, he'd have access to funds no one else in the family could touch. He never intended to stay away forever."

"I got to know Grace because she was lonely," Susanna said. "Her brother hardly said a word and Lucas had to stay at Adderly House. He couldn't risk anyone finding out where she was hiding or what he was planning. We sat and talked for hours. She told me the red hair ran in both her father's and her mother's families, and that whether she had a boy or a girl, she planned to name the baby Rowan. *Little redhead.* She didn't say as much, but I've always believed Lucas paid Tommy Ginger to travel with them until they could find a preacher or justice of the peace. He thought that once Myra discovered he'd tricked her, she'd send people to chase them down, but they'd be looking for a man and a woman on their own."

"How long did they stay with you?" Geoffrey asked.

"Not much more than a week or two. Long enough for the show to leave town and for Myra to believe her son had come to his senses. The next time I saw Lucas was when he brought Rowan to Niagara after Grace had died."

"He was a defeated man," Daniel said. "I didn't think he'd recover."

"But he did," Geoffrey said.

"Enough to make another fortune out west," Daniel agreed. "But not enough to forgive his mother or bear the sight and company of his daughter. He blamed Myra for Grace's death and saw nothing but his loss in Rowan's face."

"He visited Niagara once a year until Rowan had nearly grown into young womanhood. Then nothing."

Daniel fell silent and Susanna picked up her needle and

began threading the crystal beads again. Neither seemed able to say that Lucas was probably dead. Why else would six and a half years have elapsed since he last saw his daughter?

"You said Lucas had included tracts of undeveloped land in the trust he created for Rowan. *Multiple* tracts, as I recall. How sure are you?" Geoffrey asked.

"We think Lucas planned to guarantee a secure future for his child by tying up those portions of the family property that would rightfully come to him on his father's death," Daniel answered. "They couldn't be sold in his absence or without his consent. We know he acquired more land every time he came back to Niagara."

"You're certain of that?"

"Much of what he bought lies along the river and stretches well into the forest. It was land no one wanted at the time, uncleared and without access to the few existing roads."

"Too far from the falls to attract summer visitors," Susanna said. "Lucas had a love for the untouched forest that is seldom found among your people." She ducked her head in mute apology. "Even among some Tuscarorans."

"Lucas said more than once that he envied me," Daniel added. "Being born Tuscaroran. Having that connection to the land."

"There's a link between the threat to Rowan and the killing of Martin Fallow," Geoffrey said, when it became apparent that Susanna and Daniel had no more to add. "Whatever information you can give me will help find it."

"I'll ask among the women," Susanna offered. "Over the years many of them have worked for Niagara's white families. People like that rarely realize how much their servants know about them."

"The Adderlys have always been a powerful force in American Niagara," Daniel explained. "No one dared go up against Cyrus Adderly before his accident. Everyone assumed Lucas would prove to be the same kind of entrepreneur his father had been."

"Then Grace entered the picture," Geoffrey finished.

"And everything changed."

Susanna's skilled fingers created another sparkling green leaf.

Crazy Louie's workshop occupied an abandoned riverside factory whose owner had declared bankruptcy and sold the run-down premises to the only interested buyer he could find. Unmarked by any signage, it was nevertheless known to everyone in the area.

"Louie Whiting? You mean Crazy Louie?"

No matter who Geoffrey asked as he worked his way through American Niagara's industrial area, the answer was always the same. A smile, a laugh, a shake of the head, and then directions that ended with the assurance that he couldn't miss it. Just keep an eye out for a ramshackle building surrounded by piles of cracked, broken, disassembled, and half-built barrels of all shapes and sizes. Louie's many failures and incurable optimism were as much a part of local lore as the falls.

The factories along the river and the free state park for tourists were as different as night and day, Geoffrey decided as he skirted muddy puddles and avoided piles of smelly garbage. One area flaunted commercial exploitation at its worst, the other lauded preservation of unspoiled natural beauty. Had there been no Save Niagara movement, there almost certainly wouldn't have been a single green spot left within walking distance of the water.

He saw Crazy Louie before he recognized the old factory behind him for the workshop it had become. Hatless, coat off, a leather apron covering him from chest to knees, Louie was chopping barrel wreckage into sticks of firewood that he loaded into a wheelbarrow and carted inside. This close to the river, and with the wind blowing the direction it was today, the up-

draft from the falls coated everything with a fine layer of chill-
ing spray.

Geoffrey stood in the shelter of the open double doors, letting his eyes adjust to the gloomy interior, welcoming the heat
from the stove into which Crazy Louie was feeding the scraps
he'd just hacked into pieces. The damp wood crackled and
popped, spitting drops of water as it burned.

On one side of the large space a dozen or so barrels had been
assembled in orderly rows. Opposite the finished products
stacks of cut staves lay seasoning, filling the air with the scent
of clean lumber. Beside the staves, tangles of iron hoops curled
around one another like blackened potato peelings. Whatever
else he was, Crazy Louie's workshop proclaimed him an organized and painstakingly precise worker.

"I don't allow visitors," Louie said, turning from the stove to
see who had invaded his sanctuary. He picked up the small axe
he'd used to trim the kindling. "Best be on your way."

"I gave you my business card," Geoffrey said. "Ex-Pink?"

"I remember. I told you then and I'm telling you now. I put
a Cotswold sheep into the barrel that went over the falls.
Where it got to and why Martin Fallow rode the river instead I
haven't a clue."

"Have the police taken a statement from you?"

"Been here and gone. My answers are the same no matter
who's asking the questions."

"Someone has to be called to account for Fallow's death."

"It won't be me."

"Can you be sure of that?"

"I'm not behind bars, am I?" Louie hefted the axe in powerful hands.

"You'll find it harder and harder to keep your name clear the
longer it takes for them to make an arrest."

"What's that supposed to mean?"

"I could use your help. And in return, my partner and I will
do what we can to find out who killed your assistant."

"He wasn't an assistant," Louie said, wiping his hands on a rag he then stuffed into a back pocket. "I'd send word when I needed him, and if he didn't have anything to do that paid better, he'd come. Martin was his own man about things like that. He worked when he needed cash money. The rest of the time he hunted and fished, or he'd set up the beadwork tables when the clan mothers sold their purses and whatever else they'd made. He'd hang around to make sure nobody tried to walk away with a souvenir they hadn't paid for."

"You know a lot about someone who wasn't your assistant. It sounds as though you liked him."

"Martin was as good as his word, and there was never any doubt he was telling you the truth. He was probably a little simple in the head, but there wasn't anybody better at numbers."

"Someone told me he worked for the surveyors when the Reservation was being planned out."

"He did, though I got the impression he wasn't crazy about the job. Plenty of people didn't think much of the government claiming it had the right to buy land they didn't want to sell. Went to court over it. Lost, of course. It got so you couldn't say the words *eminent domain* without someone giving you dirty looks or spitting on your boots."

"How long did he work for the surveyors?"

"As long as it took. Months to begin with. They'd come back from time to time, and they always hired Martin. He was big and strong and kept his mouth shut. Did his work, pocketed his coins at the end of the day, and disappeared into the trees until the next time he was needed. Nobody knew these woods like Martin. He was as Tuscaroran as they come, and I don't mean anything negative by that."

"Did he have a cabin somewhere?"

"Not a clue."

"How did you let him know you needed him?"

"We had a system. I'd put one of these oilcloths in the forked branch of that tree over there, and the next morning he'd be standing in the doorway drinking coffee when I'd come walking up the road." Louie took the cloth out of his back pocket and wiped his hands again. "Guess I won't be doing that anymore."

"I don't see the barrel," Geoffrey said, not bothering to specify which barrel he meant. There could only be one.

"Police confiscated it when they took Martin's body away."

"I'd like to examine it."

"Come back in a couple of days. They won't keep it long. There's nothing to see except where the poor bastard's head got knocked around. No trick locks. No false bottoms. I built that barrel with my own two hands, and I built it solid."

"I'd still like to take a look at it."

"Suit yourself. Like I said, you won't find anything."

"There's always something, Mr. Whiting," Geoffrey said. "I'll be back."

"I'll let you poke around my barrel, Mr. Ex-Pink, but don't bring that lady partner of yours with you. I don't like women messing around in my business."

Without offering a handshake, Louie walked away.

CHAPTER 9

Daphne's sobs were loud enough to eclipse the crackle of flames in the fireplace, but neither her mother nor Lady Hamilton moved a muscle or murmured a word of comfort.

Prudence reached into her reticule for a clean handkerchief, but after a quick glance at Lady Hamilton, left the square of fine linen where it was and sat back to await whatever would happen next.

Myra Adderly's daughter was unexpectedly plain and timid, an awkwardly tall girl grown into a stoop-shouldered, apprehensive woman. Faded brown hair gathered into a tight knot at the back of her head, pale brown eyes flooded now with tears, a complexion that looked as though it had never been touched by a ray of sunlight. Her gown was a pale gray that stole every bit of color from the painfully thin creature wearing it.

Lace mittens covered Daphne's hands, but as Prudence catalogued what she was observing, she noticed that the tip of one of her subject's fingers had made a hole in the delicate filigree. The nail had been bitten down to the quick and a tiny drop of blood stained the chewed material. In the investigations undertaken by Hunter and MacKenzie, Prudence had grown accustomed to dealing with women from every social stratum, but she thought she might never have come across as miserably unhappy and out of place a woman as Daphne Adderly.

"My daughter, Mrs. Yates," Myra said in a clipped, authoritative voice. "Daphne, Lady Hamilton has brought us a woman lawyer from New York City, Miss Prudence MacKenzie."

"My practice is not restricted to women clients, so I don't believe that *woman lawyer* is entirely accurate," corrected Prudence. She had lately found herself bristling at *woman doctor, woman reporter, woman anything* when the implication was that the profession referred to was reserved for the male sex except for a few female interlopers. She'd let it go when Lady Hamilton had first introduced her to their hostess, because tipping Myra off balance had been the plan they'd agreed upon, but twice in one morning was too much.

"How are your dear sons?" Lady Hamilton asked, deftly switching back to the topic that seemed to have brought on the onslaught of tears only now beginning to subside. "I am sure they're a great comfort to you."

Prudence had noticed something else about Daphne's lace gloves, a sizable protrusion on the fourth finger of her left hand. On the right, where widows about to remarry wore the ring given them by their late husbands, was the smooth outline of a gold wedding band. Lady Hamilton spied them at the same time.

"I should be congratulating you," she said, training sharp eyes that missed nothing on the widow's strained face. "I recall reading the engagement announcement in the *Niagara Falls Gazette,* but I have a dreadful memory for details." Lady Hamilton seldom read the local newspaper. "Do we know the lucky bridegroom-to-be locally? What is his name, dear?"

Daphne turned tearstained eyes to her mother.

"Carter Jayden. You may have heard of him, Miss MacKenzie. He's a prominent investor from New York City." Myra reeled off a list of properties in which Daphne's husband-to-be had substantial equity, ending with the Fifth Avenue Hotel, where Geoffrey had long had an apartment.

"I'm not acquainted with Mr. Jayden," Prudence said. "But there are many financial and real estate speculators in the city who aren't part of the social scene."

The angry flush on Myra's cheeks told her she'd hit the mark. Carter Jayden obviously wasn't part of Mrs. Astor's Four Hundred.

A quick glance from Daphne silently applauded the remark that put both her fiancé and her parent in their places. Prudence wondered how often Myra's daughter said or did anything unsanctioned by her mother. How old was she? Late thirties perhaps, if the two sons who had been mentioned were approximately the same age as Rowan. It wasn't unusual for women wed in their late teens to have grown children while still in their childbearing years.

"Where will you and Mr. Jayden make your home?" Lady Hamilton asked.

"Here in Niagara," Myra said. "He'll have a pied-à-terre in the city, of course, for business purposes, but their chief residence will be right here." She smiled in motherly satisfaction.

"Mr. Jayden is building a house for us," Daphne said, her remark made so softly that Prudence had to lean forward to hear her.

"I'm sure that between decorating projects and planning for the wedding, you haven't a moment to spare," Lady Hamilton probed.

"Mr. Jayden makes the decisions," Daphne said. She had removed the lace mittens and now one finger stroked the diamond of her engagement ring. Too large for so slender a hand. But how would anyone know how wealthy her husband was if a woman didn't wear jewels that proclaimed his worth?

"I look forward to meeting him." Lady Hamilton smiled as though she meant it.

"How fortunate that you chose this morning to call," Myra

said. "We expect Mr. Jayden any moment, don't we, Daphne? He likes to keep us up-to-date on how things are going."

"Does he have other projects in Niagara?" Prudence asked. It was as obvious as the nose on her plain face that Daphne held no physical allure for a prospective husband, equally noticeable that she wasn't a witty conversationalist. She was, however, sole heiress to the Adderly family fortune if her brother could be proved dead and not the father of the child he'd sought to protect with what she hypothesized was a shrewdly crafted trust.

"More coffee?" Myra offered.

"Lady Hamilton had a board of trustees meeting at the Academy," Prudence said. "I wasn't terribly disappointed to be deprived of her company for a few hours."

"She can be hard to take," Geoffrey agreed, slipping his partner's arm through his. He refrained from mentioning once again how much Ernestine reminded him of Prudence's aunt; the comparison was too obvious to miss.

They were strolling the grounds of Clifton House, Prudence having returned in time to see Geoffrey arrive by hired hack. In the interests of keeping their conversation private, they'd decided on a late tea. In the meantime, there was information to exchange, plans to refine, and the fine October weather to enjoy.

"Something about Carter Jayden was nauseatingly familiar," Prudence began, "but it's taken me a while to figure out what it was."

"You've got my full attention," Geoffrey said.

"Don't tease. I'm serious."

"I know you are," he apologized.

"Do you remember my stepmother's horrid brother?"

"Donald Morley," Geoffrey said. "How could I forget him?"

"How could anyone?"

Morley had schemed with his sister to deprive Prudence of

control over the fortune her father had left her. Eventually he'd conspired to confine her to the care of a doctor who specialized in laudanum sedation of women whose male relatives wanted to be rid of them. He'd come to a grisly end, knifed outside the Haymarket, one of the most disreputable saloons in New York City's criminal underworld. In the opinion of everyone who'd ever had any dealings with him, Donald Morley had well deserved his fate.

"That's who Jayden reminded me of. He has the same heavyset frame, the same greedy look in his eyes. Just seeing him sent chills up my spine."

"What else?" Geoffrey asked.

"He's marrying Daphne Adderly Yates. I'm sure it's for the family wealth she'll come into once Myra proves that Rowan has no claim to any portion of it."

"Daniel told me that Lucas purchased land along the river before he left Niagara. He added more tracts to his holdings every time he came back."

"Jayden is a real estate speculator. According to Myra he owns a piece of a number of properties in the city, including the Fifth Avenue Hotel."

"That was a smart investment, if it's true. Anyone who had the foresight to realize that apartment hotels would take over the property market quadrupled his initial outlay," Geoffrey said. "I don't suppose Daphne chose him without persuasion."

"Jayden doesn't strike me as a man who will keep his hands off his wife's inheritance. You'd think Myra wouldn't want that kind of interference."

"She's counting on him to increase the Adderly fortunes by developing the land Lucas had the prescience to buy. Once he marries into the family, it becomes as much his as anyone else's. I don't see him agreeing to any other terms in the marriage contract."

"That only works if Myra believes she can manage and manipulate him," Prudence said. Both she and Geoffrey came from a world in which the legal niceties of property acquisition were spelled out in excruciating detail long before the engaged couple exchanged vows.

"Has she ever failed at getting what she wants?"

"I doubt it. Except for Lucas's choice of wife. She certainly has Daphne under her thumb."

"What about the two grandsons?"

"I didn't meet them. I think they're about the same age as Rowan, perhaps a few years younger. A tutor was mentioned."

"From what you've told me, I don't think the Adderly matriarch would bring an outsider into the family unless she had to. Lucas had undoubtedly been groomed to take his father's place, but when he chose Grace Malone and then disappeared, Myra had to find someone else."

"She could have waited until Daphne's boys were old enough," Prudence said.

"You'd think so. A few more years, until they'd finished at Yale or Harvard."

"I wonder why she didn't."

"There's bound to be rumors, gossip. The more important the family, the more they're talked about. We'll set Amos to finding out what Myra's hiding."

There was silence for a moment as Prudence searched her memory for anything else she needed to tell Geoffrey about the visit to Adderly House. She couldn't shake an uneasy feeling about Carter Jayden, but he hadn't stayed in the parlor long enough to engage in conversation. He'd nodded his head at Myra and Daphne, realized they were entertaining visitors, and left before anything more than cursory introductions had been made. Strange conduct for a gentleman, especially one who was shortly to join the family. He smelled strongly of pipe tobacco; so had the step-uncle Prudence had never trusted. But was that a reason to have misgivings about him?

She started to describe the odd behavior, then turned toward the sound of galloping hooves and carriage wheels grinding on the dirt and pebbles of the roadway.

"Geoffrey, is that Lady Hamilton's brougham charging up the road?"

A white handkerchief waved out one of the windows; they heard a woman's voice shouting commands as the coachman fought the sweating horses to a stop. The footman riding on the rear of the coach leaped to the ground to help Lady Hamilton descend.

"Can you make out what she's saying?" Prudence asked as they hurried across the lawn.

"Murder," Geoffrey said. "Someone's been murdered."

Hero lay at Daniel's feet on the porch where Geoffrey had left them a few hours before. His right foreleg had been splinted and wrapped in rags. Every few moments his flanks heaved as a spasm of pain rippled the length of his body, but his eyes remained dull and unfocused, tail unmoving.

Lady Hamilton sat down beside Rowan, draping her cashmere shawl across the girl's quivering shoulders, lightly touching Daniel's leg so he would know where she was. Susanna nodded a greeting to the new arrivals; she held a basket of torn and bloody rags in one hand, a recently emptied basin of water in the other.

Prudence and Geoffrey remained at the foot of the steps, appalled by what they were witnessing, but reluctant to intrude.

Lady Hamilton's carriage had hurtled across the suspension bridge and through American Niagara at breakneck speed, depositing them as close to Daniel's cabin as it could get. They'd hurried through the woods not knowing what to expect, fearing the worst. Each of them had breathed a sigh of relief at the sight of Rowan and Daniel, still alive.

"Someone set a trap a few feet into the clearing. It's never happened this close to the cabin before," Rowan said.

"My nephew had promised to come with a buggy to take me home, so I'd walked to the river to say good-bye to Rowan," Susanna explained. "I heard barking and came back as fast as I could. Rowan was faster."

"I ran."

"Someone arrived at my back door with the message that murder had been committed," Lady Hamilton said. "He took off before I could speak to him."

"My nephew," Susanna said. "A bit melodramatic." She grimaced. "But it got you here."

She disappeared into the cabin with the rags and the basin. When she rejoined them, her face was set in determined, angry lines.

"This wasn't an accident, though it was intended to look like one."

Rowan raised bewildered eyes to the clan mother's face.

Susanna laid a reassuring hand on the girl's shoulder. Her eyes lingered on Hero, then focused on Geoffrey and Prudence. "That's why I sent for you."

Prudence's first thought was to wonder what they would be seeing if Rowan had sprung the trap. Would they be looking at a mangled human foot that would have to be amputated to stave off gangrene? She knew by the quick bunching of the muscles in his jaw that Geoffrey was picturing the same thing.

"Tell us what happened," he instructed. "Everything you can remember."

"Whoever primed the trap must have done so after you left, Mr. Hunter. He waited until he saw Daniel on the porch and no one else in the clearing. Hero might have stood up when he sensed someone approaching, but he's trained not to leave Daniel's side unless he perceives an immediate threat. I think the person stepped out from the trees, did something to alarm the dog, then stood his ground, drawing Hero in the direction he wanted him to take. Some sixth animal sense must have made Hero pull back at the last minute, just enough so the jaws of the trap didn't crunch through bone and muscle the way they were designed to do. Didn't kill him right away or injure him so badly, we'd have to put him down to end his suffering."

"The trap wasn't there yesterday," Rowan said. "I walked the woods looking for mushrooms. I would have seen it."

"It was concealed under pine straw and leaves," Susanna continued. "By the time we reached him, Hero was trying to gnaw off his paw."

"Animals do that when they know they're trapped with no hope of escape," Daniel said.

"Susanna pried open the trap with an axe handle. Hero's leg was bleeding badly and at first we thought the bones were broken," Rowan said. "We tried to carry him back to the cabin, but he wouldn't let us. He set off toward the stream that runs through the trees out back, crawling and sometimes limping, leaving a trail of blood. We didn't know where he was going or why, but he wouldn't stop."

"When it became obvious that he had collapsed for the last time, we dragged and carried him to the porch. Daniel cradled his head while I bathed the leg and splinted and bandaged it."

"Will he live?" Prudence asked.

"The next few hours will be crucial," Susanna said. "I've given him something to dull the pain. It's made him sleepy, but he's coming around." She raised one of Hero's eyelids, nodding satisfaction at what she saw. His tail lifted an inch or two off the floor, as much of a wag as he could manage. "Animals have amazing resilience. They're much harder to kill than human beings."

Geoffrey had wandered out toward where the sprung trap lay at the edge of the clearing, the axe handle still holding open the steel jaws that had mangled Hero's leg. He bent over to examine the mechanism, nudged the piece of wood, and drew back hastily as the metal vise snapped closed, clamping down viciously on nothing. He used the axe to lift it, knowing from his hunting years in North Carolina how unpredictable and dangerous traps like this one could be. His father had called them the jaws of death with good reason. Many a runaway slave had lost a foot and then his life to traps that didn't distinguish between human and animal prey.

"I've never seen one of those before," Prudence said, walking across the clearing to join him. "Do you believe what Susanna said about what happened to Hero not being an accident?"

"There have to be dozens of rabbit and squirrel traps in these woods, but hunters know not to set them too close to where people are living. This one has been out in the weather for a long time. Look how rusty it is. That might have bought Hero an extra couple of seconds."

"That doesn't answer my question."

"If it was deliberate, there has to be a reason behind it."

"You don't think it was meant for Rowan?"

"I think it's more likely to be a diversion. Get the dog out of the way by killing or severely maiming it, then move on the real targets while their guard is down."

"Is that what a Pinkerton would do?"

"Pinkerton operatives working undercover have always been taught how to get rid of animals that might warn of their presence."

Geoffrey paused halfway across the clearing, studying the bloodied trail left by Hero as he'd scrabbled his way through the fallen leaves and pine straw. He laid the trap on the ground, then stepped back, hefting the axe from hand to hand as he thought through the puzzle.

"What is it?" Prudence asked.

"Let's suppose whoever set this trap didn't wear gloves when he was working on it."

She understood right away where he was going. "He left his scent behind. On the trap and wherever he walked."

"And then he didn't go back out the way he'd come in."

"He skirted the edge of the clearing and reentered the woods from behind the cabin," Prudence said, studying the path of pine straw Hero had pushed aside as he crawled.

They set out to follow the trail he'd left, Prudence keeping to the cabin side of the scuff marks, Geoffrey to the forest edge. If there had been footprints, Hero had covered them over. They moved slowly, cautiously, examining every bit of ground they trod. It took only a few minutes to lose sight of the group on the porch.

A small vegetable patch lay under a mulch of leaves. A narrow pathway led from the garden to the bank of a stream flowing behind the cabin.

"It's ice cold." Prudence stooped to dip her fingers into the water. "I think that's a cold safe," she said, pointing to a metal box tethered to a tree and trenched into the stream bed.

"This is where Hero collapsed," Geoffrey said. "You can see where they brought a blanket or piece of canvas to put him on so his body wouldn't drag on bare ground."

"He got this far and then he gave up," Prudence said, remembering the many times she'd walked and worked with the shaggy red-gold dog she and an Irish hansom cab driver had rescued from life on the city streets. Blossom had a nose that could track anything and anybody; the only time she lay down was at the end of a scent trail, when she'd reached her objective. "Hero stopped here on purpose. He was trying to tell us something."

"The lid on the cold safe is ajar. Don't touch it," Geoffrey warned as Prudence stepped toward the stream. "I'll use the axe on it."

She stood back as he sent the lid flying into the stream. Another blow hurled it out of the water and onto dry ground.

"There's a dead squirrel inside," Geoffrey said. "A cooked chicken wrapped in torn butcher's paper, a bottle of milk, a piece of cheese tied up in cloth, and two apples. The chicken and one of the apples have been gnawed on."

"I'll get the basket Susanna put the rags in," Prudence said.

"We'll need the rags, too. Some poisons can be absorbed through the skin."

"Poison? Are you sure?"

"Ask the squirrel."

CHAPTER 10

Amos Lang packed his traveling bag, then broke apart, oiled, and reloaded the gun he carried in a shoulder holster. He sharpened the knife he wore in a sheath on his belt and the one hidden inside his right boot. A medium weight pair of brass knuckles rested in a jacket pocket and the much deadlier knuckle knife got tucked into a rolled-up nightshirt. Just in case he needed it. He never went anywhere without carrying a ring of skeleton keys, and since there was no telling how long he'd be in Niagara or what he'd find when he got there, he decided on two changes of shirt and pants. Shaving mug and brush, razor and strop, toothbrush and comb. As many boxes of ammunition as would fit among the clothes.

Geoffrey Hunter's telegram had been written in a code he and Amos had modified from one long used by Pinkertons. Brief and to the point. *Get up to Niagara as fast as you can. Rendezvous as soon as you arrive.* Amos memorized the directions to the meeting place, then burned the telegram. He stopped by the Hunter and MacKenzie office on his way to Grand Central Depot to pick up a cash advance, compare messages, and coordinate travel plans with Josiah Gregory.

"I'm to stay at the Wainwright Hotel, on the Canadian side," the secretary told him.

"Where are you making contact?" Amos asked.

"I'm meeting Miss Prudence at Hamilton House. Lady Ernestine Hamilton is a longtime friend of Lady Rotherton."

"Anything else?"

"I've contracted with the Pinkertons to locate someone named Lucas Adderly, last known to be in San Francisco." Josiah shrugged and shook his head. "No address. No information except his name and a physical description from years ago that could fit hundreds of men in that city. Thousands, probably."

"If he's there, the Pinks will find him," Amos promised. "Who is he?"

"The telegram didn't say." Unlike Lang, Josiah hadn't destroyed his coded instructions. He'd filed away the yellow flimsy, as he did every bit of paper that crossed his desk. Human memory was not always reliable, but the written word was gold to an investigator. Or someone thinking about writing his memoirs.

Josiah tidied the papers on his desk, covered the Remington typewriter whose clacking gave him a headache, and locked up the office. It was going to take him longer to pack than he suspected it had taken Amos. Josiah wasn't an ex-Pink used to trekking from place to place with a single carpetbag. When he traveled, which was rarely, he could seldom make do without at least one trunk, a large portmanteau, and a decent selection of vests for every occasion.

"Do I need to remind you that if we do bump into one another up there, we act as though we've never met?" Amos had great respect for Josiah's capacity to manage paperwork, but grave doubts about his abilities in the field.

"No, you do not need to remind me," Josiah snapped.

But of course he already had.

The Traveler's Rest Hotel in American Niagara was as decrepit a place as any Amos had ever stayed in. He supposed its weather-beaten boards had been painted a dark grassy color once upon a time, but only splotches of dirty green pigment remained. The front porch boasted a pair of splintery rockers, four spittoons with generous skirts of brown tobacco juice, and an empty whiskey bottle. A stench of urine from the alley where men pissed drifted toward the narrow, unpaved street on which the hotel fronted. Someone had raked horse droppings into a pile beside the porch steps. Flies buzzed and settled on the heap despite the October chill.

It wasn't the kind of place that was ever fully booked; he had his choice of a room on the ground-floor front or the second-floor rear. Front would let him keep an eye out for whatever was going on in the street, but rear always made for an easier exit out a back window if the occasion called for it. Reluctantly, because cats usually mated and howled in rear alleyways and fistfights erupted behind saloons, he chose the room on the second-floor rear. Surprisingly large, but not unexpectedly grimy, it contained a double bed, a candlestick atop a chest of drawers, and a chamber pot set conveniently near a basin and pitcher. No water. A thin towel, grayish sheets, an unraveling rag rug, and a quilt whose stuffing had long ago begun to escape made up the rest of the room's creature comforts.

Since he had no expectation of privacy at the Traveler's Rest, Amos concealed as much of his extra weaponry around his person as he could, then used his knife to slit open the mattress along a corded seam, wedging the boxes of ammunition as deep into the horsehair as he could reach.

It was already midafternoon. He had a long walk ahead of him.

Geoffrey's directions had been concise and accurate. An hour after setting out from the hotel he had renamed the Traveler's Unrest, Amos halted a few feet from the clearing where Daniel Johnson's cabin stood. A burst of ferocious barking stopped him in his tracks.

Moments later a tall, silent form glided through the trees, stepping so softly on the forest floor that until he revealed himself, Amos was unaware of his presence. It was the first time in his career he'd been discovered before reaching his objective.

"I'm here on Geoffrey Hunter's instructions," Amos said to the figure who was keeping to the shadows.

"You're expected, Mr. Lang. The dog will not harm you. Please proceed."

He hadn't been able to get a good look at the man now walking behind him, but the voice had been well modulated, the choice of words and the delivery that of an educated individual. Judging by the absence of any verbal tremor and the ease with which he moved, Amos pegged him as younger rather than older. Armed, of course. Hunter would never post a weaponless sentry on guard. Under the circumstances, it was best to continue until told to stop, remain silent until asked to speak, and keep vulnerable fingers curled into fists. By the sound of the barking he'd heard, the dog he'd been told wouldn't harm him had large jaws and very sharp teeth.

"You made good time," Geoffrey said, stepping down from the porch, crossing the clearing with hand outstretched to welcome the ex-Pink who now and then accepted an assignment that interested him.

"Josiah arrives tomorrow."

"Good."

"I wasn't followed." Amos didn't bother adding *as far as I know,* because he would have known. He'd always been aware of when a man or woman had him in their sights. Until a few minutes ago. He turned toward the path from Niagara. No one was there. "He's good."

"As good as I've ever seen," Geoffrey agreed. "Tuscaroran."

Amos nodded. No white man could best the finest of the Indian trackers.

"I want you to meet someone," Geoffrey said, leading the way toward the cabin.

An old man with braided hair and an aged, weather wrinkled face stood up from his rocker as they approached. The closer they got, the more he seemed not to see them, until, finally, Amos understood. He climbed the steps and waited for the blind man to hold out his hand before extending his own.

"Daniel, this is Amos Lang," Geoffrey said, "the ex-Pink I told you about. Amos, Daniel Johnson."

"Mr. Johnson. It's a pleasure to meet you, sir."

"You'd best call me Daniel. We'll be seeing a lot of one another." Daniel smiled at his own jest, then asked the question he only posed to people he sensed would not be frightened or repulsed by it. "May I touch your face?"

"I'd be honored."

Daniel's sensitive fingers flitted lightly over Amos's features. It took only a few seconds for him to picture what he could not see. He understood what Geoffrey had meant when he called this man the Ferret. There was nothing about Amos Lang's face that was memorable. Only because he was blind would Daniel be able to describe him.

"The dog's name is Hero," Daniel said, sitting down again, stroking the coarse fur.

"What happened to him?" Amos gestured toward the front leg that was stiffened by rags wrapped tightly around a piece of wood stretching from paw to shoulder. He let his hand fall when he realized that Daniel could not see the motion he'd made. Then he curled the fingers into his palm and held them out for the animal to sniff. He'd never seen so large, dignified, and handsome a beast. Half dog, half wolf, he guessed, remembering all of the mutts he'd been raised with, ugly creatures who'd loved the unwanted boy more than either of the parents who'd spawned him.

"Shall I tell the story?" Geoffrey asked.

Daniel nodded.

There was an air of controlled fatigue about the elderly man that told Amos he hadn't slept well in a very long time, but that he was someone whose entire life had been built around mastery of the senses. Blindness was a defeat to which he refused to surrender.

"Someone set a trap just inside the clearing, then stepped out from the trees, knowing Hero would make a beeline for him," Geoffrey began, his wording as succinct as the report he would eventually write.

"No one saw who it was?" Amos asked.

"There wasn't anyone else here, just Hero and my grandfather," a voice from the cabin doorway said.

Amos had seen Irish redheads before, but never one as brilliantly colored as a sunset and as beautiful as the marble angels in Catholic cathedrals. He whipped the battered hat from his head, held it awkwardly in his two hands.

"Rowan Adderly," the young woman said, introducing herself as she stepped onto the porch with a tray of coffee mugs in her hands. "Susanna Landers and I—you'll meet her—were on the bluff overlooking the river. We heard the barking and came running back, but by that time, there was only Hero in the clearing.

"Susanna got the trap pried open with an axe handle. Hero's leg was bleeding badly and at first we thought the bones were broken," Rowan continued, handing coffee to Geoffrey and Amos. "He set off toward the stream out behind the cabin where we keep a cold box for food that could spoil. He left a trail of blood every time he set the injured leg down. We didn't know where he was going or why, but he wouldn't stop."

"He had the scent of the man who'd handled the trap and he was following it," Geoffrey finished. "The food in the cold safe had been poisoned. Food Susanna hadn't bought and placed there."

"How did you know?" Amos asked.

"By the time Prudence and I got here, Hero had been splinted and bandaged and carried to the cabin, but we were able to retrace where he'd gone. He'd laid down for the last time opposite the cold safe that sits in the stream."

"He'd pointed his nose at it like a hunting dog sighting a bird," Rowan said.

"There was a dead squirrel inside the safe and some of the food had been bitten into."

"But why set a trap for the dog?" With hat back on his head and a gulp of strong coffee in his stomach, Amos turned his chess player's mind back to the case he'd been summoned to Niagara to work. Time enough to dream of red-haired Irish angels when he unstoppered the brown glass bottle of laudanum that lulled him into sleep at night.

"The poisoner knew he couldn't approach the cabin without Hero barking a warning. And he needed time to arrange the food inside the safe to look as though Susanna had put it there. So he waited until he thought Daniel was alone, lured Hero to the trap, and then finished what he'd come here to do. There are rabbit snares all over these woods. Everybody who lives out here knows to watch out for them. Hero was supposed to have died. Sometime that day or the next, Rowan would have served the food that was meant to kill her and Daniel. There wouldn't have been any suspicion of foul play. Meat spoils, even in a cold safe. Nobody knows why some people get belly gripes and others who've eaten the same meal die from it."

"Susanna says we can take the brace and the wrappings off Hero's leg in two or three more days," Rowan said. "He's already gotten his bark back."

Amos stared at her.

As calm and serene as though she hadn't a care in the world. Stroking the ears of the injured dog, leaning lightly against Daniel Johnson's rocking chair, smiling affectionately at someone who couldn't see the love in her eyes. It was as though she didn't realize she'd come within inches of dying an excruciating death. How could that be?

Amos had seen the effects of arsenic, of too much morphine, of overdoses of patent medicines in corked brown bottles. Poisoners were the cowards among murderers. They left their deadly potions and walked away, many of them never to be caught. Nothing gave Amos as much satisfaction as watching a poisoner he'd apprehended dangle from a rope.

He looked over at Geoffrey and read the same thoughts on his employer's face.

Neither of them would back away from this case until they'd wrung the neck of the man who'd tried to kill the Irish angel with the sunset hair.

Jean-Baptiste Napier watched from the trees as the man he'd stalked offered his scent to Hero, his respects to Daniel, and something no one but Jean-Baptiste suspected to Rowan.

He'd been patrolling the woods around the clearing since Hero's injury, snatching sleep at odd hours, approaching the cabin only to eat and assure Daniel that he and Rowan remained safe. So far, there were no signs that whoever had lured Hero into the rusty trap and deposited poisoned food into the cold safe had returned to assess the damage he'd intended.

Susanna had maintained that it wasn't necessary to take Hero to one of the Niagara veterinarians; her years of caring for expectant mothers and their families had trained her in all manner of animal as well as human disease and injury.

But Jean-Baptiste knew there was another reason to keep quiet about what had happened. When danger threatened from an unknown source, the wise warrior drew back, concealed himself, and waited for his enemy to come out of hiding. A poisoner working on his own would eventually succumb to curiosity and the need to gloat over his success. If he'd been hired by someone else to do the job, he'd have to present whatever proof his employer demanded before payment would be made. Men who lived outside the law did not work for free.

Patience and vigilance. Two virtues Jean-Baptiste had learned as the outcast child of a French father and a Tuscaroran mother. Raised off the reservation without the security of belonging that was a vital part of the clan structure of his mother's people, he had been schooled as a European by a father who was the product of a rigorous Jesuit education.

In looks Jean-Baptiste was more Tuscaroran than French Canadian. He'd recognized a fellow conflicted soul in Geoffrey Hunter the moment he'd looked into the American's eyes. The man Lady Hamilton had summoned to rescue Rowan acknowledged a kindred spirit when he'd offered his hand.

CHAPTER 11

"He has to get money from somewhere," Geoffrey told Amos, describing Crazy Louie's workshop and way of doing business. "Passing the hat after a demonstration isn't enough for the kind of operation I saw. He doesn't make barrels for anyone else, so there's no income from that direction. He paid Martin Fallow and a few others whenever he needed them, but he didn't hire full-time or permanent employees."

"Could be he needs someone to take the dead man's place," Amos speculated.

"My thoughts exactly. What do you know about cooperage?"

"Not a thing. But by the time I meet Mr. Crazy I'll be an expert in the art and science of cask making."

Geoffrey didn't warn Amos about the danger of asking too many questions. Without seeming curious, the Ferret could coax information from a source or a suspect that not a one of them ever recalled having given up.

Nobody drinking at the saloon across the street from the Traveler's Rest remembered where Crazy Louie came from or when he'd arrived in Niagara. Just that he had a lunatic notion of being the first man to deliberately and successfully fling himself over the falls. As for choice of conveyance, that was hardly a mystery.

"I've got two empty barrels in the basement right now," the saloonkeeper said. "Taking up space until the brewery delivers again. They're all over town."

"Kids crawl into them in the winter and roll themselves down the hills as soon as we get a decent snow," someone else added.

"Well, they're round, aren't they? Stands to reason you'd have a better chance than if you shut yourself up in something that won't spin." The third speaker slammed his glass down on the bar authoritatively.

Heads nodded.

"And they float. There's whirlpools to navigate once you get to the bottom of the falls," the saloonkeeper reminded them as he refilled glasses.

"You don't want to survive the drop just to drown. That's not dying smart." The fourth customer cocked a finger at Amos. "Much obliged."

As long as he could pull coins from his pocket, the opinions would flow as steadily as the beer. One garrulous fellow described in great detail how to construct a barrel.

"It's all in how well the wood seasons and how strong the banding is," he'd declared, explaining how he'd come to the trade of cooper and why he'd had to give it up. "Snapped these here three fingers of my right hand off. Clean as a whistle. That banding steel can be as sharp as a knife. Nothing to play around with, let me tell you."

By the time the drinkers started repeating themselves, Amos knew he'd get nothing more out of them that could prove useful.

Fifteen minutes after he'd left, all anyone could remember

was that some stranger had been buying rounds. They'd already forgotten how the conversation had turned to the subject of barrels.

The Traveler's Rest Hotel was a fifteen-minute walk from Louie Whiting's workshop. Amos made it in ten, eating up the distance with a long stride that never looked hurried, but moved him along so rapidly few could keep up the pace. He lingered in the doorway long enough for Crazy Louie to notice and then stepped inside as though he belonged there.

Passing through, he volunteered, jobbing his way back along the Erie Canal to where his brother-in-law had opened a small cooperage. Specialty barrels for the fine whiskey trade, hand crafted and made to order. Not like the factories that turned out hundreds of cheap barrels a day. It was all in the handling of the white oak, he elaborated laconically, how each stave was fitted to the one next to it so not a drop of the spirits would leak. Was there any work here for a man who knew what he was doing?

It was the mention of hand crafting that got Louie's attention. Every barrel he'd made had been different from every other one. Most of them had taken on water or splintered on impact.

"I can't give you but a few days or a week at the most," Amos told him. "Like I said, I'm planning to get to my brother-in-law's shop by the end of the month, but I need traveling money."

"Can you design a barrel to specifications?"

"That's what I'm good at. Started out learning about the wood and along the way found I could pretty well sketch whatever a customer wanted." He'd tucked a yellow pencil with a thick lead into the strap of his billed cap and rubbed coal dust into his callused fingers until the stain looked natural.

"I'm working on something you might be able to lend a hand with," Crazy Louie said. He'd had an idea that morning that needed to be drawn out before wasting any wood on it. "When can you start?"

"Right now." Amos spat on the palm of his hand to seal the deal.

"Fair enough. I've got a barrel over here that came down the falls without breaking apart, but it's not as big as I'm gonna need and what was inside got beat all to hell."

"What's the stain?" Amos asked, leaning into the barrel out of which Martin Fallow's body had been pulled.

"Blood," Louie answered. "I've been trying out sheep."

"What kind of sheep did you use?" Amos took the knife from his belt and shaved off a piece of the stained wood. "Soaked right into the fibers," he said. "Must have been a lot of it."

"Cotswold," Louie said. "Most of the sheep around here are Cotswold. Thick coats, sturdy. This one weighed a hundred and eighty-five pounds. I made sure of it."

"Man weight." Amos eased the sliver of wood into a coat pocket.

Louie considered how to tell him that a sheep had gone in, but a man had come out. The blood the stranger had been scraping with his knife wasn't animal. It was human.

"This the barrel everybody's talking about?"

"What are they saying?"

"That the reason you need a new helper around here is because you killed off the last one." Amos plastered a wicked grin on his face. Conspiratorial. As if ending the life of a fellow human being was as inconsequential as drowning an unwanted litter of kittens.

"When did you say you'd gotten into town?" Louie asked.

"I didn't. But I did say I was just passing through."

"I'm guessing you've heard the whole story."

"In with a sheep, out with a dead man. There's bets being laid on how you managed it."

"Don't waste your nickel on 'em. I didn't do a damn thing

except test out that barrel you stuck your head into. Whatever else happened had nothing to do with me."

Amos shrugged his shoulders as if the topic of the sheep that turned into a man was too ridiculous to waste time over.

"You got an extra leather apron somewhere around the place?" He scanned the rough wood walls on which hung a variety of tools and discarded scraps that might have some use left in them. "You got anybody else working for you?"

"A fellow named Allen Thompkins is more regular than the rest of them, but he mostly helps out with the demonstrations and retrieves the barrel. Paddy Morgan comes by whenever he's sober and his pockets are empty. He handles the rough work and the heavy lifting, but he's not much good at building a decent barrel from scratch."

"Is he good at anything?"

"Bare-knuckle boxing. Irish stand down." Louie handed Amos a battered leather apron, scratched, stained, and pliable from years of heavy use. "If you want something to bet on, he's your man. Paddy may be a drunk, but he's got some fight left in him. He'll stand there and take punches like nothing I've ever seen. Wins more than he loses."

"Punch-drunk. Only a matter of time before he's through."

"You know about Irish stand down, do you?"

"I've seen a few matches." Amos didn't add that in his opinion it was one of the most vicious sports bloodthirsty men had ever invented. Against the law in most jurisdictions. The famous outdoor fight between John L. Sullivan and Jake Kilrain had been staged in a secret location in Mississippi where the July heat reached well over a hundred degrees. Seventy-five rounds, more than two hours of battering, vomiting, bloody fists pounding. John L. was a drunk, too, but he was also a champion.

"There's others from time to time, but it's been mainly Allen, Paddy, Martin, and me for the past few years."

Money to pay casual hires was always in critically short supply, but Louie didn't think the new man needed to know that. Nor that Allen and Paddy had often not been paid at all. Not by Louie, at any rate. Fisticuffs and cock fighting weren't the only things you could bet on in Niagara. Information was gold to the bookies who set the odds. Louie himself had been known to put a finger on the scales. The new fellow didn't need to find out about that either.

But Amos Lang had already guessed the truth of it.

They met at Daniel's cabin again, the only place in Niagara where Geoffrey felt confident of escaping notice. On his own, Amos was unremarkable, but Geoffrey's height and looks didn't afford him that advantage. For the undercover work to succeed, no one could suspect a connection between the wealthy New Yorker staying at the elegant Clifton House and the newest guest at the rundown Traveler's Rest.

Jean-Baptiste had recruited two more young men to guard Daniel and Rowan; unseen, unheard, they moved through the forest like ghostly wraiths. Amos paid them the compliment of pretending not to know they were there.

"I haven't met him, but there's a fellow named Paddy Morgan who's worth taking a look at," Amos told Geoffrey that night.

"How so?"

"He's a bare-knuckle boxer who does some of Crazy Louie's heavy work. A drunk, and punch-drunk for good measure. My sense is that information gets sold to the bookies every time Louie sends a barrel over the falls. Whether it's likely to hold together, whether the animal inside will survive, whatever can be wagered."

"Do you know where the fights are held?"

"Not yet." But as soon as he did learn their location, Amos planned to attend the next bout. Ex-boxers usually became doormen, bodyguards, and enforcers, jobs that required muscle but not much thinking. He wanted to get an idea of how far down the mental ladder Paddy Morgan had slipped before fingering him for what had happened to Hero and what had been planned for Daniel and Rowan. He'd thought more than once that it had been a sloppy job from start to finish, an assignment he would have executed very differently. But there was no telling what a drunk would do for his next bottle.

"What about Louie? Could he be deliberately sabotaging himself once in a while to fix a bet?"

"I wouldn't be surprised, especially if he's not sure the barrel he's been working on will hold up. All that effort with nothing to show for it unless he can rig the stakes? That's a temptation somebody in his situation would be hard-pressed to resist. He's not a stupid man, but he's obsessed with this quest he's set himself. One more thing. Louie's a drinker, too. Hides it better than some, but tips a flask whenever he thinks no one is looking."

"He very nearly blew up when I accused him of being paid to dispose of Martin Fallow's body," Geoffrey recalled. Heavy drinkers were notoriously short-tempered.

"Conclusion?"

"About whether he's capable of murder? Everyone is, given the right circumstances," Geoffrey said. "The bare-knuckle Irish stand downs and the betting that goes along with them add another dimension to Crazy Louie's situation. From what you've told me, Paddy Morgan has a foot in both arenas. I wouldn't be surprised if Louie does also. There's money to be made rigging fights and whatever else men bet on."

"Nothing you've told me about what happened to Hero and was planned for Rowan and Daniel smells professional. No account was taken of the effect rust would have on the jaws of that trap, and leaving the lid partially open on the cold safe smacks of panic. Pros don't panic."

"That makes the job harder. Amateurs are unpredictable."

"Have we got two unrelated cases here?" Amos asked. "A triumph of coincidence?"

"I don't believe in coincidence."

"Neither do I. Most of the time."

"I'd feel better about everything if we knew more about Martin Fallow's murder," Geoffrey said.

"It had to involve two barrels," Amos said, switching back to the only logical explanation for what had everyone making wild guesses. "Two identical barrels."

"The sheep disappeared without a trace. So did the barrel he was riding in. If it ever went into the water at all."

"Somebody made money off the stunt. Maybe a lot of money," Amos said. "We need to find out who and how much."

"It won't take Josiah long to learn who's in debt in Niagara. The deeper the hole, the harder it is to climb out of. The more desperate a man gets."

"Fallow worked with the surveyors who plotted Olmsted's free park. I'll set Josiah to combing through those records while he's digging up what he can on Lucas Adderly's holdings," Geoffrey said.

In the end, they decided that until they had more information, Amos would stick close to Crazy Louie and Geoffrey would attempt to unravel the attacks on the inhabitants of Daniel's cabin. If there was a connection between the two seemingly random occurrences, they'd find it.

Jean-Baptiste stepped into the clearing after Hunter and Amos Lang had left. They'd moved quietly down the trail to the road, obviously trained men, but no match for the skills his mother's people had perfected over centuries of adapting for survival.

Daniel left the porch for his bed as soon as he felt night fall. Age was catching up with him, as it did to everyone, even men whose eyes had not failed.

Limping, but no longer in the kind of pain that made him pant whenever his injured leg touched the ground, Hero followed his master.

Rowan made sure both her patients swallowed the medicines

Susanna had insisted they take. Sleep was nature's surest healer and the best gift she could give them.

Jean-Baptiste heard the rustle of her skirts as she stepped through the cabin doorway, closing it softly behind her, wrapping around her shoulders the luxurious cashmere shawl Lady Hamilton had insisted she keep. In the moonlight her hair shone with scintillas of red light, like sparks leaping from an evening campfire.

They walked together in the moonlight.

Neither of them spoke.

From deep in the trees just beyond the clearing, eyes watched.

CHAPTER 12

Josiah's room at the Wainwright Hotel was spacious, comfortable, and inconveniently located on the Canadian side of the river.

"It couldn't be helped," Prudence told him over tea at Hamilton House the afternoon of his arrival. "The cover we agreed upon is that you're an archivist hired by Lady Hamilton to catalog her late husband's books, personal papers, and property records."

"I was under the impression I was to find out whatever I could about an American named Lucas Adderly," Josiah said. "I've already hired Pinkertons to look for him in San Francisco. As you instructed." He decided not to add that Pinkertons came at considerable expense. Josiah prepared meticulously detailed invoices for every case Prudence and Geoffrey worked on, but he considered the casual mention of money vulgar and best avoided.

"And you will. But for the moment we want that done sub rosa. The late Lord Hamilton was a careless investor. From what Lady Hamilton has told us, he bought into whatever struck his fancy, on both sides of the river, putting his wife's name on the American properties and gifting them to her to avoid British inheritance laws. You'll start your work in Canadian Niagara, but you've got a ready-made justification for obtaining access to the American records. It's a short ride across the suspension bridge. Residents of both towns make the journey every day," Prudence assured him.

"So I'm to be a cataloger?"

"Your real work will be in what you can uncover in the records offices."

"I'll have to start by spending time in the late Lord Hamilton's library if we're to carry this off. Servants are terrible gossips. It will be all around town if the archivist at Hamilton House doesn't put in a full day's work."

Prudence handed him a key. "The room has been stocked with the special kind of boxes archivists use and there should be ledgers on the desk. If you need anything else, you're to ring for it."

While they waited for Lady Hamilton to return from an errand she'd informed the butler she had to handle personally, Prudence filled Josiah in on what they'd learned so far. She described the scene on the riverbank when Martin Fallow's body had been found inside the barrel that should have contained a Cotswold sheep. By the time she finished, he was shaking his head over the notes he'd taken in the narrow secretary's notebook that slid into a specially made inner pocket of his jacket.

"Why haven't the Adderlys gone to court yet to challenge the granddaughter's legitimacy?" Josiah asked. "They're cutting it very close if she's only a few weeks away from her eighteenth birthday."

"We don't know," Prudence answered. "Myra Adderly claims that no marriage certificate exists because her son never formalized the relationship everyone in town knows he had with Grace Malone. The story she's spread is that Grace was a harlot who wouldn't be able to name the man who fathered her daughter. My impression is that she believes the lack of confirmation may be sufficient to set Lucas's daughter aside without having to drag the family name through a court proceeding. I'm here in case she changes her mind."

"We need proof that a marriage license was issued and that a valid union took place. A signed and witnessed document. Or if it's been destroyed, the sworn testimony of witnesses."

"Exactly. We'd also like a copy of the trust Lucas established before he disappeared."

"That won't be on file anywhere except in a lawyer's office," Josiah said.

"We think Lucas suspected his family would try to deprive Rowan of her inheritance when the time came," Prudence said.

"So it's possible that he arranged for a copy to be hidden where they couldn't get their greedy fingers on it?" Josiah liked nothing more than complicated schemes hatched by venal fraudsters. And if they were family members trying to cheat one another, so much the better.

"I don't know what's keeping Lady Hamilton," Prudence said.

Speak of the devil, Josiah thought, as a brief commotion at the front door of Hamilton House announced the arrival of its owner. A woman's voice, brisk and authoritative, demanded to know if Miss MacKenzie had arrived. Moments later the parlor door was flung open. Josiah caught a glimpse of the elderly butler, a flustered maid, and a tall footman standing in the hallway surrounded by parcels.

"I am so sorry for being late, Prudence," Lady Hamilton trilled, extending gloved hands as she crossed the room. "And this must be the magician who's going to bring order out of my late husband's chaos. Mr. Gregory, I presume?"

If Josiah hadn't known better, he would have sworn it was Prudence's aunt Gillian welcoming him to Niagara. Lady Hamilton had the same graceful, willowy figure as Lady Rotherton, similarly striking features that had been exquisite in youth, eyes that bored into you like knives but could just as quickly soften and beguile. For a brief moment he wondered if all the dollar princesses had been cut from the same pattern. Beautiful, cultured, impeccably styled young women whose mothers had groomed them within an inch of their lives to capture the titles an impoverished European aristocracy was eager to exchange for impressive dowries.

A wave of French perfume washed over him as he took the hand she offered. Something else, too. An oddly farmlike scent, faint but unmistakable. Josiah glanced down and glimpsed a trace of what looked like mud or manure on Lady Hamilton's elegantly shod foot, just a trace of brown, but enough to offend his sensitive nose. What was a lady of her stature doing traipsing through that kind of muck? Surely the footman handing her out of her carriage would have seen to it that she stepped onto dry ground. He filed the incongruity in his orderly brain to be examined later.

"I imagine Miss MacKenzie has filled you in on everything," Lady Hamilton said as she led the way to the library, shedding hat, gloves, and reticule as she went.

The maid who had been sorting packages trailed along behind to catch her mistress's belongings as they were tossed aside. She flashed a conspiratorial smile at Josiah, as if to tell him his late Lordship had been no more careful of his belongings than his widow was of hers. He nodded and returned the smile with a quick nod.

Servants, maids especially, were as good at revealing what lay beneath the surface of a household as the paperwork their employers preferred to keep hidden from the eyes of the world. One question hadn't been asked and answered, and now it was niggling at Josiah's logically ordered brain. Lady Hamilton was no part of the family that had spawned Lucas Adderly, he of the questionably legitimate daughter and promiscuous working-class wife. Why, then, had she involved herself in their affairs? It didn't make sense.

And when something didn't make sense to Josiah Gregory, he had to find out why.

The late Lord Hamilton's library looked as though a careless thief had rummaged among the papers covering his desk and stacked haphazardly atop the books lining the walls.

"My husband allowed no one in here," Lady Hamilton announced, brushing one speculative finger over the dust that had settled on every surface. "Not even the maids. He insisted on his privacy."

More than likely the deceased lord was usually deep in his cups and uninterested in the orderly progression of his affairs. Josiah guessed that he'd come and gone on his own whims, accounting to no one for where he was heading or how long he'd stay away. If he was like others of his ilk, he'd plowed through the portion of Lady Hamilton's dowry that was under his control and then had little further use for his wife. Nor she for him. They might have kept up the social front required of them, but their personal lives had probably been lived in a precarious state of truce.

"I've let it be known that the late Lord Hamilton's papers contain documents attesting to the economic development of the province," his widow said. "Which makes the records he left behind valuable and deserving of a place in the official archives. Stuff and nonsense, of course. Farley didn't give a tinker's damn about anything except a full whiskey glass, a decent hunting rifle, and a brace of dogs to retrieve his kill. Canada was a last chance for him to recoup his losses. Needless to say, he wasn't successful. But this mess will make an acceptable camouflage for what we're really about."

"I'll do some preliminary rearranging this afternoon," Josiah said. "But the important work will take place in the town records office. Tomorrow or the next day would be logical."

"The sooner you can manage it, the better," Lady Hamilton

said. "I have a very uneasy feeling about what's happened in the past week. Something or someone has stirred the pot."

"I agree," Prudence said, picking up a handful of whiskey-stained papers. "It happened too quickly to be caused by our arrival on the scene, but there's no doubt in my mind that things have begun to move. And I don't like the direction they're taking."

Prudence left Hamilton House before Josiah had finished sorting the papers on Lord Hamilton's desk. By that time, he was admitting that the task before him was gargantuan and likely to be odious.

The late lord had dribbled ash and whatever he happened to be drinking over nearly every document he'd handled. Unpaid tailor bills mingled with dog pedigrees, notices from his bank, and inquiries about membership dues from his London clubs. Horse show programs, invitations to dine, notes to himself scribbled so carelessly there was no deciphering them.

Josiah set aside in a drawer the letters he had decided not to show Lady Hamilton unless absolutely necessary. She almost certainly knew and didn't care about the other women in her husband's life, but their bawdily graphic language had sent an uncomfortable flush to Josiah's face and made his ears tingle. More than one casual lady friend had written candidly of his Lordship's vigorous lovemaking and her pressing need for money.

At some point in his irresponsible life, Lord Hamilton briefly employed a secretary skilled in accounting. That ledger was the only decent record Josiah found. The entries covered a period of several months, stopped abruptly, then were taken up again by a shaky hand that dropped splotches of ink onto the pages between smudges of ash and the brown rings of a wet glass. Keeping track of what he spent was obviously not his Lordship's strong point. Josiah tore out an example of Lord Hamilton's signature, folded the bit of paper neatly, and stowed it between the pages of his notebook.

Just before he was ready to finish for the day, Lady Hamilton rejoined him. She wore a black tea gown and pearls, tendrils of fragrant smoke wreathing her upswept hair from a cigarette held in a long ebony holder.

"What do you make of Lord Hamilton's papers now that you've read through some of them, Mr. Gregory?" she asked.

She'd changed her shoes as well as her dress. Black leather beaded heels had replaced the outdoor boots with the odd odor that had lingered in Josiah's nostrils.

"I would say they pose an interesting challenge, my lady."

"You don't have to do anything more than appear to make an effort at it, you know."

"I might as well do the best I can, although I can't promise anything but the most basic organization."

"No one expects even that much. I can't think why the mess wasn't cleared away months ago."

Josiah thought it was because Lady Hamilton hadn't cared enough to bother. Or perhaps she'd known about the salacious letters and decided to avoid them.

"If you like, I'll toss what isn't important into the fire," Josiah offered, gesturing toward the leaping blaze that warmed the room.

"That would be kind of you," Lady Hamilton said.

When she smiled, the resemblance to Lady Rothington was unmistakable. Were all the dollar princesses taught how to hold their lips to reveal just a hint of gleaming white teeth?

"I wonder if you'd fill me in on Lucas Adderly," Josiah asked. "Do you know if he owned property in Canadian Niagara, for example?"

"It's possible, I suppose."

"I believe you met him shortly after you and Lord Hamilton arrived in the province," Josiah said, consulting his notebook.

"Has it been that long?"

"He was still in the habit of returning every spring or summer to visit his daughter."

"I didn't keep track of the man's comings and goings." Lady Hamilton took a last, deep inhalation, pinched her cigarette from its holder, and tossed the tobacco remnant into the fireplace.

"Did Mr. Adderly mention San Francisco during any of the conversations you or your husband had with him?" Josiah asked. He was puzzled by the curt answers he had gotten to his questions. Lady Hamilton had taken Rowan Adderly under her wing, yet she seemed to know surprisingly little about the girl's father.

"San Francisco?"

"I understand it's believed he made a second fortune in that city."

"I wouldn't know."

"If he's there, the Pinks will find him."

"The Pinks?"

"We've hired Pinkerton operatives to trace his whereabouts," Josiah explained.

Lady Hamilton blenched. "Call them off," she blurted. "There's a very good chance Lucas Adderly is dead. He hasn't visited his daughter in years."

A moment ago, she'd claimed to have nothing more than a nodding acquaintance with the man. Now, without a moment's hesitation, she was able to state categorically that he must be dead. Which was it?

Lady Hamilton fumbled a cigarette out of a silver box on her late husband's desk. Her fingers trembled when she waved Josiah away and scratched a match into flame.

Odd that so composed and imperious a woman should almost fall to pieces at the thought of Pinkertons tracking down a man she surely wanted brought back to Niagara. If he was still alive. Yet she'd said there was a very good chance Lucas Adderly was dead. Her exact words. Did she *know* he was dead?

Was she afraid of what the Pinkertons would find out about *how* he died? When? Where?

Ernestine Hamilton swept out of the library, skirts whispering against the floor, cigarette smoke snaking through the air.

Josiah locked the library door behind him and headed directly to the Clifton House Hotel.

Miss Prudence needed to be told about this conversation.

CHAPTER 13

Myra Adderly often referred to the third floor of Adderly House as *the asylum*. Never aloud, of course, and only when something tipped the equilibrium she went to great lengths to maintain. Then the unfairness of it all erupted into a bout of fury. This time it had been Ernestine Hamilton's unexpected visit and the threat posed by the woman lawyer she'd brought with her. Prudence MacKenzie was her name. As soon as Myra got Daphne in hand again, she'd write to a New York City friend asking for information.

The third floor was quiet and dim, all of the doors closed onto the central corridor, the windows at either end heavily draped. The east wing had been converted into nursery and schoolroom suites soon after Daphne and Bruce Yates married, when it became apparent that there would be no delay in starting their family. Day and night nurseries, a playroom, nanny's bedroom and parlor. Two schoolrooms and separate quarters for a tutor and governess. Myra had planned extensively for the future.

The first time Myra had allowed rage to overwhelm her self-control was when Lucas announced he intended to marry that Irish slut. She'd argued and railed at him for days, but nothing had changed his mind. He'd left Niagara in the dead of night rather than do his duty by the family name.

Reluctantly, because she'd never particularly liked her daughter, Myra had been forced to depend on Daphne to produce sons to expand the family business fortunes and daughters to marry advantageously. That was how empires had always been built. It was also why Myra insisted that the bride and her husband make their home in Adderly House. She'd learned her lesson with Lucas. Daphne would never spend another day out from beneath her mother's thumb.

Myra's grand scheme had collapsed when she'd looked into the faces of her daughter's two children and realized something was terribly wrong. She'd fixed that problem. She'd dealt with every obstacle that had come her way. Never faltering, never hesitating to do what had to be done. Daphne's second marriage would accomplish what her first had not. Myra did not entertain the possibility of defeat.

She didn't knock before entering the schoolroom where Daphne spent most of her afternoons. She knew what she would find, and it was nothing that couldn't be interrupted.

Arthur and Edward didn't look up from the tasks in which they were fully absorbed. Neither young man was deaf, but both had difficulty associating ordinary sounds with the activities that produced them. Arthur sat at a plain wooden table, gripping a pencil with fierce determination, copying the letters of his name over and over again, tongue rounded between his teeth to aid concentration. Edward lay sprawled on the floor, arranging building blocks into a pyramid shape, the stubby fingers of his right hand fumbling to lift each wooden shape and place it where it belonged. Arthur was sixteen years old, his brother Edward fifteen.

Myra had once threatened to confine both boys in the New

York State Asylum for Idiots. That was all it took for Daphne to agree to whatever her mother decreed for her. It took every bit of courage she possessed not to collapse into panic-stricken weeping every time she did something of which Myra might disapprove. Like glancing appreciatively at Prudence MacKenzie in the parlor yesterday when the lady lawyer disparaged her fiancé's social standing because Carter Jayden was not a member of Mrs. Astor's Four Hundred. Daphne feared and disliked the prospective husband her mother had chosen for her; she had enjoyed the subtle snub.

She scrambled to her feet from where she had been seated next to Edward, encouraging his block building with clucks of praise even though the structure he was creating fell apart multiple times. Myra didn't like to see her daughter too engaged with her sons, insisting that while it might be appropriate to supervise their care occasionally, it was not necessary for Daphne to interfere with the established routines that made up their daily lives. In this one thing, Daphne dared to disobey. As long as she didn't display deep affection for them, didn't clasp them in her arms or lavish kisses on their slightly flat faces, Myra accepted the unspoken compromise. It was the price Daphne paid to keep her children near her.

Myra swept an appraising eye over the large room where thick rugs muffled the sounds of awkward, ill-coordinated movements, loud voices, and stumbling speech. The nanny she had hired when Arthur was born ruled her small kingdom with a kind, but unwavering discipline. A young man trained at the Asylum for Idiots had been awarded the title of tutor. He'd recently given notice and Myra hadn't decided whether to begin looking for someone to take his place. Arthur and Edward were healthy, contented, and loving child minds in large bodies, but they would never be the grandsons Myra wanted. Education was wasted on them. She wouldn't shirk her responsibilities, but it was impossible to love them.

"Your conduct toward Carter yesterday was inexcusable, Daphne," she began. Always attack. It put your opponent off guard. Everyone, until proved otherwise, was an adversary.

"I didn't say two words to him, Mama."

"Exactly. You were as cold and silent as a fish. No wonder he left so quickly."

"He'd only stopped by to tell us the house was nearly ready to be furnished." Daphne wrung her hands. She hadn't so much as picked out a towel for the home in which she would be living. Her husband-to-be and her mother had collaborated and chosen for her. "He hasn't met the boys yet."

"Carter doesn't believe it's necessary. I explained the situation to him. He understands and is prepared to do his duty as their stepfather." What Myra had told the prospective groom was that Daphne's late husband had concealed an alarming strain of mental weakness running though his father's line and going back several generations. Unforgivable, but not uncommon among families so afflicted. Fortunately, the young man had died before siring other idiots.

"I'd hoped he could learn to love them," Daphne said wistfully. "As we do."

As soon as his wife presented him with a true son, Carter Jayden intended to commit Arthur and Edward to the New York State Asylum for Idiots, in Syracuse. As their mother's husband, he would have that right, and by then Daphne would have given birth to a new infant on which to lavish her motherly affections.

Myra was as much a party to the plan as though she had suggested it herself. She'd succeeded for years in masking the boys' true complaint under the guise of weak chests. Niagarans knew there were two Adderly grandsons but had grown used to never seeing them. It was time they disappeared from the house as well as from people's memories.

"You're not to visit with Ernestine Hamilton or that female

lawyer of hers should either of them presume to call here again."

"Miss MacKenzie seemed very nice. I've never heard of a lady becoming a lawyer before."

"*Miss* MacKenzie, may I remind you? She's not married. And I doubt she ever will be if she continues to carry on like that. No man wants a wife who doesn't put his interests, and those of his home and children, above all others."

"Why would either of them want to call?" Daphne asked. She'd long ago admitted that there was nothing about her that attracted either women or men.

"Ernestine Hamilton has some fool notion that your ne'er-do-well brother really did sire a child on the Irish girl. She's made a cause out of it."

Nineteen years ago, Daphne had sneaked out to hear Grace Malone sing at a Saturday afternoon show at the Niagara Music Hall. She'd been enthralled by the richness of her voice, mesmerized by the beauty shimmering on the gaslit stage. She'd turned to the brother who had helped her escape her mother's strict supervision for a few never-to-be-forgotten hours, and read from the look on his face that Lucas had fallen in love.

They were close, the gifted brother and disappointing sister. He'd always been kind to ordinary little Daphne. Something about him changed when he'd been forced to choose between loyalty to family and the rapture of being with Grace Malone. He'd had to become more distant than he might otherwise have chosen to be.

When he'd brought baby Rowan home, it was as though he'd handed Daphne a perfect infant of her own to love. Until he left and Myra hired a nurse for the child, hid both of them away on the uppermost floor of the house, and forbade Daphne to have anything more to do with her niece.

Then had come the emptiness of a loveless marriage and the heartbreak of babies who weren't right from the moment they were born. Long, barren years after Bruce Yates died. The growing certainty that Lucas would never return, that he, too, was dead.

Only when she had given up the last vestige of hope that her son would return so she could arrange a new marriage for him, did Myra turn her hand to planning Daphne's future again. Her daughter wasn't too old to have more children. Although there was no proof of it, she would have to gamble that the defective children really had come through the Yates lineage.

Daphne had been helpless to resist. She'd never won a dispute with her mother, couldn't imagine the bliss of victory if she ever summoned up the courage to try. So she agreed to marry Carter Jayden. She would bear healthy grandsons for Myra and do the best she could to survive. Whatever else happened, she had to be there for Arthur and Edward. They had nobody else but her.

"You aren't listening," Myra snapped. "You haven't heard a word I've said."

"Yes, I did, Mama," Daphne murmured. "I just don't know what we can do about her." She knew better than to mention her brother's daughter by name.

"You can get pregnant on your wedding night. That's what you can do. I'll take care of the rest. No redheaded bastard is going to steal the Adderly name."

"No, Mama." But Daphne wondered if there wasn't something she could do for Lucas's child now that her brother was almost certainly dead. Rowan had been a beautiful baby and a perfect little girl. Daphne hadn't set eyes on her in years. She wondered if Grace's offspring had grown up to be half the beauty her mother had been.

She knew what Lucas would want her to do. But did she have the courage?

*   *   *

The west wing of Adderly House's third floor had been given over to the care of Cyrus Adderly, immobile and mute since the fall that would have killed a lesser man. He'd fought the paralysis for years with only occasional, miniscule victories. He could nod his head, raise his right hand a few inches from the surface on which it lay, and croak barely intelligible words that Myra sometimes managed to interpret correctly. Not much more than that.

He was bathed, dressed, ensconced in a wheelchair in mild weather and rolled onto a screened balcony hidden from passersby. When his nurses judged it too cold or too wet outside, he remained in the small parlor adjoining his bedroom, maintaining the fiction that he did not need to lie abed all day.

Try as he might, he could not reconstruct what had happened to him just prior to and immediately after the devastating fall that had snapped his spine. One minute he was hale and hearty, riding a stallion that was the envy of every other man in the county, the next he had shot through the air and fallen to the ground a husk of his former self. Except that his mind, aside from the missing few minutes, never ceased working. Once he understood that he wouldn't regain control of his body, he would have killed himself had he been able. But the limbs he'd come to hate failed him in that, also.

Myra was slower to accept that her husband would never recover. She bullied, cajoled, and commanded that he move his arms and legs. He could not. What he could do was listen to her as she planned and plotted for the family's survival, especially after Lucas's defection. On days when it was too much of an effort to move his head, Cyrus blinked his eyes once for yes, two for no. The secrets Myra shared with him as she perfected her schemes could never go beyond the two of them. He was the perfect co-conspirator.

"The wedding plans have been finalized," she told Cyrus, wiping a thin strand of drool from his chin. "It will be a private ceremony, in view of Daphne's widowed state, her sons' precarious health, and your incapacity." She'd practiced the explanation so often that it rolled off her tongue without hesitation, sounding truthful and dignified. "I don't like it that Carter refused to live in Adderly House, but that was one point on which he would not budge. Arthur and Edward will stay here with us, of course. For the next nine or ten months, at least. A year at the most." Carter was determined and Daphne pliable.

Cyrus's eyelids fluttered. He was asking a question.

"If you're concerned about the newspaper announcements, you needn't be," Myra told him. "I made sure they appeared every day for a week in the *San Francisco Chronicle,* and multiple times in the lesser papers. Chicago, Philadelphia, New York, a dozen other cities as well. If Lucas is still alive somewhere, and if he reads the daily papers the way he used to, he'll be aware that his sister is marrying for the second time. And he'll know why. That should flush him out if he's still alive. Which I doubt." She waited a moment. "I didn't say anything to Carter that would imply we have any doubts on the matter. He believes we're all convinced Lucas is dead."

Cyrus's eyes filled with tears that threatened to spill down his cheeks.

"I know how fond of him you were," Myra said. "But for almost twenty years he's refused to be the son we raised him to be. It won't do to go all weak and flabby over his memory. I have a plan to deal with him and his brat if he should show up." There was no doubt in her mind that Lucas had married Grace Malone and fathered Rowan. But she'd also been careful never to admit those facts to anyone except the paralyzed mute who sat before her.

Sometimes, as now, the only thing she wanted to do was retreat to the solitude of her still room. She patted her husband's hands, folded them in his lap so they wouldn't hang down over the wheels of his chair, and pulled a drape that was letting a shaft of sunlight irritate his eyes. She heard the sound of the nurse's footsteps climbing the stairs and knew it was time for another feeding. Warm gruel and cool custard, followed by a dose of the herbal concoction that eased him into a deep sleep.

Myra's ground level still room was flooded with cold October sunlight glinting off rows of glass jars arranged on floor-to-ceiling shelves. A table for measuring, mixing, and distilling stood in the center of the room, and multi-drawer apothecary cabinets of seasoned oak lined the far wall opposite the door. She'd had plumbing installed so that buckets of water no longer had to be hauled up from the basement kitchen to the deep sink in which she soaked the herbs and roots that were then hung from special hooks drilled into the ceiling. Over the years, Myra had transformed an architect's conservatory into a laboratory that would have been the envy of any professional herbalist. But Myra shared her private sanctum and her past with no one.

As a new wife and young mother, she'd mixed cough syrups for the croup, willow distillations to reduce fever, elixirs to soothe digestive problems, and any number of nostrums whose formulas she never disclosed. She grew the herbs in a greenhouse and a walled garden where beds of flowers alternated with plants that had been used for centuries as human medicine. Over the years she'd accumulated a respectable library of books on the healing properties of wild and cultivated species. The higher she rose in Niagara society, the more secretive she kept this side of her life, until in recent years she spoke only of her prizewinning orchids and violets.

One of the apothecary cabinets had been fitted with a pair of locked doors. There was a single key, worn on Myra's watch chain, seldom used because the potions, dried leaves, and twisted roots in the small compartments were deadly poison.

She wore gloves and tied a scarf over her nose and mouth when she unlocked that special cabinet. Some poisons worked best if they were distilled, others benefited from being pounded into a paste or simmered like a broth. The deadliest simply had to be handled, preferably by hands marred by a rash or cut. But even they were outshone by the very few, very rare killers that only had to be inhaled to cause death. Working with them, though dangerous, was how Myra soothed her nerves. She could cut, chop, mix, mash, simmer, and distill while picturing the faces of the people she would like to dose.

And occasionally did.

CHAPTER 14

"Myra answered a note I sent by informing me that neither she nor her daughter would be at home should I attempt to call on either of them." Prudence had passed the offending communication to her partner. "So I've decided to attend Martin Fallow's autopsy with you."

She didn't like the feeling of being at loose ends, especially now that Amos and Josiah were immersed in the assignments they'd been given. Drinking tea and waiting for reports to come in was not something Prudence endured with good grace.

"You may face opposition." Geoffrey had had no doubt Prudence was up to the task. He just didn't like having to witness the casual insults dealt out by men who objected to women stepping outside their narrow social roles. Times were changing. But not fast enough for talented females like Judge MacKenzie's daughter.

"You're sure the autopsy is today?" Prudence had dressed in her businesslike secretarial suit and swept her hair into a tight and unfashionable bun beneath a hat decorated with a single dark blue ribbon. She carried a small briefcase into which she'd tucked the contents of her reticule, including the derringer she was never without.

"Amos verified the time and place." Geoffrey swung his cane over one arm as they walked down the crowded streets in American Niagara. There were fewer tourists in October than during the summer months, but the village sidewalks were still thronged, the boards slick with last night's rain and this morning's mud. "We have to get permission to attend from the county sheriff."

"What do we know about him?"

"Only that he was an officer in one of the New York regiments during the war. Highly thought of and can't be bribed."

The sheriff's office was also the town jail. Amos had described it as an overnight repository for obstreperous drunks and pickpockets. When the rare serious crime occurred, Sheriff Bryant moved swiftly and competently to solve it. Most of his small force of deputies were local men, content to stay in the area where they were born and raised. Like so many of the towns outside the metropolitan juggernaut of New York City, Niagara moved at a slower, more deliberate pace. Letters in the local newspaper complained that the burgeoning expansion of the village's industrial and factory area would be the death of what civility remained.

Sheriff Bryant greeted Prudence and Geoffrey like the ex-officer he was, courteous but noncommittal. He accepted the business card Geoffrey gave him, reading it carefully, turning it between his fingers as he considered their request to observe a procedure most members of the public didn't want to think about.

"Ex-Pink?" he asked. He'd worked with them during the war, helping to slip operatives behind Confederate lines, assisting the few who made it back safely. There was something about a Pink that marked him long after he'd left the agency.

Geoffrey nodded.

"What about you, miss?" The Pinks had hired the first women detectives in the country.

"Trained by an ex-Pink though I've never been one," Prudence said. "We're partners."

"You're the MacKenzie?" Sheriff Bryant looked at Prudence out of shrewd eyes that had assessed the courage of hundreds of young army recruits and the dubious talents of dozens of crooks.

"I am," she said.

"Does anyone else know who the two of you are?"

"Louie Whiting. The one everybody calls Crazy Louie. He wasn't very forthcoming the day Martin Fallow went over the falls," Geoffrey said. "I offered him protection and assistance if he decided to open up. He didn't turn me down, but he hasn't helped any, either."

"I'd call Louie one of a kind," Sheriff Bryant said, "except that Niagara attracts his type like flies to honey. There's more of them in town than I can keep track of. Huskers, charlatans, daredevils, flimflammers. They prey on the tourists who can be counted on to lose their common sense as soon as they hear the roar of the whitewater."

"We've heard he's sworn to dare the falls himself someday," Prudence commented. She had doubts about Crazy Louie's sincerity and a healthy regard for the dictum that there was a sucker born every minute.

"I hope I'm not here to see it when he does." Sheriff Bryant handed the business card back to Geoffrey. "The fewer of these going around the better."

"Nobody likes autopsies," Sheriff Bryant said as he led them through a warren of back streets to the offices of the town doctor who also served as coroner and medical examiner. "They're grisly and they don't pay much. So we get the younger men and the drunks. Too new to the profession to have learned much from experience or too bleary-eyed to be able to figure out what they're seeing. Take your choice."

"Which one will be doing Martin Fallow's postmortem?" Prudence asked. She found herself liking Sheriff Bryant's bluff affability and his forthrightness.

"Young. More idealistic and better trained than some of them I've seen. Reminds me of the doctors who volunteered for the medical corps during the early days of the war."

"The war's over," Geoffrey said quietly.

"Not until the last veteran dies," Sheriff Bryant corrected.

They traveled the blocks of unpainted wooden buildings in silence, sidestepping puddles in the dirt road.

A creaking sign swung in the breeze outside a house that sat squarely in the middle of a fenced and gated yard. A narrow porch stretched across the front and down the sides of the home. Filmy white curtains hung in all the windows.

The woman who answered their knock was wiping her hands on a small, embroidered towel as she opened the door. "Dr. Elliott is expecting you," she said to Sheriff Bryant. "He's in the back. You know where to find him." She nodded at Prudence and Geoffrey, then disappeared into a room through whose open door they could see an examining table and glass-doored cabinets filled with instruments and bottles of multi-hued chemicals.

"Dr. Elliott's father was a battlefield surgeon," Sheriff Bryant told them as they made their way down a hallway to the rear of the house. "He was killed when a shell landed on the tent where he was working. That was his widow who let us in. She was her husband's nurse and now she performs the same function for her son."

It would be at least another generation before families recovered from the pain and the practical effects of the losses they had suffered, Prudence thought.

"I was just about to start." Dr. Elliott ushered them into a sparsely furnished room that seemed to have been tacked on to the back of the house like an afterthought. Martin Fallow's sheet-covered body lay on a table in the center of the small space, with barely enough room for doctor and observers to crowd around it. Dr. Elliott had greeted Sheriff Bryant with warm formality, Geoffrey and Prudence as colleagues in the collaboration between law enforcement and medicine that violent crime begat. He seemed unperturbed by the presence of a woman detective.

Dr. Elliott handed brown cloth coats to his visitors and tied on a leather apron that covered him from chest to knees. A tray of surgical knives, bone saws, and forceps had been laid out atop a wheeled cart, alongside a basin of water in which the doctor could dip his bloody hands from time to time. The space bore no resemblance to the Bellevue Hospital morgue in New York City where Prudence had seen dozens of shrouded corpses laid out like a ghost army, but the smell was the same. Sharp, astringent, with a tang of rottenness that called for a cloth covering over nose and mouth. Dr. Elliott's face was bare of protection against the odor, and he offered nothing to his callers.

The Y incision was made, and what followed was completed quickly and efficiently. At one point, when the chest cavity lay fully open, Geoffrey passed a tin of camphorated cream. Dr. Elliott shook his head, but Prudence and Sheriff Bryant each rubbed a small amount beneath their noses to combat the smell of old blood and decaying tissues. Organs were removed, weighed, dissected, and pieces preserved in glass bottles filled with alcohol. Mrs. Elliott had glided silently into the room, notebook in hand, to write down her son's descriptions and observations. As soon as the closing stitches were complete, she laid the notebook on the table beside the bloodied instrument tray and left.

"He was unconscious when he was placed in the barrel," Dr. Elliott told them, washing his hands with carbolic soap, rinsing and drying them with a clean towel. "That's evident from one of the wounds on the back of the head. It bled heavily, meaning our subject was still alive after the blow was delivered. He was hit with something like an iron bar. It fractured the skull."

"I don't see any ligature marks on his wrists and ankles." Geoffrey commented.

"He wasn't tied up and he wasn't gagged," Dr. Elliott confirmed.

"But he wasn't dead when he went over the falls?" Prudence asked. She had to be sure.

"You saw the water in his lungs, Miss MacKenzie. Martin Fallow was breathing air until there was only water to inhale."

"And the rest of the damage?" Sheriff Bryant was also taking notes.

"He was flung violently from one side of the barrel to another. That's what accounted for most of the bruising and scrapings you're seeing. Both forearms were broken, so sometime before or during the fall he regained his senses for a short while and attempted to brace himself against the wood. It's hard to know if he realized what was happening to him. We can hope he didn't."

"I asked Dr. Elliott to take a look at the barrel the other day before we released it back to Crazy Louie," Sheriff Bryant said. "Neither of us found any evidence of sheep wool caught on the staves. Most of them had been sanded smooth when the barrel was built, but there were a few spots that were rougher than others."

"No sign that a Cotswold sheep had ever been inside it?"

"Nothing. There were two barrels, Mr. Hunter. I'd stake my badge on it."

"Then the mystery we have to solve is why witnesses swore they saw Crazy Louie send a barrel containing a sheep into the water when plainly they did not," Prudence said. "Unless there's a spot farther down the river, before the current above the falls becomes impossible to fight, where another barrel could have been launched and the original one retrieved. Is there such a place, Sheriff Bryant?"

"Not that I know of, miss."

"If there is, we'll find it," Geoffrey muttered. He was thinking of Amos Lang and Jean-Baptiste Napier, two formidable trackers from vastly different backgrounds. But Amos had gotten himself a job in Crazy Louie's workshop and Jean-Baptiste had taken on the task of protecting Rowan and Daniel from whoever had tried to poison them. He glanced at Prudence, and by the tight purse of her lips understood that she had already decided who would have to scour the dangerous riverbank. They wouldn't go unarmed. He'd see to that.

The records office in American Niagara was so much quieter than the bustling streets outside that Josiah found himself breathing a huge sigh of relief despite the tricky deception he was there to pull off. Taking care to dress in his most conservatively cut black suit, unembroidered vest, and brushed homburg, he had decided to carry an English leather briefcase of the type lawyers preferred, this one decorated with a brass lock and key. As Lady Hamilton's representative verifying her American properties, he'd vetoed the tempting idea of assuming a British accent. Mr. Hunter's dictum on disguise was always that less was better.

His credentials weren't challenged. Apparently, in Niagara, it was assumed you were who you claimed to be. A smiling clerk ushered him into a neatly organized records room, explained the filing system, apologized profusely for not being able to remain to assist, and left him on his own. With one caution. There were no longer any inkstands in the records and map rooms due to some regrettable past accidents, so the gentleman was asked to take whatever notes he required with a lead pencil, of which there were several available.

Josiah opened the drawer marked "H," and extracted several bundles of Hamilton papers. He made a show of thumbing through the folders, then carried them to a table he judged to be beyond the sightline of anyone glancing in his direction from the outer room, then closed the door the clerk had left ajar. He'd give the man twenty or thirty minutes to become absorbed in his own work before moving back to the cabinets, this time to the drawer in which he expected to find evidence of Lucas Adderly's holdings.

The Hamilton files weren't wasted time. They revealed such a jumble of purchases followed by sharply devalued sales, that Josiah wondered how Lady Hamilton could have one penny left to rub against another. If what he was seeing was an indication of how her dowry had been administered, her husband had been guilty of fraud and embezzlement as well as adultery.

The properties had all been registered in Ernestine Hamilton's name, but so had the sales. The odds that she had been told about any of them were so low as to be non-existent, and as he examined the signature purporting to be hers and compared it to the scrawl on the page he'd ripped from her husband's ledger, he doubted her Ladyship had ever put pen to paper on any of the filed documents. The late Lord Hamilton, in addition to his other crimes, was also an untalented forger.

There were a number of properties that seemed to have been taken in lieu of cash payment of a gambling debt and for which he couldn't find a subsequent bill of sale. The transactions were witnessed and therefore legal, but it appeared that Lord Hamilton had collected, registered, and then forgotten them.

Josiah knew it was not uncommon for men to request that their lost property be held until such time as they could buy it back; it was possible his Lordship had extended this courtesy to fellow card players who had never redeemed their forfeitures. He very carefully noted down the particulars, then refiled the documents. If Lady Hamilton was as astute as he judged her to be, she would understand what had happened within a few moments of his beginning to explain it.

A necessary conversation he wasn't looking forward to having.

CHAPTER 15

The new barrel design Crazy Louie was pinning his hopes on was for a longer and more almond-shaped cask than any of the others he had built. He was adding three rows of wider steel banding to secure the staves and forged iron loops attached to the inside walls for the passenger's feet and hands. Amos had sketched it out to approximate scale, using the map and drafting skills he'd learned as a Pinkerton.

"A human passenger can't hope to survive without padding," Louie reminded him, studying the drawing laid out on a worktable. "The problem is how to keep the cushioning material in place, so it doesn't slide out from under me."

"Is this the one you're planning to take your chances in?" Amos asked.

"Slip of the tongue," Louie corrected himself. "Not until I've tried it with an animal first."

"Another sheep?"

"We could tack or nail filler to the staves," Louie said, ignoring the question. "But if a nail came loose or the head snapped off, it could do a lot of damage during the rollover."

"Thick quilting sealed onto the walls of the barrel with tar," Amos suggested.

"I'm thinking about a leather belt, too," Louie said, demonstrating with his hands. "I'll be holding on top and bottom, but if I've got something to keep my midsection tight against the wall of the barrel there's less chance of being knocked loose when the ride gets rough."

"We attach it the same way we do the grips, and make sure they're all sealed with pitch. No leaking." *And you're as crazy as anybody I've ever met,* Amos thought.

"Might work," Louie agreed. "Let's think it through before we start cutting staves." He took a tape measure off the worktable and stretched out on the floor. "Figure about twelve inches above my head. We'll put the handles for my feet in the bottom of the cask so I'm standing upright when I first get in."

Amos extended the tape alongside Louie's body, scribbling calculations on the scale model drawing. He looked up when a shadow blocked his light.

"What the hell are you doing?" a voice boomed. Paddy Morgan's solid boxer's body filled the doorway. He stared suspiciously at Amos as Louie scrambled to his feet.

"It's not what it looks like," Louie reassured him, slapping dirt and sawdust off his clothes. "This is Amos Lang. He's helping me out with a new barrel design is all."

Paddy nodded his head as if finding Louie on the ground now made sense. He reached into his pocket, then seemed to change his mind.

"I came by to tell you we've got another fight tonight," he announced. "Same place, same time."

"Who are you up against?" Louie asked.

"Some fresh-off-the-boat fool who thinks he's a match for me. Flynn is his name. He's making the circuit, but he won't last more than fifteen rounds."

"Odds?"

"Good, because he hasn't fought up here yet. Plenty of people like to bet on a newcomer. They never learn." Paddy looked over at Amos.

"I'm only in town for a week or so. Working my way along the canal to a job that's waiting." He jingled the coins in his trouser pockets. "Bare-knuckle Irish stand down?"

"I trained at the same gym as John L. himself."

"Paddy's good," Louie said. "Your money's safe on him." He held out a hand. "Speaking of which."

Paddy hesitated, then laid a roll of bills on the outstretched palm.

Amos did a quick mental estimate. Not an outlandish sum, he decided, but enough to buy lumber, pay basic expenses, and keep body and soul together. He couldn't ask to attend the fight; that's not the way things were done. Either Louie or Paddy had to suggest Amos would be welcome. He bent over the drawing he'd worked up, as if trying to figure out the adjustments that had to be made.

Paddy and Louie had lowered their voices, but Amos had sharp ears; he could make out most of what they were saying. He caught the word *Pink* and knew Louie was telling Paddy there was a private inquiry agent in town. Was he cautioning him about something? The boxer laughed and Amos heard the reassuring smack of his hand against Louie's shoulder. Pinks didn't usually get involved in petty fight fixes.

"Tell the man at the door Paddy said you were all right," Morgan told Amos before he left. "I'll give him your name. You won't have any trouble getting in."

"We're releasing the body to Susanna Landers." Sheriff Bryant checked over the autopsy report Dr. Elliott had signed. "She came to me on behalf of the tribe right after Fallow's body was discovered. The clan mothers will see to him. They have their own way of doing things."

"He has no next of kin?" Prudence asked.

"Not in the way we understand it. But he'll be taken care of right and proper nonetheless."

Studying the sheriff's lined face, Prudence suspected he'd seen more than his share of shattered bodies strewn across battlefields during the war. For veterans of that terrible catastrophe, interring the remains of the dead with dignity had become a sacred obligation that stayed with them long after peace had been declared and they'd returned to civilian life.

"We've met Susanna Landers," Geoffrey said.

"Her beadwork is exquisite," Prudence contributed. She wasn't sure how much her partner intended to tell Sheriff Bryant about what they were doing in Niagara, but she'd given him an out if he wanted to take it.

"There's more to her than beadwork," Bryant said. He seemed on the verge of adding something else, but the door to the room in which the autopsy had taken place opened. Dr. Elliott and his mother stepped into the hallway. Behind them Martin Fallow's corpse could be glimpsed; the dead man had been wrapped in a coarse white linen shroud.

"Mrs. Landers is arranging transport," Dr. Elliott said. "Something should be on its way."

"It's here." Sheriff Bryant nodded toward the roadway, where a flat-bottom farm vehicle pulled by two large horses had drawn up. He tipped his hat to Prudence, shook Geoffrey's hand, and walked out to meet the men climbing down from the wagon bed.

"I want to see where Fallow lived," Geoffrey said quietly to Prudence as Dr. Elliott stepped past them to join Sheriff Bryant. "I don't know that we'll find anything that can tell us who killed him, but it's worth a look."

"Daniel will know how to get to his cabin," Prudence said.

"Under the circumstances, I don't think we need mention it to anyone else," Geoffrey said. Preparing the body of a friend or relative for burial was a ritual that should not be delayed or interrupted. "We had Tuscarorans in North Carolina when I was growing up there. I know a little about how they do things."

Prudence waited, but Geoffrey didn't elaborate.

He never ceased to amaze her. Just when she thought she understood him, he revealed something she'd never suspected. She imagined him as a boy running silently through the pine forests he'd told her about, a Tuscaroran of the same age keeping pace beside him, both of them intent on flushing out a white-tailed deer. It brought a smile to her face, but when he looked at her questioningly, she shook her head.

There were some images she preferred to keep to herself.

Documents from the Adderly file lay concealed beneath the Hamilton folders from which Josiah was ostentatiously taking notes whenever the chief clerk entered the inner records room. Twice so far. The man smiled briefly to acknowledge Josiah's presence, but didn't speak or interrupt him. He did, however, linger a little too long in the narrow aisle beside the table on which Josiah had opened his lawyer's briefcase.

The third time the clerk appeared made up Josiah's mind. When the room was empty again, he slipped the original Adderly papers into his satchel, then replaced them in the folder with documents he removed randomly from other files. A quick glance would show only that the Adderly folder contained paperwork generated in the records office. It would take a moment or two to decipher the handwritten information on the forms, and in Josiah's experience, misfiling was a common occurrence. He had the Hamilton information he'd ostensibly come for, and no qualms about leaving those documents where they were.

The senior records clerk wore a suit that fit him far too well to be off the rack and a watch and chain that were solid gold. Anyone foolish enough to dress above his salary trumpeted his dishonesty. Bribes were the lifeblood of every government office Josiah had ever dealt with. The clerk might not decide to remove the now-missing documents until he'd spoken to whoever was paying him, but there was no point taking chances.

Jean-Baptiste guided Prudence and Geoffrey through trackless forest to where Martin Fallow had built the one-room log cabin in which he'd lived his solitary life.

"He never came or went exactly the same way twice in a row," he explained as they made their way among the tall trees. "That's why there's no path to follow."

"Did he always live alone out here?" Prudence asked. At least there was a road leading to Daniel's place.

She'd had a moment of apprehension when the blind man had instructed Jean-Baptiste to lead them to Martin's cabin, but then another figure had stepped into the clearing as they left, and she understood that Rowan and the old man were well guarded at all times.

Geoffrey walked behind her, so silently that she turned her head to make sure he was still there. She could read on his face that he was enjoying this trek. Was he remembering the North Carolina that no longer welcomed him or perhaps a case he'd worked when he'd been a Pink? She wouldn't ask because she'd learned that he only spoke about his past when she least anticipated it, and almost never in answer to a direct question.

"There it is." Jean-Baptiste halted at the edge of a small clearing in the middle of which sat a cabin of untrimmed logs on whose bark grew a blanket of moss, lichen, and tiny ferns. Sturdy and unpretentious, it resembled a child's playhouse or a storybook illustration.

"We can find our own way back," Geoffrey said.

"You're sure?"

"I am."

Jean-Baptiste didn't question Geoffrey's assertion. He seemed to assess and approve the city man's abilities in a single glance that took in his easy stance and confident smile.

"I'll leave you then," he said, offering the rifle he carried.

Geoffrey opened his coat to show the Colt 45 nestled beneath his upper arm.

Jean-Baptiste nodded, turned away, and disappeared into the brown and green dimness of the trees.

"He wants to get back to her," Prudence said.

"Nothing has happened yet. No one has approached Daniel's cabin who has no business being there," Geoffrey said. "But he knows someone will come eventually, and he wants to be there to head him off."

"To keep Rowan safe." Prudence smiled.

The unlocked cabin door swung open on silent hinges, revealing a dim interior that burst into color when Geoffrey opened the shutters on its two windows. Handwoven blankets in a rainbow of multicolored stripes were draped over the bed and two chairs that sat in front of the fireplace. Rag rugs covered the plank flooring, deerskins hung on the walls, and racks of antlers decorated the corners. Beadwork decorated the dead man's moccasins that peeked out from beneath the bed and the wide belt dangling from its brass footrail. A long-stemmed white pipe lay in an earthenware dish on a narrow table where a lantern and a box of matches sat. A grammar school primer peeped out from beneath a chair cushion, reminding Prudence that Martin Fallow, though apparently able to figure even difficult arithmetical sums in his head, could barely read.

"I don't know what I expected," Prudence breathed, "but it wasn't this." The cabin was far from luxurious, but it also wasn't the spartan living space of a bachelor. She ran a hand over one of the blankets and lifted the belt to admire its intricate patterns. "I think a woman lived here with him at one time, Geoffrey. Or at least visited often and stayed long enough to make the place comfortable. The blankets are beautifully woven, and the beadwork is exquisite."

"Neither Daniel nor Susanna mentioned a wife. And Sheriff Bryant confirmed that Fallow had no living relatives."

"The way the cabin is furnished and decorated strikes me as odd for a man living alone." She set down the beaded belt and turned her attention to what they had come to do. "What are we looking for?"

"Anything that doesn't seem to belong. Or that looks as though he tried to hide it."

"Like this?" Prudence had reached beneath the bed to retrieve one of the moccasins and found a square wooden box which she pulled out and opened. "I've never seen anything like this before. It's heavy." She extracted a beautifully crafted instrument that looked like a small telescope mounted on a swivel.

"That's a surveyor's transit," Geoffrey said.

"Do you know how it works?"

"I know what it's supposed to accomplish. I'd be guessing if I tried to operate it."

"But you've seen one before?"

"When my father bought some adjoining land, he had it properly mapped and recorded at the courthouse. I remember following the surveyors around and getting in their way until I was banished back to the big house."

"What was Martin Fallow doing with a surveyor's transit? It looks expensive."

"I'd say he was verifying the figures he told Daniel didn't match up. He believed the original surveys had been altered."

"Where would someone like Martin get the money to buy an instrument like this?" Prudence asked. She twirled the dials and looked through the scope. "I can't even begin to imagine what he would have had to pay for it."

"Maybe he didn't buy it."

"Do you mean he stole it? But wouldn't he be the first one they suspected if a piece of equipment went missing? Sheriff Bryant never said a word about him ever being in trouble."

"He might not have been the only one misappropriating what belonged to the company that hired him. There's a certain amount of missing and damaged equipment that gets written off on every job. It's one of the things big outfits hire Pinkertons to watch out for. You'd be surprised how often an otherwise trustworthy employee decides he's underpaid and is owed a little something extra."

"So Martin could have gotten away with it and never incriminated himself?"

"Possibly." But Geoffrey wasn't certain enough to keep doubt from his voice.

"I don't think we should leave it here," Prudence said, nestling the transit back into the velvet-lined box. She closed and latched the top, running her fingers over the design carved into the lid. "This looks familiar. These flowers and vines. I wonder . . ." She placed the beadwork belt beside the box. "It's the same. That's odd, isn't it? You'd think the box would have the manufacturer's name on it. I think you may be right, Geoffrey. Fallow didn't buy the transit. He stole it."

"Which could mean that someone knew he had it."

"The only thing you do with a surveyor's transit is measure property lines," Prudence said. "I'm right, aren't I? It's a highly specialized instrument."

"As far as I know. To be really certain, we'd have to check with a surveyor, but I don't think it has any other use."

"Someone knew that Martin suspected the property lines were being falsified, and that he borrowed or stole a transit to prove it. That's why he was murdered."

"He would have created new survey maps," Geoffrey said. "Not even someone with Fallow's supposed mathematical prowess would be able to keep all the figures in his head."

"I'll start looking." Prudence picked up the child's reading primer and began paging through it. "Maybe all he had time for was writing down the numbers; maybe he hadn't gotten around to creating actual maps before he was killed."

"Look for notations hidden in the pictures," Geoffrey suggested. "An adult wouldn't study the illustrations too closely. He might have counted on that."

Prudence examined every page of the primer and studied each brightly colored drawing. She found no indication that anything had ever been written in the book.

They spent an hour examining everything in the cabin, from the undersides of Martin's mattress and chair cushions to the joints between the logs that had been mortared together to form the walls. Geoffrey stood on a wooden chair to run his cane across the exposed rafters. Nothing. Fallow had lived a tidy and organized life. Except for the box containing the transit, nothing else seemed odd or out of place.

Just as they had done in a live oak forest off the coast of Georgia, they explored the perimeter of the cabin and then the crawlspace beneath.

"You'll never make it under there," Prudence told Geoffrey, removing her hat and coat, tying a handkerchief over her mouth and nose. She hated small, dark places that hemmed you in on all sides, but at least she could be fairly certain she wouldn't encounter a coral snake as she wriggled her way into the spider-infested shadows. Too far north, if she remembered correctly. She sincerely hoped she did.

Squirming along on her back, hands outstretched so she could feel if anything had been fastened to the underside of the cabin flooring above her, Prudence squirmed and writhed her way back and forth until she was satisfied she'd covered every inch of the boards that were barely six inches away from her face. Nothing.

Geoffrey brushed decaying leaves, pine needles, and dirt from her blouse and skirt, not bothering to hide his smile as he did so. He hadn't thought she'd actually do it until he'd seen her drop to her knees, roll over, dig her heels into the ground, and inch her way out of sight. She'd done it without a moment's hesitation.

"Congratulations," he said, picking twigs out of her hair, "I don't think I've ever seen anything quite like that."

"Nor will you ever again," Prudence declared. "It's not something I intend to make a habit of doing." She positioned her hat atop her hair as best she could and buttoned up the jacket to her narrow-skirted secretarial suit. "There. That's as tidy as I'm going to be until we get back to the hotel and I can take a bath."

Geoffrey picked up the heavy instrument box and led the way out of the clearing.

He'd never admired her more.

CHAPTER 16

Paddy Morgan's bare-knuckle Irish stand down was taking place in a cow barn well outside the jurisdiction of local law enforcement, many of whom were enthusiastic followers of the sport. The fights were staged on Friday and Saturday nights when pay packets hadn't yet been depleted. Bookies calculated odds on instinct, years of experience, and indecipherable squiggles penciled on the back of an envelope.

Paddy was the only fighter with a reputation this week; the preliminary bouts to warm up the audience and tickle the bills out of their fingers were fought by young, upcoming pugilists eager to batter their way to fame and fortune. Every one of them dreamed of becoming another John L. Sullivan.

Amos made his way out into the countryside on a horse he rented from a livery stable near the Traveler's Rest. Like everything else in that part of town, the animal had seen better days. He was sway-backed, shaggy coated, with a mouth full of brown teeth meeting at the acute angle that was a dead giveaway to advanced age. His fastest gait was a spine-jarring lopsided trot.

Amos scanned the crowd for Crazy Louie as soon as he'd handed the horse over to a boy charging two bits to look after him. An outrageous sum, but nobody took the time or trouble to object. The fights they would cheer and the greenbacks in the bookie's fists were the main things on the spectators' minds. That, and tossing back shots of the cheap whiskey bringing exorbitant profits to the white-aproned men selling them. The crowd seemed to be made up about equally of locals and spiffed-up tourists. Not a woman in sight. And no Crazy Louie. He was either going to be late or not show at all.

Mentioning Paddy Morgan at the door was Amos's ticket into the lamp-lit barn. The bouncers eyeing the fans gave him a quick once-over, but since Paddy had left Amos's name at the gate and vouched for him, that was all the attention he got. He blended into the crowd and disappeared.

Amos had come for more than the pleasure of watching two boxers punch each other in the face and body until one of them fell bloody and unconscious to the ground. Men with money did business when they got together. Deals were initiated between bouts and matches, discussed, sometimes finalized on a handshake. Most of the talk was out of the side of the speakers' mouths, so as not to be overheard, but the noise level was so high that what should have been whispered was sometimes delivered at a volume that was close to a shout. And that was what Amos was counting on as he made his way from group to group, unnoticed by the men whose conversations he was listening to and remembering.

Everyone agreed that the future of the Niagaras lay in tourists and harnessing the energy of the falls. Since they weren't scientists or inventors, none of the speculators understood electricity, but they all knew that it was where the next wave of big money would be made. Access was the secret to success. Men like Edison and Westinghouse would fight each other tooth and nail for the property on which to build their power plants and the licenses to sell the energy they produced. Smaller fortunes would be made in the scuffle, modest riches that could multiply into vast sums. It was a question of deciding the best place to be and getting there first.

The Adderly name never came up, which puzzled Amos. Lucas Adderly might be dead or somewhere out west and his father hadn't been seen in public since the accident that had paralyzed him, but neither of those things should have substantially diminished the family's reputed wealth. Lawyers and financiers took over when a dynasty was short of talented sons to run its affairs. Until a grandson or a nephew came of age and took back the reins. If the Adderlys owned as much land along the river as Mr. Hunter had been told they did, speculators should be talking about making offers for some of it. But no one was.

Once the fights started, the noise grew deafening. Shouts from all sides of the roped-off ring echoed up to the rafters. Curses, revised odds yelled out by the bookies, howls of encouragement, bellicose cheers when the first nose was broken and blood spewed across the injured man's face. October nights were cool, but the heat inside the barn became stifling. The mingled smells of tobacco, sweat, blood, urine, cheap booze, Macassar oil, and cut-rate cologne clogged the nostrils and coated the throat.

Amos climbed to the top of the ladder that gave access to the hayloft, clinging there to keep tabs on what was happening below. Still no sign of Crazy Louie.

Paddy Morgan windmilled his way to victory over his challenger, blowing like a bull after the last round, eyes puffed nearly closed, nose streaming red-stained mucus, wide open mouth revealing gaps where he'd lost teeth tonight and in past bouts. One of the bookies saluted him with a doffed hat. Amos wondered how long Paddy had held his punches until he reached the round agreed upon to end the fight. A boxer who could win or lose on command was a profitable commodity. Their careers were short and brutal, but nobody, including the boxers, seemed to care what the future would bring.

It was well after midnight before Amos reclaimed his ancient horse and began the slow ride back to town. He'd put a decent-size roll of bills into his pocket and overheard enough conversations to make the evening worthwhile. Without a doubt, Paddy was playing the odds with one or more bookies, and it seemed obvious that Crazy Louie was probably doing the same. Land speculators had moved into Niagara like hungry ants onto a sugar loaf, but try though he might, Amos hadn't picked up on anything gratuitously illegal. They were out to cheat one another and anyone else they came across, but it was all run-of-the-mill small-time deceptions. Strangely, he'd heard only a few mentions of the sheep that wasn't in the barrel, and no one seemed to care about the dead man who had taken its place.

Amos fingered the small brown bottle he always carried with him. It was a game he played, teasing himself with how long he would wait before uncorking it, raising it to his lips, downing the first bitter drops that spread warmth and comfort throughout every inch of his mind and body. He knew the dangers of addiction but counted on his formidable willpower to stop him just short of tipping over into the pit of compulsive dependency. He'd come close to the edge more frequently than he cared to admit, but so far he'd pulled back every time.

Tonight though, with the memories of past bad moments revived by the savagery of the fights he'd witnessed, he'd allow himself a few more drops than he usually took. He needed to stay sharp, but he craved oblivion more.

"It's impressive," Prudence said, studying the house Carter Jayden had built for his bride.

Crowning one of the many hills that surrounded the town, Jayden House was situated in the center of a three-acre lot studded with tall oak and pine trees. Painters and plasterers in white overalls could be seen through the open windows putting the finishing touches on the interior while gardeners raked and smoothed perennial beds, cleaned up the outside construction debris, and pruned tangled holly bushes.

Two men dressed in rough tweeds and brown leather boiler-man caps conferred at a distance from the house. Every now and then one of them flung out an arm or turned on a heel as if to walk away. They were clearly angry. Arguing. But whether with one another or over some building issue, it was hard to tell from afar.

"I wonder," Prudence mused. The fieldstone exterior of Jayden's mansion was beautifully crafted, the chimneys rising from its roof indicating a fireplace in every room. The shed half-concealed by shrubbery hinted at the presence of one of the new electric generators that some people considered too dangerous to install in their basements.

"I haven't been able to get a comprehensive financial report on Jayden yet," Geoffrey warned. Prudence had a way of jumping to a conclusion, then setting out to prove its rightness that he hadn't yet succeeded in convincing her was antithetical to orderly investigative techniques.

"There's no time like the present," she said. "Those men aren't dressed like laborers. And they're upset about something." She didn't wait for Geoffrey to respond. Gathering her long skirts in one hand, she picked her way toward the house, carefully stepping over bits of chipped stone and wood shavings, tut-tutting when she spied bent nails and the occasional pile of broken glass. Deliberately making enough noise to warn the quarreling men of her approach. She heard Geoffrey following behind but didn't turn to exchange a look.

"Good morning, gentlemen," she said warmly. "I see we're almost ready to begin delivering carpets and furniture." She fumbled a small notebook and pencil out of her reticule. "Mrs.

Yates, or Jayden as she is soon to be, will be delighted." She did her best to simper; it was something men seemed to like and expect.

"This is a construction site, miss," the taller of the men said. "No outsiders allowed."

"I couldn't agree more. In addition to the carpets and furniture, we have windows to wash, draperies to hang, linens to unpack, the kitchen and pantries to outfit and supply—a hundred and one things to see to before the house is fit to receive its owners." Prudence waved fluttering fingers in the air at the challenging ordeal to come. "Jayden House will be the talk of the town, but I'll need some firm completion dates from you before I finalize plans with my installation teams."

She waited, pencil poised, as the two men took a few steps to one side, conferring with heads lowered and frequent glances cast her way.

"Is there a problem I need to know about?" Prudence asked, moving closer to where the contractors stood.

Geoffrey took out his gold pocket watch, opened and then held it to where Prudence could read the time.

"I know we have another appointment," she snapped, raising her voice. "But I've got a feeling something is going on here that we need to know about."

She put away her pad and pencil, drew the drawstring on her reticule, and walked the last few feet to where the two builders were huddled together.

"It looks like you gentlemen are hiding something from us that I think my partner and I have a right to be told," she said in a tone of voice that signaled she would brook no argument. "I demand to know what it is."

Both men looked at Geoffrey, who shrugged his shoulders and ambled in their direction.

"I think it's best we discover what's wrong here," he said reasonably. His easygoing air neither threatened nor raised suspicions.

"We haven't been paid," the shorter and younger man said bluntly. "Not a red cent since the contract was signed and the front money handed over. There's always an excuse and a promise, but so far Carter Jayden has ignored every invoice we've sent him."

"Does that mean your workmen haven't been paid?" Geoffrey asked.

Prudence took a step back and behind him, trying to make herself invisible.

"No pay envelope on Friday afternoon, no workmen on site Monday morning. Every man who can wield a pickaxe and a shovel can sign on to that tunnel that's being built for the Niagara Power Company."

"Tunnel digging is a dangerous job," Geoffrey commented.

"Doesn't matter. They pay on time, so we've had to do the same thing, plus a little extra for every man who completes a full week's work."

"That has to have been expensive." Geoffrey knew that most building contractors funded their projects through a combination of investor monies, their own bankrolls, and loans to which exorbitant penalties were attached for late or non-payment.

"We're about tapped out," the tall man said. "If I were you, mister, I wouldn't load up a single delivery wagon until you have cash money to carry to the bank." He slapped the rolled blueprint he carried against one leg, sending a puff of plaster dust into the air. "I'm not saying Mr. Jayden won't pay eventually, just that he doesn't seem in an all-fired hurry to get it done."

He was hedging his bets, Prudence decided, careful not to cast aspersions on the reputation of a man who was about to marry the only daughter of the richest family in American Niagara. If this town was as tightly governed as most small cities, there were few secrets among the important men who ran it. Incur the wrath of one of them and the whole coterie could turn on you.

"That's good to know," Geoffrey said. "Have the other contractors been paid?" He gestured toward the gardening and grounds crews, a few of whom were leaning on their rakes and hoes watching the confab taking place in the driveway.

"Not a one."

"How long are you prepared to wait?"

"I'd say that's nobody's business but ours," the shorter man said. He frowned as he realized he didn't really know who these strangers were. The woman had spoken out of turn and the man had only stepped in to save her bacon. Both of them had asked too many questions.

"Much obliged." Geoffrey took Prudence by the arm, guiding her down the brick driveway toward the street.

"That was close," Prudence said, glancing behind them. "They've gone inside."

"I don't think the odds of their getting paid in full very soon are good at all," Geoffrey said. "I wish we'd known about Jayden before Josiah and Amos left Manhattan, but there's another ex-Pink I can put on his trail down there."

"He's not a part of the Four Hundred and he doesn't pay his bills," Prudence mused. "But he's about to marry a very wealthy widow. I thought Myra Adderly was smarter than to let herself and her daughter be taken in by a con artist, even one as debonair and self-assured as this character."

"You're jumping to conclusions again."

"Do you think any differently?"

"He may be in dire need of a well-to-do wife, but I'm not ready to call him a con artist yet."

Prudence came to a sudden halt. "Geoffrey?" She stepped into the concealing shade of a large oak and turned back toward the house they had just left. "Do you suppose Myra Adderly is counting as much on Carter Jayden's supposed fortune as he is on theirs? The combined family wealth, I mean, as well as Daphne's dowry and whatever her first husband left her."

"All of that should have been worked out when the marriage property agreements were signed," Geoffrey said.

"But suppose it hasn't been. Worked out, I mean. Just suppose that Jayden is in well over his head and he can't afford for anyone to find out. He'd put off signing the papers, wouldn't he? Make excuses about why he can't meet at a lawyer's office, take the train down to the city on the pretext of having important business there, stay away until he can't justify his absence any longer. Come back, tell a few lies, then leave again. Once the vows have been pronounced his problems are solved."

"I'd say they may be just beginning."

"Rowan?"

"I wonder how much he knows about her."

"Sometimes I wish I'd never opened Aunt Gillian's letter," Prudence said. "Never thought an inheritance case might be a good way to launch a legal career. I feel like it's blowing up in my face."

"We're only getting started," Geoffrey reminded her.

"And I'm already floundering."

"We're in this together." He drew her out from under the tree into the sunlight.

"Don't try to make things easy for me."

"I wouldn't dream of it."

Prudence slipped her arm through Geoffrey's and leaned her head against his shoulder for a moment. Then she straightened, tensed her back, and faced forward toward where the chimney pots of Jayden House could be seen above the treetops.

"I need to pay another call on Myra Adderly," she said. "She can't be allowed to get away with whatever she's planning. For her daughter or for Rowan."

"I could almost feel sorry for her," Geoffrey said. "She's about to meet her match, and she won't take defeat gracefully."

CHAPTER 17

"How long will it take your ex-Pink in the city to get us a report on Carter Jayden's financial status?" Prudence asked. She'd agreed with Geoffrey that it would be better to confront Myra with as complete a picture of her prospective son-in-law's business reputation and financial holdings as possible. Being slow paying off the contractors working on the house he was building was worrisome, but not uncommon. There were plenty of entrepreneurs and industrialists who only parted with their money when threatened with a lawsuit.

"Two or three days at the most," Geoffrey said.

"That long?"

"We don't want any hint of what we're doing to leak out. So, no telegrams."

"I'll feel better once Josiah tells us what he's learned at the records office. He should have been here by now."

"Order tea," Geoffrey said.

He watched Prudence walk to the tall windows overlooking the river, push aside the curtains, look out for a moment, then whirl around and begin pacing back and forth across the length of the parlor, snapping her fingers as she went.

The waiter came and left, but still no Josiah.

"Should we begin worrying?" she asked Geoffrey, one hand touching the china teapot to test its temperature. "I've never known him to be late."

"You know how Josiah is," Geoffrey said, "He's going to take as long as he needs to do a thorough job."

When the knock finally came, she flew to the door and wrenched it open while Josiah's fist was still suspended in midair.

It wasn't like her to scold or complain, but Prudence's nerves were on edge. "You might have sent word if you weren't going to be on time," she said brusquely.

Josiah's left eyebrow went up, then he glanced at Geoffrey, who was shaking his head. *Give her time to settle down.* The secretary removed his hat and coat, straightened his vest and watch chain, unlocked the lawyer's heavy briefcase he was carrying.

"Is that tea?" he asked, laying a sheaf of folders and documents on the table, tapping the corners to straighten the stack.

Prudence gave up and poured. Josiah couldn't be hurried. She probably owed him an apology for the way she'd greeted him. "Sorry," she said briskly.

He added a dollop of milk and a cube of sugar to his cup, stirred without clinking his spoon, took a genteel sip, and sighed in satisfaction. There were few things in life Josiah liked more than his tea.

"I'm assuming, from what you've brought us, that your trip to the records office in American Niagara was a success." Prudence failed to keep a trace of sarcasm out of her voice.

"I think I've found what you wanted," Josiah said, continuing to sip from the bone china cup with the entwined Clifton House monogram. He held it up to the light streaming through the windows to gauge its translucence.

"Shall we begin with Lucas Adderly?" Geoffrey suggested.

"Lucas is or was a very astute investor," Josiah said.

He handed one of the folders to Geoffrey, another to Prudence.

"I decided not to leave the documents in the records office where they could easily be made to disappear," he continued. "The senior clerk is definitely on someone's payroll. His suit cost more than most office workers earn in half a year, and his watch is solid gold. He was a little too interested in the files I was examining."

"How can you be sure?" Prudence asked.

"He had no reason to come into the file room as often as he did except to catch me off guard," Josiah said. "I made sure any identifying characteristics of the papers I had on the table were well covered."

"I assume they can be returned as discreetly as they were taken?" Geoffrey asked.

Josiah nodded.

"This is theft." Prudence held the unopened folder on her lap, waiting for Geoffrey to agree. Her newly acquired law license was in jeopardy. She couldn't think of a single legal argument to justify perusing records stolen from a government office. She caught the suggestion of a smile at the corner of Geoffrey's mouth as he began studying the pages Josiah had given him. "Well?"

"You'll do a lot worse in your career," Geoffrey said. "You might want to think about getting used to it."

She muttered a string of words she'd heard her partner use one afternoon when he thought she was out of earshot. Then she began reading the first of more than half a dozen records of substantial land purchases.

Josiah finished his tea, poured a second cup, and munched contentedly on crustless ham-and-watercress sandwiches. He was reaching for a slice of pound cake when Geoffrey handed the documents he'd been reading to Prudence and accepted hers in return. For another ten minutes the only sounds in the parlor were the soft rustle of turning pages and the occasional clink of silverware against china.

"I assume you've looked at all of these," Geoffrey said. He'd gathered both stacks of deeds and assembled them in order of date of purchase.

Josiah nodded.

"I have a map of the area." Prudence took it from between the pages of one of the guidebooks she'd purchased and spread it out on the table, pushing tea things aside. As Geoffrey read off the geographic coordinates, she penciled in the boundary lines. "I'm not doing this in ink yet," she explained, frowning in fierce concentration. "In case I make a mistake. What were those last two numbers, Geoffrey?"

He repeated them slowly, watching as the visual representation of Lucas Adderly's land purchases grew. "He knew what he was doing," he said as Prudence laid down her pencil. "He's made it nearly impossible for anyone else to put together a large parcel of contiguous lots near the water without including one or more of the plots belonging to the Adderly family."

"And I imagine he counted on the selling price to be whatever the traffic will bear," Prudence commented, quoting a phrase she'd often heard her father use when discussing the financial cases that had come before his bench.

"Who controls the trust? That's the missing piece," Geoffrey said. "Which brings us back to where we were when we first agreed to take this case. We have to assume that Myra Adderly has reason to believe Rowan has been named primary trustee and will begin receiving substantial disbursements on her eighteenth birthday."

"Provided she can prove she's Lucas Adderly's legitimate daughter," Josiah said, folding his napkin neatly.

"And she's still alive," Prudence added grimly.

"Agreed," Geoffrey said. "If that were all, the courts would easily and quickly settle the case. But there's more to it than filing paperwork if the plats have been tampered with. Why kill Martin Fallow and try to hide the fact of his death by consigning his body to the falls? What happened to him was neither accidental nor coincidence."

Prudence began going through the surveyor's reports again, ending up with three different piles. "It looks as though he used several companies," she said. "Wouldn't you have thought Lucas would employ the same firm for all his transactions if their work was satisfactory to begin with?"

"What are the dates?" Geoffrey asked.

Prudence shuffled and reshuffled the documents several times while Josiah wrote down the categories into which she grouped and regrouped them: by date of purchase, by the name of the firm performing the survey, by the individual acting as chief surveyor. "Two more divisions," she said, "I think we need to establish who notarized the authenticity of the signatures on the plats and then list the identity of the city clerk who accepted and filed them. We're looking for patterns," she added. "Discrepancies that can't be explained."

By the time they'd finished, Prudence was nursing a headache. Peering at barely legible signatures and deciphering the language of formal surveys was hard on the eyes and a brain not used to describing parcels of land in terms of degrees of longitude and latitude.

"What have we learned?" Geoffrey asked, flexing shoulders cramped from leaning over a low table.

"I'm not sure any of it directly affects the case," Prudence declared. "Lucas Adderly apparently used three different firms in order to prevent any single one of them from learning how extensive his land ownership was. That's the only logical reason I've come up with. As far as I can tell, he alternated by date, again so as to seem a casual purchaser rather than someone systematically putting together a monopoly. All of the deeds are recorded in the name of the Adderly Trust."

"This plat is marginally different," Geoffrey said, putting the others aside as he smoothed out the creases and flattened it on the table. "The ink looks a shade lighter in places and the surveyor's name doesn't appear on any of the other filings."

"Maybe he wasn't with the firm when the rest of the commissions were made," Prudence offered.

"If I may," Josiah interrupted. "Any clerk worth his salt learns to write a precise script that can be easily read. The typewriter is becoming ubiquitous and printed forms are common, but it will be a long time yet before deeds and other legal instruments aren't at least partially written out by hand." He traced a finger over the calligraphy he was analyzing. "Some of these letters and numbers have been deliberately made difficult to read. Look at the o's and the a's. The u's, n's, w's, and m's. The fives and the sixes. The ones and the sevens. Can you always tell them apart with any certainty?"

"Where is this parcel on the map?" Prudence asked, her pulse quickening.

"We've put it on the riverbank because that's where it logically belongs," Geoffrey said, consulting the outline Prudence had drawn. "And at first glance that's what the figures seem to indicate. But a good case could be made for it being here as well." He pointed to an area farther back from the Niagara.

"Use this," Josiah said, pulling a magnifying glass from his briefcase. "You're looking for any sign that the original inked notations have been scraped off or written across."

Prudence crouched over the plat in question, moving the magnifying glass back and forth to study the numerical figures, bringing the lens closer then farther away from her eyes. "I don't see anything suspicious," she said, handing document and glass to the secretary. "You're better at this than I am."

But even Josiah could find nothing wrong with the only deed they'd singled out to question. "Baffling," he said when he finally gave up searching for proof of tampering. "Either this is the best forgery I've ever seen, or someone has taken the precaution of recreating the entire survey from scratch. That would take a lot more time and expertise than changing a few numbers and perhaps a signature." He hefted the empty teapot and frowned.

"I'll telephone for more," Prudence said, realizing as she stood up that she'd been bent over and tense with the effort for more than an hour.

"What about the Hamilton properties?" Geoffrey asked, standing up also, working the muscles of his arms and shoulders.

"Lady Hamilton's late husband made a mess of their finances," Josiah said, laying a sheaf of papers on the table. "There wasn't any point removing those plats or deeds from the records office, but I took copious notes because that's what I was expected to do. I didn't want to jeopardize my cover."

"Could you sum up the situation?" Geoffrey asked. No one could read Josiah's shorthand except the secretary himself.

"He bought high and sold low."

"That doesn't make sense," Prudence exclaimed. "Shouldn't it be the reverse? Buy low, sell high?"

"Should be, but the late lord had the business acumen of a compulsive gambler. Plus an uncontrollable drinking habit. I saw that in the papers I sorted through in his study, but the proof of how badly he muddled things was in the records office."

"Meaning?" Geoffrey had known more than one high roller who'd taken the plunge from wealth to straitened circumstances. None of them had shouldered any blame for the poor decisions they'd made. Circumstances had always been against them.

"He bought properties and put them in Lady Hamilton's name, just as we were told. But he managed to lose every one of them before he died. Signed over to someone with whom he'd been playing cards or sold outright to stake himself to bad business propositions. A logging company that went bankrupt before it cut down a single tree, a railroad spur going nowhere, a gold mine with neither shaft nor gold."

"Women?" Prudence asked. She knew if she didn't bring up the topic, neither of the men would mention it.

"All I have are first names gleaned from what I found at Hamilton House. I'm assuming he handled those expenditures in cash."

"How careful of him," Prudence said. "But whether she admits it or not, every wife suspects when her husband is straying."

"Is there any way to tell whether he was using his own funds or siphoning off money from his wife's dowry?" Geoffrey asked.

"Not from the documents I was able to look at. Bank records would tell that story, but unless Lady Hamilton gives us access, no reputable institution will open them to us."

"Remind me about the conversation you had with her after I'd left Hamilton House," Prudence directed. "The lady's husband may have been cheating her in more ways than one, but that doesn't affect the case. You said she turned pale when you mentioned hiring Pinkertons to find out where Lucas Adderly had gone and what happened to him after he disappeared."

Josiah's detail-oriented mind recreated the scene in the late lord's library. He had a gift for remembering conversations verbatim, unconsciously mimicking cadences of speech as he spoke the words. "Did I mention before that I detected what I'm positive was a whiff of manure when Lady Hamilton joined us in the parlor after the errand that made her late?" he finished.

"You may have," Prudence said. Every lady got used to the occasional misstep when she descended from her carriage or crossed a city street. Horses were everywhere, and so were the piles of dung they left in their wake. "Is it important?"

"It's not a scent you fail to notice," Josiah said, recalling the many times he'd screwed up his nose at the smell of his own shoes after a day of walking New York City's streets and sidewalks. "But she didn't remark on it."

"No, she didn't," Prudence agreed. "But I don't think I would have mentioned it either, if I had guests waiting for me in the parlor." She put aside the image of Lady Hamilton's daintily shod foot stepping into a pat of manure. "Did she give you any information on what you might find in the Canadian records office?"

"I expect to find much the same thing as in the American files," Josiah said. "But it's also likely there are family properties in England that he couldn't touch because of an entailment or some other legal stranglehold on ownership. His Lordship gambled and speculated with whatever could be converted into a liquid asset, but no wealthy family allows all of its holdings to pass into the hands of a spendthrift. Entailed estates would devolve to the male heir, not his widow. Probably a cousin, since the marriage didn't produce any children."

"My grandfather saw to it that my aunt Gillian's fortune was well protected when she married," Prudence volunteered. "Surely Ernestine Hamilton's father made it impossible for her husband to drain all of her resources." Marriage contracts between men and women of means had always been detailed agreements on everything from which spouse inherited the furniture to who had control over their sons' schooling.

"We'll know better after I've finished going through the Canadian property listings," Josiah said. If the results were as bleak as those he'd already found, he pitied the lady. To go from wealth to near penury would be a shock from which it would be difficult to recover.

"I think we'll send Amos to follow up on our mysterious surveyor," Geoffrey said, dismissing Lady Hamilton's financial problems. "He's good at appearing scruffy and forgettable. All we want to know is whether the man still works for this firm."

"And if he lives in Niagara," Prudence added.

"Or if he's a licensed surveyor at all," Geoffrey said. "Forgery is more art than mathematics."

CHAPTER 18

Carter Jayden waited until he knew all of the workers had left the building site. Then he bided his time until darkness fell and the moon rose, giving just enough illumination to make his way onto the grounds without the bobbing glow of a lantern to give him away.

In recent weeks, despite its being nearly completed, the house had sat unguarded during the nighttime hours. The watchman and his two large dogs no longer patrolled the shadows, checking the mansion's windows and locked doors on hourly rounds, their presence a deterrent to anyone looking for a place to shelter out of the October chill. The security guard had taken himself and his animals elsewhere after his last two bills had gone unpaid despite repeated demands.

It was cold and still, the sound of the falls a distant murmur in a sleeping world. Carter walked quickly along the grass verge of the road, alert to the muffled noises of hungry predators and luckless prey. He was listening for another set of approaching footfalls, but heard none, despite stopping every now and then to concentrate. He'd deliberately come early to the rendezvous, but he thought it likely that the man he was meeting would have had the same idea. It was always better to lie in wait than to arrive when expected.

Jayden House's curtainless windows gleamed in the moonlight, three perfectly aligned rows topped by attic dormers behind which servants would live in tiny rooms alongside storage spaces that would gradually fill up over the years. He paused to admire his creation, expensive and grandiose; some would say intimidating. A miniature version of the palaces being constructed along faraway Fifth Avenue. Which was what the house was intended to be. Carter's undistinguished family background meant he would never be welcomed into the Four Hundred; he'd reluctantly accepted his exclusion. And decided to create his own kingdom outside the closed world of New York City society. It was second best, but his only alternative. And it would have to do.

Daphne Adderly Yates was a healthy if unattractive woman, a little mature for his tastes, but a proven child bearer with a few more years of fertility ahead of her. There had been several others who might have served his purposes, but none with a father conveniently incapacitated and close to death, and no other male relatives to oversee the substantial fortune coming her way. He'd done his homework and was satisfied with his choice. The only niggling worry was the lack of clear evidence that the brother was dead, but since everyone else seemed to take his demise for granted, Carter had decided to ignore that potential problem. His instincts for self-preservation had always been good. He saw no reason not to trust them now.

The girl Rowan was another situation entirely. Myra, his future mother-in-law, had downplayed the threat, but Carter had taken his own precautions. Unfortunately, the scheme he'd hatched hadn't worked, and now the redheaded bastard was closely guarded. No marriage license for the parents and no birth certificate for the daughter meant no legal standing in a court of law. That should be enough, but what if a piece of paper attesting to her legitimacy did turn up? The lawyers who held the trust agreement were playing it close to the vest.

The Adderly matriarch controlled how the family trust funds were spent, except that large sums had to be approved by the law firm named as administrators. Everything was due to change when Rowan came into her own, but no one knew what those changes would be except the lawyer who was executing his client's wishes. He wasn't talking, and the addendum to the trust was locked away in a safe, not to be opened and read until the appropriate date. It was the most annoying predicament in which Carter had ever found himself. Utterly ridiculous. He thought Daphne's brother must have been a thorn in everyone's side to have come up with an arrangement this shrouded in intrigue.

Carter didn't trust the man he was meeting tonight, but he needed him as much as the hired killer needed the money he would be paid. Carter wouldn't ask for details. Best not to know the fine points; he'd be genuinely surprised and more than a little shocked when the news broke. Myra might guess that he'd had a hand in it, but she'd never betray her suspicion by word or deed. The woman knew how to keep secrets.

The front door stood open, only a few inches, but enough to tell him that even though he'd come early, the man he'd hired had preceded him. He should have known the mistrust would be mutual. He fingered the pistol he'd concealed in his trouser pocket, readying himself to use it if he had to. A momentary worry about what he'd do with the body ran through his mind, so outlandish a thought that he dismissed it. Money would change hands, the individual he was paying would melt back into the darkness, and a day or two from now would come the news he wanted to hear. Nothing would go wrong. Despite past disappointments and thwarted ambitions, Carter never believed his current venture would fail. Whatever it was.

He stepped into the house and closed the front door behind

him. The latch snicked into place. He waited, listening to his own breathing, straining his ears for anything that would indicate the man he had come to meet was nearby. It was too dangerous to call out a name, even if he'd had one. There was always the chance that a bum sleeping raw had heard about the empty house and decided to make it his own for a night.

Carter moved into a pool of moonlight and took out his gold pocket watch. He could just make out the ebony hands and numbers against the white face. Not as early as he'd thought. He must have slowed his pace without noticing it, distracted by thoughts of how he'd manage Daphne and how soon he could dip into her money. Dealing with Myra was going to be more difficult, but he hadn't met a woman yet, young or old, who didn't eventually succumb to his charm. Or his bullying. He had a gift for mixing the two of them so adroitly that his victim was hard put to realize she'd been bamboozled.

A scrabbling noise came from somewhere overhead. A squirrel or a mouse on the second floor? Carpets hadn't been laid, so there was nothing to dull the sound of scampering claws. It sounded like fingernails scraping against bare wood planks. After a moment or two, the scratching sound faded and then died out. A heavy night silence settled over the house. He felt a waft of cold air across his cheeks and realized that a window or door had been left open.

Carter drew the gun out of his pocket, holding it down by his side. Out of sight in the darkness, he hoped, then worried that if someone was indeed hiding in the shadows, he might have seen the brief glint of the gun barrel. Nothing happened. No one whispered his name. No one approached.

Carter moved to one of the tall windows that looked over the front lawn and the driveway. He stood to the side and slightly back where he wouldn't be glimpsed as he peered out. He wasn't frightened yet, but he wasn't comfortable either. Punctuality had been stressed when the arrangement to meet had been made. He'd been told that if he didn't show up on time, the deal was off, although he hadn't quite believed it. Bluster, he'd thought, because the man he had hired obviously needed money. Why else would he put himself in such jeopardy? He held off for as long as he could before pulling out his watch again. A full fifteen minutes beyond the agreed-upon time. What the hell was going on?

Out of the corner of his eye he saw a figure appear in the doorway to the formal dining room. As he turned to get a better look, he realized that something was very wrong. The man he'd come to meet was of medium height, slender, dressed like a workingman so he'd blend into a crowd. This person was well over six feet tall, with shoulders nearly the width of the door frame. Without thinking, Carter raised his gun hand. The weapon shone silver in the moonlight, and before he could pull the trigger, if that was even his intention, he saw a bright flash and felt the slam of a bullet entering his chest.

He went down like a felled tree.

The gun slipped from his hand. He felt the heat of blood flowing over his shirt, his vest, the coat he'd unbuttoned to get at his watch. It dripped and pooled onto the floor on which he lay. Even as he fought against it, he knew death was coming and it was too late to stop it.

The man who had fired the single bullet stood over his target, nudged the head with an elegantly booted foot, waited until Carter exhaled a last breath. He debated whether to take the gun with him, then contemplated the most likely interpretation of the death scene here and the one upstairs if he left the firearm after shooting a round into the heavily wooded lot outside.

Made one further adjustment. He took the handkerchief from Carter's pocket, dipped it in the dead man's blood and carried it to the staircase, deliberately leaking red drops as he climbed. He saturated the handkerchief twice more as he laid the blood trail. When he was satisfied, he wrapped the stained handkerchief in a clean cloth taken from the body cooling on the second floor. Stood for a moment thinking through what he'd done. Ruffians didn't count, but a gentleman never left his home without a clean handkerchief. A small error, but with luck it wouldn't be noticed. He positioned the gun he'd just used to kill Carter Jayden beside the dead man and slipped the victim's unfired weapon into his pocket

And then he left, closing the front door behind him so no creatures of the night would be attracted by the scent of death.

Prudence and Geoffrey had put off searching the undeveloped riverbank below where Crazy Louie had launched his barrel because it was likely to be a fruitless endeavor in which neither of them placed much stock. Tourists crowded into any spot that offered a free view of the falls, and outdoor enthusiasts tramped enthusiastically through wooded areas and along trails carved out years ago by deer and lumbering bears. It didn't seem possible that any place remained where a second barrel could be concealed and then secretly tipped into the river. Someone was bound to have seen something.

Prudence would gladly have left the exploration to Amos Lang, but the ex-Pink was spending the daylight hours in Crazy Louie's workshop and exploring Niagara's shady nightlife for as long as he could remain on his feet. He never complained about lack of sleep and never explained how he managed to do the work of several trained men. Josiah in the woods was too outlandish an idea to contemplate. She and Geoffrey were the only ones left.

This time, instead of renting horses from the Clifton House livery stable, they decided to walk the riverbank, setting out before the hotel's dining room opened for breakfast. It was an absurd undertaking, Prudence thought, but one that had to be checked off their list.

"There isn't that much ground to be covered," Geoffrey reassured her, glancing at the map he'd sketched out. "We know where spectators gathered." He pointed to areas he'd shaded with a pencil. "And there's no point going back over places we've already been. That leaves out the promontory where Crazy Louie waited to see the descent over the falls and the site where the barrel containing Fallow's body was pulled ashore."

"We've been through this so many times," Prudence complained. She was heartily fed up with disappearing Cotswold sheep and daredevils without an ounce of common sense. She'd never been drawn to P.T. Barnum's oddities, and Crazy Louie's notions seemed cut from the same cloth. If it weren't for an instinctive affinity with another young woman who had lost her mother at an early age and suffered abuse at the hands of an arrogant female relative, Prudence would have been sorely tempted to withdraw from the case and take the next train back to New York City. There were too many false trails leading in conflicting directions, nothing definitive to hold on to.

"We'll find something," Geoffrey said, as if he'd read her mind. "It takes patience and not giving up. No one can commit a crime and not leave something of himself behind. Or take something away, even if it's as small as a smear of dirt or a piece of a leaf stuck to the bottom of a shoe."

Prudence smiled with what she hoped was a show of confidence, but privately all she wanted was a swift return to the hotel and a cup of hot coffee.

Every now and then they spied someone hurrying to work, but it was too early in the morning for tourists to be out, and there were fewer of them this time of year anyway. For the most part, Prudence and Geoffrey had the woods and the riverbank to themselves. It was a beautiful and serene setting in the clear sunlight filtering through trees that hadn't lost all of their leaves yet. Squirrels scampered above them, rabbits sat like statues in the shadows, believing stillness made them invisible. Birds pecked the damp ground for insects and worms.

None of the undergrowth on either side of the path they were following appeared to have been disturbed by the passage of a large, heavy barrel.

Until, finally, they spied a spindly pine sapling neatly snapped off as though by a sharp axe. Pale, exposed wood among the greenery, a barely two-foot-tall trunk rising up from the forest floor, six feet of dying tree stem lying where it had fallen. Unnoticed in someone's hurry to consign Martin Fallow to the river. This had to be the spot they'd been looking for.

"Whoever did it rolled the barrel then dragged branches behind to erase any flattening of the soil or natural debris," Geoffrey said, sweeping his cane lightly over the tracks that became apparent as soon as he explained them.

They worked their way from the broken tree to where a narrow portion of the bank sloped down to the river, an entry point unimpeded by the rocky outcroppings that made some areas too dangerous to explore. Standing there, studying the flow of the Niagara and assessing the distance from the falls to the landing spot where Crazy Louie had sent his recovery team, they mentally mapped out the route the barrel had to have taken.

Prudence tossed pieces of fallen branches into the swirling water, calculating their spin and drift, puzzling out what had to have happened, trying to step into the mind of whoever had conceived the scheme.

"It had to have been someone who thought he knew what he was doing," she decided. "The barrel containing the sheep was rigged to break apart in the whirlpools or against the rocks at the bottom of the falls but not disintegrate entirely. No one would have seen it shatter and they certainly wouldn't have noticed that a second, much flimsier barrel had been pitched into the river and swept toward those same rocks by the current. Pieces of the sheep's body and a few wooden staves should have been swept downriver to the landing spot, where the crowd would interpret them as proof that Crazy Louie had miscalculated again. Nobody would be looking for a second body, so even if they saw more bits and pieces swirling by, they'd ignore them. The whole thing was engineered so that no trace of Martin Fallow would ever be found. It wouldn't be the first time a human being had been swept away and never seen again."

"Overkill," Geoffrey said. "Too many chances that something could go wrong. I don't like it."

"The locals are speculating that Fallow planned to steal Crazy Louie's thunder. That he intended all along to launch himself into the river, and that he thought he'd garner more publicity for the stunt because no one was expecting a man to spring out of the barrel where a sheep had gone in. I overheard two of the bell boys talking about it this morning while you were checking for messages at the front desk."

"That's the cover-up," Geoffrey said. "Logical and titillating enough to satisfy the tourists without unduly alarming anyone."

"The Niagara newspaper describes the body as being severely battered. End of discussion." Prudence had spent two cents to buy a copy of the paper from the boy hawking them in the lobby.

"I'll let Amos know what we've discovered," Geoffrey said. He didn't sound like a man who'd just cracked a difficult case.

"I wonder if they got the barrels mixed up," Prudence speculated. "Put Martin into the wrong one."

They'd found what they'd been searching for and established a logical interpretation of the evidence. Yet neither Geoffrey not Prudence felt satisfied.

"Could we be looking at this wrong?" Geoffrey ventured.

"How so?"

"What would be the easiest way to get rid of a body around here?"

Prudence studied the raging river and the miles of forest stretching off into the distance. She'd wanted their discovery to be the solution they'd been looking for, but it wasn't. "I'd toss it into the river at night or bury it in a shallow grave in the wilderness. By the time the water and the rocks or predators finished with it, there'd be only bones left. No possible identification."

"Then why didn't our killer take the easy way out? Why go to all this trouble?"

Sheriff Bryant and his deputies interrogated the skilled craftsmen engaged to complete the final decorative plastering and the installation of the last bits of carved wood paneling. They all swore that no one had shown unusual interest in the house and that the doors and windows were routinely locked when they left the premises. They might be disgruntled at the uncertain state of their wages, but not a one of them fell under suspicion for a murder that only made their financial situation worse.

Two murders. Carter Jayden downstairs, and another, unidentified man found upstairs at the end of a trail of bloody droplets.

"Looks like a falling-out among thieves," a deputy said, staring down at the unknown dead man. "Jayden was making for the front door, but he was wounded worse than he knew." He nodded toward the small dark splotches staining the floor.

"That's what it looks like," Bryant agreed.

But he thought that something about the scene appeared staged, and that's why he'd send a message to the ex-Pink and his partner staying at the Clifton House Hotel. Three suspicious deaths within days of each other was not something he and his deputies were likely to solve without experienced outside help.

The Niagara force could deal with drunks beating each other up, theft, and domestic disputes, but what had happened at the falls and now in this opulent mansion had him tugging at his mustache and shaking his head.

Somebody would have to inform Myra Adderly and her daughter that there wouldn't be a wedding after all.

He didn't envy the person who had to break the news.

CHAPTER 19

Geoffrey sent a telegram to New York City as soon as Sheriff Bryant's message reached them. With Carter Jayden dead, there was no need for secrecy. It no longer mattered that inquiries were being made into his financial standing. Whatever new ventures Jayden had set into motion had come to a crashing halt with the bullet that took his life.

"I only met him once, the day Lady Hamilton took me to call," Prudence said as she and Geoffrey waited for a response to their cable. "He was in and out of Myra's parlor so quickly, there was barely time for an introduction. My first and last impression of the man is that he made me uneasy. Daphne couldn't repress a slight shudder when he touched her. On the shoulder. More to insist on her attention than as a gesture of affection."

Neither partner had done more than briefly congratulate themselves on locating the spot where the second barrel had been launched into the river. That small victory in the case paled beside the finding of two bodies in American Niagara's newest and finest mansion.

"What do you make of this?" Prudence asked, handing over a second note Sheriff Bryant had addressed to her. "I'll do it, of course, because it's the best opportunity we're likely to have to get back inside the Adderly house, but it's unusual."

" '*In view of the delicacy of the situation,*' " Geoffrey read aloud. "Bryant is likely to deliver the news, ask a few questions if the ladies are up to answering, then leave you with them while he gets on with the investigation."

"I doubt either of the Adderly women will confide in a stranger," Prudence said, "but I think you should be there also." She paused for a moment. "Lady Hamilton needs to be told what's happened."

"I thought she and Myra didn't like one another."

Prudence shrugged as a tap on the parlor door brought her to her feet.

"That was quick," she announced, opening the flimsy yellow telegram. She scanned the message, then handed it to Geoffrey. "Worse than either of us thought."

" '*Up to his ears in debt. Outstanding loans about to be called in.*' According to this, Jayden has been surrendering properties or selling them at rock-bottom prices to creditors. He ran up a huge hotel bill and left town without paying it. Carter Jayden's world was about to collapse. He desperately needed to marry an heiress. And quickly."

"I don't know about the New York City press, but his engagement to Daphne had been announced in the Niagara paper," Prudence said. "All his creditors had to do was wait until after the vows were pronounced. He could have paid all of his outstanding debts and barely made a dent in the Adderly family fortune."

"There's no mention here that any marital prospects were rumored." Geoffrey glanced through the telegram again, then handed it back to Prudence. She'd need it when she and Sheriff Bryant broke the news to the erstwhile bride and her mother.

"I'll telephone Lady Hamilton," Prudence said. She'd grown so used to the convenience of the instrument that she often wondered how they'd managed without it.

The hotel switchboard put her through to Hamilton House with only the customary short delay, but she was frowning when she put down the speaking tube and earpiece. "She's not at home. The butler says her Ladyship's gone out, but he couldn't or wouldn't say where or when she'd return. That's odd."

"Why odd?"

"It's as though she's hiding something. From her own household. And from us." Prudence reached for her hat and reticule. "It's happened at least once before. When I met Josiah there for the first time. She'd left on some mysterious errand even though she knew I was coming, and when she got back it looked as though she'd been out shopping. Why attempt to conceal something like that?"

"Maybe she has reason to be discreet," Geoffrey said, slipping the crook of his cane over his arm.

"Don't be ridiculous." Prudence stared at him for a moment, then turned to leave the suite. She heard him chuckling behind her. Could Lady Hamilton be having a liaison no one knew about? She remembered some of the scandalous stories her aunt Gillian had told about the Prince of Wales's set. No names, of course. But Prudence's ears and cheeks had turned red, and she'd been hard-pressed to believe what she was hearing. Titled ladies and royal gentlemen behaving like libidinous fictional characters in a cheap romance.

She glanced back as her hand touched the doorknob.

"Really? Do you think so?"

He smiled.

Sheriff Bryant was waiting for them outside Adderly House, sitting his horse in the roadway, out of sight of the front windows. He wore a black frock coat, broad brimmed black hat, and narrow riding trousers over polished boots. Clearly this was more than a routine notification of death. Carter Jayden was an important businessman from America's most celebrated city, come to Niagara to marry the daughter of one of the town's wealthiest families.

The office of sheriff was an elected position. Politics was everything.

"Shall we tell him about the telegram before we go in?" Prudence asked.

"We could, but I'd rather not chance him revealing Jayden's duplicity to soften the blow of his death," Geoffrey said. "People react differently if they've been informed that the deceased was not who they thought he was."

"You don't think . . . ?"

"Not Daphne. But from how you've described her, Myra Adderly is cut from different cloth. Some of our most famous murderers have been women," he reminded her.

"I'll take that as a left-handed compliment to the equality of the sexes," Prudence said. She had scandalized Josiah by declaring that she was in agreement with the Woman's Suffrage Movement although she had yet to take part in any of their marches.

Geoffrey directed the carriage driver to wait for them. Before they approached the door they stood at the bottom of the steps while Sheriff Bryant described what he'd found and the condition of the bodies.

"It looks as though Jayden surprised someone who had broken into the house. We may never find out why he went there alone after all the workmen had left. Shots were fired on the second story. Jayden was badly wounded but managed to make it down the central staircase and toward the door before he collapsed. There were drops of blood on the stairs and across the floor. The gun he was carrying dropped from his hand when he fell. We haven't identified the other dead man yet, but he was also armed."

"Was the front door locked?" Geoffrey asked.

"Closed when the on-site crew boss got there this morning, but unlocked. He swears that the last thing he does every day is check that all the doors are secured and the windows latched. The victims have been taken to Dr. Elliott's surgery, but the cause of death in both cases is obvious. The best he can do for us is dig out the bullets so we can match them to the guns we found."

Prudence would have liked to ask why the sheriff was including them on such an open-and-shut case, but she held her tongue. If it was nothing more than a gut feeling that something about the crime scene didn't make sense, Bryant might be reluctant to admit it. Especially in front of a woman.

The front door of Adderly House opened, a puzzled butler peering out at them.

Sheriff Bryant identified himself and asked to see Mrs. Adderly and Mrs. Yates. Together. Whether it was his somber tone of voice, or the badge pinned to his jacket that made the difference, the butler did not hesitate. He ushered them into the parlor, stayed for a moment to stir the fire, then left. They heard soft footsteps ascending the staircase to the second floor.

Geoffrey retreated to a spot in front of a window whose curtains he opened, letting a flood of light into the room. Sheriff Bryant stationed himself close to the warmth of the fireplace, hands clasped behind his back, rocking gently back and forth on his heels. Only Prudence sat, choosing a love seat where she hoped Daphne would join her.

The house was so silent that even before the parlor door opened, they heard the rustle of silk skirts across the floor and Myra Adderly's querulous voice demanding to know why the butler had admitted visitors at such an early hour.

"This is most irregular," she said, coming to an abrupt halt. Her daughter, following dutifully behind, almost stumbled into her. "I demand to know why you think you can barge your way into my house without invitation."

"I think you've already met Miss MacKenzie," Sheriff Bryant began smoothly. "This is Mr. Hunter. I asked them to accompany me this morning because what I have to tell you will be difficult to hear." He stepped to one side to address Daphne, half-hidden behind her mother. "Mrs. Yates, I regret to have to inform you that Mr. Carter Jayden was found dead of a gunshot wound a few hours ago."

If he expected her to cry out or totter into a faint, he was disappointed.

Daphne Adderly Yates smiled.

Prudence patted the empty space beside her on the love seat, taking both Daphne's hands in hers when the no-longer bride-to-be sat down. The smile with which she'd greeted Sheriff Bryant's announcement hadn't left her lips. If anything, her expression had brightened, as though the news had been welcome instead of catastrophic.

"That can't be right," Myra protested. "You've identified the wrong person."

"There's no mistake, Mrs. Adderly," Sheriff Bryant assured her. "He was found on the ground floor of the house he was building for himself and Mrs. Yates." He nodded in Daphne's direction. "The man who found him manages all the building crews. He spoke to Mr. Jayden often. Two of the contractors have verified the identification. They'd been working with the deceased for months, reporting to him at every phase of construction. Neither of them doubted for a moment who it was."

Myra grasped the back of a wing chair to steady herself, then sat with straight back and clasped hands, staring blindly at her daughter. "A vagrant must have done it," she said. "How could this happen? Where was the watchman?"

"No watchman on duty," Sheriff Bryant said. "Hadn't been anyone there overnight for several weeks."

"That doesn't make sense. No one leaves a valuable property unguarded," Myra raged. Her eyes snapped again as she demanded answers to a calamity she hadn't anticipated and could do nothing to reverse. She glared at her daughter, who sat with bowed head beside the lady lawyer. "Don't you have anything to say?" she demanded.

"Such a tragedy," Daphne murmured through lips that curved more than they should have.

"What is Miss MacKenzie doing here?" Myra demanded, as if noticing her presence for the first time.

"I'm glad she came, Mama. I'd like her to stay for a while." Daphne looked at Prudence out of dry eyes that pleaded for understanding. "If you can, that is," she added.

"I'll remain for as long as you need me," Prudence replied. "If your mother has no objection."

Myra waved a beringed hand as though to brush away a fly. "I still don't understand what happened."

"Mr. Hunter has made some inquiries you should know about," Prudence said. "You need to listen to what he has to say."

Geoffrey held out a Hunter and MacKenzie business card. When Myra didn't take it, he handed it to Daphne.

"Miss MacKenzie and I are partners in a private inquiry firm," he began. "We sent a telegram to an associate in New York City. The information he relayed to us may shed some light on why Mr. Jayden met the end he did." He glanced at Sheriff Bryant, whose features had gone blankly rigid. *Trust me*, he telegraphed, hoping the lawman would understand why he hadn't revealed the contents of the cable until now.

Myra's face burned with fury and embarrassment as she learned how badly she'd misjudged Carter Jayden, how close the Adderly family had come to being duped and swindled. She shook her head and refused to read it for herself when Prudence opened her reticule and tried to give her the telegram she'd brought with her.

"We don't have all the details yet," Geoffrey concluded, "but we'll be receiving a comprehensive report within the next day or two."

"I don't imagine any of the society families in New York City would allow him to pay court to their daughters," Daphne said. "So he came to Niagara to find a rich bride." She managed to imbue the statement with a triumphant ring, as though proving her mother wrong gave her great satisfaction. She squeezed Prudence's hands in quiet jubilation.

"That's enough," Myra snapped. "Not a word of this is to be leaked to the newspapers." She stared pointedly at Sheriff Bryant's badge.

"They'll be all over the story," Bryant warned. He wasn't happy about it, but he recognized the stratagem Geoffrey had employed. He'd often used it himself. The less you shared with a suspect early on in an investigation, the more likely you were to catch him or her off guard. And sometimes you had to keep things from a colleague whose face might give away too much. "There isn't any way to stop reporters when they smell scandal."

"I won't have it!" Myra exploded. "I will not have our family name mocked and dragged through the mud."

Daphne clasped a hand over her mouth as the laughter she could no longer repress poured out, a string of amused chuckles quickly escalating to a full, unladylike chortle.

Sheriff Bryant stared. Geoffrey studied the patterned oriental rug.

Prudence never took her eyes from Myra, who raised an arm as if to slap her daughter as hard as she could across the face. At the last moment she ground her teeth, surged to her feet, and fled from the room, slamming the parlor door behind her.

"The marriage was my mother's idea," Daphne said as the sound of angry footsteps and banging doors reverberated through the otherwise silent house. "I never liked Mr. Jayden very much. I'm sorry he had to die that way, of course."

"So unexpected. And so shocking," murmured Prudence. "I'm sure you're as overcome by the tragedy as we all are."

Daphne hesitated, raising a hand to conceal the suggestion of a smile she couldn't hide in any other way. "How kind of you to offer your sympathy, Miss MacKenzie."

Sheriff Bryant coughed, then stepped away from the fireplace, seating himself on the chair Myra had vacated. "I wonder if you feel up to answering a few questions?" He waited politely, notebook and pen in hand.

"I'll do whatever I can to help find the person who committed this horrible crime." Daphne folded her hands primly in her lap and concentrated on keeping her face expressionless. "You may ask me anything you like."

"That's very brave of you, Mrs. Yates." Sheriff Bryant thumbed through his notebook until he found an empty page. "When was the last time you saw Mr. Jayden?"

"You were here, Miss MacKenzie," she said, turning to Prudence. "It was the day you and Lady Hamilton came to call. He stopped by to tell us how the house was progressing, but he left when he saw that Mother and I had company."

"What about the most recent conversation you had with him?"

"I might have to consult my daybook," Daphne said, a perplexed frown creasing her forehead. "There were last-minute decisions to be made about the wedding."

"Did Mr. Jayden ever mention his business affairs? I realize this may be a difficult topic, but anything you can tell us could be important."

"He never spoke of anything to do with commerce." Wellbred ladies did not admit to knowing anything about financial dealings. They left monetary discussions to the fathers, brothers, and lawyers who hammered out the details of their marriage contracts and dowries.

"Our associate in New York will be sending information as

soon as all the details can be put together," Prudence volunteered, curious to see what Daphne's reaction would be.

"I'd like to see that report," Daphne said, stepping into the snare Prudence had set. Curiosity among ladies was considered a fault rather than a virtue.

"We'll bring you a copy of everything," Prudence promised, curious how much Daphne knew about the way her brother had tied up the family fortune.

"Did Mr. Jayden have any relatives?" Sheriff Bryant asked.

"He told us his parents were dead, as was a brother who hadn't married. He never spoke of aunts, uncles, or cousins."

"What about wedding guests?"

"It was to be a quiet family gathering," Daphne said.

"No one on his side?"

"No one."

Stranger and stranger, Prudence thought. A man on the verge of bankruptcy who passes himself off as wealthy by spending money he doesn't have. If he lied about that, couldn't he have falsified his family background as well?

"Where did he come from?" she asked softly, more the inquiry of a concerned friend than the question of an interrogator.

"I don't know, Miss MacKenzie," Daphne replied. "There's so much I never dared ask. Too much, I realize now."

"Didn't dare ask?"

"Mr. Jayden had a temper. If I put myself forward, he said I was being inquisitive and intrusive, that no real lady would dream of conducting herself in that way. I think he meant to imply none of the grand ladies of his acquaintance in New York City. His lips would fold in so tightly they disappeared into a straight line and his eyes could turn as cold as ice." Daphne ducked her head, then lifted it with a determined shake. "He frightened me."

"He was a con artist and a bully, Mrs. Yates."

"Please call me Daphne. I feel we could be friends, Miss MacKenzie."

"Prudence."

Geoffrey nodded to Sheriff Bryant.

It was time to leave his partner to her work. She'd learn everything there was to know about the Adderly family and the face Carter Jayden had presented to them. But only after the men were gone and Daphne could open up to her new confidante over cups of sugary tea and slices of raisin cake.

CHAPTER 20

"Did you win big last night?" Crazy Louie asked, tying on his leather apron.

"I didn't have enough cash to make it worth my while," Amos said, setting out the drawing of the new barrel he'd been working on.

"Did Flynn go down in the fifteenth round?"

"Like a rock."

"When Paddy drops a number, you can count on it." Louie thumbed his nose in the universal gesture of one trickster to another.

"I'll remember that if there's a next time."

"Did he get hurt bad?"

"Swollen nose, black eye, a cut cheek. Maybe a couple of loosened teeth." It had looked to Amos as though Paddy deliberately walked into some of the wild blows Flynn swung at him, but he thought it best to keep that opinion to himself.

"Fight fans like to see the blood fly," Louie said. "They need to feel they've gotten their money's worth, or they won't come back."

That confirmed what Amos had suspected. The fight was fixed. Paddy had been paid to wait until an agreed-upon round before taking down his challenger. The only question was whether Flynn had been in on it, but Amos couldn't afford to seem too curious. He'd wait a while before trying to find out.

"I used red oak on the last barrel," Crazy Louie mused, shrugging off the previous night's bout. "But I think the white oak staves curve better." He headed off toward a pile of lumber at the far end of the shop.

"Need some help?" Amos called.

Louie waved his arm and continued walking.

Keeping an eye on Louie, who was setting aside some white oak planks and rejecting others, Amos moved toward the stand-up desk where the shop's receipt book was kept. He'd seen Louie flick through it more than once, muttering to himself and making notations on some of the columned pages. If he was as obsessed with his mission to shoot the falls as Amos thought him to be, odds were good that Louie was keeping track of every piece of lumber and animal he used to bring him closer to his goal.

Red oak and a Cotswold sheep. Those were the words Amos was searching for as he skimmed the most recent entries. Every few seconds he glanced up to make sure Louie hadn't left the shadowy depths of the area where the wood was stored to season. He caught a glimpse of the words *red oak,* but nothing more than a notation about price and delivery. No record of a barrel having been built. The most up-to-date record of animals sent into the whitewater was of a pair of leghorns, one rooster, one hen.

Still keeping an eye on Louie, Amos ran a finger along the ledger's inner binding, searching for signs that a sheet had been ripped out. Sketches and what looked to be haphazard jottings had been stored between some of the pages, but they didn't seem to be much more than random ideas never acted upon. He paused at a drawing of a ram's head, but there was nothing to tell him when the rough picture had been made. Another slip of paper bore a single word—*Samuelson's*—and a question mark.

Amos had stepped away from the desk and was frowning over his much-modified drawing when Louie rolled back a wheelbarrow on which he'd balanced a dozen thin staves of white oak.

"I started getting these ready a while back," he said, carefully checking each piece of wood as he unloaded it. "What do you think?"

"Nice. Very nice." Amos hefted a stave, bent it between his extended hands to test pliancy and the degree of the arc. "Do you have enough of them?"

"Not of this quality. But I know somebody who might." Louie took off his apron, shrugged into a coat, slapped a hat on his head. "I'll be back." He handed Amos a broom. "Shop needs sweeping."

"I don't want to talk about him," Daphne said after Geoffrey and Sheriff Bryant had left. "Can you understand that?"

"Of course I can. Under the circumstances." All she had to do was wait, Prudence thought, and eventually Daphne would begin to open up. She'd want to share her feelings about Carter Jayden with someone. Definitely not with Myra.

"I usually take tea with my boys around this time of day. Would you like to meet them?"

"Very much. How old are they?"

"Arthur is sixteen. Edward is fifteen."

"How fortunate that you haven't had to send them away to school," Prudence said. *And how unusual.* "I understand good tutors are difficult to find." Most of the boys she'd known had attended Phillips Academy before admission to Harvard or Yale. Fathers insisted on it, pointing out that today's school friends became tomorrow's business associates.

"They are very special children," Daphne said.

Shouldn't she have referred to them as young men? Surely Arthur and Edward would object to being called *children,* even if in their doting parent's eyes they were always her babies. "Will your mother be joining us?"

"She's not fond of her grandsons."

"I'm sure that's not true," Prudence said.

"You'll see," Daphne replied. "Hard as it is to accept, I know my own mother. She isn't like most women."

Which was another reason Prudence was choosing to remain close to Daphne for as long as she could. Myra had been furious when she'd stormed out of the parlor; at some point she'd remember that she'd left her daughter and the lady lawyer sitting side by side on the settee.

They stopped outside the schoolroom door. Hand on the knob, Daphne paused as if to say or explain something. Then she changed her mind, turned the knob, and led her new friend inside.

"That's Arthur," Daphne said, pointing to a squat young man sitting at a tea table with place settings for three. A white linen napkin had been tied around his neck. "And this is Edward." Slightly younger and heavier, awkward on his feet, he lumbered toward his mother and slipped his hand into hers. "We have a visitor today," Daphne said in a voice that was louder than her normal speaking tone. She pronounced each of her words slowly and clearly. "Say hello to Miss MacKenzie, boys."

"Hello, Miss MacKenzie."

"Hello, Miss MacKenzie."

They looked at her expectantly.

"I'm happy to meet you, Arthur and Edward," Prudence said.

"We have bread and butter sandwiches." Arthur showed her the full plate, crustless sandwiches arranged in a pyramid shape.

"They're his favorite," Daphne explained. "Aren't they, Arthur?"

He nodded.

The nursemaid laid a fourth place setting and brought another chair. She poured tea for Daphne and Prudence, removing the hot teapot before bringing juice for Arthur and Edward.

When Prudence would have put a sandwich on Edward's plate, Daphne shook her head.

"I get my own sandwich," Edward told her.

"Of course you do," Prudence said. She stirred milk and sugar into her tea, sipped and smiled, unable to think of anything to say.

The boys concentrated on their sandwiches and slices of cake, lifting their glasses with both hands so as not to make a spill. They laughed at their mother's questions and competed loudly with each other to tell what they had done so far that morning.

As she watched and listened, Prudence realized that notwithstanding whatever was wrong with them, Arthur and Edward were happy and well cared for. There was no doubt that the strong bond between mother and sons stretched both ways. Never by word or gesture did Daphne express sadness, disappointment, or impatience. She loved her boys for who and what they were. Not despite it.

Until he came to work for Crazy Louie, Amos wouldn't have known wood of a red oak from a white from any other kind of oak. But he had memorized the grains and the subtle colorations as Louie paced the length of the workshop, pointing out the piles of lumber he'd gathered to season. He watched when Louie pulled out a plank, remembered where it came from, and hoped to hell he'd identify it correctly if asked. So far, he had.

The act of barrel making was going to prove a bit more ticklish. All Amos knew was what he'd absorbed in the bar near the Traveler's Rest where he'd stood two rounds of drinks. He considered it money well spent, but it was only a matter of time until Louie caught on to the fact that his expert hire could talk a good game but had no practical experience in what he proposed to do. He figured he had at most another day until he'd need to disappear.

The stack of red oak Amos hadn't had an excuse to inspect was next to the white oak from which Louie had pulled the staves he'd brought to the front of the workshop. If his employer came back and found him rooting around in the seasoning piles, he'd say he was just checking to make sure the white and red oak stores hadn't gotten mixed up. A weak explanation, but the only one he thought stood a chance of being believed.

What he was looking for was red oak staves with a few threads of white sheep fleece stuck to their splintery surfaces. He didn't think Louie would leave the duplicate barrel whole for somebody to find; he'd have broken it up as soon as he got it back to the shop. But raw wool was hard to get rid of, oily and usually matted with twigs, dirt, and insects. The Cotswold sheep Louie had put in his barrel must have left pieces of its fleece behind every time it rubbed against the staves. Even sedated, the sheep's body had to have been slammed hard against the curved surfaces as the barrel bobbed and bounced in the rough water.

If Louie had used all of the staves for firewood, there'd be no way to prove the barrel substitution. Amos had examined the cut pieces piled in the basket beside the stove and poked among the coals, but he'd seen no sign of fresh or burned fleece. He was hoping that even if most of the lengths had been split for kindling, a few would have been overlooked or set aside for later use.

Amos stood at the foot of the pile of red oak, studying the structure of the stack. Wood that was being seasoned was never thrown haphazardly into a heap. It was important to create a symmetrical pile that would allow for good air circulation and keep individual planks from being bent into unusable shapes. He compared the red oak arrangement to the white oak beside it, and both of them to the layered planks of maple and walnut that Louie had said he'd bought when he'd briefly flirted with the idea of furniture making to fund his over-the-falls ambition. The only thing that differentiated one stack from another, other than the nature of the woods themselves, was the way dust had settled on the planks. Nothing had disturbed the maple and walnut surfaces except the occasional rat. Tiny paw prints mingled with scattered droppings in the furred dust.

Louie had rearranged the pile of white oak when he'd chosen staves for the new barrel, but he'd carefully restacked the planks he hadn't taken out. It looked as though he'd burrowed through most of the pile because some of the wood appeared dust-free, as though it had lain in the center of the heap before being moved. It would have been easy to slide in some red oak staves, but Amos didn't find any.

The dust on the surface of the red oak pile looked as though someone had taken a broom to it recently. Streaked in places, swept nearly clean in others. The planks were of various sizes, all of one long length at the bottom, then pieces that differed by several feet. If this was the pile from which Louie had built the barrel containing the sheep and the one into which Martin Fallow's body had been placed, it looked as though he'd restacked the unneeded wood. Some of the pieces were too short for anything but the stove.

Amos picked up one of them, about eighteen inches long. It seemed heavier than the wood he'd already handled. Damp. Waterlogged? He picked at the splinters that came off easily when he pulled at them with his fingernails. The air in Niagara was always moist from the mist of the falls, but not wet enough to thoroughly soak a length of wood. He felt his heart skip a beat as he realized that he was holding a piece of the missing barrel, the one that had contained the Cotswold sheep. He turned it over several times, searching for a trace of wool, even a single fiber. Then he scrabbled through the pile, setting aside three more lengths that seemed heavier than they should, damp enough to leave traces of moisture on his skin.

Louie was predictable. He'd cut up the barrel into lengths that would fit into his stove and hidden the ones he couldn't burn right away, probably intending to reduce them to ashes within a day or two. Nobody would question a lit stove in October. Amos managed to find another half dozen of the eighteen-inch-long sticks, and on one of them he spotted several fingernail-sized clumps of wool. So dirtied that they looked brown until he pulled the fibers apart and a stray sunbeam lit up the white.

Gotcha!

Sheriff Bryant stood in the doorway of the back room where Dr. Elliott performed his autopsies. One wrapped corpse lay on the long wooden table. The sling containing the second body had been deposited on a rolling cart by two of his deputies. Sling and body were no longer there.

"What happened?" he asked, eyes flicking from one side of the narrow space to the other, over to the cart, back to the table, to the cart again. No matter how many times he looked, the missing corpse didn't materialize.

"I found the door unlocked when I came to start the autopsies," Dr. Elliott said. "Neither Mother nor I had noticed anything wrong before then. I'd gotten home from being with a patient most of the night just in time to let your deputies in and then I'd left again on another call. Mother had gone out right after her breakfast."

"So the house was empty this morning?"

"Only for about an hour and a half," Mrs. Elliott said. "I'm sure of that because I looked at the clock before going on my errands and then again when I returned. I'd covered my son's breakfast and left it on the kitchen table for him. It was still there. He came in before I finished putting away what was in my basket."

"We sat down together. Mother heated up my food and drank a cup of coffee with me."

"That would have been around nine-thirty. There were no early-morning appointments, so we took our time."

"Thank you, Mrs. Elliott. You can go on about your business now." Sheriff Bryant waited until she'd left, then he stepped deeper into the room where Dr. Elliott stood beside the shrouded corpse. "Let's make sure this is who we think it is," he said, closing the door.

The canvas covering had been tightly wrapped but not secured with rope or a strap. Working together, Sheriff Bryant and Dr. Elliott loosened and then folded back the heavy material until Carter Jayden's face lay in full view.

"That's him, all right." Sheriff Bryant continued unfolding the canvas. "There's the bullet hole. Can you tell if the slug is still in there?"

Dr. Elliott used a narrow-bladed scissors to cut through Jayden's silk vest and shirt, then reached for a probe. "It's in deep, but I can feel it."

"How soon can you start working on him?"

"Right away, if you like."

"I don't suppose you took a look at the other man?" Sheriff Bryant asked.

"I didn't," Dr. Elliott said, taking off his jacket, rolling up his shirtsleeves, and donning the apron that would protect his clothing from blood splatters.

"He was wrapped up tight when my men brought him in?"

"They both were. Like I said, I was on my way out again, so I didn't do anything but show them where to put the bodies and lock the door after they'd left."

"Where do you keep the key?"

Dr. Elliott reached into his trouser pocket and pulled it out. "Mother has a duplicate on her housekeeping ring. We're the only two who usually come in here." He waved at the rows of brown and dark green bottles lined up inside a glass-fronted cabinet. "I keep the strong drugs where nobody can get at them accidentally. I checked. Nothing's missing."

"Somebody got in. Two somebodies, I'd say. Whoever they were, they didn't want the fellow they were taking away to be identified."

Dr. Elliott picked up a scalpel.

Sheriff Bryant stepped away from the table.

CHAPTER 21

The mutton stew Amos bought from an outdoor vendor was tough and full of gristle. The potatoes tasted of black spot and the carrots had lain in a root cellar for so long, they'd lost most of their color. But the price was right and the woman stirring the pot didn't mind answering questions.

"Not too many farmers raise sheep around here," she told him. "But Samuelson's wife comes from a family of weavers in the old country. She sets up a table by the suspension bridge every few months to sell blankets to the tourists. Makes decent money at it, or so I hear."

Amos walked three miles out into the country, found the old hanging tree with a weathered wooden plaque nailed to its trunk, took the fork to the east, and walked another half mile.

It was nothing more than a hunch, but he'd learned over time to trust his instincts. He also needed to walk off the stew if he was going to make it through tonight's fights. According to Crazy Louie, who had come back with a wagon load of white oak that needed more seasoning before anything could be done with it, Paddy Morgan's rematch with Flynn had been scrubbed.

Replaced with amateur night. Not to be missed. In a rare good mood, he'd approved the neatly swept workshop floor and told Amos he wouldn't need him for the rest of the day.

Cross-bred sheep with horns could batter through the curved staves of a barrel. That was one of the reasons Louie had gone to the trouble of finding a Cotswold for his experiment. He'd launched into a long explanation when Amos had asked why the new barrel he was designing would also be tried out by a sheep. "Cotswolds have scurs," he'd said, "but they never have horns. Good dispositions, thick coats, long fibers. Not the kind of animal to bolt unexpectedly. Relatively easy to locate one about the weight of a man."

And then he'd abruptly fallen silent. The next time Amos asked about sheep, he hadn't answered.

Amos spotted the newly sheared ram as soon as he turned down the track leading to the Samuelson house. A dozen or more sheep grazed in a fenced pasture, all but one of them with coats that looked as though they were the result of a few months' growth. White fleeced, white faced, with black hooves, they might have stepped from a painting.

Everything about the farm was neat and prosperous looking, from the fields and gardens that had been readied for winter, to the red barns and white house with wide verandas and green shutters. A pair of black-and-white dogs ran out to greet him, keeping their distance and barking loudly to warn that someone was approaching. A woman appeared in the front doorway, broom in hand, calling to the dogs when Amos halted and took off his hat so she could see his face.

"I'm looking for the Samuelson farm," he said, pitching his voice loud enough to be heard but not sound threatening.

"We're not hiring," the woman answered, firmly but not unkindly.

"I'm not looking for work, ma'am," Amos said, taking a few tentative steps closer. "I bought some stew a while back from a lady who told me Mrs. Samuelson wove the best wool blankets in the area."

"Callie Westover?"

"I didn't get her name."

"She's a good woman, and a terrible cook. But she's a widow lady, so everyone buys a bowl from her now and then." She clucked at the dogs, who lay down without taking their eyes off the newcomer. "I'm Betsy Samuelson."

"Amos Lang. Please to make your acquaintance, ma'am."

"What can I do for you, Mr. Lang? Sell you a blanket?"

"I have a question or two about that ram over there," he said, turning toward the pasture. "The one who looks like he just got shorn."

"What about him?" Mrs. Samuelson's voice had gone cold and sharp. The dogs stood up, their ears pricked forward.

"I'm wondering why he wasn't taken care of when the others were clipped."

"That isn't any of your business, is it, Mr. Lang?"

"What I'm thinking is that someone paid you a nice bit of money not to shear him in the summer, like you'd planned. This person had a use for the animal that required a thick, wooly coat. He bought the ram, and maybe you and Mr. Samuelson thought that was the last you'd see of the animal. You had a younger male coming along in time for lambing season. Why not sell the old one while he still had some value?"

He paused, but she neither interrupted nor corrected him.

"Then he shows up again, hardly the worse for wear, and this time you're paid to take him back and keep quiet about it. No explanation offered, but you agree. You shear him right away, not as close as you would have a few months ago, figuring no one will notice or care. Maybe in another few weeks, you'd be right. But I could tell the difference just by looking, and I'm no sheep expert."

From the way she kept the dogs near her, Amos figured

Mrs. Samuelson's husband wasn't home. He hadn't seen a figure out in the fields, and no one had walked into the yard from the barn.

"I think you'd better be on your way, Mr. Lang."

One of the dogs growled.

"All I need is confirmation that you or Mr. Samuelson sold that ram to Louie Whiting—Crazy Louie—and that when he brought the animal back, he made some sort of deal to keep the return a secret."

"I have no idea what you're talking about."

"A man was killed, and his body placed in a barrel identical to the one your sheep was supposed to take a ride in."

Mrs. Samuelson leaned the broom against the porch railing and turned as if to go back into the house.

"I'd stay right where you are, ma'am," Amos said quietly. "I'm sure you've got a weapon inside that you'd like to get to, but that would be a serious mistake."

"What do you want from me?"

"Like I said." Amos unbuttoned his jacket. He'd worn two guns today.

She nodded.

"And a piece of that ram's wool," Amos added. "The barrel's been found. There's fleece caught on the staves."

"All he told us was that he needed a sheep that weighed about as much as he did," Mrs. Samuelson said. Her words were slightly garbled, her breathing quick and shaky. "We heard about what happened, how the sheep disappeared, and Martin Fallow showed up in the barrel instead. Folks figured either Louie had paid him to go over or Martin decided to steal his thunder. The least said about it the better. We didn't want to be any part of whatever it was."

"When did Louie bring the animal back?"

"The ram was grazing in the field the morning after the accident."

"You knew what it meant?"

"Wouldn't you?"

Amos rebuttoned his coat and gestured toward the pasture. When she'd cut a handful of fibers from the ram's coat and handed them to him, he tipped his hat and set off down the road, alert to the noises behind him, but not overly worried.

Mrs. Samuelson hadn't seemed the type to shoot a man in the back.

"When was the last time you saw Rowan?" Prudence asked as the carriage taking her and Daphne to Daniel's cabin reached the end of the road.

"The year my mother decided she would no longer spend holidays and vacations at home with us," Daphne said, glad she'd followed Prudence's suggestion to put on a warm coat and change into outdoor boots before leaving the house.

The path into the woods was narrow and muddy where the tree canopy grew so thick overhead that the ground was in perpetual shade. Daphne carried a large woven basket packed with delicacies a mystified cook had hastily retrieved from the kitchen pantry. Basic good manners required bringing a gift when paying an unexpected call, and Daphne had been raised on the importance of obeying the social conventions.

"She's grown-up now," Prudence said. She'd done her best to keep a nervous but determined Daphne distracted during the drive. Asking questions, encouraging her to delve into the memories she'd been unable to share with anyone else.

"I remember her being a beautiful little girl. Striking red hair, hazel eyes that changed color with the light. And a voice that was always magically on key."

"Did you ever hear her mother sing?" Prudence asked.

"I did. Lucas took me to a performance when Grace first came to Niagara."

"Rowan's voice isn't trained, of course, but she can bring tears to your eyes when she sings a ballad."

They fell silent as the path slanted upward toward the ridge overlooking the Niagara River. Prudence hadn't told Daphne about the attempted poisoning nor that the cabin was guarded night and day by a young half-French, half-Tuscaroran man and the friends he'd recruited to keep Rowan and Daniel safe. She wasn't sure yet how much information she could share without endangering the case. For all her apparent interest in her brother's child, Daphne was still Myra's daughter. It was impossible to know whether the newfound resistance to her mother would last.

As they paused to catch their breath, Prudence heard footsteps behind them. She pulled Daphne from the path, hiding her behind a screen of holly bushes, shushing her surprised exclamations with a finger across her lips.

"Be quiet," she hissed, darting out to pick up two small packages that had tipped out of the wicker basket.

Derringer in hand, Prudence waited.

And then breathed a sigh of relief as she recognized the figure walking through the trees in their direction.

"How did you know where we were?" she asked, stepping out onto the path, weapon dangling from her fingers.

"I saw the carriage go by and followed it. Are you all right?" Geoffrey asked. He nodded at Daphne, whose frightened face regained some of its color as she struggled through the undergrowth and back out onto the path.

"What's happened?" Prudence asked quietly.

"The unidentified body disappeared from Dr. Elliott's before he could perform the autopsy."

A sharp gasp told them Daphne had overheard what he'd said.

"How could that be?" Prudence asked, tightening her grip on the derringer, eyes sweeping through the trees.

"Sheriff Bryant believes the house was broken into when Elliott was out on a call and his mother had gone into town. A window of about an hour and a half."

"So whoever took the body waited until the house was empty."

"Then moved quickly. So far there aren't any witnesses."

"Why steal a corpse?" Prudence asked.

"To prevent identification that could be traced back to whoever hired him," Geoffrey said. "And maybe to make sure the bullet that killed him couldn't be matched to someone's gun."

"We assumed it was Jayden."

"But now we have a third party in the mix."

"What did the dead man look like?" Daphne asked. She was trembling from head to foot as though the slightest breeze might blow her over, but her eyes were dry and determined. "I saw Carter in conversation with a very frightening-looking man. He didn't know I was watching him."

"When was that? And where?" Geoffrey asked.

"In front of the Gustavson Hotel, about two weeks ago. I wanted to see the progress on the house, and he'd agreed to take me, but only if I promised to make the visit brief. Mother insisted on coming with us, but at the last moment she changed her mind. I was alone in the carriage and a few minutes early. Carter was standing on the hotel porch, so absorbed in whatever he was discussing that he didn't notice I'd arrived. When he did look over at where the carriage had pulled up, he said something dismissive to the man he was talking to, and the man turned on his heel and left. I didn't see where he went, but I remember feeling shivers run up my spine. I'd never seen anyone who rattled me so badly just by the impression of him."

"Can you remember what he looked like?" Geoffrey had ignored Daphne's request to describe the dead man, not wanting to put words in her mouth or images in her mind's eye. He held out his arm to steady her.

"I'm all right," she insisted. But when Prudence reached for the heavy basket, she surrendered it gratefully. "He wasn't as tall as Carter. Medium height, I'd say. That was the first thing I noticed about him. Thin, clean shaven, dark-skinned with very sharp features and the coldest eyes I've ever seen. He glanced at me when Carter realized the carriage had pulled up. Something about the deadness in his eyes chilled me to the bone."

"Anything else? Did you hear his voice?"

She shook her head. "They were too far away. His clothes were shabby. I remember wondering why the doorman hadn't sent him away. Then I realized he must have used Carter's name, that he had an appointment with him."

"Did you ask your fiancé who the man was?" Prudence asked.

"Carter didn't tolerate questions," Daphne reminded her. "They made him angry."

"It's the same man," Geoffrey said. "Sheriff Bryant had one of his deputies write down a description before the body was removed from where it was found. No beard, dark complected, sharp nose. Medium height, slender build."

"So there's nothing to worry about," Prudence said. "He can't threaten you, and whatever scheme he was involved in with Jayden is as dead as they are." It wasn't true, but if the lie comforted Daphne, it had been well worth telling. Geoffrey's quick nod told her he agreed.

"We'll need permission from Lady Hamilton before allowing you into the records room," the Canadian clerk told Josiah firmly.

"They're public documents," Josiah protested.

"Are you a Canadian citizen?"

"No, but that shouldn't make a difference. Public records are open to the public."

"As I said, you'll need her Ladyship's written authorization."

"Is there someone else I can talk to?"

The clerk glanced at the clock hanging on the wall. He closed the ledger in which Josiah had written his name and request. Shelved it out of sight below the counter.

"The office is closed," he announced. "Come back tomorrow."

Josiah had only been to one bare-knuckle fight, eight years ago at Madison Square Garden. The Englishman Tug Wilson had danced, run, rolled, deliberately fallen, and otherwise avoided heavyweight champion John L. Sullivan's fists for four exhibition rounds, earning himself a thousand dollars and the boos of a crowd that felt cheated out of the bloody contest they'd paid good money to see. He explained all of this and how much he despised the sport to Amos Lang, then gave up and agreed that two pairs of eyes scanning a crowd were bound to be better than one.

"Tell me again what or for whom I'll be looking," Josiah said as they sighted a gathering crowd and lantern light pouring through the open doors of the barn where the ring had been set up.

"Crazy Louie, for one," Amos said. "There's also a boxer named Paddy Malone. Not fighting tonight, but bound to be here nonetheless. He may be with Louie, but if not, I'll watch out for him. What I really want to know is who's running the operation. I've asked around, but I'm not getting any answers." He briefed Josiah on what he'd discovered at the Samuelson farm that afternoon.

"Do Mr. Hunter and Miss Prudence know?"

"There wasn't time to find them. It's what we suspected, so no real surprise except that Crazy Louie was stupid enough to take the sheep back to where he bought it."

"So what exactly do you want me to do?"

"Circulate through the crowd. Listen. Watch as bets are placed. See if you can spot the bookies checking in with someone." Amos paused. "Just remember every name you hear. We can sort them out later."

"What else?"

"A feeling. Something's on the verge of happening, but I don't know what."

Josiah went in first, so well-dressed and prosperous-looking a customer that even though no one had left his name with the bouncer, he was waved through. Amos followed ten minutes later, losing himself in the crush as soon as he sighted Crazy Louie and Paddy Malone standing together beside the ring. Neither of them paid any attention to the slender, slightly older man in the bespoke suit who had eased his way beside them. Two for one. Amos left Josiah to it and circled the outer ring of the crowd where the bookies were noisier and the bets smaller and more desperate.

The drinks flowed faster there also, from flasks hidden in pockets as well as off trays laden with finger-smudged glasses. From the smell, the waiters were hawking rotgut whiskey, greasy gin, and skunked beer. After the second or third round, nobody cared.

Bouncers leaned against the barn walls, ready to bang heads and twist arms at the slightest provocation. Brass knuckles on their hands, clubs hanging from their belts. If trouble erupted, it was likely to start in the back rows, far enough away from the toffs to throw the troublemakers out before any real damage could be done.

Amos wove his way from one end of the barn to the other, up and down all four sides of the ring. There was a tang in the air that tasted metallic in his mouth. Something was stirring, but as he'd told Josiah, he didn't know what.

"It's amateur night again," someone said, wiping beer froth from his mouth. "I've a mind to put my name on the list."

"You don't need no more broken teeth," his friend said, hawking out tobacco juice and missing the spittoon.

"Anybody can fight?" Amos asked.

"Ten bucks'll buy you five rounds. Plus half of what the bookies win off you."

"Not a bad deal."

"Depends on how good you are. How good are you?"

Amos faded back into the crowd.

An hour later he was ready to call it quits. Maybe amateur night didn't attract the kind of fight fans who could supply the information he wanted. Maybe it wasn't lucrative enough for whoever was calling the shots to put in an appearance. Then why were the hairs on the back of his neck still itching? He signaled Josiah to make his way over to where he waited.

Josiah never got there. He stopped halfway between the ring and the door where the entrance fees were collected, turning a desperate look in Amos's direction. Then he began pushing his way toward where two bouncers were holding a couple of men by the collars of their coats, hustling them out the back exit. Feet dragging in the straw, arms and hands limp and hanging by their sides, the captives were obviously unconscious. And when Amos caught a glimpse of their faces, he understood why. They'd been savagely beaten, eyes swollen shut, blood dripping from mouths where teeth had been knocked out, noses crushed and oddly off center.

"That's the clerk from the records office in American Niagara," Josiah whispered when Amos finally caught up to him. "And the other man is the one who wouldn't let me into the records room in the Canadian office." He was having trouble speaking, his voice cracking and teeth chattering with cold or nerves. Or both. "I've never seen anything like that. What happened?"

"I told you something was brewing," Amos said, taking Josiah by the arm, steering him toward the entrance, away from the bloodbath no one had bet on. The cries no one had heard in all the enthusiastic yelling and cheering and smacks of fists on flesh.

"Are they dead?"

"If not already, they soon will be. We need to get out of here before somebody recognizes you as the man who was seen asking them questions."

"What's going on, Amos?"

"We've stirred up a hornets' nest, that's what. And hornets are deadly when they're mad."

CHAPTER 22

Lady Hamilton put two bottles of a very good French burgundy into the saddlebags she carried, then locked the wine cellar door behind her. In the kitchen she packed thick slices of three different cheeses, a decent hunk of ham, and a packet of biscuits. Added four large apples, a small loaf of newly baked bread, and a tinned fruit cake.

This was the quiet hour, when staff took the only break afforded them during the long workday. Shoes were removed, corsets loosened, naps taken before preparations began for tea and then dinner. The only sounds in the empty basement rooms were the ticking of the kitchen clock and the meow of the old mouser who these days preferred being fed scraps to hunting down his dinner.

Her horse stood saddled and waiting in the rear courtyard, not a speck of yesterday's dust and mud anywhere on hooves or curried coat. The stable boy had ambitions to become a groom and then a coachman someday and a genuine love for the animals he was learning to care for.

He snatched off his cap as she approached, tied the heavy saddlebags across the mare's withers, and stood respectfully by as her Ladyship settled herself into the sidesaddle. Lady Hamilton was a much-admired horsewoman, known for her perfect seat, steady hands on the reins, and erect, almost military posture. It made him proud to work for so regal a rider, even though setting out alone as she did wasn't really the done thing. He couldn't think of another lady in Niagara who rode without a groom in attendance.

"I'll be back by teatime," she said as she did whenever she went out in the early afternoon.

The saddlebags would be empty, and her pale skin flushed with color when she returned. She wouldn't explain where she'd been, and it wasn't the stable boy's place to ask. He'd brush the mare's coat and hooves clean, add an extra measure of oats and fresh water to the evening feed, and keep his suspicions to himself.

The Canadian records office was hushed and empty of customers when Josiah approached the counter behind which stood a cluster of clerks who should have been sitting at their desks. He couldn't make out what they were saying, but he didn't doubt it had to do with the death last night of their head clerk. And his American counterpart. Nothing like that had ever happened. Two respectable civil servants beaten to death at an illegal bare-knuckle boxing fight somewhere outside the city limits. No details about exactly how or why it happened, just rumors of savage battering that rendered the faces of the dead men nearly unrecognizable. It didn't bear thinking about. But how could they not?

He was ushered into the inner records room without argument and without the customary cautions about not using an ink pen and leaving folders he had finished with in a basket for the clerks to refile correctly. The young man who unlocked the file room for him went back to his whispering colleagues and didn't notice that the new arrival had closed the door that usually remained partially open.

Josiah's first foray was into the Hamilton folders since os-tensibly he had been hired by Lady Hamilton to organize her late husband's affairs. Within the first hour he had found much the same evidence of frequent purchases followed by ill-advised sales as he had discovered in the American office. But there was something about the pattern of land and business deals that seemed unnecessarily complicated. A parcel of land or an investment property might pass back and forth between Lord Hamilton and a series of buyers several times before end-ing up titled to a holding company. When Josiah located the firm's file, he found one company officer's name repeated many times over. E. Corcoran.

He was tempted to ask a clerk in the outer office if the name was a familiar one in Canadian Niagara. He could see through the glass panel in the door that they had drifted back to their desks, though every now and then one of them glanced up. He couldn't shake the annoying feeling that he'd stumbled over something whose importance he should have grasped immedi-ately but hadn't.

He picked up a pencil and began doodling on the pad where he'd taken his notes. Not something he usually did, but then Josiah wasn't often befuddled. He played with rearranging the letters of the name Corcoran, trying to fit them into an ana-gram he would recognize. None of the combinations he tried worked. He added the *E* and tried again. Still no success.

He wrote upper case *E*'s with and without curlicues and flourishes, standing tall, bending forward, slanted back.

And then, without conscious thought or effort on his part, the elaborate calligraphy petered out and the name Ernestine appeared. Though he'd never heard them used together, Ernes-tine and Corcoran flowed so smoothly, so naturally, that he understood he'd discovered Lady Hamilton's family name be-fore she married.

Unbeknownst to her alcoholic, philandering husband, Lady Ernestine Hamilton had used her maiden name to reclaim the money he was throwing away with both fists. When he borrowed from and then paid back loans with interest to the holding company she'd set up, he was doing business with his wife. When he surrendered property for lack of payment, he was giving it over to the woman whose entire dowry he would have squandered if her slick businessman father had not protected it. Lord Hamilton might have nearly bankrupted himself, but Lady Hamilton was exceedingly rich. He'd have to make a second visit to the records office on the American side of the river to confirm that the same stratagem had been used there as well. He needed more and better notes. *Shame on you, Josiah!*

He remained in the records room for another hour, following cleverly disguised trails that meandered here and there but always led back to E. Corcoran. Lady Ernestine Hamilton. He was puzzled for a while by another name that cropped up in the earliest documents. Lucas Adderly. Listed as a witness to E. Corcoran's signature and occasionally as an officer of one of the many holding companies that Josiah understood were subsidiaries of a single operation. Then Adderly disappeared, as neatly as though he'd never existed. Was this the link between Rowan and Lady Hamilton that neither Miss Prudence nor Mr. Hunter had been able to find? Had Lucas helped a fellow American navigate the choppy waters of financial duplicity in return for her promise to look out for the well-being of his daughter?

Josiah was not a romantic, so when an unwelcome image popped into his mind of a desperate dollar princess in dishabille with a man whose face he could not make out, he shook the notion out of his head and packed his lawyer's leather briefcase. Some episodes in the past were best left lying where they belonged, in a dead man's memory where they could do no harm to anyone.

Daphne Adderly Yates was listed on Carter Jayden's death certificate as the individual who had provided information in lieu of next of kin. There was precious little she could tell Dr. Elliott and Sheriff Bryant about the man she had been about to marry. She mostly shook her head at their questions, biting back the words she would have liked to let fly. *Swindler, cad, confidence man, trickster, charlatan, rogue.*

Myra, embarrassed and angrier than her daughter because the marriage had been her idea, also held her tongue. Ill-considered speech had a way of leaking out into the community where it would give rise to derisive laughter and contempt. As if the Adderlys deserved to be duped. Daphne would be pitied, but Myra would be judged as being *no better than she ought to be.* There were too many Niagarans who might remember her less-than-sterling origins.

Carter Jayden needed to be buried quickly and without public notice. Since he had no known religious affiliation, Myra secured a plot in the city graveyard, choosing a burial site that was cheap and out of the way, unlikely to be noticed by visitors once the mound of dirt had settled and the grass grown back. Out of sight, out of mind. The Adderlys would see that all was done circumspectly, properly, and with dignity. As expected. But once the interment was over, they would wipe him from their minds as though he had never existed.

The coffin was draped in a black pall and carried to the cemetery in a glass-paneled hearse. Not Ferguson Funeral Parlor's largest vehicle, but the casket hidden beneath the drapery wasn't their most expensive coffin. Myra and Daphne rode in a closed family carriage, garbed in black, faces covered by mourning veils. As was customary, men raised their hats and women lowered their eyes as the two conveyances passed, but Myra had given instructions that the most direct route to the cemetery be taken, so very few Niagarans witnessed Jayden's last ride. Tourists paused for a moment, then got on with the business of amusing themselves.

Neither Geoffrey nor Sheriff Bryant wore black mourning bands around their arms; their presence at Carter Jayden's obsequies was strictly professional. Prudence had chosen a dark gray gown to show respect for the dead but not the grief of personal loss. They, along with Myra, Daphne, and the two Ferguson attendants, made up the entirety of the party escorting the deceased to his final resting place.

"I'm not sure why I do this," Sheriff Bryant remarked as he watched the hearse make its slow journey from cemetery gate to open grave. He scanned the grounds, empty except for the gravediggers standing off to one side, shovels in hand, heads wreathed in cigar smoke. "No murderer with the common sense God gave a rat would turn up at his victim's funeral. Yet here we are, every last badge-wearing one of us, eternally hopeful that our quarry won't be able to stay away. Have you ever known a guilty man stick his neck out like that?"

"There's always a first time," Geoffrey said, meeting Bryant's rueful smile with one of his own. "But I have seen a man contemplate murder while the funeral hymns were being sung."

"We could read it on his face," Prudence added. "And we were right. He took his vengeance in due time. Not that anything was ever proved against him." It had been the second important case they'd worked together.

"Jayden took a single shot to the chest," Bryant said. "At close range. From what I was able to tell him about the body that's disappeared, Dr. Elliott thinks he gave as good as he got. He believes the two men were facing each other, each of them holding a gun he thought was concealed by the darkness. Probably not much more than a couple of yards apart. We'll never know who shot first, but it was impossible to miss at that distance. Jayden only made it down the stairs because the bullet didn't go directly into his heart. As far as Elliott is concerned, that's the end of it. Two men and two bullets. He may be right, but a body doesn't get up and walk out of an autopsy room on its own two legs. I can't help wondering if a third figure was lurking in the shadows on that second floor."

The hearse rolled to a stop on the graveled road that wound

through the cemetery, the feathery plumes atop the horses' heads gradually ceasing to wave. The funeral parlor attendants nodded to the gravediggers, who meandered over and pocketed the extra coins agreed upon to help carry the coffin. Ropes were slung beneath the box to lower it into the ground, then gravediggers and attendants stood back in respectful silence.

Myra and Daphne stepped to the graveside. Neither woman raised the veil hiding her face, but Prudence caught a glimpse of their expressions as each bent forward to deposit a single red rose atop the coffin. Myra's lips were pursed tightly closed; there was no mistaking the anger in the way she held her head. Daphne wore the same slight smile with which she had greeted the news of her fiancé's death. A decorous joy, if there could be such an emotion.

The silence stretched into an embarrassingly long hush. There was no clergyman to recite prayers for the dead, no relative to weep, no business associate to mourn the loss of an able partner. There didn't seem to be a protocol for how to end a service that had never begun.

One of the gravediggers coughed and then hawked tobacco juice into the grass.

Myra turned away from the open grave. "It was very thoughtful of you to come," she said to Geoffrey and Prudence, the words as meaningless as the tone of voice with which they were uttered. But if asked, the funeral attendants would bear witness that Mrs. Adderly, despite the difficulty of the situation, had behaved with the formal dignity commensurate with her station. Reputation always came first. The appearance of good breeding was at least as important as the actual fact.

She nodded to Sheriff Bryant, who was not her social equal. If she wondered why he'd shown up, she didn't ask.

Daphne whispered her thanks into Prudence's ear, the grip of her fingers on Prudence's hands painfully tight. "Will you come back to the house for tea?" she asked. It was what you did after a burial.

Myra's head whipped around. "Do come," she urged with no trace of warmth in her voice.

"That's very kind of you, Mrs. Adderly," Sheriff Bryant said, although he clearly hadn't been included in the invitation. "But I think I'll be stopping by when we have enough information about Mr. Jayden to ask more questions."

"We've told you everything we know about him," Myra said stiffly. "My family and I cannot be held responsible for the way he chose to lead his life and conduct his business if those choices contributed to the manner of his death." It was as far as she would go to acknowledge that the man she'd chosen for her daughter had not been worthy of her.

"I'm sure you believe you have," Sheriff Bryant continued smoothly. "But you'd be surprised how much you remember about a person when you set your mind to it. If the right questions are asked." He tipped his hat to her and to Prudence and Geoffrey, then strolled away, pausing to speak to the funeral parlor attendants, having a slightly longer conversation with the gravediggers, who nodded agreement.

"He's asking them to keep an eye out for anyone who visits the grave," Geoffrey said, taking Prudence's arm for the walk back to the entrance gate.

Myra and Daphne had climbed into their carriage and lowered the shades as it drove away. The hearse stood empty while the attendants waited for dirt to cover the casket before leaving.

"You don't think it's over, do you?" Prudence asked.

"Do you?"

"Too neatly tied up for my liking," Prudence said. "And we still have the problem of a missing body."

CHAPTER 23

Amos Lang, dressed in a white butcher's apron and carrying a quarter haunch of beef on his shoulder, entered the Clifton House Hotel through the rear kitchen entrance. It was an odd time for deliveries, but it was also the peak of the dinner hour. No one paid him any attention. He followed a cook with a fileting knife in his hand to the meat locker, deposited his burden on an empty hook, and waited until he was alone. Then he stripped off the meat seller's garb and climbed the back stairs to the guest rooms above. When he exited the stairwell, he was wearing the uniform of a room service waiter, balancing a drinks tray on one hand.

Josiah, who looked like a respectable guest even when he wasn't, took a more direct route to the suite where Prudence and Geoffrey were waiting. No one noticed him, either.

"Should I ask where you found the uniform?" Prudence said as Amos set down the tray.

"Every hotel keeps racks of extra uniforms in all sizes," he answered. "For emergencies and accidents. It won't do to have your waiters serving guests in food-stained pants or ripped jackets." When Amos grinned, his ordinary-looking face took on an elfin glow.

"It becomes you," Josiah said, well aware that his bespoke suit, silk vest, and gold watch were the equal of his employer's.

"I'd like to get down to business." Geoffrey pulled the drapes over the floor-to-ceiling windows. It was unlikely anyone would be outside on the falls side of the hotel after dark, but he was taking no chances. "Amos, let's hear from you first. What did you find out about the two clerks?"

"No one saw anything." Amos rarely used the kind of small notebook in which most detectives kept their case notes. He relied on memory and mental images that had the clarity and accuracy of photographs. "The story told to Sheriff Bryant is that the two clerks were arguing. One of them struck the other and a fight broke out. A couple of bouncers waded in, separated the men, dragged them to an exit, and threw them outside while the boxing match was still going on. Told them not to come back, that their money wasn't good anymore. The supposition is that the clerks continued to batter each other until they lost consciousness. Since they were out behind the barn none of the fight promoters or fans saw them when they shut down the ring for the night and left. The farmer who owns the place discovered the bodies shortly before dawn this morning when he took a lantern out to check on his stock."

"Does anybody believe that?" Geoffrey asked. He'd heard many stories in his time, most of them so ridiculous, he wondered why the fools who told them thought they bore any resemblance to the truth.

Amos shrugged. "The facts are that they were beaten almost to death and then left out in the night cold to make sure they didn't recover. The other half of the story is that no one saw anything. Period. End of tale."

"Case closed?" Prudence asked.

"Open and shut," Amos agreed. "From what I've heard,

fights outside the ring are commonplace. The only thing different about this one is that nobody would have expected two government clerks to engage in drunken fisticuffs."

"They were drunk?" Josiah looked doubtful. "I only caught a glimpse of what was going on when the bouncers were dragging them away. I barely recognized who they were, but I wouldn't have thought either of them was a drinking man."

"That's the popular opinion."

"What did the autopsies show?" Geoffrey asked.

"Stomachs full of rotgut. Their clothes had been drenched in it. Like they'd flung whiskey at each other."

"That's what it was supposed to look like," Prudence speculated.

"The only good thing to come out of the mess is that I was able to get into the Canadian records files without any questions being asked," Josiah said. "All anybody in that office wanted to talk about was what had happened to their senior clerk."

"What did you find out?" Geoffrey asked.

"Lady Hamilton is shrewder than we've given her credit for. While the late lord was spending money like there was no tomorrow, she was swindling him as thoroughly as he was fleecing her. And she wasn't doing it alone. Lucas Adderly's name appears on some of the documents I examined. He verified her signature on deeds that needed witnessing and served as chief officer of the holding companies she set up. Does the name Corcoran sound familiar?" he asked Prudence.

"It does," she answered. "I remember Aunt Gillian talking about some of the other dollar princesses who went to England around the same time she did. Not about the young women so much as the family fortunes that were enriching the empty coffers of the British aristocrats they married. The Corcorans own a transatlantic shipping company and coal mines."

"Lady Hamilton is using E. Corcoran to conceal the identity by which she's known socially, but I've no doubt it's on the up and up," Josiah said. "She strikes me as the kind of woman who researches everything very carefully before committing to an investment or a course of action."

"So does Aunt Gillian," Prudence confirmed. "I think they discovered early on that they were only valued for their wealth. Even if they were young and naïve when they left the United States, they soon found out that love was never going to factor into their marriages. They had to learn to look out for themselves."

"So the link between Lucas and Ernestine is older and stronger than she led us to believe," Geoffrey said.

"Given what Josiah has uncovered, I can't help but wonder why Lady Hamilton took the risk of bringing a lawyer onto the scene. Surely she must have known private investigators would be used."

"A moment of panic, I think," Geoffrey said. "She made the mistake of telling your aunt that she was in desperate need of an attorney. Lady Rotherton, being who she is, acted upon the information. And voilà, here we are."

"She seemed glad to see us when we first arrived," Prudence said.

"She was probably anticipating that you'd choose to broker a quiet out-of-court settlement. Enough to protect Rowan's future, but not provoke an all-out counterattack by Myra Adderly."

"The first death occurred after we got here," Prudence mused.

"And changed the entire complexion of the case," Geoffrey said.

"Crazy Louie is involved," Amos volunteered. "If not directly in Martin Fallow's murder, at least in the cover-up. I found the farm where he bought the sheep he sent over the falls. The animal is back in its pasture. The farmer's wife claims it was returned during the night so neither she nor her husband saw who left it."

"What made her talk?" Josiah asked.

Amos shrugged and touched the revolver hidden in his shoulder holster.

"You didn't?" Josiah had a nightmarish image of Amos holding his gun on a frightened woman and threatening to use it if she didn't answer his questions.

Geoffrey smiled. He'd known the ex-Pink for three or four years and by reputation for longer than that. Amos had never hesitated to pull a trigger or use a knife when the situation warranted, but the quiet menace in his eyes and the flat deadness of his voice usually made killing unnecessary.

Amos pulled two separate tufts of wool from a trouser pocket. "The small one is from the cut stave of a barrel in Crazy Louie's workshop. Most of the wood has been burned, but there were a few pieces left." He placed both balls of wool on the palm of one hand. "The other one is from the ram in the Samuelson pasture. Recently shorn but made to look like the shearing was done at the same time as the rest of the flock."

"They look alike," Prudence said.

"I had Mrs. Samuelson explain wool to me," Amos said. "She's a weaver who sells blankets in Niagara. A practiced spinner can tell one fleece from another by things like color, fiber strength, staple length, degree of crimp, and purity." He rattled off the terms she'd used as though he'd been familiar with them all his life. "Even the amount and kind of twigs and dirt the sheep gets into and then carries around. She took this larger chunk from the ram and I showed her the bit I'd found at Crazy Louie's place. She wouldn't go so far as to say they're from the same animal, but they're definitely from the same breed. And raised somewhere around Niagara. No doubt about it."

"I'm less concerned about how Louie managed the switch than I am about who hired him to do it," Geoffrey said.

"The same person who arranged for the two clerks to be killed?" Prudence asked. "And orchestrated Carter Jayden's murder?"

"Five deaths," Josiah murmured.

"Add the failed attempt on Rowan and Daniel." Prudence

glanced at the penciled outline taking shape in Josiah's note-book.

"Was there anything special about either of the clerks?" Geoffrey asked. "Anything that made them stand out?"

"Other than the fact they were both almost certainly taking substantial bribes?" Josiah finished his diagram with a dramatic flourish, laying the opened notebook down for everyone to see.

"Careless of them to wear their double dealing on their backs," Amos said. "Anyone who thought about it would realize how out of place expensive clothing and watches were in that kind of office. Why wait until one or the other of them started telling tales out of school? Much safer to get rid of them when they were no longer needed."

"When can you get into their rooms?" Geoffrey asked.

"As soon as we finish here," Amos answered. "Sheriff Bry-ant sent deputies to search them after the bodies were identi-fied, but I doubt they found anything. You would have heard."

"He signals that he'd like our help, but then he doesn't in-clude us in new developments until his own men have run up against a stone wall," Geoffrey said.

"Daphne saw Carter Jayden deep in conversation with a stranger when she went to pick him up at his hotel recently," Prudence said. "From the description Sheriff Bryant provided, she thinks it could have been the man whose body was stolen from Dr. Elliott's house. After what happened with Martin Fal-low, I doubt the corpse would have been dumped into the river."

"Buried in the woods?" Geoffrey asked.

Prudence nodded.

"Jean-Baptiste and his friends know the forested areas around here better than anyone else," Geoffrey said. "If there's a newly dug grave out there, they'll find it."

"Could Lady Hamilton take Rowan to her house while they search?"

"I doubt she'd leave without Daniel," Geoffrey said. "And

there's the dog, too. Can you imagine either of them in one of Lady Hamilton's elegant parlors?"

"If it weren't for Myra, I could ask Daphne to bring Rowan to Adderly House," Prudence said. She thought for a moment. "I don't believe Daniel is in danger if he's by himself. Rowan is the target."

"Isn't Rowan a threat to the inheritance Mrs. Yates expects for herself and her sons?" Josiah asked.

"You would never have guessed there was anything between them but a natural family fondness," Prudence said, remembering Daphne's visit to Daniel's cabin. "I know I told you it went well, but I've had time to think about what they said to each other. I don't believe there's ever been any hard feelings between Lucas's sister and his daughter."

"Rowan doesn't blame Daphne for Myra's harsh treatment?"

"She understands that Daphne was also her mother's victim. I won't go so far as to say that Carter Jayden's death has set her free, but Daphne seems stronger and on the verge of declaring her independence. She doesn't fight Myra, but she no longer bows her head as quickly as I saw her do when Lady Hamilton first introduced me to them." Prudence considered everything Daphne had told her. "She adored her brother. I'm certain of that. She was as mesmerized by Grace Malone's voice and beauty as he was. Things might have been very different for Rowan if Daphne had not had two sons who would never be able to fend for themselves. Caring for them, defending them against their grandmother, drained her of energy. She devoted every ounce of tenacity she possessed to guarding their welfare; there wasn't anything left over for Rowan. Something she deeply regrets."

"What next?" Amos asked.

"See what you can find in the clerks' rooms," Geoffrey said. "We need the trust document that's at the root of everything that's happened and why we're here in the first place. Josiah, can you find it?"

Josiah's teeth clenched in determination as Prudence, Geoffrey, and Amos studied him.

"I can't begin to imagine where he might have hidden it, but I'm positive Lucas wouldn't have disappeared out west leaving behind only one copy of a document that important," Prudence said. "I've wracked my brain about it, and so has Geoffrey, but other than to search all of the obvious places, we're as puzzled about where he would have hidden it as Myra must be."

"Why Myra?" Josiah asked.

"She doesn't know whether somewhere in it her son acknowledged Rowan as his true and legitimate daughter. If he did, and depending on the language he used, it could make the existence of marriage and birth certificates unnecessary."

"I'll find it," Josiah promised. He had no idea how to keep that pledge, only that nothing and nobody would be allowed to stand in his way.

He knew their names, but Amos preferred to think of the men he'd seen dragged from the bare-knuckle Irish stand down as the American clerk and the Canadian clerk. Neither man was important in himself; their only roles in all this had been to file falsified documents in government offices. The sole thing missing was the link between the hireling who had carried out the forgeries and whoever had ordered it done. In Amos's experience, amateur thieves often gave in to the temptation to keep some part or token of what they had stolen. Nothing was as satisfying as fingering an object that rightfully belonged to someone else.

Amos waited in the shadow of an elm until well after two o'clock in the morning before he picked the lock on the Canadian clerk's rooming house. It was clear from the moment he stepped inside that this official had been in the business of accepting bribes for years. The kitchen didn't smell of boiled cabbage and burned coffee and the downstairs parlor and dining room were fashionably furnished. The carpeted stairs and upper hallway were dimly lit by gas lights turned low but left on to burn throughout the night. The occupants' names had been inked in fine calligraphy onto calling cards fitted into brass plates on their doors. It made finding the Canadian clerk's room easier that he'd anticipated. Somewhere toward the rear of the house a woman snored daintily in the silence.

Sheriff Bryant's men had already searched the place, so Amos left the obvious for last, finding and examining all the places no one else would suspect. When he finally turned his attention to the armoire, he decided that this clerk had a love of fine clothing that almost matched Josiah's. In Amos's world, two of anything was enough. One to wear, one to wash. The man whose private life he was rummaging through had enough suits, shirts, shoes, cravats, and underwear to keep a gentleman in style for years.

Some of the trouser pockets had remained turned out after the deputies rummaged through them, and the shoes that had probably been meticulously arranged on the floor of the armoire now lay in a disordered heap.

But a wardrobe could contain more than clothes. Tapping lightly with the sensitive tip of one finger, Amos covered the surface of the rear and side walls, listening for the hollow sound that would tell him a hidden panel had been worked into the design. He found it at the bottom of one of the elaborately scrolled doors, a square of wood that could be lifted out by inserting a pen or pencil into a crudely gouged out hole that had been concealed with a wad of inked paper. Clever, but not professional.

There wasn't time or light enough to read the papers that tumbled into his hand, so Amos folded them into a packet that would fit into the inside pocket of his jacket, then replaced the wood panel and the crumpled paper that stopped up the hole. To be sure he hadn't missed anything, he sifted through the contents of the desk that stood against one wall of the private parlor connecting to the bedroom.

He made the short walk to the river without having to step into the shadows more than two or three times. He doubted whether the late-nighters would remember a man who slid out of sight between buildings, but Amos thought it foolish to take unnecessary chances.

The interior walkway of the suspension bridge was closed at night, a single watchman on duty to open the gates in case of an emergency. Amos didn't bother waking him.

He walked along deserted sidewalks to the boardinghouse where the American clerk had rented a bedroom and adjacent private parlor. From the outside and in darkness softened by gas streetlights, the house looked as though it had once been a gracious single-family home. Years ago probably. Now it needed paint on windowsills and porch railings. Weeds crowded into the flower beds and the few straggly bushes Amos could make out were in need of a good pruning.

Again Amos waited in the shadow of a whispering elm, listening to the soft rustle of the leaves above his head. He heard nothing, saw no lit candle moving from bedroom to water closet. Fifteen minutes after beginning his watch, he picked the lock of the kitchen door. The windows of only two rooms in the house did not have their curtains drawn; Amos had judged them to be the clerk's quarters, marking them on the second-floor layout of the mental map he hypothesized, locating them on the first try. Door locked but yielding to his pick after less than half a minute.

With the shaded light of a bull's-eye lantern to guide the search, he felt between every one of the clerk's folded garments, probed the pockets of trousers and jackets hanging neatly in the wardrobe, examined every piece of furniture, the rugs lying on either side of the bed, the curtains hanging at the bedroom's only window. He moved on to the parlor, the horsehair-stuffed armchair and matching ottoman, stack of wood piled by the fireplace, small round table on which a tea service sat.

As with the Canadian clerk, both rooms had already been searched, anything obvious carted off. Amos found nothing the authorities had overlooked despite exploring hiding places he knew they hadn't found. He guessed by the excessive neatness that the landlady had set everything to rights again as soon as they'd left. The only unstraightened spot was the interior of the rolltop desk. She'd be back for that in the morning, when the light was better and she had the time to read through the papers her guest had left behind. Rooming house owners paid lip service to the privacy of their guests but knew more about them than their own mothers.

He found what he was looking for stuck to the back side of a narrow drawer that resisted his first efforts to pull it out. All of the desk drawers had stops, but only this one appeared to be glued in place so that it took the thin blade of a knife to dislodge it. A small key in a tiny brown envelope had been fastened firmly in place, probably by the same glue that prevented the stop from being turned. No markings on the envelope and only a number on the key. He put both in the pocket where his watch nestled, relocked the door, crept down the stairs, and let himself out onto the back steps. A quick adjustment with one of his picks, and the house was secure again.

Amos had done a good night's work. A small brown bottle of laudanum waited for him in the mean room at the Traveler's Rest.

He'd have to limit himself to a few blessed drops, though. Three or four hours of sleep.

The investigation was picking up speed, the way cases did once they began to unravel. Amos had always preferred to work alone, but Mr. Hunter was expecting him at Clifton House again by midmorning. And Josiah, too, he remembered.

Next steps were tricky at this point. Likely to change at the flip of a coin.

The only living things moving with him through American Niagara's streets were stray dogs and feral cats.

CHAPTER 24

Geoffrey gave the key Amos found to Josiah, with instructions to visit the local banks and security companies on both sides of the river. "It's small enough to be used in the drawers of a desk, but the number suggests a vault somewhere."

"There aren't many banking and security companies in either Niagara," Josiah said, pocketing the key. "It shouldn't take long to find the one that issued this. Gaining access may be tricky if the clerk's signature is on file and he was known by sight."

"Do the best you can," Geoffrey said. "We'll worry about warrants later. Get back to looking for the trust document as soon as you can, but this takes priority."

Prudence accompanied Josiah to the parlor door, glancing out into the empty corridor as he left. No one would ever take him for anything but a distinguished older gentleman of means. She smiled as he disappeared down the stairway to the lobby, then closed the door to the suite, planning to let a good five minutes pass before leaving.

While she waited, Prudence poured the last of the coffee, handing half-full cups to Geoffrey and Amos, whose eyes looked reddened and puffy. She remembered her own reflection in the mirror after a night of heavy laudanum-induced sleep and wondered if Amos had found in the drug a way to forget an unbearable past. And how deep into the addiction he'd fallen. She'd mention the observation to Geoffrey, but not now, not when they could all feel they were drawing closer to the tantalizing end of a particularly confusing case.

"With any luck I'll be able to persuade Rowan to stay with Lady Hamilton for a few days," she said, checking the tiny gold watch fastened to her shirtwaist. "Long enough for Jean-Baptiste and his friends to search the woods for our missing and unidentified corpse."

"Whoever is behind all of this wouldn't have tried the river again," Amos agreed. "He has to assume Sheriff Bryant doesn't have the manpower to search every inch of the forests around here, so that's where he's hidden the body. It takes luck and good tracking skills to identify an area in the wild that's been disturbed and covered over."

"If he'd done that with Martin Fallow's remains, we'd all have assumed Fallow had taken off for parts unknown," Geoffrey added. "Like Lucas Adderly did."

"I'll remember that," Prudence said. "When you need to pull off a deception, the obvious is sometimes the best choice." She picked up her reticule, checked the angle of her hat in the mirror, then closed the parlor door behind her with the determined click of a woman on a mission.

It was risky, but Geoffrey had decided it was time to confront Crazy Louie on his own turf, the workshop where he had crafted two identical barrels and dreamed up the stunt that had gone so wrong. It would reveal Amos's deception, but both ex-Pinks agreed that the journeyman traveling to his brother's barrel factory had probably learned all he was likely to uncover.

"If you're right about Louie's involvement with rigging bets," Geoffrey said as they crossed the suspension bridge into

American Niagara, "the bare-knuckle fight setup is the tip of the iceberg. Sheriff Bryant may be clean, but most local police and sheriffs turn a blind eye and hold out a greedy hand for what they consider victimless crimes. Gambling and prostitution being the two most lucrative pastimes."

"I saw Paddy Morgan deliver some of Louie's winnings," Amos said. "It wasn't a big pot by the looks of it, but my guess is it was only one of many."

"Paddy is the boxer you were telling me about?"

"He is. I saw him again the night I took Josiah to the fights. The way he shakes his head when he's talking or trying to remember something reminds me of the older boxers I've seen in the Garden. The ones I've heard have blackouts so they can't recall what they've done or said. They can appear normal when they're sparring, but when you ask a question, whole chunks of a day or night have gone missing."

"Drunks have blackouts, too."

"Louie let slip that Paddy's hardly ever entirely sober, so you've got a punch-drunk bare-knuckle boxer who can't stay away from the booze. The only thing that makes him an unlikely candidate for killing Martin Fallow is that it took some imagination to figure out the barrel switch."

"Which didn't work," Geoffrey said.

"I'm not so sure about that anymore," Amos said. "If the idea was to get rid of Fallow and make it look like an accident, then it succeeded. Most of Niagara believes Martin was trying to beat Louie over the falls and saw his chance with this new, sturdier barrel.

"The story I've heard more than once is that Martin was biding his time. Louie had been telling everyone that as soon as he proved a large animal could survive, the next step would be a human being. He was confident the sheep would make it, and if so, Louie would follow. So Martin supposedly got one step ahead."

They halted by the open doors of Crazy Louie's workshop.

Smoke drifted out from the lit stove inside and they could hear the rasp of a saw biting through wood.

"He'll be here alone at this time of the morning," Amos said. "Paddy never shows up until late in the afternoon."

"Were you supposed to work today?" Geoffrey asked.

"Open the shop, start the fire, sharpen the saws, and finalize the drawings for the next barrel. He'll be in a rare mood because I didn't show, and he had to do the setting up himself."

"A man in a temper is likely to say more than he should."

Geoffrey set off for the workshop's dim interior, Amos at his heels.

Crazy Louie spun around as soon as he heard their footsteps over the scrape of his saw. "I don't care what kind of excuse you have," he shouted as soon as he spotted Amos. "Get out of my workshop. Don't come back and don't expect to get paid for a day not done."

"Amos works with me," Geoffrey said. He waited until the look on Crazy Louie's face told him the barrel maker realized he'd been suckered. "I volunteered my services, if you remember, Mr. Whiting. You should have taken me up on the offer."

"What's that supposed to mean?"

"It means we have proof that there were two barrels. Identical. Built by you. You destroyed what you could find of the one that had ram's wool on the staves, but you didn't complete the job."

Amos, who had gone to the rear of the workshop, returned with two short pieces of still-damp red oak, both of them spotted with threads of white fleece. He handed them to Geoffrey.

"If there was only supposed to be one barrel, where did these staves come from? You've never used a sheep before." Geoffrey pointed out the tufts of white fleece caught in the splintery wood.

"The story of Martin trying to beat you over the falls won't work," Amos said. "The sheep you bought from the Samuelsons is back in the pasture."

"I shouldn't have believed the story you told," Crazy Louie snarled at Amos. "You watched me too closely before you did anything, and you asked too many questions."

"Put down the saw," Geoffrey said.

"Or else what?"

Geoffrey slid the polished sword halfway out of the cane in which it was sheathed.

Crazy Louie paled. He held on to the saw for a few more moments, then laid it down atop the wood he'd been trimming, stepping back and holding up both hands to show they were empty.

"Start at the beginning," Geoffrey ordered. "And don't leave out anything."

"You'll never be able to pin it on him," Louie said. "There weren't any witnesses."

"At the beginning," Geoffrey repeated. "Pin it on who?"

"I had a bet laid on that the barrel and the sheep would both survive the drop," Louie began, ignoring the question he didn't want to answer. "I needed the money."

Amos scanned the workshop, mentally checking off the supplies and equipment.

"I know what it looks like," Louie said. There was the beginning of a whine in his voice. "Good lumber doesn't come cheap."

"So you financed the operation by betting on every attempt," Geoffrey said.

"I covered the odds both ways by using different bookies. It worked for a while."

"Then they got on to you."

"The deal was I could continue to rake in what I needed, up to a point, if I guaranteed the odds. Betting on the barrels was a cash cow and the people who run the operation knew it. The tourists love the thrill of it. Some of them come up just for that."

"What about the fights? Are they fixed, too?" Amos asked.

Louie shrugged. "I don't have anything to do with that angle."

"Paddy Morgan throws a fight when he's told to. I've seen him do it," Amos said. "He's in deep and he'll never get out. The time when he might have made a name for himself at the Garden is long past. He's finished. He just hasn't admitted it yet."

"Tell us about Paddy," Geoffrey said. "What's a washed-up boxer doing working for a barrel maker?"

"I never should have agreed to hire him," Louie said. "He's been nothing but trouble from the day he walked through the door."

"Whoever's running the fight game and the gambling uses him to keep you in check, is that it?" Amos asked. "You never had a choice. Paddy may be a drunk, but his fists could knock you senseless if you stepped out of line. He helped you out around here when he was sober, and the money you paid him was enough to tide him over between fights. He doesn't put two and two together very well anymore, does he?"

"He knows who he works for."

"Tell us what happened." Geoffrey said. He slid the sword in and out of the cane a few times, the thin sound of sharpened steel cutting through the sputter of burning wood.

"I wasn't there," Louie said, "so I have to go by what I could get out of Paddy. He isn't all that clear about it." The whine became more noticeable.

"Let's have it," Amos said softly.

"The only way I could be sure the fix would work was to use two barrels and two sheep," Louie explained. "The barrels I was able to manage easily without anybody knowing, but the sheep had to be bought at different farms."

"You had plenty of witnesses to the launch of the first barrel. They'd all seen the sheep bolted inside," Geoffrey prompted.

"Paddy had the second barrel and the second sheep ready to go in case the first barrel broke up when it went over the falls. I had a feeling it would. I get those sometimes. I know when something's going to go wrong. I can't explain it." Louie wiped a hand over his eyes, then blurted out the rest of the story. "So he's waiting to see what happens because I guaranteed success and the odds were set for that.

"Martin comes along through the woods. Paddy doesn't know what he's doing there, but Martin figures out the fix right away. He says he's gonna tell the sheriff what's going on, so when he turns away Paddy picks up a rock and hits him hard in the back of the head. Martin goes down. Doesn't move or make a sound. Paddy knows he can't leave him lying there in case somebody else stumbles out of the trees, so he shoves Martin into the barrel. Puts the lid on. The sheep is tied to a tree and Paddy figures he'll have time to make the switch if the barrel I'm sending over breaks apart. Only he can't remember what happened next. He never goes anywhere without a bottle, so I'm thinking he started drinking and didn't stop until he blacked out. He bolted the head tight and shoved the barrel into the river all right, but the sheep was still tied to the tree."

"Who took it back to the Samuelsons' farm?" Amos asked.

"Paddy. That's where he got it, so in his stupor he figured that's where it belonged."

"Where's Paddy now?" Geoffrey asked.

"I've told you everything I know."

"Where can we find him?" Amos flexed his fingers, balled them into fists. He wasn't a big man, but the air of menace he could summon at will had cowed many a suspect.

"His shack isn't far from here. I can give you directions. You won't have any trouble locating the place."

"You're coming with us," Geoffrey informed him. He patted down Louie's pockets, checked to be sure he wasn't carrying a knife in his belt, ran his hands over a jacket he took from a hook in the wall, tossed him his hat. "If Paddy backs up your story, we'll see. If not, you can consider yourself under arrest."

"You can't do that. Private inquiry agents don't have jurisdiction unless they've been sworn in by a sheriff. You don't have a badge."

"I have this," Geoffrey said, revealing the Colt in its shoulder holster.

Amos patted the gun he carried. And smiled.

Louie broke. He was a daredevil and a gambler, but he wanted fame and glory, not broken bones and bullet holes in his body.

They walked in silence, Geoffrey beside Louie, Amos two paces behind in case the barrel maker decided to make a run for it. Every now and then someone raised a hand in greeting because Louie was a well-known local figure. When he didn't stop to talk, they moved on, wondering what new scheme had him so absorbed he hardly said a civil hello.

They passed the Traveler's Rest and the saloon where Amos had bought a few rounds and a lot of information. Boardinghouses, cheap hotels, and seedy places of business were gradually replaced by empty lots and ramshackle shanties sitting on bare, muddy ground. The wooden sidewalk gave out and there were fewer people in the roadway, then none.

"That's Paddy's place over there," Louie announced, pointing to an unpainted shack that looked more like a lean-to than a place fit for human habitation. A smokestack stuck out of the roof, but there were no windows to let in light and air. A narrow door hung crookedly on its hinges. "He'll be there if he's still passed out from last night."

"Is he armed?" Geoffrey asked.

"He pawned his gun a long time ago. He doesn't need anything but his fists. Paddy didn't mean to kill Martin, you know. He was just buying himself some time the only way he knew how."

"You first," Amos directed, one strong hand on Louie's arm. "He's less likely to come at us out of a dead sleep if he recognizes the person who woke him up."

Louie pulled the rope handle that opened the door. A smell

of old booze, vomit, and unemptied piss pot hit them as hard as Paddy's still powerful left hook. The men raised the lapels of their coats over their mouths and noses, standing back to let the stench dissipate in the fresh air.

"Paddy," Louie called out. "Paddy, wake up. There's some here as needs to talk to you." He took a faltering step forward, turned toward Amos and Geoffrey as if to ask what he should do next.

Geoffrey picked up a water bucket from beside the door, checked to be sure it was full, and handed it to Louie. "Use this on him."

But it wasn't needed. Louie disappeared into the shadowy interior of the shack, then burst out into the open moments later, wide-eyed and retching. He fell to his knees, spewing the contents of his stomach into the dirt, waving his arms wildly.

Amos stayed inside only long enough to verify what Louie's reaction had already told them.

"Paddy's throat's been slit," he reported. "Sometime during the night. He's already cold and stiff."

"That's makes number six," Geoffrey said. He waved to a boy and his dog running along the road. Handed over a coin big enough to make the boy's eyes goggle. "Sheriff Bryant. As fast as you can. Another one of these if you bring the sheriff back with you. Understood?"

The boy nodded and took off like a jackrabbit, dust puffing out from under his feet.

"What do we do with Louie?"

Geoffrey shrugged. "That's up to him."

CHAPTER 25

Lady Hamilton was more than willing to take Rowan into her home. "I've never been entirely comfortable knowing she was out in the woods with a blind man and a dog for protection," she told Prudence as the carriage turned into the narrow road leading to Daniel's cabin. "But I thought she was safe there from Myra and the malicious gossip that labeled her illegitimate."

"It won't be for long," Prudence said. "Only until Jean-Baptiste and his friends have searched the woods for the body that was stolen from Dr. Elliott's clinic."

"Is that so important?"

"It could lead us to the person who hired him."

"Carter Jayden did. We know that now," Lady Hamilton said. "Thieves fall out, and when that happens, they kill one another."

"Someone doesn't want the dead man identified."

"I think you and Mr. Hunter are making a mountain out of a molehill. Let it go, I say." Lady Hamilton climbed down from the carriage and shook out her skirts. "Are you coming, Prudence?"

Prudence stared at her for a moment, wondering what had provoked this sudden pullback from the active investigation that had become so important a part of the case for which Lady Hamilton had hired them. On two occasions her Ladyship had disappeared for several hours, giving no credible explanation of where she'd gone or why. The butler hadn't been able to do anything but repeat the excuses he'd been given. What was Lady Hamilton hiding? Something was definitely off. In the meantime, and for her own safety, Rowan had to be persuaded to leave Daniel's cabin. It wasn't going to be easy.

For a few minutes, as they climbed out of the carriage and walked through the woods, there was such a sense of serenity that Prudence could easily forget the clearing had been the scene of the attempted poisoning of two human beings and the mangling of a dog. Like so much else about this case, contradictions abounded.

"If Carter was behind what went on here," Lady Hamilton said as she raised an arm to wave at Rowan and Jean-Baptiste, "then I don't understand why you think Rowan is still in danger. The man's dead. And good riddance. I'm sure Daphne is relieved she doesn't have to marry him."

There didn't seem to be any point attempting to explain what seemed so obvious to Prudence and Geoffrey. In the strange mood she was in, Lady Hamilton selected the facts she was ready to accept and ignored the others.

"I've come to take you home with me, my dear," she said to Rowan, kissing her on both cheeks, then holding her at arm's length in anticipation of a happy smile and a grateful hug.

But Rowan stepped away. "I can't leave Daniel," she said softly.

Lady Hamilton's silence and the stiffness of her back were clear signals that neither Daniel nor Hero would be welcome at Hamilton House.

"You're not to worry about me," Daniel said from his spot in a rocking chair on the porch. "I'm not deaf, remember. Just blind." He patted Hero, who had stood up at the approach of visitors, wagging his tail vigorously as soon as he caught Prudence's scent. "No one can get close enough to do any harm as long as this fellow is by my side."

"You've had one intruder that we know of," Jean-Baptiste said. "The location of your cabin is no secret."

"I'm an old man. What harm can I do? The only person here who's in danger is Rowan. Guarding her is why it's been as crowded around this clearing as a tourist lookout below the falls." Daniel chuckled. "You and your friends are very good, Jean-Baptiste, but you can't fool an old tracker. If I can hear a spider tiptoe across a leaf, I can certainly hear young men stomping through the trees."

"I have an idea," Prudence said. They were at an impasse. Neither Lady Hamilton nor Daniel were of a mind to give in, which put Rowan squarely in the middle. "Jean-Baptiste, you took us to Martin Fallow's place when we wanted to search it for clues that could tell us why he was killed."

"You and Mr. Hunter."

"That's right. There was no trail leading to the cabin and you said that was because Martin never went the same way twice in a row. It's so isolated that not even Crazy Louie knows where Martin lived." She had their attention now. Even Hero seemed to be listening. "Suppose we hide Daniel and Hero there for the few days you think it will take to find the unidentified man's body? They'd be safe, and you or one of your men could check on them from time to time."

"I don't want to leave Daniel," Rowan repeated. "If he and Hero will be safe at Martin's cabin, why can't I stay there also?"

"Why don't we compromise?" Lady Hamilton interrupted. "Daniel can go to the cabin and Rowan can see that he's settled in. Make sure he'll be comfortable and walk him around until he knows where things are. Then she'll come back with me and Miss MacKenzie. There's no place in Niagara she'd be safer than at Hamilton House. If we pull the carriage around to the back stable yard, no one will see her go into the house. I think it's the perfect solution."

She'd said her piece so authoritatively that Daniel nodded his head in agreement and even a reluctant Rowan showed the hint of an acquiescent smile.

Without waiting for more discussion, Lady Hamilton strode into the cabin, emerging a few minutes later with a small carpet-bag in her hand. "All you need are a few changes of clothes, Daniel," she said. "And Hero's feed and bowls."

He seemed to agree with her, getting to his feet and reaching for the stick he used to feel his way.

It wasn't until they were following Jean-Baptiste through the trees that Prudence realized Lady Hamilton had assumed Martin Fallow's cabin would have everything in it Daniel would require, including food and the means to prepare it. Yet she hadn't known Martin except as a familiar face around the town. Why did she take it for granted that a cabin she'd never visited would be suitable for an elderly blind man? Would have a comfortable bed, a decent fireplace and supply of cut wood, candles or lanterns he could light to signal to the men checking in on him that all was well. She should have been dubious about sending Daniel off to an unknown dwelling that could very well be nearly uninhabitable. Unless she'd been there. Unless she was as familiar with Martin Fallow's home as she was with her own.

Except for the occasional flapping of wings as startled birds rose from their nests, the forest was silent. Jean-Baptiste and Daniel walked without stirring up the leaves beneath their feet or brushing against a single twig. Prudence could hear her own footsteps despite every effort to imitate their guide, but as they grew closer to their destination Lady Hamilton's progress became as noisy as that of a lumbering animal.

She snapped the small branches of the bushes against which she veered, and her feet shuffled loudly through pine needles and dry October leaf falls. Several times she called out for Jean-

Baptiste to slow down. She whistled to Hero and bawled his name when he lifted a leg against a tree. It was as though she were making sure that someone would know they were approaching. Try as she might, Prudence could not imagine who that person might be. Martin Fallow's cabin had presumably remained empty after he left it on the day he died in a barrel. It had certainly been deserted when she and Geoffrey had searched it. Surely Jean-Baptiste would have said something if the Tuscarora clan mothers had decided it should not remain untenanted.

Prudence wasn't out of breath from the easy trek through the woods, but her heart was beating faster than it normally did. She halted, bending over as if to remove a stone or a burr from her boot, forcing Lady Hamilton to pass her by. She thought they might be close to the cabin, and for the rest of the way she walked behind the older woman, watching and listening intently.

When they reached the clearing, Jean-Baptiste said something to Daniel, who nodded and sent Hero trotting ahead of them, nose to the ground as he circled the cabin, sniffed its steps, bounded up onto the porch and finally stood there waiting for them, tail wagging and tongue lolling from his mouth. As close to smiling a welcome as a dog could get.

Rowan ran appreciative fingers over the soft, colorful blankets, nodded satisfaction at the woven rugs that brightened the wood floor, and approved the kitchen and indoor water pump. "You'll be well sheltered, Grandfather," she said, placing her hands between Daniel's before they left. "Jean-Baptiste will tell the clan mothers you're here. Someone will come to cook for you and stock the cold safe."

"It will be good for you to live for a time in the house of a rich white lady," Daniel said, smiling in Lady Hamilton's direction so she wouldn't take offense. "That's what you'll be yourself one day." He placed a finger over Rowan's lips when he sensed she was about to argue with him. "Hush now. You know I'm right. When I'm gone, you'll have to make your way in that world. Lady Hamilton can teach you how."

Jean-Baptiste disappeared into the forest while one of the other young Tuscaroran men escorted Prudence, Rowan, and Lady Hamilton to where the carriage waited to take them back to Niagara.

The last thing Prudence saw when she looked back over her shoulder was a glistening trail of tears running from the blind man's eyes.

Before the carriage trundled through the covered lower level of the suspension bridge, Prudence asked Lady Hamilton to take her to Adderly House.

"I want to see how Daphne is doing," she explained.

"And there are questions you want to ask her. You don't need to make excuses to me," Lady Hamilton said. "I hired you and Mr. Hunter to look out for this child's interests, and the Adderly family is very much at the center of the problem we're trying to solve." She patted one of Rowan's hands, then held it in her own as if the young woman were a small girl in need of comfort and reassurance.

"Shall I come with you?" Rowan offered.

"I don't think so," Prudence said, "though I thank you for the suggestion."

"We need to get you home and out of sight." Lady Hamilton's briskly delivered statement left no room for argument.

As the carriage left the Adderly house driveway, Prudence turned her mind away from Rowan and toward the two women she had come to talk to. Myra was a largely unknown though antagonistic quantity, while Daphne was very much her mother's opposite, open and friendly, seemingly without resentment toward the niece who might come into wealth that far eclipsed her own.

Carter Jayden was dead, but there were issues that needed to be resolved. Had he written a will naming his wife-to-be as his primary beneficiary? If he had, would she still inherit even though the marriage had never taken place? What would happen to the magnificent house that was only days away from completion? Were there funds to pay off the contractors in an account that Carter had been reluctant to deplete? Or had he really been on the verge of bankruptcy? Was the late Carter Jayden somehow essential to Rowan's case or just an annoying distraction?

"The property is so encumbered by debt that it will have to be sold to pay off what's owed," Daphne informed Prudence when they'd settled in the parlor to talk.

"What does your mother say about the situation?" Prudence asked, knowing that Myra Adderly ran the family finances with no advice or interference from either her husband or her daughter.

"She's withdrawn into her still room," Daphne said. "She waved me off and locked the door when I tried to ask her what needed to be done."

"Is it really any of her business?" Prudence asked softly. She thought Daphne seemed to be taking short steps toward independence, only to hesitate and fall back when decision-making frightened or overwhelmed her. "You were about to embark on a new life that only included her on its fringes."

"We're a sad house, Prudence," Daphne said, "a house of suffering and disappointment. I think my mother's withdrawal is an attempt to come to grips with the disappointment of knowing that everything she planned for me and for herself has once again been destroyed."

"For herself?"

"Grandchildren she could love and be proud of," Daphne said. There were tears in her voice if not her eyes. "The establishment of a dynasty she's been obsessed with for years. My brother shattered her hopes, and she was bitterly disappointed when it became obvious that Arthur and Edward would never be able to live on their own. This marriage with Carter was a way of starting over, her last chance."

"She was playing with your lives, yours and Lucas's," Prudence said. "I know how that's done and how damaging it can be."

"I think she's softening," Daphne said. "I really do. Before she retreated to the still room, she spent more time with my father than she usually does. I could hear her voice through the door when I went up to have tea with the boys. Sometimes it takes great sorrow and repeated failures to teach us the lessons we must learn."

And some people never learn those lessons, Prudence thought. Their hearts and minds remained closed to them.

"When Carter's lawyer came to see me, he seemed to think I would regret having to give up the house," Daphne said matter-of-factly. "But I don't want to live in a home I never designed and that would always remind me of a marriage I didn't want. It will be on the market as soon as he's drawn up the paperwork."

"I think that's a sound decision."

"So did the lawyer. He's a local man, not part of the firm my family has always used, but I like the idea of keeping transactions that have to do with Carter away from anything that might affect me or my boys as members of the Adderly family. Do you understand what I mean?"

"I do," Prudence replied.

"I'm so sorry," Daphne suddenly exclaimed, one hand flying to her mouth. "I forgot you were also a lawyer. I should have consulted you professionally, not gibbered on about my personal problems."

"Perhaps we can just be friends," Prudence suggested.

"Would you like to meet my father?" Daphne proposed, getting hastily to her feet to dispel the embarrassment of failing to remember Prudence's legal credentials. "He has very few visitors, as you may imagine, but I think it does him good to see a new face from time to time."

She was halfway out of the room before Prudence could answer. She had no option but to follow.

Cyrus Adderly sat immobile in his wheelchair. He wore a full suit of formal clothing, including a gold watch he could not reach for and highly polished leather shoes that would never touch the floor. His eyes flickered into life when Daphne came through his sitting room door, bringing with her a young woman he'd never seen before.

Handsome rather than beautiful, dressed conservatively in a plain gray walking ensemble, a modestly feathered hat tilted above elaborately upswept light brown hair. Myra had told him of a lady lawyer with whom Daphne had struck up an acquaintance. Was this she? He blinked his eyes several times to indicate that he was awake and alert.

"Father, I want to introduce you to Prudence MacKenzie. Lady Hamilton brought her to Niagara from New York City to help Rowan prove she's Lucas's daughter." Daphne turned to Prudence. "He can hear and understand what we say, but he won't be able to speak." She leaned over and patted one of her father's hands, then seated herself in a chair placed where the paralyzed man could see her, gesturing to Prudence to do the same.

"I've very pleased to meet you Mr. Adderly," Prudence said. She understood how important it was to conduct a conversation that appeared to be in no way out of the ordinary. In the days following Geoffrey's return to consciousness after he'd been shot, when it wasn't certain he would live, she'd schooled herself to wear a calm and confident smile no matter how difficult or grim the situation.

"I'm sure Mother's kept you up to date about everything concerning Mr. Jayden's death," Daphne began, "but there is one additional development now." She glanced at Prudence, who nodded encouragement. "My late fiancé wrote his will in such a fashion that I inherit the house he was building despite our never having gotten married. Unfortunately, everything he touched turned not to gold, but to empty promises. I've told his lawyer to sell it and pay the contractors what they're owed. It's the right thing to do."

Cyrus's eyes blinked slowly. Once, twice, three times. *I agree.*

"He blinks once for yes, twice for no, and three times to indicate like-mindedness," Daphne explained. She smiled fondly at her father.

"The lawyer was here this morning. Carter left a mountain of debt, but I'm not liable. I'm sure Miss MacKenzie could explain it if you want?"

Cyrus blinked twice.

"Something else has happened that's a little odd," Daphne continued. "I didn't mention this when we were downstairs, Prudence, because I'm not sure it's worth spending time over."

Cyrus's eyes fluttered rapidly. *Tell me.*

"I haven't had a chance to talk to Mother about it because she was locked in her still room when the phone call came, and even though I knocked on the door, she refused to answer." When Myra did not want to be disturbed, she ignored any and all efforts to get her attention.

"I have an appointment at the offices of the firm that handles our family legal affairs and business transactions," she told Prudence. "The secretary called to ask me and Mother to come in at our earliest convenience. I don't remember that ever happening before."

"There must be paperwork detailing which assets you and Mr. Jayden would have owned jointly and which you would have retained in your own name," Prudence said. "A marriage contract, to put it bluntly and succinctly. Have you signed anything?"

"Mother and Carter saw to all that," Daphne said. "I asked, but every time I tried to bring up the subject of who would control what, Carter got angry and Mother got even more infuriated." She thought for a moment. "But no, Prudence, I don't recall having signed anything. In fact, I'm positive I didn't."

Cyrus's eyes blinked furiously.

"If Mother isn't ready to leave her still room, I'll go by myself," Daphne said. "Or Prudence, could you come with me?"

"I can't represent you in anything having to do with your brother's trust. It would be a conflict of interest."

"As a friend then? Could you come along to help keep up my courage?"

"We'll see."

Cyrus was staring at his daughter as if desperate to tell her something.

"You're not to worry, Papa," Daphne told him, stroking the motionless hands. "No matter what Mother says, I think it's time I became involved in the family finances. I've never been taught how to handle money, but I can learn. There won't be another Carter Jayden. I've made up my mind not to be pushed into something I don't want to do. I will not marry again. And that's final." Two red spots bloomed on her cheeks.

"Bravo," Prudence whispered, clapping her hands soundlessly. When she looked at Cyrus, he had focused his eyes on her instead of his daughter. The furious blinking started again. "What does it mean?" she asked Daphne.

"He's trying to tell you something. You have to ask *yes* or *no* questions. Sometimes I don't manage to get it right and I never learn what he wanted to say. It can be very difficult for both of us."

Prudence cast her mind back over everything that had been said since she and Daphne had closed Cyrus Adderly's sitting room door behind them, sending his attendant off to the kitchen for a well-deserved cup of tea.

"I think he became agitated as soon as you mentioned that

you'd been contacted by the family lawyers," Prudence said, watching Cyrus's eyes for signs of agreement.

He blinked once. Slowly.

"And we talked about your mother and Mr. Jayden arranging your marriage contract."

Cyrus blinked again. Once. Then the eyelids fluttered.

"Are you worried about something, Mr. Adderly?"

Yes.

"Does it have to do with Mr. Jayden?"

No.

"What else could it be?" Daphne asked. She bent forward as though getting closer to her father would somehow enable her to understand what he was thinking.

"Are you worried about the family finances?" Prudence asked. The question had come out of nowhere, except that there had to have been a reason that Lucas Adderly constructed the trust Myra was so determined Rowan would not receive. And Prudence had witnessed the swift fall of many a New York family whose fortune had been tied up in risky speculative investments.

Yes. The eyes blinked faster than before, as though to push through to something even more harrowing.

Daphne's face lost all color. She reached for Prudence's hand and held it so tightly Prudence felt her fingers start to go numb. "Are you afraid of Mother, Papa? Is that it? You're afraid of what she might do?"

One long, slow blink.

And a tear gathering, but not falling because Cyrus Adderly could not cry.

CHAPTER 26

"I'm not sure exactly what he's afraid of," Daphne said as she and Prudence left Cyrus Adderly's rooms. She glanced back as the nurse who had brought a tray of food tied a napkin around her patient's neck and began to feed him the way you do a baby. Spoonfuls of something that looked like oatmeal, bits of it falling off his lips onto his chin, scooped up and inserted into his mouth again. Tears filled her eyes as she watched for a moment. Then she closed the door quietly. "I don't know why I asked if he was afraid of Mama. It's an absurd idea. She's devoted to him."

"He may think there will come a day when she decides he'd be better off being taken care of professionally."

"In an institution?"

Prudence nodded. Most of the families she knew kept their invalids at home, hiring nursing staff to keep them comfortable until the inevitable end. There was no telling what happened in hospitals and care homes where there wasn't a vigilant wife or daughter to make sure things were done properly. You heard horror stories of patients whose skin broke down from lying in their own waste or who tried to swallow their tongues to end suffering unrelieved by morphine or laudanum.

"I don't think that's what it is," Daphne said.

"He blinked *yes* when I asked about the family finances."

"You said you'd come with me when I go to the lawyer's office," Daphne reminded her.

"Are you sure about that? I doubt your mother will approve," Prudence said. She'd been careful not to make a promise she couldn't keep, but Daphne had heard only what she'd wanted to hear.

"I won't tell her."

Daphne insisted on sending Prudence back to Clifton House in her carriage. It was late afternoon, the streets of both Niagaras crowded with tourists hurrying to get in one more activity before returning to their hotels for dinner. The sky was that special October azure, a bright and cloudless display of color before winter's gray crept into everyone's life.

At the last moment, while Prudence and Daphne were standing together in the foyer, Myra had emerged from her still room, coldly angry and implacable. She knew that her daughter had made an appointment with the family lawyers, guessed that Prudence had agreed to accompany her. And was furious that an outsider would become privy to confidential information she had no business learning about.

Daphne had lost the verbal battle; she was no match for her mother's sharp tongue and vitriolic attack. Prudence had stood aside from the fray and then smoothed things over as best she could. When Daphne hesitantly decided that her new friend's presence would no longer be necessary, Prudence had withdrawn as gracefully as possible. She'd seen tears in Daphne's eyes as she'd left the house, but she'd also seen determination. Daphne might have to go it alone with her mother, and might not win every verbal sparring match, but she would hold out for some small victories.

And that was a step forward in and of itself.

Geoffrey was entertaining a guest Prudence had never seen before. A nondescript man of unremarkable features, yet whose eyes were sharply observant before he shuttered their intense brown gaze.

Something about the visitor reminded her of Amos Lang— the ordinariness of him, she thought. Too unexceptional to be anything but another of the Pinks or ex-Pinks Geoffrey hired when a particularly dangerous or delicate job needed to be done.

"Prudence, I'd like you to meet Gustave Schneider. He's from the Pinkerton Agency's Chicago office."

Schneider nodded politely. "It's a pleasure, Miss MacKenzie."

"Mr. Schneider has had a report from the San Francisco office that he thought important and delicate enough to deliver in person," Geoffrey explained when they were all seated.

She raised her eyebrows inquiringly. Geoffrey shook his head.

"Mr. Hunter preferred to wait until you could both hear it together," the Pink said. He glanced at the pair of them, as if assessing their working relationship, but gave no indication of the conclusion he reached. Hunter and MacKenzie had hired the Pinkerton National Detective Agency; it wasn't necessary to dig any further into the clients' affairs than had already been done before the contract had been approved.

"Please continue," Prudence instructed.

"We found traces of your man in San Francisco, as you had suspected." Schneider paused, as if to reorder his thoughts. "Lucas Adderly was wanted for murder. Still is, for that matter."

"Murder?" It was the last thing Prudence had expected.

"A little over a dozen years ago," Schneider continued. "Our operative wasn't able to get his hands on one of the posters put up at the time, but the newspaper that covered the story keeps a decent morgue of back issues. An unnamed passenger stabbed the eldest son of a wealthy and politically connected family during a robbery on board an arriving train. He got away from the station before the body was discovered, but he'd shared a compartment with the dead man and was described by the conductor and one of the porters. The victim's family offered a reward, but nothing ever came of it. The trail was cold from the beginning."

"So that's the end of it?" Prudence asked.

"Just the beginning," Schneider said. "Adderly covered his tracks well, but . . ."

"Not well enough?" Geoffrey offered.

"That always depends on how much you want to find somebody," Schneider continued.

"*We never sleep.*" Geoffrey chuckled, quoting the famous Pinkerton motto.

Schneider took a large brown envelope from his briefcase, shook out a few newspaper clippings, and flattened one of them on the table around which they were sitting.

"Beautiful," breathed Prudence. The three-story turreted house rivaled anything she had known in New York City before the Vanderbilt mansions transformed Fifth Avenue. "'*The William Murphy mansion on Russian Hill*,'" she read.

"It's conjecture, of course, but our operative is convinced that the murder suspect from the train, Lucas Adderly, and William Murphy are one and the same. It's a logical assumption, given the facts that we *can* document."

"Which are?" Geoffrey asked.

"Adderly arrived in San Francisco on the same train as the dead man. We've traced his movements from when he left the East until he stepped onto the platform in San Francisco. Then he vanished for six months. We assume he disappeared into the mining camps somewhere in Northern California or Nevada. Our operative believes he changed his name because he couldn't be sure someone from his past wouldn't recognize the sketch on the poster and name him to claim the reward. There were so many Irish in the gold fields that one more Murphy didn't attract any attention.

"When he resurfaced in San Francisco as William Murphy, in addition to buying up land and investing in shipping interests, Adderly became one of the biggest suppliers of food, clothing, and equipment to the mining camps. Gold is elusive and finding it is a gamble, but men always have to eat. Their clothes wear out and their picks and shovels need replacing. That's where the sure money gets made."

"No one here in Niagara has a photograph of him," Prudence said.

"You won't find a likeness in any of the San Francisco papers, either."

"Rich and important men don't usually avoid publicity," Geoffrey said.

"This one does."

"That's a very large mansion for one man," Prudence commented, mentally counting the rooms behind the lace-curtained bow windows. "New York society bachelors usually live in hotels or in one of the new apartment buildings like the Dakota. Spacious luxury without the bother of having to deal with a dozen or more servants."

"He doesn't live alone, Miss MacKenzie," Schneider said.

"He remarried?"

"We don't think so. There's no record of a marriage certificate issued either to a Lucas Adderly or to the right William Murphy."

"I don't understand."

"His situation seems to have changed about seven years ago."

"Around the time the mansion was built." Prudence studied the date on the newspaper clipping.

"What's interesting is that Murphy, or Adderly, whichever you prefer, didn't commission the house. It had been built by a banker for his socialite wife and five children, but they hadn't moved in yet. The story goes that Murphy came back from one of his periodic trips to the mining camps and made the banker an outrageously large offer to take immediate possession, including the furnishings and the staff that had been hired. The deal went through without any publicity until the transfer deed was recorded and an alert reporter picked up on it."

"What else did the reporter find out?" Geoffrey asked.

"Nothing his editor was willing to print."

"But there's definitely a story hidden behind those windows," Prudence said. She and Geoffrey had worked with enough newspaper people to know that what made it onto the page was usually only a fraction of what a good journalist had discovered. "So Adderly goes to the mining camps, comes back to San Francisco, and pays an exorbitant amount of money for a house he wasn't interested in before he left. I agree with your operative, Mr. Schneider, Adderly isn't living alone. He brought a woman back with him from one of the camps, but he can't introduce her to society, so he keeps her hidden."

"He's hired a nurse to look after her."

"She's ill? Or old?" Prudence asked.

"The reporter who broke the original story has moved on. Nobody at the paper seems to know where, but the current editor was around back then. And willing to talk on the provision that anything newsworthy we discover goes to him as an exclusive. Our operative agreed."

"We've come to that kind of arrangement before," Geoffrey said.

"Whoever the lady is, she never leaves the house unaccompanied. When she does go out, it's in a closed carriage."

"Shopping?" Prudence asked, naming one of the favorite occupations of New York socialites.

"Not that we've been able to confirm. She's always heavily veiled and the carriage rarely stops."

"What else do you have on Adderly?" Geoffrey asked. He wouldn't dismiss the mysterious woman who lived with the man calling himself Murphy, but neither did he want to allow her to distract from the main thrust of the investigation.

"Rumor has it that he absents himself from San Francisco periodically without revealing where he's going. He has a private railway car and an associate who takes his place running the businesses. Our operative says everyone who works for him is well paid enough not to be willing to answer questions."

"He could have used the private car to travel to Niagara," Prudence hypothesized. "Under whichever name he wanted to use."

"There's no proof of that, but based on the information you provided and everything else we've dug up, it's a logical explanation for what I have to tell you."

"Go on," Geoffrey urged.

"He's disappeared. And so have the veiled lady and the nurse. The house is fully staffed, but Murphy and the two women are gone. Our operative's sources have dried up. It happens."

"Where is your man now?" Geoffrey asked.

"On another job."

When a Pinkerton operative reported back to headquarters that he wasn't able to obtain any more intelligence on the case he was working, no one argued with him. They were the best of the best.

"Your secretary emphasized the need for haste and secrecy," Schneider said. "That's why I'm here." He set another large brown envelope on the table. "Copies of bank and business records, more clippings from San Francisco newspapers, statements from the people we interviewed. The William Murphy who made a fortune in California is almost without a doubt the

Lucas Adderly you asked us to find. We don't know how long he's been gone from San Francisco or where he is. Whether we continue the search is up to you, but we don't think it's likely to produce results within the time you need them."

I don't like this, Prudence telegraphed to Geoffrey.

Neither do I.

"I think we'll need to discuss our options," Prudence said, gathering up the materials she planned to go over in detail.

"I'm leaving tomorrow morning," Schneider said.

"We'll have made a decision by then," Geoffrey assured him.

"Do you suppose Adderly caught on to the fact that a Pinkerton operative was investigating him?" Prudence asked that evening over dinner.

"Anything's possible," Geoffrey said, "but agents are trained to be discreet and virtually invisible when they're tracking someone."

"At least we know he's still alive."

"He's either on the move or he's gone into hiding."

"This may sound far-fetched, Geoffrey, but could his disappearance have something to do with Rowan's upcoming birthday?" Prudence looked around the Clifton House dining room. No one was paying them any special attention, but she pitched her voice to a near whisper just the same. "What I'm trying to say is that it's not entirely unthinkable that Adderly might be traveling to Niagara to be here when Rowan claims the trust he set up for her."

"It's not at all far-fetched. It's the first thing I thought of when Schneider said he'd disappeared."

"The operative didn't know when Adderly left San Francisco, which means it could have been weeks ago."

"It takes less than a week by private rail car," Geoffrey said.

"San Francisco to New York?"

He nodded.

"Are you sure?"

"Close enough. Maybe as little as four or five days if the tracks are clear all the way."

"So we don't need the Pinkerton Agency anymore?" She was loathe to say it aloud, but Prudence had a gut feeling that Lucas Adderly, aka William Murphy, had come east to make sure his daughter's inheritance would be safe. "Someone had to have warned him that Myra was planning to challenge the trust."

"Someone did."

"Lady Hamilton?"

"She strikes me as a woman who doesn't leave things to chance. She had to have known your aunt would write you as soon as she knew your legal talents were needed. And if that wasn't good enough, who better to testify to Rowan's legitimacy than her own father?"

"Where is he?"

"I think we'll be told that when he and Lady Hamilton decide the time is right."

"I don't like being manipulated, Geoffrey."

"Neither do I."

"After everything is settled, I plan to have words with Ernestine Hamilton."

"The case has blown up in her face, Prudence."

"And in ours, too."

"But we're used to it. Unraveling that kind of complication is what we do best."

CHAPTER 27

Jean-Baptiste tried to imagine himself in the mind of whoever stole the body of Carter Jayden's unidentified killer. Where would he take and bury the corpse? Throwing it into the Niagara River wasn't possible; the incident of a sheep going into a barrel and a man's body coming out had attracted too many curious onlookers to the riverbanks. Much like a daredevil stunt at a carnival, people were determined to figure out how the trick had been done.

Miles of forest surrounded the two towns on either international side of the falls. Land had been cleared and cultivated over the years, but there were still stretches of virgin timber inhabited only by wildlife. Somewhere in those regions lay a shallow grave that Jean-Baptiste hoped had not yet been disturbed by a bear, a cougar, or a pack of wolves. You couldn't drive a wagon through closely growing trees and bushes, so the burial place would have to be located close to a road, preferably a seldom-traveled dirt track.

It didn't take long to locate the wheel marks of a lone wagon making its way out of American Niagara toward a sparsely populated area of the county. And when Jean-Baptiste and his trackers saw the unmistakable evidence of a horse at rest, they knew they had found a likely spot. They fanned out along the roadside, keeping one another in sight as they walked into the woods, pausing every now and then to examine their surroundings.

They found footprints, heavily sunk into the damp earth. Then marks of dragging, heels plowing up twin furrows the width of a man's body. Deer scat, but no signs that a carnivore had caught and followed the scent of death.

The grave itself was barely three feet deep, the body in it wrapped in canvas. Jean-Baptiste pulled back the covering just enough to be sure it was a man they'd found—and a recent burial—then they lifted him from the hole, shoveled dirt, leaves, and pine straw over the disturbance, and brought him back to Niagara.

To the same autopsy room from which he'd been taken.

"The bullet that killed him has been excised," Dr. Elliott said, indicating the hole in the corpse's chest wall that had been dug with a broad-bladed knife. "Whoever did it sliced through tissue and muscle until the tip of his knife struck metal. It looks as though he started gouging then, until he got it out."

One of Jean-Baptiste's men had driven the newly exhumed body to Dr. Elliott's surgery; the others had disappeared into the forest to resume watch over Daniel.

"Then there's no way to be certain about the caliber of the gun that killed him," Geoffrey said.

"None at all," Dr. Elliott agreed. "This is butchery, plain and simple." He began filling out a death certificate, identifying the dead man as *Unknown*. "I'll open him up and check the stomach contents, but I don't expect to find anything that will tell us who he is."

A shadow fell across the autopsy table as the broad figure of a man in uniform filled the doorway.

"I have someone with me who might be able to help with that," Sheriff Bryant said.

He nodded to Prudence and Geoffrey, ushering in a heavily made-up woman in a blue dress that was several shades too bright for daytime wear. "This is Mrs. Tansy Scott. I believe you already know Dr. Elliott."

"He takes good care of my girls when needs be," she said, smiling at the doctor and casting a quick glance around the small room.

"Mrs. Scott came by the office this morning looking for a missing person," Sheriff Bryant said.

"My bouncer," she explained. "He hasn't been seen since close of business three days ago. Didn't sleep in his bed that night, didn't show up for breakfast or work the next morning. Same story last night and today. When a man like him skips free meals, it's because he's left town or he's gotten himself into trouble. I figured the law might have him locked up and I'd bail him out."

"The timing is right," Sheriff Bryant said.

"Is that him?" Tansy Scott asked. "Why is there a cloth on his head?"

"Dignity," Dr. Elliott said. A corpse's eyes sometimes remain partially open during an autopsy. It could become unnerving. "We cover over the portion of the body that isn't being examined." He slid the sheet up to shield the gaping hole in the dead man's chest.

"I can't identify him if I can't see what he looks like."

Dr. Elliott lifted the white linen towel from the dead man's face.

Tansy Scott sidled alongside the table until she reached a point where she could stand and study what lay before her.

"That's him, all right. Pete Narolly was the name he was using, but I can't swear to whether it's the one he was born with. He liked to be called Big Pete, though that's an exaggeration, if you want the truth of it." She flicked a flirtatious grin in Geoffrey's direction.

"What else can you tell us about him?" Sheriff Bryant asked.

"I wasn't the only one he worked for. He told me when he took the job that he wouldn't tolerate any questions about what he did on the one night a week we didn't entertain clients. So I never asked him any. But he had more money than I paid, that's for sure and certain."

"How do you know that?" Prudence asked.

The three men in the room stared at her. Sheriff Bryant had very deliberately avoided anything that might be interpreted as an introduction to one of the town's foremost madams.

"Searched his room, didn't I?" Tansy replied. She smiled convivially. "More than once. I like to know what's going on under my roof."

"Do you know who else he did jobs for?" Sheriff Bryant asked.

"Big Pete was closemouthed. He didn't give anything away unless you paid for it."

"When did he start working for you?"

"It hasn't been that long. Five months maybe. The bouncer before him married one of my best girls and they took off out west. We had a hell of a going-away party for them." Tansy's eyes lit up and she chuckled, a richly throaty sound that explained part of her success.

Dr. Elliott scored through *Unknown* and printed *Pete Narolly* on the death certificate.

"You let me know when he's ready to be put in the ground," Tansy Scott said. "Pete was a mean son of a bitch even when he wasn't drunk, but nobody deserves a pauper's grave."

W.J. Duhring had decided that it wouldn't help matters to soften the blow.

"The simple fact, Mrs. Adderly, Mrs. Yates, is that the investments in the family's portfolio have not paid off. Several of the companies in which there were considerable holdings have gone bankrupt. Their stock is worthless."

"What about the rest of them?" Myra asked. Her whole body trembled, not with dismay, but a sweeping flood of anger.

"I'll get to those, but I must remind you that the bankrupt stocks I mentioned and some others that are on the verge of insolvency were purchased against our advice. We didn't feel they were sound at the time you evinced interest in them. I regret to say we were right."

"And I was wrong? This disaster you're describing is my fault?" Myra's voice was shrill with rage. She wanted nothing so much as to lift up the heavy ledger lying before her and fling it at Duhring's bald head.

"What do we have left?" Daphne asked softly.

"Your income from your late husband's estate and the marriage settlement are and always have been protected. Nothing to worry about there. The firm has acted as trustee since Mr. Yates's passing. Conservative investments. Steady growth of the principal. Nothing spectacular. Nothing dangerous."

"You're lying," Myra snapped. "There isn't anything wrong with the choices I made. The way to grow money is to speculate. Only a fool sits back and lets the world pass him by. I refuse to be anybody's fool."

"You can see for yourself, Mrs. Adderly." Duhring laid out a sheaf of papers one by one, side by side, as if they were enormous playing cards. "I had our bookkeepers copy these figures for you to study at your leisure. You'll see that everything I've said is true. Numbers don't lie. More's the pity."

"Summarize it for me," Myra demanded. Tiny drops of moisture appeared on her forehead. Daphne handed her mother a handkerchief. "I want to know the worst."

"If Mrs. Yates continues to live at Adderly House and undertakes all of the household expenses and upkeep of the property, you'll see no change in your daily life. Should that become the case, then the firm will insist that the property be retitled in Mrs. Yates's name."

"No. Never."

"As trustees of her holdings, we can mandate the title change. In court, if necessary."

"And if I don't agree?"

"The house and the property on which it stands will be sold to pay your outstanding debts, of which, I am sorry to say, there are a goodly number. In fact, as of today, the firm has authorized your bank to refuse any more withdrawals or requests for credit."

"That's scandalous. You can't do that."

"We can and we have."

"You're insolvent, Mama," Daphne said, not even realizing that she'd used a term she'd only read in newspaper articles about speculators.

"What about the trust my son established before he disappeared? Surely I can tap into that?"

"Details of the trust remain undisclosed until Miss Rowan Adderly's eighteenth birthday. The funds are not available to pay your personal debts."

"Come on, Mama," Daphne urged, picking up the financial documents that had been prepared for them, tugging at her mother's arm to bring her to her feet. "We'll talk about all of this at home."

"I am always available to answer any questions you might have," Duhring said, escorting them into the outer office, gesturing to a clerk to see the ladies to their carriage.

"Thank you, Mr. Duhring," Daphne said.

Myra tightened her lips and sailed through the outer door without looking back. She was badly shaken, but not beaten. Myra Adderly never admitted defeat.

They heard the commotion from upstairs as soon as they walked through the front door.

"What on earth is that caterwauling about?" Myra demanded of her butler, unpinning her hat, flinging gloves and reticule onto the polished surface of the entryway table. She'd already stormed off in the direction of her still room when his hesitant reply caught her attention.

"It's the boys, Mrs. Yates," he was telling Daphne as quietly as he could. "Something's happened in the nursery that set them off."

"I'll soon put an end to that," Myra declared, stopping dead in her tracks before whirling around to storm up the mansion's central staircase.

"Mama, please," Daphne pleaded, following quickly behind. "I'll see to whatever's gone wrong. There won't be any more fuss."

"You spoil them. You've always made excuses for their behavior. All I ask is that you keep them quiet and out of sight. You can't even manage to do that!"

It wasn't the time or the place to mention that Daphne's money would soon be the only source of income to keep the mansion and its inhabitants' way of life afloat. Her mother's anger, kindled in the lawyer's office, had smoldered all the way home, needing only another spark to set it aflame again. *Later, when things have calmed down.*

"I didn't do it. I didn't do it." Edward's husky voice shouted his innocence in tones that penetrated the nursery's closed door and reverberated down hallway and staircase.

They heard the heavy thud of tramping feet and knew that one or both boys were stomping in panic or temper.

"I didn't mean to. I didn't mean to." Convulsive sobs punctuated Arthur's howls.

It sounded like a crowd of terrified children instead of two boys whose mental ages did not match their physical development.

Myra flung open the nursery door, deliberately letting it slam against the wall. There was a moment of shocked silence as Daphne shot past her mother, Nanny, and the young man hired from the New York State Asylum for Idiots to where Arthur and Edward were flailing their arms and legs aimlessly. Then the hysterical shouting picked up again. Daphne tried to put her arms around her sons, but an outthrust limb, she didn't know whose, knocked her to the ground, stunning her.

Myra strode across the floor and slapped each of her grandsons across the face. Hard, loud blows that cracked against their cheeks and left imprints of her hand on their skin. They stopped wailing. Slumped and stood as still as statues.

Nanny and the young male assistant steered Arthur and Edward toward the table where colored pencils and large sheets of paper had been laid out for the day's lesson.

"We're going to draw trees," Nanny murmured. "Green on top and brown below. Nice and full and round where the green is and long and slender where you put the brown."

"What started this?" Myra demanded of the nursemaid who was wringing her hands in the folds of her apron, cap askew and tendrils of hair hanging down alongside her face. "Answer me, girl."

"Mr. Arthur spilled his milk," she said, hiccupping her answer, bending to help Daphne to her feet, seating her in Nanny's rocker.

"All that noise over spilled milk?" Myra raged. "Where?"

The nursemaid pointed toward the rag rug that was Arthur's favorite play spot, where he liked to balance lead soldier figures between the rounded braids.

"Get it up. Take it downstairs. Make sure it's thoroughly washed and hung out in the sun to dry. Milk smells when it spoils."

The maid dropped to her knees to roll the rug into a cylinder she could carry. Puddles of milk had pooled beneath it.

"That looks like he spilled the whole pitcher. Who was stupid or careless enough to let him hold it?" Myra stared at the offending white liquid as though it had done her irreversible, personal damage.

"It was an accident, Mrs. Adderly. I swear it won't happen again." The maid reached for tea towels drying on a rack beneath a window.

"Wait! Stop!" Myra watched as one of the pools of milk seeped through the wood floor. The other pool didn't move. "Get me the poker from the fireplace," she commanded. "Stay where you are, Daphne. I don't want you fainting on me. Things are bad enough already without you adding to the confusion."

The nursemaid stepped across the floor to the fireplace, tiptoeing past the wet places on the floor, returning with the poker in her hand.

Myra snatched it from her grip. "Get out. Take that rug downstairs as I told you."

She waited until the nursery door closed, then turned to assess what was happening on the far side of the room. Nanny and the tutor were bent over Arthur and Edward's shoulders, each of them absorbed in successfully guiding the drawing lesson. Someone, probably Nanny, had wiped the tear- and mucus-stained faces. It was as though nothing had broken the tranquility of their small world.

When she was sure no one except Daphne was watching, Myra wedged the narrow end of the poker between two of the floor planks, in a spot where she'd seen the spilled milk disappear the quickest. She pushed until it wouldn't go in any further and then stepped on the upper handle with her booted foot. Without much more than a muffled *crack*, a piece of floorboard broke off, revealing a hole beneath it that measured no more than a foot long by six inches wide.

"What is it?" Daphne breathed. She'd ignored her mother's orders and now stood beside her, not quite believing what she was seeing.

"I knew he'd have to have hidden another copy around here somewhere. Your brother was never the type to leave things to chance. He liked to back up his bets by fixing the odds."

"What are you talking about, Mama?"

Myra bent down, slid one hand into the hole, and pulled out a canvas-wrapped pouch spotted with spatters of milk. "It's the trust document, the one we suspect gives everything to Lucas's bastard."

"A copy of the one in the lawyer's office?"

"I told you Lucas was cautious. He hid this here in case we managed to get the other one thrown out without being read or acted upon. Don't ask me why exactly, unless he thought the girl would turn out to be smarter and more ambitious than we think she is."

"Rowan?"

"Who else would I be talking about?" Myra slid the piece of plank back into place, stepping hard to make it secure.

Then without another word, she turned and left, never once glancing toward her grandsons.

CHAPTER 28

It took Josiah most of a day to identify the key Amos had found in the American clerk's room. He knew from its size that it was designed to fit a very small lock. The number incised on one side suggested a safety box like those banks had begun offering their customers. The trick was in locating the bank vault that housed the right box. By the time a teller recognized the key, Josiah had almost given up hope.

"It's definitely one of ours," the teller said. "You'll have to speak to our vice president. We don't handle those transactions at the windows." He beckoned to the customer waiting in line behind Josiah.

The problem was that Josiah had no identification to prove he had the right to inspect the contents of the safety box. He assumed the clerk had rented it under his own name, but whether as a front for someone else or a safe place to hide the bribes he'd been taking was anybody's guess. Josiah waited, watching the desk at which a fussy-looking fellow wearing a pince-nez sat shuffling papers and occasionally copying information into a ledger. He had *vice president* written all over him. When he finally left his station with the heavy ledger in his arms, Josiah seized a moment that might not come again.

"I'm in a terrible hurry," he said to the female secretary who looked up from her typewriter keys with startled eyes behind thick lenses. He tossed the key onto her desk, took out his pocket watch, snapped it open, and did an impatient sidestep.

"Mr. Barton should be back in a few minutes," she said.

"I can't wait for Mr. Barton. My key is right in front of you. I insist that you get my box out of the vault."

"I don't have the authority to do that, sir."

"I'm not going to tolerate an inexcusable delay. I have important things to do and no time to waste." If there was anything Josiah hated, it was a bully, but he made a good one when he had to. Lord knows he'd been a victim often enough in his life. He picked up the key, grabbed the young woman's hand, and slammed it into her palm. "Now get my box!"

She scurried away like a mouse with a cat on her tail.

He followed, glancing back just once to assure himself that Mr. Barton had not, in fact, returned to his desk.

She put the numbered box on the table that took up most of the small space in the private room where customers could pore over their papers and valuables without anyone seeing what they were doing.

"The card?" he demanded, gambling that this bank, like many others, kept separate signature cards for each box owner.

"Yes, sir."

She picked it out of a narrow file drawer, then immediately dropped it on the floor.

"Get out of my way," Josiah said, doing his best to imitate a thoroughly nasty customer.

She stepped outside the cubicle, taking off her spectacles to wipe the smudged lenses.

It took him less than a minute to read the name on the card and open the box.

E. Corcoran. The box was empty.

*   *   *

Myra harvested and dried the sap from her milkweed garden in late summer, when the plants were bursting with life and the allure of the monarch butterflies who fed on them. Farmers knew that milkweed was poisonous to their grazing animals, but settlers desperate for greens had learned over time that they were also delicately flavored and harmless if the leaves were repeatedly boiled and rinsed. Like so many other things in the natural world, they were useful, beautiful, and dangerous. Not unlike Myra herself.

She kept the dried milkweed in the locked drawer whose key she wore on her watch chain. It wouldn't do for an accidental poisoning to reveal the existence of an arsenal of harmless-looking powders as lethal as bullets. Milkweed could have a bitter taste; it needed to be mixed with honey or maple syrup, dissolved in a strong-tasting broth, or stirred into a powerful cognac. For Cyrus, she'd chosen the beef broth that had become his favorite food. Easy to swallow, flavorful, and so concentrated that it turned into a firm gelatin when cooled.

The nurses who attended Myra's husband welcomed her visits to his rooms. Caring for a paralyzed man was not an easy task, involving as it did heavy lifting and the frequent cleansing of bodily wastes. Though she never stayed long, Mrs. Adderly always dismissed the caretaker on duty to the kitchen where hot tea and conversation helped make the sick room's long hours of silence bearable. His wife was a hard person to read and sometimes Mr. Adderly seemed agitated after she'd left, but the nurses who tended him knew from experience that private patient care was far preferable to emptying slop pails and changing pus-drenched bandages in the wards of a public hospital.

"I've brought some of the broth you like so much," Myra crooned, draping a large white linen napkin around Cyrus's neck. She dipped a silver soup spoon into the steaming liquid where the milkweed powder had dissolved without leaving a trace, then feigned sipping from it. "Perfect. Still warm from the kitchen." It was important that Cyrus not suspect what she was doing. He couldn't move, but he could clench his teeth, toss his eyes, and make loud, grunting noises. Myra had been careful to doctor the broth where he couldn't see what she was doing.

"Now then," she said, settling herself into the cushioned chair by his bedside. "You'll have a nice nap after you've drunk all the broth. And I have good news to share. Daphne and I went to the lawyers' office and all is well. A tiresome matter about the provisions of Carter Jayden's will, but nothing to be concerned about." The lie came easily; soothing Cyrus was as much a part of her routine as using him as a sounding board when she needed to voice the ideas and plans forever swirling in her brain.

The first spoonfuls went down quickly; hardly a dribble to stain the white napkin.

She thought for a moment that she might tell him she'd located a copy of the trust document their perfidious son had left behind when he disappeared, then decided against it. Much as she would have liked to celebrate her triumph, the provisions of inheritance that Lucas had laid out were also a schematic for murder.

If Rowan died before her eighteenth birthday, and Cyrus and Daphne were also dead at that time, the entire trust passed to Myra. All of its assets under her sole control, with the provision that she continue to provide for Daphne's sons should that become necessary. But if Rowan died before she came of age, and Cyrus and Daphne survived her, then the trust passed irrevocably under the management of the law firm that had drawn up its particulars. Myra would become a pensioner, subsisting on whatever dribbles of cash her son's lawyers chose to accord her. The solution to averting such a catastrophe was simple.

Husband, daughter, and granddaughter had to die.

Cyrus first, because his passing was the simplest and most convenient to accomplish.

Myra continued spooning beef broth into her husband's mouth, humming softly as he swallowed. She read in his eyes the small physical pleasure of tasting something delicious, and then the moment of doubt when his heart gave an unexpected flutter. Milkweed in a concentrated dose could stop the human heart and paralyze the lungs. Cyrus had to ingest enough to kill him cleanly, without the interference of vomit or diarrhea that might lead to awkward questions. No one, including his doctor, had expected him to live as long as he had; death by cardiac failure would not surprise anyone.

Myra's hand moved rhythmically between the soup bowl and her husband's mouth. Almost done. She tilted the bowl to gather the last few drops.

When she rinsed the bowl and the spoon with a splash of water from the drinking pitcher and tipped the liquid into the chamber pot, Cyrus knew.

He'd always suspected Myra would find a way to get rid of him when she didn't need him anymore. And so she had.

Cyrus closed his eyes. Thought despairingly of his daughter, Daphne. Sent a prayer and a plea for mercy winging heavenward.

Myra stepped into the bathroom she'd had installed for the use of the nurses. She emptied the chamber pot, rinsed it out, then pulled the handle on the wonderful new flushing toilet. Watched as the evidence of what she'd done swirled away.

Left Cyrus to die alone in his bed.

Told the nurse she met in the corridor that her husband had drunk his broth and was sleeping comfortably. No need to disturb him.

Lady Hamilton had left Rowan alone in the big house.

"I'm sorry, my dear, but it can't be helped," she'd said before ordering her horse to be saddled. "You brought your beadwork with you. That should keep you busy."

Rowan had nodded, reassured her hostess that she would be quite all right, and settled herself on one of the parlor's silk upholstered settees. Basket of beads beside her, a half-finished purse in her lap, needle flashing busily when Lady Hamilton, clad in a black wool riding habit and wearing a veiled riding hat, came in for a final word before leaving.

"Ask one of the servants if you need anything," she instructed Rowan. The girl wasn't used to being waited on and needed to be reminded of her status as honored guest. The hand she brushed over Rowan's bright hair was gentle and affectionate, but she couldn't hide that she was impatient to be on her way. She waved a cursory good-bye from the doorway, her mind already set on where she was going. No one had asked, because by now they all understood she would not answer.

Half an hour passed without interruption. Rowan almost drifted off as she beaded, nearly pricking her finger more than once. She'd slept badly the night before, waking at the slightest creak of floor or windowpane. At the scrape of a branch across a shutter. The hiss of the gas lights in the hallway. She'd missed the comforting smell of Hero's thick fur, Daniel's broken snore, the occasional howl of a wolf, the quick flight of prey running to safety through the trees.

Lady Hamilton had stood indecisively at the foot of Rowan's bed before turning out the light and wishing her good night. And at breakfast, she'd frowned absentmindedly over her boiled egg and toast as though puzzling through a vexing problem. Whatever it was, Rowan decided, couldn't be any more disconcerting than being abruptly whisked away from Daniel and Hero. She hadn't realized how much she'd grown to care for them until they were no longer there.

And Jean-Baptiste. She couldn't think his name without a hint of a smile appearing on her lips.

"Miss Rowan?" The butler stood in the doorway, a shadow moving behind him in the hall. "Miss Rowan, you have a visitor."

How could that be? No one was supposed to know she was here.

Before she could decide what to do, a figure brushed past the startled butler and barreled down on the equally surprised Rowan.

"You won't need these anymore," Myra said, plucking the beadwork purse from her granddaughter's hands, stripping needle and thimble from her fingers, depositing all of it in the bead basket.

"How did you find me?" Rowan stuttered.

"I always know where you are." Myra reached for the shawl draped over a nearby chair. "It's cold outside, but not enough to need a heavy coat. Come along. The carriage is waiting."

"Where are we going?"

"Back to Adderly House, where you belong."

Rowan hadn't lived in her father's old home since childhood. The woman tugging her off the settee was the same one who had had her removed from Our Lady of the Falls Academy and kept in the orphanage from which Lady Hamilton rescued her.

"I don't belong there," Rowan said. She didn't raise her voice or allow anger or discourtesy to creep into her tone. She had been raised to respect authority and her elders.

"I say you do."

"What does Daphne say?"

"She has nothing to do with this."

"She came to Daniel's cabin. We talked."

"You're wasting time. Get up."

"Daphne apologized for what she said was the poor way the family had treated me."

"You have your mother to blame for that."

"She died when I was born. How could she be to blame for anything?"

Myra tightened her grip on Rowan's arm until the girl could feel her grandmother's nails through her sleeve. "It's time to forget the past, time to forge a new future. And for that, you'll need to be a part of the family."

"My father's daughter?"

Myra stiffened, but kept the smile on her face. "Exactly."

It was a tremendous concession. Rowan couldn't fathom what had made this woman decide she wasn't the bastard offspring of a whore, wasn't a child whose sire could never be known with any certainty because of who her mother was. Rowan had been so hurt the first time she'd heard the ugly stories Myra had spread that she'd thought she would die with the pain and the shame of them. But she hadn't. She'd learned to live quietly out of sight of those who would mock her, ignoring the cruel reach of people who rejoiced to see her suffer. And grown strong because she had survived.

But Rowan was also trusting. She wanted so much to be loved by someone that she'd never grown the instinct that smelled out a lie.

Myra's hand on her arm fell away when Rowan stood up and reached for her shawl. Wrapped it tightly around herself and smiled at her father's mother.

"If you really want me . . . ?"

"Of course I do," Myra said, bustling her toward the front door. "It will be as if all these difficult years had never happened."

Rowan had one moment of doubt as the carriage rolled down the hill toward the suspension bridge. Lady Hamilton hadn't been home to hear what had been said and the promises that had been made. How would she react when the butler told her who had come to call in her absence? Rowan wished, too, that she could have talked over with Daniel this surprising turnabout. They'd grown close over the months of living together. He was the wisest person she'd ever met.

All on her own, Rowan had made the only decision that called out to her heart. She had never felt she belonged anywhere. Now she had begun to hope that she did.

Prudence and Geoffrey went directly from Dr. Elliott's office to Canadian Niagara.

The man who had shot Carter Jayden had been identified and would soon be in the ground again. The mystery of who had stolen his body would have to wait. Rowan and the threat to her safety was uppermost in their minds.

"I recognize that carriage," Prudence said as they emerged from the suspension bridge tunnel. "It's the Adderly brougham. What's it doing on this side of the river?"

"Did you see who was in it?" Geoffrey asked.

"Two women. But it went by so fast I couldn't make out who they were."

"Myra and Daphne?"

"I can't imagine who else it could be. I wonder if they discovered that Carter Jayden had banking or property interests here as well as in American Niagara." Prudence thought for a minute, then dismissed Daphne's late fiancé from her mind.

"Lady Hamilton has been lying to us," Geoffrey said, urging the horses to pick up speed.

'I've been trying to sort through what can be believed and what can't," Prudence agreed.

"Lucas is alive. Pinkertons don't make mistakes. Lady Hamilton has known it all along, but what doesn't make sense is why she's been concealing the truth from us."

Lady Hamilton was dismounting from her horse as Geoffrey drove the rented two-wheeled cabriolet into the stable yard behind the house. She handed the reins to the groom, gave him a few quick instructions, and waited for Geoffrey and Prudence to climb out of the carriage.

"You're just in time for tea," she said cheerily. "I'll change and join you in the parlor."

"We have some questions for you," Prudence began.

"I'm sure they'll wait until I've put on a proper tea gown," Lady Hamilton declared. She set off across the stable yard, swinging her riding crop quickly and confidently. She'd disappeared inside the house before Prudence could catch up to her.

"She's in a good mood," Geoffrey commented. "I wonder what's happened to put her in such high spirits."

"She's rescued Rowan and gotten the upper hand over Myra Adderly." Prudence grimaced. "Society ladies are the same the world over. You can never have two queens in a single anthill."

"I don't know why you're called the gentler sex," Geoffrey said. "Any one of you could give the most experienced military man a run for his money." He handed hat, gloves, and cane to the waiting footman.

"I wonder if I might have a word, sir." The butler waved off the footman and opened the parlor door.

"Is something wrong?" Prudence asked.

"Not wrong exactly, miss. But perhaps not quite what was expected. Under the circumstances, I'm not sure I should wait for Lady Hamilton to come down before mentioning it."

"I think you'd better get to the point," Geoffrey urged.

"Miss Rowan left with her grandmother. Mrs. Adderly said she'd send for Miss Rowan's things later."

"Say that again?" Geoffrey thought he couldn't have heard the man correctly.

"Mrs. Adderly came to call a little while ago," the butler repeated. "She and Miss Rowan talked together in the parlor, then they left in Mrs. Adderly's carriage."

"Just like that? No message?" Prudence asked.

"Nothing, miss. I only mention it because Lady Hamilton was quite specific about not letting strangers into the house while Miss Rowan was here."

"But Mrs. Adderly is not a stranger," Geoffrey said.

"Precisely, sir."

"And Miss Rowan seemed willing to go with her?"

"I'd say more than willing, sir. Happy. She was smiling. I heard her call Mrs. Adderly *Grandmama.*"

"Send a maid upstairs to ask Lady Hamilton to join us as quickly as she can," Prudence instructed. She turned from the now-anxious butler to Geoffrey. "You don't suppose Rowan is in any immediate danger, do you?"

"Someone tried to poison her, and we don't know who it was," Geoffrey reminded his partner. "I don't think they've given up."

"Myra? Her own grandmother?"

"I sincerely hope not."

"Hope not what, Mr. Hunter? And why did you send a maid to tell me to hurry up? It's most extraordinary." Lady Hamilton looked as bandbox perfect as if she'd spent hours preparing for tea with her guests.

"Rowan is missing. Myra came and took her away," Prudence said.

CHAPTER 29

It took more than an hour for the imprint of Myra's hand to fade from Arthur's and Edward's cheeks. Arthur told Nanny he saw black dots dancing in front of his eyes and Edward's right ear rang. Daphne hummed, sang, and rubbed the places that hurt. Nanny's lips drew tight across her teeth; she didn't like interference in the nursery, and she especially disapproved of the way Mrs. Adderly treated her grandsons.

The handprints gradually faded; the boys stopped shaking their heads and looking questioningly at their mother. They didn't ask in words why Grandmama had hurt them, but their eyes spoke volumes.

The maidservant who had taken away the milk-soaked rug returned with a bucket of soapy water and a basket of rags. She scrubbed and wiped until no trace of the spill remained.

Except for Arthur's and Edward's mumblings, there wasn't much talk in the nursery schoolroom. The adults had been shocked into silence by Myra's anger and the crack of her hand across her grandchildren's faces. Every time there was a noise in the hallway, heads swiveled toward the door.

When Daphne at last rose from the chair where she had been sitting, her legs trembled, and she clutched the fireplace mantel to maintain her balance.

"Are you all right, Miss Daphne?" Nanny asked. She'd been with the Adderly family since Lucas had been a baby.

"I'm fine, Nanny. I may go lie down for a while, but I'll be back this afternoon for tea."

"I'll ask Cook for bread-and-butter sandwiches."

"The boys will like that."

So much remained unsaid.

Daphne had heard the carriage pull into the driveway and leave again, but she had no idea where Myra might have gone. Perhaps back to the lawyer's office, triumphantly waving a copy of the trust document she wasn't supposed to have access to yet? But what good would that do? It was more likely that her mother had hidden the carefully wrapped bundle some-where in the house where she didn't think Daphne would find it. Myra was secretive even when there was no need for con-cealment.

Myra's bedroom door was shut but not locked. Daphne turned the knob with fingers that trembled at the audacity of what she was doing. Even as a child she had been forbidden to enter her mother's bedroom without invitation. She'd come to regard it as a secret chamber that was as mysterious and irre-sistible as Aladdin's cave. Every foray completed without Myra's knowledge was an adventure about which she told no one, not even Lucas.

The room was dim and still, smelling faintly of the lavender scent that accompanied Myra wherever she went. Like the woman who slept there, everything was immaculate and in per-fect order. Not a single garment left over a chair back, not a trace of powder on the glass top of the dressing table. The book she was reading was place marked and positioned precisely where her hand could find it if she happened to wake in the night. A pitcher of fresh water and a crystal glass sat on one of the bedside tables.

Only one object was where it shouldn't be. Next to Myra's glove box lay the small gold watch she usually pinned to her shirtwaist. Beside it pooled the thin gold chain that secured it, and on that chain two keys, one very small, the other slightly larger. Daphne had never seen them anyplace but on her mother's bosom. It was inconceivable that Myra had gone out without the timepiece and the keys. Until Daphne looked closer and saw the broken clasp.

She might never have this opportunity again.

Daphne folded her hand over the watch, chain, and keys, scooped them off the dressing table and left her mother's bedroom, closing the door behind her. Down the central staircase as quickly and quietly as she could go, past the parlors, library, and dining room. A sharp turn to the right and she reached the short hallway that connected the main part of the house to the still room. The larger of the two keys slid into the lock, turned almost without effort.

Sunlight filtering through pine trees swirled through the room like eddies of silent water. Nothing lay atop the counters except tidily arranged jars and bottles, recently washed, dried, and set out to be filled with crushed herbs, liquid medicinals, and soothing skin creams. At first glance it didn't look as though Myra had hidden anything in here.

But Daphne remembered what she'd observed the few times her mother had insisted she learn something of what every woman with a family should know about healing nostrums. Myra kept ledgers in which she recorded what she was working on, and she'd collected a library of books so old the pages sometimes crumbled at the touch. There was also a locked cabinet Daphne had been repeatedly warned away from.

She shuffled through the drawers first, finding the ledgers, stacks of paper, and boxes of fragile instruments. The special glass-fronted shelves next. Rows of leather-bound books but no canvas-wrapped package smelling of spilt milk. Then the special cabinet into whose lock the tiny key fit perfectly. The moment she swung open the door she knew she'd found what she was searching for.

Myra had taken the trust document out of its canvas wrapping, putting the pages into the cabinet after skimming each one, flinging the black ribbon that had been tied around the document atop the scattered papers. Daphne spread them on the worktable where Myra conducted her experiments, arranging them in the right order. She began to read.

When she'd finished, she understood why her mother had relocked the still room in such a fulminating rage that she'd broken the clasp on the chain that held the keys. Lucas had created a twisted plan Myra could never have imagined a son of hers designing. The blow that must have struck the hardest had to be the provision that if Rowan died before her eighteenth birthday, but either Cyrus or Daphne were alive on that date, the bulk of the principal and the revenues of the trust holdings would be left to the sole survivor or divided between the two of them. Myra would get nothing.

Only if her husband, daughter, and granddaughter were all dead would she control what Daphne knew she considered rightfully hers. It seemed as though Lucas had played the cruelest possible joke on his mother. She had refused to consent to a marriage with the woman he loved and had later proved unyieldingly cold to the baby he brought home to her. She could only inherit if everyone she loved was dead. *And what good would money do her then?* he must have thought.

The weak point in Lucas's elaborate scheme was that Daphne knew her mother had never loved anyone, not in the way Daphne loved her boys or Lucas had loved Grace and Rowan. She thought that people who had known the joy and the pain of loving could never understand a creature like Myra. She was a woman who considered love a weakness, who maintained the wifely façade demanded by society, but crushed every feeling that might have sprung to life within her fallow heart.

As Daphne started to put the trust pages back into the cabinet where she had found them, she pushed aside some of the tightly corked bottles, then took one out and read the label. Foxglove. She read another. Water Hemlock. Another. Nightshade. More. Castor bean. Milkweed. White snakeroot. Death Cap. Destroying Angel. Arsenic.

And now she knew why the cabinet was always locked, why her mother carried its key on her person. Each of the beautifully labeled jars contained a poison that could stop a heart or cause it to flutter uncontrollably, erode or burn out the lining of a stomach, cause severe vomiting, dizziness, weakness— bring agonizing death to the person who ingested the harmless-looking powder.

In order for the trust to pass into her hands, Myra had to be the only member of her family who remained alive on the date of Rowan's majority. Which was rapidly approaching. Rowan. Daphne. Cyrus. They all had to die.

Daphne snatched back the pages of the trust, forced her shaking fingers to arrange the bottles of poison as close to the way she'd found them as she could remember, closed and locked the cabinet. She felt as dizzy and sick to her stomach as though she'd accidentally brushed against milkweed and sucked the white sap from her skin. Milkweed grew wild in pastures. Myra cultivated it in her greenhouse.

Clutching the papers she'd taken, Daphne closed and locked the still room door. She wasn't thinking, wasn't planning, wasn't doing anything but reacting instinctively to a threat she could hardly bring herself to contemplate or accept. She placed the watch and the chain with the broken clasp on her mother's dressing table, then left Myra's bedroom with its cloying scent of lavender, taking faltering, unsteady steps down the hallway.

"Are you all right, Mrs. Yates?" The day nurse who sat with Cyrus and prepared him for bed every evening slipped a supportive hand beneath Daphne's elbow.

"I'm fine. A bit of a spell, but nothing serious." Daphne tried to focus on the kind, smiling face. Her mind and her eyes seemed to be playing tricks on her, as though she were still in the throes of a nightmare.

"Your father is sleeping. So if you need me, I'm available."

Then it all made sense. Blindingly logical sense.

"I wonder if you would get me a cup of tea?" Daphne asked. "I'll just sit here until you bring it back."

"Tea's just the thing when you've had a spell," the nurse agreed. She helped Daphne into the chair outside Cyrus Adderly's bedroom door and set off briskly for the kitchen.

As soon as she was out of sight, Daphne sped to her room, hid the trust document inside a hatbox atop her armoire, then nestled her riding hat and veils over it, fitting the lid down snugly. She stacked two more hatboxes atop the important one, put the chair she'd climbed on back where it belonged, then stepped to the middle of the room to study her handiwork. It would have to do until she could think of something better.

It had taken all of two minutes. Surely that nearly infinitesimal amount of time would make no difference.

She opened her father's bedroom door, praying silently that he really would be sleeping, that her imagination and her fears had played a cruel trick on her.

"I was lucky, Mrs. Yates," the nurse whispered from the doorway behind her. "Cook was sending up an early tea, so I didn't have to go all the way down to the kitchen." She set down the tray. "He's still asleep, but I can wake him if you like. You can have your tea together."

Daphne's eyes had fastened on her father's chest, watching and waiting for its rise and fall.

"Mrs. Yates?" The nurse followed Daphne's gaze. She frowned, crossed to the bedside, pressed the fingers of one hand to

Cyrus's wrist. The back of her hand moved to his cheeks, his forehead, the artery in his neck. One finger raised and lowered the eyelids. She sighed and turned to face the woman who stood as still as a statue and seemed to know already what she had to tell her.

"I'm afraid he's gone, Mrs. Yates. In his sleep. As peacefully as we all wish to pass over." She reached for the edge of the sheet to draw it over his face.

"Not yet," Daphne said. "I'd like to sit with him for a while."

"Of course you would. I'll telephone the doctor." There was a death certificate to sign, funeral arrangements to be made, the widow to be informed when she returned. Another private nursing post to be found. She closed the door behind her and went downstairs to begin the work of attending to Cyrus Adderly's remains.

"I hope that's how it was, Papa," Daphne whispered, massaging her father's cool fingers in her own warm hand. "I hope it wasn't foxglove. I hope you didn't feel your heart racing until it burst from the strain of it." He didn't look dead. Until you touched him. Then you sensed the awful stillness and the cold spreading across his skin.

It wouldn't occur to the doctor to order an autopsy. Cyrus Adderly had been his patient ever since the fall that paralyzed him. Myra had been warned more than once that her husband's heart was failing. It was a near miracle he'd lived as long as he had.

Daphne's husband had also suffered a fatal heart attack. Unexpected in a man so young, but far from unknown. There'd been no autopsy ordered in that case, either. And no more feeble-minded children born.

Before the nurse could return, Daphne went to her room again. She unscrewed the lid of a jar of Mrs. Anthony's Vanishing Formula, then slipped the key to the poison cabinet into the cream and pushed down until she felt it lie on the bottom of the jar. She returned the still room key to her mother's dressing table, slipping it back onto the chain. Let her try to figure out where and how the missing cabinet key had disappeared.

Beside her father's body once more, Daphne tried not to contemplate the unthinkable.

The last time Rowan set foot in Adderly House had been when Myra had informed her that she would be living at Our Lady of the Falls Academy year-round, including the seasonal vacations when most of the other boarders returned to their families. There was a small group of girls who never left the convent, either because the journey to a faraway home was too long and dangerous or because their parents or guardians couldn't be bothered with their inconvenient presence. Rowan had felt sorry for them.

When she had been removed from the Academy and consigned to the workhouselike atmosphere of the orphanage, Rowan had been more puzzled than angry, more accepting than rebellious. She had believed it was all a dreadful mistake that her long-absent father would return to correct. Told that her grandmother's every spare moment was taken up with the declining health of her paralyzed husband, Rowan had said prayers for the grandfather she barely remembered and for her father's mother.

The rescue by Lady Hamilton and her sojourn at Daniel's cabin in the forest had seemed like answers to prayers voiced more and more fervently the harder she was worked and the lonelier she became. The father she had never ceased mourning had not suddenly materialized, but a dignified and beautifully dressed woman, an old blind man, and a half-wolf dog had taken his place. It was enough. She gave them the love she had kept bottled up for so many years and told herself to be content. Most of the time she was.

*　*　*

Daphne kept vigil beside her father's bed while the vestiges of his long illness were tidied away.

The nurse opened Cryrus's window to let a few inches of fresh air into the room while she disposed of the medicines that were no longer needed and removed the glass and spoon used to administer them. She emptied the pitcher of water and stacked the linen napkins tidily on a bedside table, lighting the customary candle to beat back the darkness of death.

Daphne heard the carriage circle into the driveway, her mother's voice instructing someone to climb out and follow her inside. She set aside her teacup and rose from where she was sitting, standing to one side of the curtain to look out and down.

Rowan. Her niece's flame-red hair glowed in a shaft of sunlight. It didn't make sense. The girl had seemed so settled when Daphne visited her at Daniel's cabin. Composed, serene, as if she'd found the place she belonged. How had Myra persuaded her to come to Adderly House?

"Shall I tell her, Mrs. Yates?" the nurse asked. "Or would you prefer to do it?"

For a moment Daphne didn't know what the woman was talking about. Tell who what?

Then she stared behind the nurse to where her father's body lay, hands folded across a chest that no longer rose and fell with the breath of life. And suddenly she understood why Rowan had been brought to the home where the girl's father had once thought she would be safe.

Two lives now stood between her mother and the fortune Lucas had tried to deprive Myra of controlling. Hers and Rowan's. Daphne pictured the tiny key lying at the bottom of the jar of Mrs. Anthony's Vanishing Formula. The only way Myra could reach the poisons in her special cabinet was by prying or breaking it open.

It wouldn't be easy because the cabinet's doors were solid, cured oak, the hinges hand crafted by a blacksmith. The lock itself might appear dainty, but it, too, had been made to order by an expert smithy. She doubted her mother would take a hammer or a fireplace tool to the cabinet. She'd look first for the key, assuming she had dropped it somewhere in her rush to leave the house in search of Rowan. Would Myra summon a locksmith? If she did, and if he succeeded in opening the cabinet, Myra would know that the trust document had been taken and that the poisons she'd gone to such pains to conceal were no longer secret.

There would be no doubt in her mind that her daughter knew everything.

Daphne's head was spinning. She hardly felt the nurse leading her toward the door, down the hallway to her bedroom, easing her onto the pillow, slipping off her shoes. The last thing she seemed to see before everything went black was Rowan's concerned face bending over her.

CHAPTER 30

"I had no choice but to tell them about you, Lucas," Lady Hamilton said. "Rowan has been kidnapped."

"Myra is her grandmother," he said. "She may not love her as I had hoped, but she won't harm her."

Lucas Adderly was tall, broad shouldered, with piercing blue eyes above a thick black beard streaked with gray. He had an air of composed strength about him that could only have come from a lifetime of fighting a legion of demons.

"There's already been one attempt to poison your daughter," Geoffrey said bluntly. He wasn't sure how much this man knew, only that he'd gone to extraordinary lengths to hide his presence in Niagara. Despite their meticulous search of this cabin after Martin Fallow's death, Prudence and Geoffrey had found nothing to indicate that Lucas Adderly had been staying there.

"That was engineered by Carter Jayden," Lucas answered. "I made sure it wouldn't happen again."

"It was you in the house the night Jayden was killed?" Prudence asked. She didn't have to add that something about the way the two bodies had been arranged had gnawed at Geoffrey's training and her instincts. No matter how many times they'd discussed the supposed falling-out between thieves, they'd come to the same conclusion. *Staged.*

Lucas nodded. "They were armed, waiting for one another. I disrupted their plans, but I shot in self-defense. I'm not a murderer. Not now, not ever."

"Myra has changed," Lady Hamilton interrupted. "I was never afraid of your mother, Lucas. But there's something about her now . . ."

"If you'll submit an accounting, I'll see that you're well compensated for your time and effort." Lucas ignored Lady Hamilton, looking from Prudence to Geoffrey, blue eyes cold and sternly purposeful. "There won't be any reason to take Rowan's case to court once I make myself known."

"It's not that simple," Geoffrey said.

"You were hired to perform a service that is no longer required."

"There are too many loose ends," Geoffrey continued. "You and Lady Hamilton may decide you don't need us on the case, but we don't walk away that easily."

"I presume you've known that Lucas was alive all along?" Prudence asked Lady Hamilton. She looked pointedly around the comfortably furnished cabin that had been home to the late Martin Fallow. "Did Martin move out every time Lucas came back to Niagara?"

"He slept in a bedroll on the front porch," Lucas said, cutting off whatever answer Lady Hamilton had been about to give. "He acted as my bodyguard when I needed him."

"Why *did* you hire us?" Prudence asked. She had her temper under control, but she could feel the suppressed anger burning her ears nonetheless.

This was supposed to have been her chance to prove herself in court before men who doubted women could or should attempt to claim a professional life. She felt used. And now she was being tossed aside. It didn't sit well.

"I apologize, Prudence," Lady Hamilton began. "No, Lucas, let me explain. We owe them that much." She held up one hand in an imperious gesture that demanded silence and acquiescence. "The plan was always that Lucas would return to ensure that Rowan came into the trust he created for her. But during the past few years, things became complicated. In a moment of weakness and indecision I confided in your aunt. Not everything," Lady Hamilton hastened to reassure Prudence. "Only that I had been unable to secure an attorney to represent Rowan if her case had to be pleaded in a court of law. At one point I really did believe that was more likely than not. You know your aunt Gillian, Prudence. I imagine she wrote you by return post and then traipsed off to Scotland where neither of us could reach her."

"Why didn't you tell us all this when we arrived? Why pretend?"

"Martin Fallow. I knew his death wasn't an accident. Suddenly there was a presence out there more threatening than anything we had imagined."

"I always knew there was a possibility my mother would try to deny Rowan," Lucas interrupted. "She hated Grace. But I thought I'd protected my daughter with the trust I created. The idea was to make her too valuable to be mistreated. I failed in that. Ernestine made me see the truth of it."

The way he said Lady Hamilton's name told Prudence and Geoffrey all they needed to know about the relationship between the woman who had tried to safeguard Rowan and the man who was her father.

"Your mother claims you never married Grace Malone," Prudence said.

A muscle twitched across Lucas's cheekbone, but he said nothing.

Lady Hamilton's sigh was loud and prolonged. "Poor Grace," she murmured.

"Start at the beginning," Geoffrey said.

"Why should I tell you anything?" Lucas asked.

"It's the price you have to pay for our absence," Geoffrey answered. "And our silence."

"I can tell them," Lady Hamilton offered. She wouldn't say aloud that speaking about the woman he'd loved pained Lucas more than she could bear.

"And then you'll leave?" Lucas asked.

"Maybe," Geoffrey said. "I make no promises."

The silence stretched on until finally, Lucas nodded. Shook his head when Lady Hamilton would have spoken for him.

"Grace almost died when Rowan was born," he began. "We'd planned to go to San Francisco, but Grace wasn't strong enough. We found a preacher who married us and a cabin where we could stay until the child came. My sweet Grace grew so weak during those months that I feared she wouldn't survive the birth. Headaches so severe, she wept with the pain of them. Spells of dizziness so strong, she couldn't walk unaided. There wasn't a doctor in the area and Grace refused to be taken back to Niagara. A midwife delivered her when the time came. Rowan was born as healthy and strong as we could wish for."

"She's grown into a beautiful young woman," Prudence said.

"Grace had a brother. Tommy Ginger, they called him. Not so much because of the red hair as the freckles that covered every inch of his skin. He was her accompanist and manager. He couldn't read a note of music, but he played piano like no one I've heard before or since. Tommy had helped Grace and me leave Niagara on the sly and he was a witness when we married, but he had restless feet and a love for the bottle that was the ruin of every good thing he tried to do. He helped us settle into the cabin and then he left to find work. Promised he'd return before the baby was due. He came back all right, but he was a week late. And he brought the smallpox with him."

A wave of tiny quivers sped over Lucas's features. He closed his eyes for a few moments before opening them again and continuing.

"He wasn't ill himself, so he didn't know he was carrying it, but he'd played piano in a town where thirty or more people had been quarantined. We didn't understand all of this until Grace became feverish and the rash broke out. I realized right away what it was. If you've ever seen smallpox, you never forget what it looks like. Both of us were terrified our daughter would catch it. Babies almost never survive the pox. Grace begged me to take Rowan back to my mother's, and God forgive me, I did. Tommy Ginger stayed to nurse her through the worst of it. He said it was the least he could do.

"I'll never forget standing in the cabin doorway, cradling Rowan in my arms as my wife sank into delirium. There was nothing I could do but take the baby to safety. Tommy Ginger closed the door behind me and that was the last I knew until his letter came. Three weeks later. By that time, I was almost mad with worry. He wrote that Grace had died, and he'd buried her in the woods behind the cabin. He said the end came quickly and she didn't suffer. I knew that was a lie. Daphne and Mother cared for Rowan while I went to look for the grave. He'd dug it in a pine grove and carved her name on a wooden cross. Grace Malone Adderly. Tommy had disappeared, but not before burning down the place where Grace passed. It was the only way to keep the infection from spreading."

"And then you returned to Niagara," Geoffrey prodded.

"I did. The heart went out of me when I stood where only ashes remained of the future Grace and I had planned. For the next five years I did the best I could to be the father Rowan deserved. As she grew out of babyhood she looked more and more like her mother. Seeing a miniature Grace every day grew too difficult to bear."

"That's when you went to San Francisco," Prudence said.

"My father became an invalid after his fall. I had taken over the businesses and made sure they would continue to prosper with the management I put in place. My lawyers set up Rowan's trust. I turned over her guardianship to my mother."

"Then what happened?" Geoffrey asked. They had heard the Pinkerton agent's version of Lucas Adderly's life in California, but there had been holes in the narrative that only the man himself could fill in.

"You're an ex-Pinkerton," Adderly said.

"I am," Geoffrey admitted, certain now that Lady Hamilton had shared everything they had told her.

"Then I'd venture to guess that very soon after getting this case you hired the Pinks to find out what they could about me."

"We did."

"I was accused of murder within hours of getting off the train in San Francisco," Adderly said bitterly. "The man assaulted me as we were pulling into the station. He had a knife. So did I."

"There weren't any witnesses to what happened?" Prudence asked.

Adderly shook his head. "He'd planned it that way. When I realized he was dead, I knew no one would believe I'd acted in self-defense. I took his identification and everything else in his pockets. To give myself more time I set the corpse in a sitting position in the compartment and pulled his hat down over his face as if he were asleep. Grabbed my carpetbag, stepped down onto the platform, and got lost in the crowd."

"There were wanted posters with sketches of your face," Geoffrey said.

"I found out the next day that the man I killed was the ne'er-do-well son of a family with political ties to Sacramento. The story was in all the newspapers. Casting him as an innocent victim rather than the assailant allowed the family to rehabilitate him and clear their name of any disgrace. The conductor and one of the porters swore up and down that they'd been suspicious of me from the moment I boarded. I knew then that I had to become someone else."

"The poster that circulated claimed you were an Irishman," Geoffrey said.

"The blue eyes and black hair." Adderly chuckled. "If there was Irish blood in our family woodpile, I was glad to have it. Half the men drawn to the gold mines were Irish. Most of them stayed on after the strikes began to peter out. I grew a beard, changed my name, and disappeared."

"How long before you felt safe?" Prudence asked.

"I got comfortable in the new identity after a few months. No one doubted I was who I claimed to be," Lucas said. "But I was always careful not to let anything slip, even after I knew no one was looking for me anymore."

"And then he found Grace," Lady Hamilton said. Her eyes swept from Prudence's to Geoffrey's, their look challenging and accusatory at the same time.

"Grace was dead," Prudence exclaimed, turning toward Lucas. "You saw the grave and the ashes where her brother burned down the cabin."

"They lied," Adderly said. "Both of them." He rose from his chair, walked toward the cabin door, hesitated, then wrenched it open and stepped out onto the porch.

"Give him a moment," Lady Hamilton said. "He'll be back. He needs to tell this story to someone other than me."

"How long have you known?" Prudence asked.

"About Grace? Only a few years. After Lucas and I . . ." She didn't complete what she had begun to say.

Prudence would have asked the obvious question, but Geoffrey laid a restraining hand on hers.

Lucas left the cabin door open when he returned, set a new log in the fireplace, and stirred up the coals. Reseated himself. Clasped both hands together. Took up where he had left off.

"I built a cargo business in San Francisco, shipping supplies into the port and then hauling a good portion of them into the mining camps. That's where the real money was made, but it was never easy. Wagon wheels fractured, mules and oxen foundered, rivers overflowed their banks, and my partner and I had to post guards around the clock to keep what we were carrying from being stolen. Twice a year I toured the camps myself to make sure my factors weren't robbing me blind. They were rough places, brutal and dangerous when the mining was good, savagely violent when it wasn't. I reveled in those trips. They challenged my wits, kept me fit for whatever came my way, and helped me forget everything I'd lost. I drank hard in those days. Everybody did. We all fought one another. A man whose nose hadn't been broken wasn't worth his salt.

"I was up north on the Merced River. It was winter. Cold and miserable. Sleet falling so hard, it sounded like rocks against the canvas that was all we had between us and the elements. Every man jack miner in the camp took himself off to the saloon tent when it got dark. So did I. There was whiskey and cards and a wagonload of traveling prossies. Just about what you'd expect. But that night there was something else. A singer who called herself the Black Swan and wore a veil to hide her face. She'd been traveling the camps and small opera houses for years, but I'd never come across her before."

"Grace," Prudence breathed.

"Grace," Lucas confirmed. "I knew the moment I heard the first notes she sang. Tommy Ginger had gotten older and his hair had faded, but that freckled skin was the same. He looked out over the saloon audience about the time I caught sight of him, and he recognized me. Fumbled the keys for a moment, then carried on as if nothing had happened. I faded into the crowd so Grace wouldn't see me. Let her sing into the silence until the show was over and every man in the place got to his feet. They like to have collapsed the tent with the noise they made."

"The veil was because of the smallpox," Prudence said.

"She was badly scarred. Not just her face. Her whole body."

"Our Pink told us there were rumors of a woman living with you," Geoffrey said.

"I gave Tommy Ginger more cash than he'd ever dreamed of earning. He took off in the middle of the night with everything they possessed, stranding Grace in that mining camp with no accompanist and no money. She came back to San Francisco with me, on my sworn oath that she would have her own quarters and we would never live together as husband and wife. It wasn't until years later that I saw how much damage the small-pox had done to her body."

"How ... ?" Prudence choked off the question she'd blurted out.

"She was often ill, falling into fevers and unconsciousness. I hired a woman to look after her, a good woman whom Grace eventually trusted. I only broke my word to her once, when we thought she was dying and I forced my way into her room despite my promise never to look at her uncovered face."

"I've seen smallpox victims," Geoffrey said.

"Then you have some idea of the horror the disease can leave behind. Grace recovered, and as the years passed, we got comfortable with one another again. As long as I kept my distance and never spoke of love. That kind of pretense eventually wears you out. Whatever passion had been between us withered and died."

"Where is she now?" Prudence asked, picturing in her mind a once-beautiful woman now broken, disfigured, and alone.

"She's here in Niagara."

"I found a widow who cares for the sick and elderly in her home," Lady Hamilton said. "She's about five miles out of town, on the small farm she and her husband worked until his death."

"Grace traveled with her nurse," Lucas contributed. "I hired the woman to stay on as a companion after the illness I told you about. Grace depends on her. They've become friends."

"Why?" Prudence asked. "Why come back to Niagara after all this time?"

"To see Rowan. To see her child in the flesh," Lucas answered.

"I don't understand. Surely, if she's scarred as badly as you claim . . ."

"I sent photographs," Lady Hamilton said. "The Academy began hiring a photographer a few years ago to capture the likenesses of its graduating classes. He earned extra by taking the special pictures I commissioned."

"Grace doesn't intend to reveal herself to Rowan. She only wants to see for herself the child whose face the photographer captured. It's become an obsession. She spends hours every day poring over the photographs."

"Only three of them," Lady Hamilton said. "We couldn't risk more."

"She begged me to bring her to Niagara, and once she explained how she planned to manage things, I agreed. She'll remain in her carriage outside their office on the day Rowan presents herself to my lawyers. Ernestine will be accompanying Rowan. She'll see to it that they remain within sight for several minutes before going inside. That's all Grace claims she wants. A glimpse of the child she hasn't seen in eighteen years."

"How terribly sad," Prudence said.

"She's always veiled," Lucas reminded them. "Even if Rowan notices the carriage and wonders why it's there, she won't see her mother."

"Then what?" Geoffrey asked.

"That's all," Lucas said. "The story ends there. Grace and I return to San Francisco."

"And Rowan?"

Lucas shrugged his shoulders. "I haven't planned that far."

This was a man who had spent his entire life negotiating and maneuvering. Impossible that he hadn't concocted a strategem for his only child's future.

Why was he lying to them?

CHAPTER 31

"Nanny gave her a few drops of laudanum in a cup of tea to calm her after the boys had their upset, Mrs. Adderly," the nurse said. "Unfortunately, she didn't tell me or Mrs. Yates what she'd done."

"So you gave her a few more," Myra said, looking down at the composed face of her unconscious daughter.

"On doctor's orders," the nurse huffed. It was a dose often administered to female relatives of the recently deceased.

"I'm sure it was," Myra said. She laid a comforting hand on Rowan's shoulder. "I know you and Daphne have grown fond of one another, but there's nothing to worry about. She'll sleep a little longer and then wake up refreshed and ready to assume the burden of mourning her father. Why don't you sit with her for a while?"

"If you want me to, Grandmama," Rowan said.

"Then I'll check back on the two of you when I've seen to the doctor and given instructions to the staff."

Myra leaned down to kiss Rowan lightly on the forehead.

Daphne's eyelids fluttered. Her mother passed a hand over them to still the quivering.

*   *   *

"He looks very peaceful," Myra said. "After enduring the paralysis for so long, you could see in his eyes that he was ready to go." She touched Cyrus's clasped hands to make sure they were cold, then glanced around the room to reassure herself there was nothing she had forgotten.

"I think that's Dr. Elliott's carriage," the nurse said, peering out the bedroom window. "Shall I go downstairs and bring him up?"

"If you would," Myra agreed. "I'd like a few moments alone with my husband."

As soon as the nurse had left the room, Myra slid a finger between Cyrus's lips. Nothing should remain of the milkweed powder she'd dissolved into his broth, but she couldn't be sure that Dr. Elliott wouldn't examine the inside of the dead man's mouth. A very small trace of white adhered to her skin. She poured water into a glass, swished her finger in the liquid, then ran it along her husband's teeth. Satisfied that nothing was left, she blotted a drop or two of water from Cyrus's chin, rinsed her finger in the water glass, then sat back in her chair.

When Dr. Elliott entered the death chamber, Myra was weeping quietly into a handkerchief edged in black lace.

He palpated his patient's carotid artery. "The nurse was right to call me, Mrs. Adderly. He's gone."

Myra nodded, patting the tears from her eyes. One of her girlhood talents had been the ability to cry on command.

"I'll sign the death certificate and notify Ferguson's." There was only one funeral parlor in American Niagara.

"Arrangements were made with them some time ago," Myra confirmed. There had been frequent health scares over the years.

"May I?" Dr. Elliott placed two fingers on Myra's wrist. "A little fast, but that's not unusual under the circumstances. I'll see to Mrs. Yates now."

"She's lying down in her room, Doctor," the nurse volunteered. "I didn't know that Nanny had already dosed her with laudanum when I spoke to you on the phone."

"All the more reason to check on her." It was sometimes astounding how much liquid morphine women could get in the habit of consuming without obvious undue effects other than drowsiness and vagueness of speech. Daphne Yates was relatively young and healthy, but she had lost a husband-to-be and a father within a few days of each other. Accidental overdosing was a not infrequent consequence of deep bereavement.

"Someone is with her," Myra said, attempting to divert Dr. Elliott from Daphne's bedside. The fewer people who knew Rowan was in the house the better.

"And who would that be? Not Nanny with more laudanum, I hope." Dr. Elliott realized it was the wrong thing to say as soon as the words left his mouth.

"I'll see you out." Myra snatched the laudanum bottle from the nurse's hand and marched stiff-backed toward the door, turning to glare at Dr. Elliott until he closed his medical bag and followed her from the room.

"Three more drops when she begins to wake up," Myra said, explaining how to mix the laudanum with a little sweet sherry to disguise the taste. "Doctor's orders. Can you remember to do that, Rowan?"

"Yes, Grandmama."

"I know you want your aunt Daphne to recover fully from the losses she's suffered."

"Yes, Grandmama."

"She collapsed just before we arrived. It was fortunate the nurse was nearby."

Rowan nodded. She thought Daphne looked ethereally composed as she lay sleeping, hands lying palms up at her sides, bosom rising and falling rhythmically, her breathing light and effortless.

"Don't forget to give her the laudanum. I'm counting on you."

"Yes, Grandmama." But Rowan wasn't sure. At the orphanage, when girls misbehaved or answered back, they were sometimes liberally dosed and then locked in a closet. The laudanum kept them quiet for a while, until they woke up in darkness and discovered they were confined in a space no wider than a coffin.

Sometimes, even now, Rowan's dreams were haunted by their screaming.

Crazy Louie met Myra in the greenhouse, as instructed. He'd brought two more of the kerosene lanterns that were advertised as small stoves because they threw off heat as well as light. That made a total of eight of the devices, placed strategically at the corners and along the walls. The kerosene he poured over the plant-covered wooden tables and racks smothered the rich smell of well-rotted compost with an acrid stench that made his nose smart and his eyes sting.

"You're sure no one saw you?" Myra asked.

"I came through the woods."

Myra smelled liquor on his breath. "Do you remember what we agreed on?"

"You've told me more than once. I don't like it." It was too late and there was too much at stake to back away, but that didn't mean he couldn't voice an opinion. He'd been blackmailing the nose-in-the-air hoity-toity Adderly bitch for years now, but the money she'd pay him after this night's work would make everything he'd already collected seem like pocket change. He needed it, especially since it looked like he was going to lose his income from the fight fixers now that Paddy Morgan was dead.

"I'll bring her out here, ostensibly to help me cut flowers to arrange around my late husband's coffin. You'll have to grab her from behind and hold the rag over her nose until she loses consciousness. It shouldn't take more than a few minutes. Chloroform works quickly."

"I'd rather knock her out with this," Louie said, hefting a shovel.

"There can't be any broken bones, especially not a cracked skull. It has to appear to be a believable accident. She knocked over one of the heaters and couldn't escape the fire."

"I still don't like it."

"Remember to wait at least fifteen minutes before you push over the lanterns. I have to have time to get back inside and down to the housekeeper's room."

"You'll need more than that for a believable alibi."

"The servants will be finishing their meal. They'll see the housekeeper leave the table to meet me in the hallway. She'll have preparations for the funeral that I'll have to go over and approve. No one will notice the fire until it's too late to put out. And no one will suspect that there's anyone in the greenhouse until we realize that my granddaughter is no longer inside, and I remember that she mentioned wanting to pick out some of the flowers to lay atop the coffin."

Myra smiled. She'd thought of everything.

"I want my money now," Louie demanded.

"You'll get it when the job is done," Myra snapped. "As agreed."

"Now." Crazy Louie took a box of lucifers from his pocket. He looked around at the kerosene-saturated wood, opened the box, and pulled out a single phosphorus-headed match.

"Half now, half later," Myra offered. She'd pay him because she had to. But that wouldn't be the end of it.

"Bring it out when you come back with the girl."

Daphne stirred, opened her eyes, then struggled to sit up.

Obedient to her grandmother's instructions, Rowan measured a scant three drops of laudanum into the crystal glass a maid had left on the bedside table. She reached for the decanter of sweet sherry brought up from the parlor. The scent of the strong Portuguese wine filled the room as soon as she removed the stopper.

"What is that?" Daphne murmured, wrinkling her nose against the tingle of alcohol, flailing her unresponsive arms and legs.

"Grandmama said I was to give you this if you woke up," Rowan said, holding up the brown bottle of laudanum. "Does your head hurt?"

Daphne rubbed fretfully at her temples until the throbbing eased.

Rowan helped Daphne sit up and plumped the pillows behind her. "Perhaps this will help," she murmured, holding out the glass.

Daphne pushed away the medicine. "I'm groggy," she murmured.

"Maybe the nurse gave you more than you're used to," Rowan said. She'd learned not to swallow what was doled out in the orphanage every night before bed, holding the bitter liquid in her cheek until she could move out of her place in line and spit it into the dark-colored apron the orphans wore over their work dresses.

"What do you mean? What did she give me?"

"Laudanum," Rowan replied. "So did Nanny. That's why you were in your bed when I arrived."

"I don't remember falling asleep," Daphne said. She had felt drowsy, then pleasurably calm and no longer a part of what was going on around her. She remembered Nanny's smiling face, the sudden flare of energy when she entered Myra's still room, the sense of otherworldly understanding when she discovered the trust document and the locked cabinet of poisons. *Poisons.* She shook her head to dispel the foggy confusion from her brain, reaching out to dampen her handkerchief in the carafe of fresh water that always sat on her bedside table. "They gave me laudanum?"

Rowan nodded. She set down the crystal glass from which Daphne had refused to drink.

"Where is my mother?" Daphne pressed the wet handkerchief to her forehead, her eyes, her cheeks, the back of her neck.

"Grandmama went downstairs with the doctor." She had heard their voices in the hallway. Now Rowan wondered if she should remind Daphne that a death had occurred in the house. Surely her aunt hadn't forgotten.

"We don't have much time," Daphne said, throwing off the quilt, leaning against Rowan to steady her legs. "Listen to me, and don't interrupt.

"You're in danger. We both are. This is important, Rowan. You have to leave this house right now. Don't ask questions. Just go. Not out the front door. Down the servants' stairs and through the kitchen door. Run as fast as you can. Bring Mr. Hunter and Miss MacKenzie back with you. Do you understand?"

The girl stared at her.

Daphne clenched her fists. She pushed herself off the bed, knocking Rowan off balance. Her niece stumbled, eyes widening with fright, but she didn't fall.

"What on earth is going on here? Daphne, what are you doing up?" Myra stormed into the room, thrusting Rowan aside as she knocked her daughter down onto the bed. She grabbed the glass of laudanum-laced sherry and held it against Daphne's mouth, the fingers of one hand pinching shut her nostrils. When Daphne gasped for air, Myra forced the liquid down her throat.

Within a few moments, Daphne's struggles had subsided.

"I'm sorry," she whispered, her eyes fastening on Rowan's.

"You should be, causing all this ruckus when your father has just left us," Myra said. She wrapped the quilt around Daphne and tucked the ends in tightly.

Rowan tried to help, but Myra shooed her off. "I have something else for you to do," she said when Daphne had lapsed into immobility. "Would you like to help choose the flowers to put around your grandfather's casket?"

"I hardly remember him." Rowan recalled being taken into Cyrus's rooms a very long time ago, but the visits never lasted more than a few minutes.

"I'll take you to say good-bye," Myra decided, "and then we'll go to the greenhouse together."

"I'll cut the flowers," Rowan stammered. She wasn't afraid of looking at a dead person; she'd passed by more than one deceased orphan lying in a cheap pine coffin in front of the chapel altar. What disconcerted her now was her grandmother's brisk efficiency. Daphne's warning hadn't fallen on deaf ears, but neither had it made much sense.

She glanced once more at Daphne's serene face. What possible harm could come to her in the home where her father grew up and where her grandfather Cyrus had been lovingly nursed for so many years? Perhaps the death of her fiancé *had* unhinged her aunt. It wasn't unknown or even unusual for a grieving woman to weep herself into hysteria. Hence the laudanum.

More than anything, Rowan wished she could sit at Daniel's feet, one arm around Hero's neck, and tell them both how confused and conflicted she felt. The dog would lean his warm bulk against her, and Daniel's carefully considered words and weighty silences would answer the questions she wasn't sure how to ask.

She followed Myra down the stairs and past the locked still room, out the small door no one else used, alongside the hedge between the greenhouse and the mansion. A carriage sat in the street, half-hidden by the trees that grew along the edge of the property. Rowan wondered briefly who was inside and why the carriage wasn't moving, then she dismissed it from her mind.

"The lilies grow at the far end," Myra said, standing back from the greenhouse's open door, encouraging Rowan to precede her. "I'll get the secateurs and join you there."

"It's warm," Rowan said, feeling a flurry of hot air against her skin as she stepped inside.

"The gardeners will have turned on the heaters to encourage more of the lilies to bloom," Myra explained. "Go ahead. I'll be right with you."

She waited until she heard the rustle of skirts against thrashing feet and then the soft laying down of a body onto the packed earth floor.

"Remember," she told Crazy Louie as she handed him half the payment they'd agreed upon. "Wait fifteen or twenty minutes until you turn over the lanterns."

Rowan lay unconscious at her grandmother's feet.

Myra kicked the girl's skirts out of the way as she left.

CHAPTER 32

"Something's happening," Grace Malone said to the nurse companion sitting opposite her. One gloved hand rested on the uncurtained carriage window.

It had been almost an hour since Grace recognized her daughter seated beside the woman who had made her life so miserable and ordered their driver to follow the Adderly coach. The carriage had been parked within sight of the mansion ever since.

"That was a doctor who just arrived," the companion said.

"How can you tell?"

"The bag. They all carry one." Leila Reid had been a nurse since the last dark days of the war, more than twenty-five years now. Widowed and childless, she'd left hospital work to care for Lucas Adderly's reclusive wife when the long shifts became too emotionally demanding and physically exhausting. In time, the relationship between Grace and Leila had grown to be close and trusting. Both women understood suffering and the value of silence.

"He was called to certify a death," Leila declared when the doctor climbed back into his buggy twenty minutes later. She offered Grace a mint from the large purse that also contained a bottle of tonic, smelling salts, and extra handkerchiefs. "He didn't stay long enough to attend a living patient."

"The husband?" Grace asked.

"Very possibly."

People confided things to nurses they wouldn't tell anyone else. The farmer's widow in whose care home they were staying had answered all of Leila's questions and chattered on until Grace and her companion knew as much about the Adderly family history and scandals as though they'd grown up in Niagara. The story of Cyrus's fall from his favorite horse and the paralysis and failing health that followed had been of particular interest to residents, as had the mysterious disappearance and presumed death of Myra's only son.

"Look, there she is," Grace exclaimed, leaning forward with excitement, then abruptly forcing herself to move away from the carriage window. "And that's Myra with her."

Myra and Rowan had left the mansion by a side door and were walking toward a greenhouse unshaded by the towering oaks and pines studding the rest of the property. Myra seemed engrossed in conversation with her granddaughter, reacting to Rowan's smiles with laughter and quick, affectionate glances.

"You recognize her?" Leila asked.

"Everyone in Niagara knew Myra Adderly by sight," Grace explained. "She was the town's society queen in her day, and I don't suppose much has changed. Lucas brought me to the house one afternoon when he still thought there was a chance his mother would accept an Irish saloon singer into the family. It was a polite, frozen, devastating disaster. She made it clear I wasn't welcome. Not then, not ever. I doubt she's changed much in all the years since she rejected me and everything I stand for. Her kind never does."

"Your daughter is more beautiful than any of the photographs you've shown me."

Rowan's red hair caught and reflected glimmers of the fading

sun, bathing the girl's pale face as though with golden candle-
light. She walked with the graceful steps of a born dancer, turning once to look curiously at the carriage parked in the road.

It was the first time Grace had seen her daughter in person
since the day she put the infant into Lucas's arms and begged
him to take her to safety.

Tears slipped down the pitted cheeks hidden behind the
black veil.

Leila reached for Grace's hands, holding them comfortingly
in her own as Rowan and Myra disappeared from sight. "Shall
we go back to the guest house?"

"Just a little longer," Grace pleaded. "I'd like to stay while
there's still light or until she comes out."

Shadows appeared on the greenhouse glass. Grace and Myra
saw the outline of a man's figure. Then the door opened and
Myra emerged. Alone. She paused as if giving instructions to
someone inside, the gardener perhaps, then made her way
along the flagstone path leading back to the house.

"Something's wrong," Grace said, struggling to open the carriage door.

"There's nothing to worry about." Leila kept one hand
firmly on the door latch. She had strict instructions not to
allow Lucas's wife to excite herself. "You'll see. Just be patient
for a few more minutes. Rowan will be out before you can say
Jack Robinson."

Grace sank against the cushioned seat, but she never took
her eyes from the structure into which her child had vanished.

Crazy Louie had seen the carriage in the road outside Adderly House as he made his way from the shelter of the woods
across the open grounds to the greenhouse. He'd paused for a
moment, then swigged another mouthful of whiskey from his
flask and dismissed it. He had other things on his mind besides
an unfaithful spouse parking on a quiet street to enjoy an adul-
terous rendezvous.

He wasn't a stranger to violence, but burning a young woman to death wasn't something he could do without the support of a considerable amount of alcohol. He'd been almost sober when he'd demanded an advance of half the sum Myra had agreed to pay him, but the large flask he carried was close to empty as he lit one lantern after the other, gulping a fortifying slug every time he struck a lucifer. He tried not to look too closely at the girl lying unconscious on the ground. He probably should have sprinkled her clothing with extra kerosene, but he hadn't been able to bring himself to go that far, even with the whiskey.

He'd lit six of the eight lanterns when he remembered that he was supposed to wait a while before setting the structure ablaze. Myra, damn her eyes, had claimed she needed time to establish her alibi. Better leave the last two unlit until he was ready to tip them all over and make his escape. He looked at his watch, then stepped outside to smoke a cheroot.

The carriage was still parked in the street, none of its side lamps burning. Whoever was inside was trying not to attract attention. Louie caught a glimpse of the top-hatted driver and chuckled to himself. Somebody always knew your secret. That was just the way of things. The smoke from the cheroot plumed into the dusk. He was impatient to get this over with. He fingered the cash money in his pocket, and wished he'd thought to bring a second flask of whiskey.

There'd been only one hitch so far, but it seemed to have resolved itself, so he hadn't mentioned it to Myra. Somehow the cork stopper in the bottle of chloroform she'd given him had come loose. Or maybe he hadn't put it back in tightly enough when he'd taken an inquisitive sniff back at the workshop. By the time he got to the greenhouse the volatile liquid had all but evaporated, so he'd poured some water into the bottle, shaken it well, and used that to moisten the rag he'd held over the girl's nose. It seemed to have worked. Through the smoke of the cheroot and the fogged-up glass, he could just make out her body.

Louie checked his watch again. The hands hadn't moved

since the last time he looked. No ticking sound. The tiny winding knob kept slipping out of his fingers, but he finally got it going. Myra was probably going to get a few extra minutes. He hoped she'd be worrying while she waited for the hullabaloo that always accompanied fire.

He leaned against the greenhouse door, imagining his name in huge black letters splashed across the nation's newspapers when he made his successful ride over the falls. The money Myra was paying him would make that dream a reality. It always came down to money when you were trying to do something no one else had ever achieved. Inventors starved themselves and committed suicide for lack of financial support. Crazy Louie had decided long ago that he wouldn't be among those failures.

He'd do whatever he had to in order to achieve success.

Rowan's head hurt. She raised a hand to rub her aching temples and discovered that her fingers were clutching dirt. She pushed herself to a sitting position, wiping her palms against her skirts. Flickering lantern light illuminated a man-made forest of exotic plants set atop rows of wooden tables. A man's silhouette was outlined against the far wall of what she realized was her grandmother's greenhouse. Why was she lying on the ground?

Daphne's warning rang through her muddled thoughts.

You're in danger . . . Run as fast as you can. Bring Mr. Hunter and Miss MacKenzie back with you.

Rowan forced herself to breathe deeply and concentrate on what she had glimpsed of the interior of the greenhouse before everything went black. Chloroform. She smelled a faint whiff of it lingering on the lower part of her face. She rubbed at it with her sleeve, glancing toward where the man stood, the glow of his cheroot arcing through the dusk outside. A narrow aisle bisected the length of the glass enclosed room, doors at either end. She would have to take a chance that her only way out wasn't locked. If it was, she decided, reaching for a hand trowel lying beneath one of the tables, she'd break the glass.

The most important thing was not to stumble and fall once she got to her feet.

Moving stealthily, she crawled out of the smoker's line of sight, then stood and made her way along the row of tables, each step a little more steady than the previous one. She'd just grasped the door handle when she felt a draft of outside air and smelled the unmistakable stench of cheap tobacco.

He'd waited a little longer than Myra had instructed, but Louie had been enjoying his cheroot, the last full swallow of his whiskey, and the notion of his name in bold print across a newspaper's front page. Crazy Louie's whole life had been spent pushing his way into the limelight, only to be shoved aside, rejected, and repeatedly mocked. Niagara and the falls wouldn't break him. Not with more money to create the perfect barrel than he'd ever earned before.

The six lanterns he'd already lit burned steadily if a bit fitfully. Kerosene was like that, the impurities it contained causing sparks to fly within the safety chimneys. He hummed to himself as he walked from one lantern to the next, turning up the feed, wondering if he needed to bother striking a lucifer to the last two. Maybe he could just knock them over and make his escape before the flames got dangerous.

No. Myra wouldn't pay him if things didn't go exactly as she'd planned. He knew her well enough to be certain of that. Light all of the lanterns, then tip them over one by one, she'd told him. Wait until he was sure the greenhouse would erupt into a blaze the firefighters wouldn't be able to put out, then make his way out the door, through the garden, across the lawn, and into the safety of the trees. It was only a fifteen-minute walk to his workshop. He'd be drinking a cup of hot coffee laced with more whiskey before the staff at Adderly

House realized what was happening. He'd seen wires strung into the house. That meant a telephone connection. No matter. He'd be long gone before anyone picked up the instrument to call for help.

He left unlit the lanterns closest to where he intended to make his escape. There'd be flames behind but not in front of him. Louie drained his flask of its last few remaining drops, tucked it into a coat pocket, and took out a box of wooden matches. He was unsteady on his feet, but not more so than the many times in the past when he'd needed a little Dutch courage. Once he finished this job and built the quintessential barrel to get himself safely over the falls, no one would be able to touch him. He'd be a celebrity, as famous as any of P.T. Barnum's oddities or Buffalo Bill's Wild West riders. Fame was within his reach.

He kicked over the first lantern, almost losing his balance as it crashed to the dirt floor and a pool of flame licked at a wooden table leg. Another lantern. A third. The individual fires crackled and whooshed, spreading quickly into one all-consuming blaze. Still low to the ground, but creeping upward, reaching hungrily for the kerosene he'd splashed everywhere he'd been able to fling it. The fourth, fifth, and sixth lanterns.

He stood for a moment, box of lucifers in hand, enjoying the spectacle of leaping flames. Safety a few steps away. And then he realized that he hadn't had to avoid the girl's body as he'd walked the greenhouse aisle, knocking over each lantern in turn. She should have been lying beneath his feet, unconscious, her skirts fanned out around her legs, red hair spilling down her back. Hair as bright as the fire that would consume it.

She wasn't there. He would have remembered brushing by her. Stepping over her.

The door at the far end of the greenhouse slammed in the gust of a flaming updraft.

A dark shadow seen through leaping flames fled through the deepening dusk, unbound hair reflecting blood red highlights, upswept skirts revealing the flash of bare white legs sprinting toward the darkening tree line.

Crazy Louie howled like a hungry wolf scenting escaping prey. He kicked at the two remaining lanterns, spilling their kerosene across the floor. A river of fire ran from one to the other and the burning greenhouse roared with the turbulence of the flames spiraling upward through the exploding glass roof into the evening sky.

He had to catch her. He had to drag her back before Myra and the Adderly servants surged out of the house to stare open-mouthed at the conflagration. The girl named Rowan had to die in the fire. Otherwise, he wouldn't get paid. And without the money he'd been promised, his life's dream would end in failure and ignominy.

Too late. He'd waited too long.

She'd disappeared into darkness, sheltered by close-growing trees in the heavily wooded area that stretched between here and his workshop.

Louie took off at a dead run. Nobody knew those woods as well as he did. The girl had to be feeling the effects of the chloroform, weakened though it had proved to be. Her legs would falter, she'd give out of breath, lose her sense of direction and become lost. With any luck, she'd stumble over a windfall branch, sprain an ankle, lie in the leaves whimpering until he caught up to her.

Then what?

The only safe place to hide was the workshop. That's where he'd take her, tied up, maybe shoved into one of his failed barrels.

He'd never put a woman in a barrel.

He laughed aloud as the forest swallowed him up.

Grace and Leila spied the flames from the tipped-over lanterns long before anyone else suspected a fire had been started.

They saw Rowan burst into the open, bolting toward the woods at the back of the lot with the speed of a frightened deer.

"She made it," Grace breathed when her daughter had disappeared between the tree trunks. "But why didn't she run back to the house?"

The carriage driver jumped down from his perch, urged his passengers to stay where they were, then sprinted up the driveway to raise the alarm.

"I've seen accidents and I've seen deliberate burnings," Leila said. "Someone set this fire. It wasn't caused by an overfilled lantern."

They watched, mesmerized, as plumes of red snaked upward, hanging against the glass walls of the greenhouse like curtains that suddenly whipped together to form a solid barrier of scarlet.

Grace leaned out the carriage window, searching beyond the burning greenhouse for Rowan to emerge from the trees. "I didn't see the gardener leave. I hope he got out in time."

"He was smoking a cigar or a cigarette outside. The fires only blazed up after he went back in," Leila said. "And he was drinking from a flask or a bottle." She mimicked the lift of a drinker's arm.

The sound of galloping horses and clanging bells drowned out Grace's response as the Niagara volunteer fire brigade charged up the hill, followed by a crowd of curious and frightened men and women carrying buckets and blankets to drench and beat out any flames spreading toward the roadway. Servants flooded from the doors of the Adderly mansion, flapping aprons against the heat, clutching one another as sparks flew through the air.

Myra Adderly stood in the house's grand doorway, a regal figure outlined by the light of the hallway behind her. She watched the noisy confusion and frantic firefighting efforts with no expression on her face. People who got close enough to get a good look at her remembered later that she looked as though she were waiting for something.

On the nursery floor, peering out from behind a curtain, the two Yates boys stared down at the pandemonium. Nanny and the young man from the New York State Asylum for Idiots stood beside them.

Lady Hamilton's carriage forced its way through the throng making its way up from the village. It stopped beside the carriage Crazy Louie had thought contained two lovers enjoying a guilty tryst. Geoffrey Hunter stepped out and looked toward the mansion's front door. He turned to say something to the other passengers.

Myra smiled. She looked forward to telling them they were too late.

CHAPTER 33

The fire scene was barely organized chaos. Volunteers arrived on foot and horseback, shrugging into rubber coats and protective headgear as they ran toward the engine spewing water onto the flames. Some of the crowd along the roadside climbed over the wrought-iron fencing onto the Adderly property. A few children danced and capered in the light of the flames until parents cuffed their ears and dragged them to safety.

It very soon became apparent that the fire was confined to the metal-and-glass greenhouse slowly collapsing in the flames. Except for the Adderly mansion, there were no structures nearby and the trees were saturated with early-evening mist from the falls. The firefighters in their rubber coats relaxed their efforts and began mingling with the spectators. No fatalities and no damage except to the destroyed greenhouse. The fire would burn itself out.

The villagers began to lose interest, slowly detaching themselves from the scene to return home to their interrupted dinners.

Lucas wrenched open the carriage door. "Why are you here?"

he asked the veiled figure inside. "Are you all right?" he added in a softer voice.

"We'd gone out for some air," Grace said. "I saw a carriage go by and recognized Myra. There was a flash of red hair and I knew the girl sitting beside her had to be Rowan so I told the driver to follow them. I couldn't help myself. I had to catch a glimpse of her."

"I promised I would take you to the lawyer's offices so you could see Rowan go in. You said that would be enough, that was all you wanted." Lucas fought to keep control of the fear roiling in the pit of his stomach. He didn't want to alarm the woman who was still his wife, but he desperately needed to assure himself that the burning greenhouse had nothing to do with their daughter. He didn't know why Myra had as good as abducted Rowan from Lady Hamilton's house, but at least he could assume she was safe inside the mansion.

"You don't always . . . keep your word."

One hand crept from Grace's lap to the large needlepoint bag on the seat beside her.

"Not too much," Lucas cautioned, recognizing the elaborate label on the brown bottle she raised to her lips.

Dr. James's Elixir and Brain Restoration Tonic soothed Grace's nerves and eased the bouts of convulsive hiccupping that made it hard for her to breathe. She was sure there was opium in the popular patent medicine, but she didn't care. It worked. Most of the time.

"I'm sorry, Lucas," she apologized. "I couldn't wait any longer."

"You wanted everyone to believe you were dead," he reminded her. "This was taking a chance." He'd been reluctant to bring Grace with him from San Francisco, but she'd begged and pleaded. *Just this once.* She so seldom asked for anything other than to be left alone.

Better dead than disfigured. She had made him swear he would never betray her.

"What if someone had seen you? Recognized you?"

"It's been years," Grace said.

"You were the most famous woman in Niagara. No one who heard you sing would forget you."

"I never lifted the veil," Grace said. She had sewn tiny lead beads into its hem. Not even a strong wind could blow it upward and away from her face. Her eyes drifted from Lucas to the man standing beside him. She nodded politely, as though someone had just introduced them.

"Lucas has told us what happened. You've nothing to fear from me or from my partner," Geoffrey said, "May I ask how long you've been sitting here?"

"Well over an hour," Grace said.

Leila nodded agreement.

"Did you see her?" Lucas asked. "Did you see our daughter arrive with her grandmother and go into the house?" His voice had gentled, but though he leaned closer to the woman in the veil, he did not reach out or touch her.

Grace hesitated. "I saw her twice. Once when she and Myra walked to the greenhouse, then again just a few minutes later. By herself. She ran out of the greenhouse and into the woods just before the fire took hold."

"You're sure the figure you saw was your daughter?" Geoffrey kept his voice low and reassuring, trying to gauge the emotional well-being of the woman who had chosen the pretense of death over ordinary life. He had felt Lucas stiffen beside him and knew it was all Rowan's father could do not to set off immediately for the tree line. They needed more information.

"Tell us everything you saw. Think your way through it slowly. Don't leave anything out," Geoffrey urged, glancing over his shoulder to where Prudence was climbing out of Lady Hamilton's carriage. She caught his eye and nodded.

"Rowan and Myra came out of the house together," Grace began. Her voice from behind the veil sounded raspy, as though her throat was sore. "They walked to the greenhouse. Someone else was already there. I'm sure of it. A man, to judge by the shadows cast by the lantern light. A gardener? Myra stayed inside for a few minutes, then went back to the house. When I looked at the greenhouse again, I didn't see Rowan's shadow on the wall. Just the gardener's. I don't know how much time passed. Then suddenly Rowan burst out of the far door and ran into the woods."

"That was all?" Lucas's hands had gripped the carriage door so tightly, the knuckles turned white. Now he relaxed his grip.

"The man went after her," Leila said. "He had been standing outside the greenhouse for a while before the fire broke out, smoking something and drinking from a flask. We could smell the tobacco. I told Grace he'd find Rowan in the woods and bring her back if she'd gotten lost."

"You're sure he was a gardener?" Geoffrey asked.

"Who else could it be?" Leila asked.

"She can't have gone far," Lucas said, removing the side lanterns from Lady Hamilton's carriage, handing one to Geoffrey. "There hasn't been time."

"If she's frightened, she may have run deeper into the woods than she intended." Prudence had heard nearly all the conversation, enough to believe Rowan was still in danger and that Geoffrey and Lucas intended to set off after her. She motioned Geoffrey aside for a moment while Lucas instructed his wife's driver to take Grace and her companion back to the guest house she never should have left. "I'll take care of things here. Sheriff Bryant has arrived. And Myra needs to be questioned."

"Be careful," Geoffrey cautioned.

"I will," Prudence promised.

"Keep an eye out for Amos."

"He'll find me."

"Send him to Daniel's cabin. He and Jean-Baptiste can start searching for Rowan from that end in case that's the direction she's taken."

Prudence laid a hand on Geoffrey's arm. "I don't like that there was someone else in the greenhouse."

"Neither do I."

"Myra had to have known he was there."

"What are the odds he wasn't a gardener?"

"I thought when Carter Jayden was out of the picture there wouldn't be any more attempts on Rowan's life."

"Don't push Myra too far when you question her."

"Would she do away with her own granddaughter?" Prudence had encountered wickedness in many incarnations, but this kind of murder was beyond ordinary evil. "I don't think there's a special word for the crime we're talking about."

"There isn't," Geoffrey said. "Or if there is, I haven't come across it."

They stood close to one another for a few more moments, not speaking, the touch of Prudence's hand on Geoffrey's arm as tight a bond between them as they'd ever managed. They only broke apart when Lucas stepped back from the carriage.

"Are you ready?" he called to Geoffrey.

Prudence watched the bobbing lanterns cross the lawn, thinking they looked for all the world like two errant sparks that had escaped an inferno.

As soon as Lucas was out of sight, Grace countermanded his order to return to the guest house, determined to stay until Rowan emerged from where Grace devoutly hoped she was hiding. It hadn't escaped her notice that Mr. Hunter did not seem to share Leila's belief that the man chasing after her daughter was a gardener intent on bringing her back safely.

Lady Hamilton resisted the idea that she remain with Grace and Leila while Prudence confronted Myra.

"I've known Myra for years, which means I've also figured

out how to get under her defenses. We don't like one another, but we've fought enough skirmishes for me to know I can best her when something is really important."

"That's the point," Prudence explained. "Her defenses will be up before you have a chance to ask the first question. I'm a relatively unknown quantity. She's suspicious of me and displeased by her daughter's friendliness, but she hasn't had years of practice in how to handle me. I can throw her off balance."

Torn between wanting to do battle with a longtime adversary and the opportunity to satisfy her curiosity about Grace Malone, Lady Hamilton hesitated and then gave in. She snapped an order at her driver to sit tight, then climbed into the other carriage, seating herself across from Grace and her nurse. The silence inside was profound.

None of the remaining spectators noticed the determined woman making her way toward the mansion's open door where a bevy of servants clustered at the foot of the steps.

When she finally broke free of the dwindling crowd, Prudence looked up to discover that Myra no longer stood as if on guard in the entryway to her home.

The butler, the housekeeper, and the group of servants clustered around them had no idea where she'd gone.

"Mrs. Adderly was right there a moment ago," the butler said, turning to stare at the empty spot where his employer had been standing. "I'm sure she was."

"Perhaps she went to check on Mrs. Yates," the housekeeper suggested.

"Is something wrong with her?" Prudence asked. She looked up to see Arthur and Edward staring at the remains of the fire from a nursery window, flanked by the adults who were in charge of them. Their mother was nowhere to be seen.

"Mrs. Yates had a spell. After Mr. Adderly passed on." The housekeeper wasn't about to tell this recent visitor that too much laudanum had rendered Mrs. Adderly's daughter unconscious for most of the afternoon. "I believe she's still lying down."

"I'll go up," Prudence said, advancing through the front door before anyone thought to stop her. A flustered hall boy pointed in the direction of the family bedrooms, but when asked if Mrs. Adderly had come inside, shook his head and stammered that he didn't know.

As she climbed the staircase to the second floor, the outside noises fell away. Reflections of the fire flickered on some of the windowpanes, but many of the drapes had been drawn. The second-floor corridor was dim and silent. Daphne's suite was the second on the left, according to the hall boy.

The door was closed. And locked.

Prudence knocked. Waited. Knocked again. Removed the small wallet of picks from her reticule. She was almost as fast at breaking a lock as Geoffrey.

The gaslights had been dimmed and the fire in the grate was little more than live coals. Prudence could make out the figure of a woman lying on her side in the four-poster bed, but not much else. She turned up the gas, then stirred the coals and laid on more wood for warmth. October evenings in Niagara very swiftly grew dark and cold.

She shook Daphne's shoulder gently as she called her name. "Wake up, Daphne, wake up."

A pitcher and a glass stood on the nightstand. Prudence wet a handkerchief and squeezed drops of water over Daphne's face.

The sleeping woman pawed the air. Prudence held both hands in her own, murmuring reassuring words as Daphne swam out of the laudanum fog that had trapped her in unconsciousness.

"It's me, Daphne. Prudence. I need you to wake up. You have to tell me what happened here this afternoon." This time Prudence laid the damp handkerchief across Daphne's forehead, then wiped the crustiness of sleep from her eyes. She helped Daphne sit up, held out water to drink, propped her against a pile of pillows.

"Rowan. Where is Rowan?" Daphne struggled to get off the bed, then fell back as dizziness overwhelmed her. She pressed the wet handkerchief against her mouth and closed her eyes.

"Stay as still as you can," Prudence urged. "The nausea will pass." She'd almost forgotten how confused and sick the drug could make its unwary victim.

Daphne leaned against the pillows without moving. Except for her resolute swallowing and deep, measured breaths, she might have been asleep again. When her eyes opened and focused on the woman seated on the bed beside her, Prudence knew the worst had passed.

"How did you find me?"

"The greenhouse is burning. The fire engine is here, as well as half the population of Niagara. Rowan is safe, we think. But Myra has disappeared." A squeeze of the hands to bolster Daphne's courage. "All we know is that Myra took Rowan from Lady Hamilton's house, where we thought she was safely hidden."

"She brought her here," Daphne confirmed, continuing to pat her eyes and mouth with the damp handkerchief. "I saw them from the window, and then the next thing I knew I was in my bed and Rowan was bending over me. Nanny had slipped laudanum into my tea and Father's nurse gave me another dose. They meant well, but . . ."

"I know," Prudence said. "No matter how hard you fight against it, you rarely win."

"I warned Rowan. I told her to get out of the house, but then my mother came into the room. She held me down. I tried not to swallow, but she was pinching my nose and I couldn't breathe." Daphne pushed herself off the pillows, then managed to get to her feet, Prudence holding her steady as she took the first steps to walk off the effects of the drug. "I have to tell you what I found." She choked on the words.

"As much as you can manage," Prudence said. She tried to keep impatience from her voice, but time was running out. If Myra had gone in search of Rowan, there was no telling where she would take the girl if she caught her before Geoffrey and Lucas tracked her down.

"I found poisons in a locked cabinet in Mother's stillroom," Daphne said. "Dr. Elliott told the nurse my father's heart stopped. So did my husband's. After the boys were born and it became obvious there was something very wrong with them." That was as far as she could force herself to go, short of an accusation, but close to an inference. "There's more. We found a copy of the trust document where Lucas had hidden it in the nursery. If we are all dead—my father, Rowan, and I—before the trust goes into effect, my mother inherits and controls everything. If even one of us is alive, she gets an allowance to be administered by the lawyers." Daphne's eyes pleaded for understanding. It wasn't in her to say the words aloud that would accuse her mother of murder.

"Your mother is not a woman to surrender whatever power she wields," Prudence said, leading Daphne back to the bed. "The housekeeper will send up your maid, but I can't stay."

"You have to get to Rowan before my mother does." Tears gathered in Daphne's eyes, began to roll down her cheeks.

"I will," Prudence said. "I promise."

"Leila and I will be fine by ourselves," Grace said. "Miss MacKenzie is right, Lady Hamilton. Someone has to sit with Daphne."

Prudence had brought an Adderly servant to escort Lady Hamilton back to the house.

"I don't like leaving you alone." What she really meant was that there hadn't been time to pry more than a few sentences out of Lucas Adderly's wife, certainly not the entire story of her years hiding from a world she felt would deride her for the disfigurement of smallpox. Lady Hamilton had heard Lucas's side of the tale, but she suspected there was much more to it than he had divulged.

"I've been alone nearly all my life."

"That was your choice," Lady Hamilton said.

"The driver knows the way back to the guesthouse," Grace said, ignoring the remark. She opened the carriage door and gestured Lady Hamilton out.

Lady Hamilton huffed off toward the Adderly mansion, her back rigid and the heels of her shoes digging into the ground.

"What do I need to do?" Amos Lang stepped out of the dark. He tipped his hat to Prudence and then to the shadows in the carriage that began slowly moving away.

"Thank goodness you're here," Prudence said. "Geoffrey wants you to alert Jean-Baptiste that Miss Rowan may be trying to make her way through the woods to Daniel's cabin."

"He's afraid she's lost?"

"It's more complicated than that," Prudence said. She filled him in on the sudden reappearance of Lucas Adderly, then explained what Grace had told them and what she'd learned from Daphne.

"What can you tell me about the man in the greenhouse?" he asked.

Prudence repeated Grace's description. "She saw him smoking a cheroot and drinking from a flask before the fire broke out. He ran into the woods when it looked like the greenhouse would collapse. That was after Miss Rowan escaped," she finished.

"He wasn't a gardener," Amos said. "No gardener would risk losing his job by tipping a flask where anyone looking out a window could see him."

"Geoffrey and I agree." Prudence turned to watch Grace's carriage make its way through the spectators still crowding the road. "But we don't know who he is yet."

"I'd better get going," Amos said. "It's cold and dangerous out in those woods. Jean-Baptiste and the men he has guarding Daniel need to be put to work as soon as I can get to them."

The words were hardly out of his mouth before he was gone, leaving not even a whiff of bayberry rum or Macassar oil behind.

She had done what Geoffrey asked her to do—sent Amos to warn Jean-Baptiste that Rowan was wandering the forest and needed to be found.

Daphne had told her story and was being looked after by Lady Hamilton. Grace was on her way back to the seclusion of the guesthouse where Lucas had hidden her.

Myra had disappeared. It was up to Prudence to find her.

Irresolute and increasingly unsettled by a feeling that something important she ought to remember was dancing just beyond her mental grasp, Prudence stared at what remained of the fire. The silhouettes of the firemen and onlookers looked like black paper cutouts. Arms stretched to point toward where another portion of the greenhouse had caved in on itself, hats waved away heat and sparks, dippers poured water into thirsty mouths and over children who scampered too close to the coals. Here and there a man drank from a flask.

Drank from a flask.

She'd seen it before, that twist of the wrist and backward toss of the head. Recently. Someone who apparently emptied his flask more than once during the working day. Smacked his lips. Carried a faint scent of whiskey with him wherever he went. She'd even remarked on it to Geoffrey.

How can he hope to survive the falls if he goes over with a bellyful of whiskey?

Crazy Louie!

Crazy Louie who was never without a flask or a bottle, who poured a tot of liquor for good luck over every barrel he sent into the water.

As she ran, the words thundered in her head.

Crazy Louie! Crazy Louie!

Lady Hamilton's coachman had climbed down from his perch to check the blinders that kept the horses from being spooked by the flickering light. Then he stepped away, not too far, to get a better look at the plumes of smoke billowing into the evening sky.

He sprinted as soon as he heard hoofbeats and the creak of turning wheels, but it was already too late.

Hair flying as she picked up speed, shoulders hunched over the reins, boots firmly planted on the footrest, Prudence MacKenzie drove her Ladyship's brougham hell-bent for leather toward Niagara.

CHAPTER 34

Rowan remembered that the clearing in which Daniel's cabin sat was somewhere alongside the river, so when she stopped to catch her breath, she listened for the sound of rushing water. She peered through the deepening dusk but all she saw was far-off glimmers of light from Niagara's hotels. She'd crawled, stumbled, and then bolted out of the greenhouse like an animal escaping from a cage. No plan except to run as far and as fast as she could.

She bent over to quiet the gasps she was afraid would give her away in the stillness. He'd come after her, the man whose face she hadn't clearly seen, but whose intent was obvious. She'd glanced back just before reaching the shelter of the forest and spotted his outline against the flames, arms pumping as he ran toward her, teeth gleaming in his open mouth. A moment only, when their eyes met, and then she'd whirled around and plunged into the woods.

The sounds of the fire had faded with the light of the flames. Rowan didn't know where she was, but if she couldn't see in the gathering darkness, neither could her pursuer. She slid down the trunk of a large tree, cradling herself in a nest formed by its roots, scooping leaves around her so she would blend into the forest floor. All she had to do was control her breathing, stay quiet, remain motionless.

Until morning. Until Miss MacKenzie and Mr. Hunter realized she was missing and set out to find her. She fingered the small gold Celtic cross that had once hung around her mother's neck. Rowan had no memory of Grace Malone, but her father had shown her a photograph before he'd disappeared. It was like looking into a mirror.

She pressed the cross between two fingers and pretended she wasn't lost and alone.

Before he'd become obsessed with barreling over the falls, Crazy Louie had been a scrub farmer, eking out a precarious living on a few inherited acres, his chief source of meat the rabbits he snared, the deer he hunted, and the occasional wild turkey he shot. He was as at home in the woods around Niagara as in the workshop where he built his barrels and dreamed his dreams. The girl he was chasing had no chance of eluding him. It was only a question of time before she gave up and sat down to rest. Then he'd have her.

The faintest of early moonlight broke through the clouds, but it was enough to catch the flash of white hands moving through a heap of fallen leaves. She'd caught her breath and made herself go silent, but she hadn't reckoned with the rustle of the dry autumn foliage. Louie waited for the clouds to part again; he had to be sure of exactly where she was. If she skittered out from under him and took off running, he might not have a second chance.

The knife with which he could have slit her throat lay somewhere between where he crouched and the burning greenhouse, as did the flask he'd emptied. A fondness for the drink had led him into uncertain situations in the past, but he'd always bulled his way out of them. No reason to think he couldn't do it again. He still carried the rope he'd grabbed when he sprinted away from the Adderly greenhouse.

He launched himself through the air as soon as a ray of light slid over the mound of leaves under which the girl had tried to hide herself. When Louie pounced, it was with the full force of his weight and the added heaviness of the airborne assault. He heard and felt the breath knocked out of Myra's granddaughter as he pulled at her wrists, pinning them to the ground above her head. With his free hand he shoved a filthy rag into her mouth. He wedged a knee between her legs, then hit her so hard across the face that her head lolled to one side, and he knew she'd lost consciousness.

Quickly, before she came to, he wound the rope around her body, securing her arms against her sides. It wasn't a long piece, but it did the job. He left her legs free so he wouldn't have to carry her the mile or so to his workshop. Pleased with his handiwork, he stood Rowan against a tree trunk, holding her there as she opened her eyes. The fear he read in them in was almost as exciting as the prospect of propelling himself over the falls.

Myra wouldn't pay him unless he supplied proof the girl was dead. He slid a thick finger under the gold chain she wore and tugged until it broke against her neck. In his hand lay a small gold filigree Celtic cross. He'd never seen anything as fine. For sure and certain Myra would recognize it. When he looked into Rowan's eyes again, they'd changed. She'd changed. The fear was still there, but there were flashes of as hard an anger as he'd only ever seen in the fight ring. If Rowan had been a man, he might have grown wary. But she was just a girl.

He'd kill her, but only after he'd made her pay. She'd very nearly ruined the job he'd promised to do for Myra. Deprived him of the money he would have earned. Wreaked havoc on the dream of a lifetime.

Louie jerked Rowan onto the narrow track leading to the

bluff where his workshop stood. "Don't fight me," he hissed. "You'll only make it worse."

He amused himself on the walk by imagining what he would do to the girl stumbling before him. Should he remove the rag so he could hear her scream? Regretfully, he decided against it. Sound carried in the night, and sound above water was magnified. He'd have to settle for silent screaming.

As they grew closer to the workshop, the moonlight grew uncertain and the night darker. Clouds were piling up above them, thunder rumbled in the distance, and forks of faraway lightning cracked in the hills.

A storm was brewing.

He chose a barrel he knew would split open as soon as it struck the water, one of several he'd constructed early on, when he was new at the business. Instead of Horseshoe Falls, where he intended to make his own attempt, he'd send the girl over American Falls where no one and nothing could survive the huge boulders littering its base. The gold chain and its filigree Celtic cross would be left at the spot where it would be assumed Rowan had made her despairing leap, clearly visible but wedged under a rock.

Louie hummed to himself as he moved around the workshop, rolling out the barrel, locating the hammer and nails he'd use to secure the head, running through the plan over and over again to make sure he'd gotten everything right. He couldn't afford to make a mistake this late in the game.

When Myra strode through the doorway, riding crop in hand, Crazy Louie nearly threw the hammer in her direction, catching himself at the last moment.

"I th-thought you were someone else," he stammered, letting his arm go slack.

"Who were you expecting?" she snapped.

"Bums sometimes come looking for a place to sleep." It was the only thing he could think of.

"What went wrong at the greenhouse?" Myra angled the riding crop at something rolled in a blanket on the ground. "I assume that's her?"

"The chloroform you gave me wasn't strong enough," Louie said. *Always shift the blame to someone else.*

"There was nothing wrong with it," Myra said. "If it didn't knock her out it was because you didn't use enough." She pointed at the rolled blanket again. "I don't like repeating myself. Is that her?"

Louie nodded. He nudged Rowan with one booted foot and pulled back the edge of the blanket so Myra could see for herself. The girl's face was bruised and dirty, the rag lodged in her mouth. She was awake, hazel eyes blazing as she looked from Louie to her grandmother.

"It has to be a believable accident," Myra said, flipping the blanket over Rowan's face.

"Suicide," Louie corrected. He held out the gold chain and cross. "They'll find this where she went in."

"You don't need a barrel for that," Myra informed him.

"It'll break open and the pieces of wood will float downstream. It won't leave any traces."

"I said you don't need a barrel."

"If the body's found, there can't be a rope or a gag," he argued. "It's too dangerous to carry her out far enough into the river to be sure she goes over the falls. If she's conscious she'll fight me, and if she's out cold, she'll be too heavy to manage. I can roll the barrel into the water in the direction I want it to take. It floats," he explained.

Myra stared at him. In her mind's eye she could see the scene he'd described, and she realized he was right. The best solution to her problem would be both Louie and the girl losing their footing and tumbling over the falls, but Louie was too canny to let that happen. He knew the dangers of the falls better than anyone else in Niagara. "When?" she asked.

"Now. While the whole town is distracted by the fire."

"You'll have to go across the bridge."

"Not this time. I'm sending her over American Falls. From this side."

"That's impossible."

"I know a trail that leads to a spot where even if someone were looking up at the falls from below, they wouldn't see what we were doing."

"We? What am I paying you for?"

"I can't manage this alone. Together or not at all," Crazy Louie said. He didn't know where he'd suddenly found the courage to stand up to Myra Adderly, but his veins were singing with the thrill of it.

Prudence knew there had to be a faster way to Crazy Louie's workshop than down the main road to Niagara, but she didn't dare take any of the narrow dirt side tracks. She had a good memory for places, but all she had to go on tonight was what Geoffrey had told her. She thought she could find it by what he'd described, but only if she kept to the streets he'd named. She was driving the brougham as fast as she dared. If one of the wheels hit a rock and the vehicle rolled over, she'd likely be thrown from her perch and badly injured. Geoffrey would be furious. She'd promised him she'd be careful.

A slow-moving carriage just ahead of her was blocking the road, but there was enough room to edge by if Prudence reined in the horses and edged past cautiously. Perhaps the coachman would veer to the right as he heard her approach.

Eyes fixed ahead instead of on the ditch into which she didn't dare slide, Prudence whistled and clucked her two-horse team around the carriage that pulled to a halt to let her by. She was vaguely aware of a passenger peering out the window and the angry expression on the driver's face, but she couldn't stop for even a moment. As soon as her rear carriage wheels were once more in the center of the road, she whipped up her team and sped on.

*   *   *

"Follow that carriage," Grace said to her hired coachman. "I'll double what you're being paid if you don't lose it."

The road leading to the factories lining the Niagara River was wide enough for two wagons to pass one another, but unpaved and heavily rutted. Prudence reined in the horses pulling the brougham, slowing them to a walk. The buildings she passed were dark, but a few boasted gaslights burning at their entrances. She tried to remember how far after the turnoff Geoffrey had said Crazy Louie's workshop was located. Had he mentioned the names of any of the other factories along the road? It hadn't seemed important at the time; she hadn't paid much attention.

The last thing she wanted was to come upon the workshop unexpectedly. She guided the team into a dark yard and hauled on the carriage's brake until she was sure it was holding. She'd lost her hat somewhere along the main road and been in such a hurry to set off after Crazy Louie that she hadn't put on her coat or a pair of gloves. Her hands were sore and blistered from handling the reins the way she had, and she felt the night cold settle in around her as she started walking. She could hear the distant roar of the falls, but no sounds that would indicate anyone was still working in any of the factories.

So be it.

Prudence checked the Remington Model 95 over-under double-barreled derringer in its small holster sewn inside her boot. The gun and the holster had been gifts from Geoffrey, who also insisted she carry a smaller single-barrel derringer in her reticule. Easily concealed, they were only deadly at close range.

There was a light off in the distance. Moving along the side of the road, Prudence approached cautiously. If it was Louie's workshop, she couldn't risk being heard or seen.

There wouldn't be any backup.

No one knew where she'd gone.

Careful to stay clear of the lantern light spilling out of Crazy Louie's workshop, Prudence circled around until she could approach from the opposite direction. A horse and cart stood in the yard, and in the bed of the cart she saw a single barrel, anchored to the sides with rope so it wouldn't roll.

She listened but heard nothing from within. She crept closer to the door, pressing her back to the side of the building. She could just make out Louie seated on a sawed-off piece of tree trunk. He was smoking a cheroot. Rowan was nowhere in sight.

So perhaps he hadn't caught up with her? Perhaps she'd made it through the forest to Daniel's cabin after all. And Prudence had gone tearing through the countryside on a wild-goose chase.

She backed away from the door, edging her way toward the road and safety. But as she passed the cart with the barrel in its bed, she heard noises that stopped her cold. The sound of feet thumping against wood, of a body rolling from side to side, and strangled cries from deep in a female throat. She glanced behind her. The doorway stood empty.

Prudence hoisted herself onto the cart and crawled to the barrel. She curled her fingers into a fist and knocked softly. Twice, so whoever was inside would know it was a signal. The thumping stopped.

Pressing her mouth to what felt like a knothole, Prudence called softly, "Rowan. It's Prudence. Thump once if it's you."

And it was. She'd imagined all sorts of things Louie might demand for Rowan's release, but she hadn't thought he would be cruel enough to send her over the falls to certain death.

And then everything went black.

CHAPTER 35

Prudence regained consciousness in a dark, confined space, unable to move her arms or call out for help. Her head ached, a filthy rag had been stuffed in her mouth, and in the blackness surrounding her she couldn't tell if the blow that had knocked her out had also blinded her. It was a terrifying thought. *Breathe. Breathe.* She could hear Geoffrey's voice coaching her. *You have to remain in control no matter the circumstance. Breathe. Breathe.*

As she fought back the initial panic, Prudence gradually became aware of a rocking motion. A picture flashed through her brain—the cart parked outside Crazy Louie's workshop, the barrel lying in its bed, roped to the sides. Suddenly she knew where she was and that she wasn't alone. She'd found Rowan, but now there were two barrels in the wagon. A single horse pulled the vehicle along an unpaved road—she heard the clop of its hooves—which could only mean that Louie was driving it to the falls.

Figure out what your enemy will do. Plan your counterattack. Then you'll know the chances you'll have to take to defeat him.

She didn't think Louie would toss the barrels into the water without untying the ropes around the bodies and pulling the rags out of their mouths. Not if he planned to make the deaths look like accidents. Or suicide.

If she was going to chance a break for freedom, Prudence knew it would have to be in that split second between being untied and shoved back into the barrel. Once the lid was nailed on, there would be no hope of getting away. She concentrated on contracting and loosening the muscles in her arms, hands, and legs, fighting numbness and the prickly sensation of pins and needles. The ropes were tight, but her clothing prevented them from rubbing her raw. The palms of her hands throbbed, but she'd have to ignore the blisters and the blood.

Two people were talking. One male—Crazy Louie. One female—Myra? Who else could it be? Prudence couldn't make out what they were saying, but from the sound of their voices, they were arguing. Myra seemed to be berating Louie. He, in turn, swung from a cajoling whine to a sudden, staccato burst of self-defense. What was it Amos had said about him? That he was a hard one to figure out, and not to be underestimated because he seldom let on what he was thinking. Like so many men, he drank too much.

Figuring out whatever it was they were pitching into each other about might tell her what they planned to do when the cart arrived at the spot Louie had picked to launch the barrels. Prudence's greatest fear was that a chloroform-soaked rag would be slapped over her nose and mouth before the ropes were cut from her body. Aside from holding her breath for as long as she could, there was no way she could fight off breathing in the fumes. Not if she was wrapped up like an Egyptian mummy.

She wondered who had heard her approach the workshop and which of the two conspirators had come up with the idea of having Louie sit on a log and smoke a cheroot. The plan had worked. She'd let down her guard. Her over-under derringer was still in its boot holster, but there was no way to tell if the bullets had been removed.

Something hard and lumpy was wedged against her side, but she'd pressed her single-shot derringer into Daphne's hand before leaving the bedroom. The lockpicks! The sharply pointed steel picks she'd used a few hours ago to open Daphne's bedroom door. They were inside the reticule whose strings she'd fastened tightly around her wrist when she picked up the reins to the Hamilton brougham. Her fingers could feel the pointed outlines through the silk of the reticule. They'd fallen out of the case she must not have shut securely. How much time did she have?

Don't think about time. Concentrate on working the point of one of the picks through the silk. Let it slide down her hand to where two fingers and a thumb could grasp and hold it. Lodge the point under a strand of the rope and saw for all she was worth.

Careful! Don't let go of the pick. Don't let your mind wander. Picture the rope and the pick, the fibers giving way and snapping. One by one. Ignore the pain. Don't think about the blood every time the sharp metal pierces skin instead of rope.

Don't faint. Don't stop. Faster. But don't drop the pick!

"The heads aren't nailed shut," Louie explained. "I can pry them open with the claw of the hammer."

"Then what?" Myra demanded.

"Pull them out by the feet, untie the ropes, take the rags out of their mouths, shove them back in again, nail down the heads, and we're done."

"They'll fight you."

"I'll have a hammer in my hand."

"If I'd known you'd bungled things so badly, I would have brought more chloroform."

"We don't need it," Louie promised. "They'll be dazed from

being bounced around inside the barrels and they won't be able to move their arms. I tied those ropes tight."

"We take them out one at a time."

"Agreed. But they go over the falls together." Louie's voice was shrill with barely suppressed excitement. He'd never launched two barrels at once.

"You should have strangled her while you had the chance," Myra complained.

"Your granddaughter?"

"She's no granddaughter of mine."

"You said it had to look like an accident."

"And you just promised me back at the workshop that the body would be unrecognizable if it was ever found."

"You can't predict what the falls will do. The last thing either of us could want is signs of strangulation around the girl's neck."

"What's the point of going to all this trouble if you can't be certain?" Myra raged.

"We're here," Louie said, cutting her off and reining in the horse.

The track he'd been following was too narrow to be called a road. At times it ran so close to the edge of the bluff that one false step could have sent them tumbling into the rocky river below. It opened unexpectedly into a small clearing so close to American Falls that they had to shout over the roar of the water. There was barely enough space to turn the cart around.

Lightning knifed through the sky and a rumble of thunder set the horse to dancing in its traces. Louie grabbed a burlap sack from beneath the driver's bench, handing the reins to Myra as he leaped down and stretched it over the animal's head. His heart was racing, and his blood seemed to be surging through his veins. He loved storms, enthralled by what high winds and heavy rains did to the falls. It was as if the world were wrenching itself apart, spewing waterspouts upward to crash into the cascades pouring down over the cliffs. More than anything else he wanted to leap into the raging torrent and feel himself borne downstream in currents that swirled him safely around the rocks that tore everything and everyone else to shreds. It was a wild, crazy dream that he was confident would someday come true.

But not yet. Not tonight.

Myra tied the reins to a small pine, hobbled the horse's front legs, then joined Louie at the rear of the cart. Shouting directions to her, he lowered the tailgate and propped a narrow ramp against the back of the wagon, then watched as she untied the ropes securing the barrels. He opened a wooden toolbox, took out a hammer, and crammed a fistful of nails into his pocket.

"All right," he yelled. "Go ahead. But be careful. Those things can get away from you."

Myra nodded, then nudged one of the barrels with her foot. The cart was on enough of a slant to start it rolling in Louie's direction. He leaped up onto the wagon just as the barrel reached the top of the ramp, pushing and shoving until he had it positioned the way he wanted it.

The rolling thunder had quieted, and most of the lightning strikes moved off into the distance. It had begun to rain, but not hard yet. They had time before the leaf-strewn ground beneath their feet grew slippery.

"Whichever one this is, she's out cold," Louie said, listening for the pounding of feet against staves or cries of terror and despair. He gave the barrel a calculated shove, then stood back as it slid down the ramp onto the ground. "Too fast," he muttered as it rolled and the head popped off. If this had been an ordinary trial run, he would have had Paddy Morgan at the bottom to steady it.

A bolt of lightning lit up the sky and hit the ground close by. The horse whinnied inside its burlap sack, stomping its hoofs, pulling against the reins securing it to the tree. The cart lurched forward, throwing Louie off balance, sending him sprawling against the remaining barrel. Myra grabbed for the side of the wagon to steady herself and missed. Her outthrust legs sent the second barrel lurching down the ramp, hitting the ground and the first barrel with a hard crack of splintering wood.

The double-shot derringer rolled out, the picks, and then the rope that was no longer securely wrapped around a helpless Prudence MacKenzie. She was on her feet in seconds, tugging and pulling Rowan from the barrel that had split open and rolled perilously close to the falls. Louie scrabbled for the hammer that had fallen from his hand while Myra crawled and slid from the cart that had lurched to one side. She'd spied the derringer and was making a leap for it, Louie close behind her, hammer upraised to strike.

Prudence clawed at Rowan's ropes and pulled the girl away from the precipice toward the woods, steadying her when she stumbled, searching for a stout branch with which to fight off whoever reached them first. The rain suddenly came down in windy gusts, turning the leaf littered ground slick and hazardous.

Prudence and Rowan were no more than a few feet into the trees when a black-clad figure surged toward them, screaming through the thunder and the torrential cloudburst.

Grace Malone charged past her helpless daughter and into Crazy Louie's outstretched arms, wresting the hammer from him as he staggered backward, tripping over his own feet, struggling to keep his balance. Myra whirled, her sense of danger momentarily distracted from the two younger women she was sure were no match for her. Weaponless, the derringer still somewhere in the mud beneath her feet, she grabbed for the billowing black cloak, yanking with all her strength to pull the attacker off Crazy Louie.

The three of them were locked together in the pouring rain like figures lurching across the screen of a zoetrope. Barely visible in the darkness, black against the foaming white spray of the falls, they swayed clumsily back and forth, never releasing their holds on one another, pummeling and grunting like maddened fighters in the ring.

Prudence's fingers tore at the loosened ropes holding Rowan's arms against her sides until they fell free. "Rub some feeling back into them," she ordered. "I'm going after the gun." She thought she'd spied a glint of metal on the ground. She wasn't sure the barrel wouldn't be full of mud, rendering the derringer useless, but it was worth a try.

Rowan nodded and pulled the rag from her mouth, choking out a desperate question. "Who is that?"

"It doesn't matter," Prudence said, not quite believing it could be the veiled woman she'd last glimpsed as her carriage left the Adderly House grounds. "Whoever it is needs help. Stay here."

She darted out from the shelter of the trees and was immediately soaked by the storm. Her hair streamed down her face, the deluge soaked her skirts, and her boots became stuck in the mire. She fell to her knees and used her hands to grope for the gun she thought was somewhere within reach, barely able to see what she was doing.

"Prudence!" Rowan shrieked. "Prudence, they're going over!"

It was Grace who was forcing the way toward the edge of the cliff, toward the spot where the barrels were supposed to have gone in. She dragged Louie and Myra with her, never ceasing to fight them for a second, though neither of her assailants seemed aware of the direction she was taking them.

Prudence leaped to her feet, derringer clutched in one hand. She slogged her way through the mud sucking at her feet, desperate to tear Grace away from Louie and Myra. She didn't dare fire the gun for fear it would blow up in her fist, but the sight of it should put the odds in her favor. If she could get to them in time.

She felt a body brush against her and realized that Rowan had struggled through the rain to help. Hands outstretched, she was reaching for the black cloak billowing in the wind. A step ahead of Rowan, Prudence caught the hem of the cape and pulled on it as hard as she could. It came away in her fingers, sending her and Rowan tumbling back down into the mud. The wearer of the cloak had unfastened it, then clasped both hands around the arms of the pair now struggling to get away from her. Held them tight in a death grip.

Seconds before the rim of the precipice gave way beneath their feet, Grace Malone shook the veil from her face and looked triumphantly in her daughter's direction. Lightning lit up her features, but not the scarring. The brilliance of the flash smoothed out the smallpox pits; they disappeared into the raindrops coating her skin. For a few moments, Grace looked eerily beautiful. And young again.

Then they were gone.

CHAPTER 36

The storm that broke out the night Crazy Louie, Myra, and Grace went over the falls whipped through Niagara with pounding rain, winds that uprooted trees, and lightning that struck a church steeple. Roofs leaked, streets flooded, and debris choked the river until the force of raging water swept it downstream. When the sun broke through the remaining clouds the morning of the following day, tourists and Niagarans alike poured out of their hotels and homes to assess the damage. Only the falls looked exactly as they had before the downpour.

Sheriff Bryant sent a note to Prudence and Geoffrey in their suite at the Clifton House, then showed up in person an hour later. He was freshly shaved and wearing a clean uniform, but his haggard face and red-rimmed eyes testified to a sleepless night. He'd gotten the bare bones of what had happened from an exhausted and soaking wet Prudence, who had unhitched the horse from Louie's cart and ridden the animal back to Niagara. Leila had put a shaken and bewildered Rowan into Grace's hired coach and taken her to Adderly House where Daphne insisted they both remain.

"I'd like to go over the whole story again, Miss MacKenzie," Sheriff Bryant said. "If you're up to it."

With Geoffrey seated beside her, holding one of her hands in his, Prudence recounted every detail she could remember from the discovery that Myra had taken Rowan from Hamilton House until the terrible moment when Grace and her daughter's assailants had disappeared into the waters of American Falls.

Sheriff Bryant listened attentively, took notes from time to time, but did not interrupt her with questions or comments. Even with only a few hours of rest, Prudence was as good a witness to what she and Rowan had endured as any he'd heard testify in court.

"The bodies haven't been recovered," Sheriff Bryant told them. "Nobody who knows the falls expects to find them. That means that yours and Rowan's accounts are all we have to go on. The nurse can swear to having seen Grace go over the cliff, but that's all. She didn't see much of the struggle or the faces of the other two victims, and the storm destroyed any evidence we might have found."

"Has Louie's wagon been recovered?" Prudence asked.

"My men got it out of the mud, repaired a wheel, and drove it down to the village, but the barrels must have rolled into the falls. There wasn't any trace of them."

"Have you questioned Lucas Adderly?" Geoffrey asked. "About how Grace came to be in Niagara and what she meant to do here?" The woman had been believed dead for nearly eighteen years.

It was an abrupt change of subject, but by the look on the sheriff's face, not unexpected.

"I remember when he and Grace Malone eloped," Sheriff Bryant said. "Mrs. Adderly demanded that I hunt them down and bring them back. I don't think she ever forgave me for refusing. But as I told her at the time, they were adults who presumably knew their own minds. I informed Lucas this morning of his wife's death and how it came about, but for the rest of it, he's not talking."

"He was with me last night when we searched the woods for Rowan," Geoffrey said.

"He did tell me that much. And that the two of you ended up having to shelter in Daniel Johnson's cabin when the lightning got bad."

"We didn't leave until daylight."

"I'm not sure he has much to tell us that's immediately relevant to the situation," Sheriff Bryant said cautiously. "There's no reason to believe Lucas is implicated in what happened. I'll speak to him again if it's warranted, but I can't force him to submit to hard questioning."

"So case closed?" Prudence asked. In her opinion, it was far from ended. Too many questions remained to be answered.

Sheriff Bryant hesitated. "I think what we have here is two crimes masquerading as one. Martin Fallow, the records clerks, and Paddy Martin never had anything to do with the Adderlys."

"How do you figure that, Sheriff?" Geoffrey asked. He'd decided to reveal as little as possible of what his team had discovered. Josiah and Amos's methods teetered on the edge of irregularity, sometimes slipping into illegality. Best not to involve them.

"Fallow thought the surveyors had been bribed to alter some of the plats Lucas had purchased," Sheriff Bryant began. "That's what he told Daniel and what Daniel passed along to you. He was wrong. I think we'll learn that one or two of the surveyors *had* been paid to change boundary lines and file false documents, but it was for larger interests than young Miss Rowan's. The clerks had to be eliminated because they knew which papers were fraudulent. Where and when they'd been filed. Who fabricated them. Eventually they wouldn't have been able to resist blackmail or selling what they knew to the press. I wouldn't be surprised if one of them hadn't already been knee-deep in extortion. It's a dangerous game to play."

It had been a well-thought-out scheme. Nothing of what Geoffrey, Prudence, and Sheriff Bryant suspected could be proved.

"Niagara will be developed," Sheriff Bryant predicted. "There's no doubt of it. I've lived here all my life and I see the handwriting on the wall. Fortunes are going to be made by whoever can harness the power of the river and turn it into electricity. But turbines and generating plants have to be built on land, the closer to the water source the better. When big money sets out to grab property away from farmers and small landholders the safest thing to do is get out of the way. You should know that, Mr. Hunter, being an ex-Pink."

"We weren't always on the side of right," Geoffrey admitted.

"Paddy Morgan had outlived his usefulness," Sheriff Bryant continued. He could have said a lot more about the moguls who hired Pinkertons to keep their workers in line and break up strikes, but there wasn't any reason to bring up sore points neither he nor Geoffrey Hunter could do anything about. "He was close to not being able to last long enough in the ring to throw a fight in the right round. Paddy was drinking himself to death and doing too much talking along the way.

"You can't stop men from wanting to drink and gamble, Miss MacKenzie. Bare-knuckle boxing and Irish stand down are vicious and sometimes deadly sports. That's why it's better to let the rings be set up outside the town limits. The men who run the events and the betting are in it for profit, pure and sim-ple. They regulate the fights, in their own way."

"And you stay out of it?"

Sheriff Bryant shrugged. "I don't have the manpower to do anything else."

It was a difficult question to phrase, but Prudence had to find out. She had the feeling that Sheriff Bryant had been sidelining her and Geoffrey with the distraction of gambling and graft. "Two well-known citizens can't just disappear one night without people wanting to know what happened to them."

"It was a tragedy, Miss MacKenzie." Sheriff Bryant's head dipped briefly, like that of a mourner acknowledging grief and unfathomable loss. "Mrs. Adderly set off in search of her granddaughter when she realized that Miss Rowan had run out of the burning greenhouse into the woods. I think there's more than one of her staff who will remember that's what probably happened."

"She was afraid the girl would lose her way and inadvertently follow one of the pathways leading up to the falls," Geoffrey took up the story. "There aren't any guardrails in most places."

"We know Louie liked to watch the water whenever there was a storm," Sheriff Bryant continued. "Mrs. Adderly came across him on his way up to American Falls and persuaded him that Miss Rowan might be in danger. The cliff gave way beneath their feet. That explains why we found Louie's cart there."

"But not the horse?" Prudence asked.

"Nobody saw you ride it into town." Sheriff Bryant smiled. "It was a good thing I was at the station to catch and put him in our stable. The poor beast was terrified by the storm and managed to break out of his harness. Everybody knows horses don't like lightning."

"Why?" Prudence had to know why the sheriff would lie to cover up the truth.

"Daphne Yates doesn't deserve to be known as the daughter of a murderess," he said. "She's had a hard enough life as it is." The sheriff put away his notebook and reached for his hat. "Miss Rowan needs to be able to put last night behind her. She won't be able to do that if everyone in this town knows her grandmother tried to kill her."

"And Grace Malone?" Geoffrey stood to shake hands and show the sheriff out.

"Her story is as close to legend around here as recent history can get. I'd like to keep it that way."

"Truth has a way of getting out eventually," Prudence reminded him.

"Mrs. Yates knows how to keep a secret and so does Miss Rowan," Sheriff Bryant said, moving toward the door. "Lucas is a past master at it, and unless I miss my guess, he'll buy the nurse's silence. All my deputies know is that they recovered Crazy Louie's wagon during the worst storm we've had in years. It's over, Miss MacKenzie. You won't be reading about murder in Niagara in your New York City newspapers."

"I didn't feel we should leave without checking on Rowan one last time," Prudence said as the hired carriage rolled to a stop in the Adderly House driveway. "She's the reason we came to Niagara."

"I agree." Geoffrey held her hand a moment longer than necessary as he helped Prudence out.

Their bags were packed, train tickets purchased, a telegram sent so they'd be met at Grand Central Depot. Josiah and Amos had already left.

"I wonder if we'll see Lady Hamilton here," Prudence speculated. They'd telephoned, then driven by Hamilton House before crossing the suspension bridge to the American side. Neither her butler nor her lady's maid knew where she'd gone or when she'd be back.

Half an hour on the cabin porch with Daniel and Hero, then a walk back through the forest to where the carriage waited to take them to their last stop before catching the train. Tying up loose ends was how Geoffrey described what they did at the end of every case. By the time they arrived at their office near Trinity Church, Josiah would have already put away the files.

"Mrs. Yates and Mr. Adderly are in the large parlor," the butler informed them, leading the way to the room where Prudence had paid her first call on Myra. Where she'd watched, astonished, as Daphne burst into tears at the mention of her sons and their cousin.

Today Daphne met her with bright eyes and a warm hug. "I wish you didn't have to leave right away," she said, leading them toward where Lucas stood by the fireplace. "My brother and I have so much to thank you for." Her voice had a ring of confidence and genuine affection.

Tea was waiting for the ladies. Lucas poured whiskey for himself and Geoffrey.

"I was hoping we might find Lady Hamilton here," Prudence began, then stopped.

Lucas had frowned at the mention of Ernestine's name and Daphne's eyes dropped to her teacup.

"I'll write her a note as soon as I get back to the city," Prudence said quickly, glancing at Geoffrey for help breaking the awkward silence. Surely he'd noticed it? "Will Rowan be joining us?" She hadn't been at Daniel's, and the butler at Lady Hamilton's had been sure she wasn't with his mistress, wherever that was. Which left the Tuscarora beading ladies or Jean-Baptiste, whose name she was reluctant to mention while Lucas was still frowning.

"She's upstairs with the boys," Daphne said, the moment of discomfiture brushed aside as if it had never occurred. "Rowan is wonderful with them. It does my heart good to see how quickly they've responded to her. I've worried so much about their being lonely all these years with no friends or companions their own age. She should be down soon."

"We're a little early," Prudence apologized.

"That's all to the good," Lucas said, glancing at his sister. "Daphne and I have talked about it and we agree that I owe you some explanations. Rowan will have to know eventually, but not yet. And I won't put on paper what I'm going to tell you."

He looked toward the parlor door as if hoping his daughter would interrupt the confession he was about to make.

"No one blames you for what happened," Daphne said softly. "Just tell them."

"The deaths of Carter Jayden and his hireling were self-defense. That I can swear to."

Lucas emptied his whiskey glass, set it down, and began speaking.

"I was determined to prevent Jayden from marrying my sister, but the most I hoped for was to confront him and bribe him to leave Niagara. I was willing to part with whatever it took. I couldn't let anyone see me, so I waited until nearly midnight then went to his hotel. I saw him come out as I arrived. The rest you can guess at. As soon as I realized where he was going, I beat him to the house, but Narolly was already there. He drew on me from the top of the stairs as I came in the front door, but his shot went wild. He was already dead when Jayden arrived. It wasn't until the next morning that I realized I couldn't let Dr. Elliott remove the bullet from Pete Narolly's chest. Sheriff Bryant would have known right away that the same gun was used on both men."

"How did you manage it?" Geoffrey asked.

"Hardly anyone notices a scruffy laborer wearing dirty boots and rough clothes." Lucas grimaced. "I learned to disguise myself years ago in the mining camps. I didn't count on Jean-Baptiste and his trackers finding the body so quickly. Underestimating them was a mistake." He sat for a moment without speaking. "I like that young man, Jean-Baptiste. He's talented, well-educated, and principled. Society will never forgive that his mother was Tuscaroran, but I doubt he'll have much use for society."

"How did you learn what Jayden was up to?" Geoffrey was usually the one to steer a wandering conversation back to what was important, but this time it was Prudence.

"You're not the only ones who act on their suspicions, Miss MacKenzie. When Ernestine wrote me about the man my mother had chosen for Daphne to marry, I asked my associate to look into his background. What he learned convinced me that Daphne would be better off without him."

"Did you have him followed?" Geoffrey asked.

"No. That was another mistake I made. Jayden was a liar, a cheat, and a thief, but I didn't think he was also a murderer. If I'd imagined he would pay someone to poison Rowan and Daniel, I would have strangled him and his henchman with my bare hands before either of them got anywhere near the cabin. He signed his own death warrant when he drew on me."

"We think he wanted to get Rowan out of the way in case the trust worked to Daphne's disadvantage." Prudence said. "He was desperate for money."

"We met with Sheriff Bryant this morning," Geoffrey said. "He's convinced the other four deaths had nothing to do with your family. He's accepted the truth of what Miss MacKenzie told him happened at Crazy Louie's workshop and the falls, but the public will be told that your mother and Louie met tragic and accidental deaths while searching for Rowan. He'll keep his silence and his word."

Daphne touched her handkerchief to her eyes. It really was all over. Myra would never be able to hurt her again.

"I've hired your Pinks," Lucas said.

"My Pinks?"

"The Chicago office will direct their San Francisco operative to make sure my name is cleared. I don't want to spend the rest of my life pretending to be William Murphy."

"So you'll return to San Francisco?" Prudence asked.

"We'll see. I'm not sure I want to leave Daphne and Rowan on their own just yet."

He stood as light footsteps could be heard tapping down the staircase and across the foyer's marble floor.

Rowan's face lit up when she saw Prudence. She sped into the parlor and the arms of the new friend who had rescued her from certain death.

As the three women relived the series of awful events that only time would blur into healing, Prudence stole a quick look at Lucas, still standing, back to the fireplace. His look of fierce protectiveness told her everything she needed to know about Rowan's future.

EPILOGUE

"A miniature Christmas tree?" Geoffrey asked, looking at Josiah's otherwise-immaculate desk.

"He's been inspired by Macy's windows." Prudence smiled. "They've become quite the crowd pleasers. People stand outside gawking at all hours, no matter the weather." Macy's was on Sixth Avenue, occupying an entire city block between 13th and 14th Streets, a short walk from the MacKenzie mansion on Fifth Avenue. "They really are spectacular."

Spectacular but not as elegant as the Tiffany display in Union Square. Geoffrey had spent an hour there this morning, wondering whether Prudence would prefer diamonds or emeralds, leaving without having made a purchase. The question hadn't been asked. He preferred not to speculate about what Prudence's answer would be.

"He sorted the mail before he left," she said, "but I haven't looked at it yet."

"It's not like Josiah to take time off during a workday."

"I didn't ask where he was going, and he didn't volunteer the information." She picked up a stack of envelopes, glancing at the return addresses as she briefly considered each one. "Here's something from Niagara, Geoffrey." The envelope was bordered in black. Cyrus and Myra Adderly had died within days of one another, and while one would be sincerely grieved and the other not at all, the public face of mourning had to be observed.

"Is it personal?"

"From Daphne." Prudence skimmed the letter, then sat down at Josiah's desk to read it again, slowly.

The last time she'd seen Daphne Adderly Yates had been more than six weeks ago.

"Lucas stayed," Prudence said, holding the black-bordered notepaper loosely in her hand.

"For Rowan's sake, I imagine," Geoffrey mused. "I remember that he spoke very favorably about that young man who guarded Daniel's cabin. Jean-Baptiste Napier."

"Daniel is dead." Prudence ran one finger over the line announcing his passing. "Hero spends most of every day with Edward and Arthur in the nursery and schoolroom. Daphne doesn't mention Jean-Baptiste."

They sat for a moment in silence, contemplating Josiah's miniature Christmas tree, sharing silent remembrances of their brief but never to be forgotten stay in Niagara Falls.

"Lady Hamilton sailed for England a month ago," Prudence finally announced. "I suppose that means we'll never know what really went on between her and Lucas. How long it lasted. Why it ended."

"Grace," Geoffrey said.

"Lucas loved her deeply once," Prudence agreed. "But even great love can't always survive tragedy."

"Lady Hamilton didn't throw herself off a cliff to save Lucas's daughter. That's a debt Lucas can never repay."

"I wonder if Grace knew about her husband and Ernestine Hamilton."

"Does it matter?" Geoffrey asked.

"I don't suppose so." Prudence folded the letter and slipped it back into the envelope. "Do women always have to sacrifice themselves to be remembered?"

Diamonds, Geoffrey thought. *Definitely diamonds.*

AUTHOR'S NOTE

Much of this book was written during the earliest and most difficult days of the Covid-19 pandemic, when hardly anyone traveled, groceries were delivered, and Zoom became more than a casual experiment.

Traveling to Niagara Falls was out of the question, but the memories of two previous trips served me well. I had only to close my eyes to hear the roar of the water and feel the mist on my skin. No one who visits ever forgets the wonder of seeing American Falls, Bridal Veil Falls, and Horseshoe Falls for the first time. The shock of all that raging power. The awe as you stand and stare. And then the inexplicable magnetism of stepping closer and closer to the edge, of imagining oneself tossed down the river, hurtled through air and cataracts, plunging into the rapids below.

In a barrel.

In October 1901, Annie Edson Taylor, a 63-year-old widowed schoolteacher desperate for money, did just that. *The New York Times* reported that several thousand people watched the plunge, and that apart from a cut on her head and the aftereffects of shock, Mrs. Taylor was apparently fine. Except that the daredevil feat didn't bring her the fortune she'd hoped for. She hawked her picture and her autograph around Niagara Falls for years, then died impoverished and forgotten.

Surely, I told myself, Annie Edson Taylor hadn't been the only one crazy enough to attempt a stunt hardly anyone believed was survivable. So I sent Prudence MacKenzie and Geoffrey Hunter to Niagara Falls to meet Crazy Louie. Eleven years before the widow Taylor rode the falls.

ACKNOWLEDGMENTS

As always, writing a book is only the beginning. My thanks to John Scognamiglio, editor *extraordinaire*, and to Jessica Faust, agent *incomparable*, for their enthusiasm and support. To the art department for the beautiful cover and to Larissa Ackerman for making sure readers know where to find it. A special thanks to copyeditor Pearl Saban for putting the final touches on what I thought couldn't possibly need any more correcting.